Kevin Rozzoli's interest in horses began when he was asked to be the timekeeper for the Tom Quilty Gold Cup, a 100-mile endurance ride. This was followed by timekeeping for the NSW Horse Trials Association. After his election to the New South Wales Parliament, Kevin took on the role of Chair of the Hawkesbury Race Club Trust. Later he filled the position of Shadow Minister for Racing, and in recognition of his involvement in the racing industry he was made a Life Member of the Hawkesbury Race Club. After his retirement from Parliament, Kevin attended Roland Fishman's Writers Studio and completed the novel writing course, putting his rich and diverse background to good use.

AGAINST THE ODDS

A SECRET THAT COULD JEOPARDISE THE HORSE RACING INDUSTRY

Kevin Rozzoli

BROADCAST

A catalogue record for this work is available from the National Library of Australia

ISBN: 978-1-7638250-4-8 (Paperback)
ISBN: 978-1-7638250-5-5 (Ebook)

Produced by Broadcast Books, www.broadcastbooks.com.au
Cover design by Luke Causby/Blue Cork
Cover images: Nhan/Adobe Stock (Horse & jockey)
Oleh Slepchenko/Adobe Stock (stable)
Typeset in Adobe Garamond Pro 12.5/17pt by Matthew Oswald, Like Design
Printed by IngramSpark

1

THE AIR HUNG HEAVY with the blend of tobacco smoke, horse sweat and manure. Dusty Rhodes – thirty-five years old, lean of limb, face indented by exposure to sun and wind – drew in a lungful, coughed, scanned the crowded sales ring, trying to find some comfort on the hard wooden seat, and looked again at his catalogue. He heaved a sigh. Almost there, he thought. In the sea of faces around him nobody smiled, poker-faced professionals.

The hammer fell on Lot 31. For the umpteenth time, his fingers flicked the glossy pages of the Warrianderra Annual Yearling Sale Catalogue. Lot 32 emerged from the race opposite, dancing at the end of its halter, the skill of the groom showing its qualities to maximum advantage.

This was it. The horse he desperately wanted, The Conqueror.

Bidding opened at ten thousand, rising quickly until, at twenty-five thousand, only two bidders were left. He'd hung back hoping to gain a psychological edge. His limit was fifty. Time to move, his bid came flat, unemotional. 'Twenty-eight.'

The auctioneer's voice lifted a few decibels, excited by the prospect of fresh money. Ferret eyes darted between the two men who had carried the bidding so far.

Out of the corner of his eye, Dusty saw the shake of a head. The auctioneer called to the other man, 'You, sir, on my right?'

'Thirty thousand.'

Back to Dusty. 'Against you now, sir.'

Impassively, but with quickening pulse, he said, 'And three.'

'Thirty-five.'

'Thirty-eight.'

A pause. 'Forty.' The bid echoed off the galvanised-iron roof. A hush settled over the crowd.

Dusty's pulse raced. He sensed his opponent weakening. The prize was almost his.

'And two.'

'Forty-two,' the auctioneer repeated, his voice a notch higher. 'I have forty-two from the gentleman on my left.' His finger stabbed in his opponent's direction. 'Against you, sir.'

The man said nothing.

'Going once. Going twice!'

Dusty watched the hammer rise. Perspiration trickled down his face.

In the centre of the ring, the horse stood stock still.

'Forty-two, I have forty-two. Do I hear forty-five from you, sir?' The question was flung at the other bidder. Seconds seemed like minutes. No response.

A whistle of air escaped Dusty's mouth. He began to relax. The hammer rose. 'All done then. The bid stands at forty-two thousand.'

The auctioneer paused to savour the drama.

From somewhere behind him Dusty heard a new voice, hard and arrogant, cut the air. 'Fifty.'

Dusty's body locked rigid; his mind momentarily numbed with disbelief. His grip on reality faltered and his field of focus narrowed until he could see nothing but the horse in the ring. At that moment, it reared high and proud, challenging him to respond. Dusty wiped the saliva from the corners of his mouth. Reason left. He had to have the horse. His wife Jenny, God bless her, had agreed, if it was necessary, to chance another five. Would it be enough? Wild thoughts raced through his mind. Squeeze a bit more out of the mortgage and borrow against the value of the horse. His dream, something he indulged only in the inner recesses of his mind, won out. His teeth clenched as he heard the auctioneer's almost servile voice. 'Fifty, thank you, sir. Is there any advance on fifty, do I hear fifty-five?'

He struggled with his conscience, then raised five fingers, unable to trust his voice to not reveal his desperation.

'Thank you, sir. We have fifty-five.'

The same deliberate voice rang out. 'Sixty.'

Three fingers.

'Sixty-three.'

The voice behind him, like a rifle shot, delivered the final blow. 'Seventy-five thousand.'

Dusty slumped forward, his face buried in his hands, fighting tears of frustration, crushed by those three words and an all-pervading sense of failure.

Yet if his mind had been clearer, he would have acknowledged, somewhere in the turmoil, a tiny ripple of relief eddying against the tide of despair and defeat. His catalogue slipped to the floor.

'Going once, going twice; for the third and final time; are we all done? At seventy-five thousand then.' The hammer fell. Again, in the somewhat servile tone, 'Congratulations, Mr Murphy, an excellent investment.'

Dusty jerked upright, twisting around for a glimpse of the man who had so effectively crushed him. Like a flash of lightning on a dark night, he now understood that he'd been trying to outbid the racing manager of Mowbray Park, the biggest racing stable in the district.

The auctioneer rattled through the last three lots. Shell-shocked by what had happened, Dusty registered little until those around him started shuffling away and an excited babble of conversation filled the air. It was all over.

Stumbling through the exit, he blinked in the afternoon sunshine. For a few moments the normality of the world around him was unsettling, like coming out of a movie matinee when he was a kid.

Not wanting to face anyone he knew, he dropped his head and trudged to where his ute was parked, at first not noticing the figure leaning against the driver's door. A hard-edged voice jolted him into the present.

'No hard feelings I hope, son.'

Dusty stared into a face that matched the voice, hard and arrogant.

'That's the way it goes. You've more in the bank than me,' he said, unable to hide his resentment. 'That horse has loads of potential but won't be the easiest to handle.'

He reached out to open the ute door. The man didn't move.

'You reckon the horse has real potential?' the man said.

'I don't think. I know,' Dusty said softly.

'I've heard a lot about you. The knack you have with horses. Uncanny like your dad, the old timers say.'

Dusty's eyes widened. For the first time he took stock of Murphy, the man. A few inches taller than him, close to six feet, and carrying a bit too much weight, but with an aura of strength and authority.

'Want to come on board and train him and a few other horses? Perhaps we can strike a deal.'

The dream that had been shattered a few minutes earlier now reincarnated in front of him, but a note of warning jarred his brain. For some time, rumours had been circulating about Mowbray Park and its reclusive owner, Donovan Malek. What lurked behind this extraordinary offer? And what's more, it seemed too good to be true.

His mind spun. His immediate instinct was to say yes, for crying out loud, yes, but that was because he so desperately wanted exactly what was on offer. Yet he hesitated. He'd just had a sharp lesson on the difference between dreams and reality. And he was not sure he wanted to work for Mowbray Park.

'I'll think it over. Talk to the wife.'

'Look, son, I'm sticking my neck out, but I saw how disappointed you were and I know enough of your reputation. I can't be sure the boss will see it my way but if I know where you stand, I can probably sell him the idea. Still ...' His words trailed off in a shrug.

'What sort of a deal?'

'A month's trial, a thousand dollars a week, and, if it works out, full-time work on two thousand.'

The balance swung the way of reality.

Murphy waited for an answer.

'Come off it, I earn better money working for stingy builders.'

Murphy allowed himself a bleak smile. 'Two thousand a week and if we sign you up, three thousand a week.'

'That's more like it.'

Murphy extended his hand. 'Done?'

'Done.'

With the deal settled, Murphy started to walk away, but had gone only a few paces when he turned back. Reaching into his jacket, he took out a wallet from which he extracted some notes. 'One more thing,' he said, counting them out. 'Here's a grand to start with, a gesture of good faith.'

Dusty shook his head. 'Thanks, but no thanks.'

With a wink, Murphy took Dusty's left hand, thrust the money into it and closed his hand. 'Don't be a fool, it's tax free. Ring me next week and we'll work out when you can start.'

Dusty's fingers stayed clamped around the notes. They seemed to have taken on a life of their own. As he watched Murphy stride away, he thrust the notes into his jeans pocket.

'I'll ring on Monday,' Dusty called out.

Murphy waved an acknowledgement without looking back and climbed into a black four-wheel drive utility with 'MOWBRAY PARK STUD' emblazoned on the side.

Dusty watched him drive off. A cloud of fine dust blew over him.

2

THROUGH HALF-CLOSED EYES Dusty watched Jenny peel potatoes and then shell peas for dinner. From the back verandah of their modest home on the outskirts of Warrianderra, they had a commanding view of the Great Dividing Range. The afternoon sun was already casting long shadows across the back lawn where their two boys Jem, six, and Rafe, four, played with a soccer ball.

He'd been married for ten years to this woman with curly blonde hair, amazingly blue eyes and strong principles. Over the years, she had changed him from a loner who worked seven days a week – because he didn't know what else to do – to an industrious husband and a loving father.

He enjoyed these moments when the family were together, but today he had something on his mind. He'd sensed her relief when she heard that his bid had failed, so he hadn't dared tell her how high he had gone, nor that he had accepted the job offer from Murphy.

'Dusty, I've been thinking.'

He opened his eyes wider and sighed. The determined jut of her jaw meant something serious.

'I ran into George Mitchell the other day and he's thinking of putting you in charge of one of his teams. Isn't that good?'

George, an old friend of the family, owned the largest building company in town and had put Dusty through his apprenticeship.

'Not sure I'm cut out for it,' he said.

She went on as if she hadn't heard him, 'The extra money'll be handy, otherwise we'll have to stop putting the $50 a week into your horse account.'

This was the account he'd opened the day he started work, hoping one day, to buy a promising racehorse. Over the years it had grown to quite a substantial amount.

Dusty smiled at her. 'Think of that account as a savings plan.'

'I know, love,' said Jenny. 'And I agreed to take out some of our mortgage for the auction, but as that didn't happen, I thought we need to do things a little differently.'

Why did she always have to be so practical? He leaned over the verandah rail and called out to the boys. 'Another few minutes and then inside for your bath.'

By now she'd finished the vegetables. 'What started out as a good habit has now become an obsession.'

'It's still a good habit and one I just won't break. It's there for a purpose, for our future. One of these days you'll be glad we made the sacrifice.'

Jenny's response was patient but firm. 'I know, I know. You keep saying that, but the fact is we're stretched. It's hard to meet our regular commitments.'

With that she got up and went into the kitchen.

It was just as well she didn't wait for a reply because he didn't have a decent answer.

◆

Sunday turned out to be stifling hot, so Dusty had taken his family to the river. He and Jenny sat on the grass watching the boys playing happily.

Jenny finally broke the silence. 'Have you given any more thought to what I said last night?'

Dusty hedged. 'About what?'

'The foreman's job. With the extra money we could still put something into your precious horse account.'

Dusty's attention became absorbed by a couple of birds squabbling on a branch, nature mirroring life. He'd need to be careful how he phrased his reply.

'You're right, but ...'

He let his words hang in the air, waiting for her reaction.

'But what? Please, Dusty, I really want you to give it serious consideration.'

'I know, I know.' He sighed. 'And it makes a lot of sense. But try to see it from my point of view. If I'm going to crack a chance in the racing game it'd be good to be close to the action.'

Jenny was silent. Dusty ventured a discreet look. He could tell she wasn't convinced.

'Why are you so obsessed with being a trainer? I know you love horses, but there's many ways to be involved without putting us through hell.'

Dusty gritted his teeth. Emotions tumbled through him. A flair of anger; why did she have to throw that in his face? Aggravation; because he knew she was right. Disappointment; that all his effort so far had produced nothing. He despaired that his dream was slipping away.

'A few stables have hinted they might offer me something. I'll go and talk to them, push the issue a bit. Give me three months and if I haven't got anything I'll do whatever you want. Jen, please try to understand.'

'I do understand. For God's sake I've understood since before we were married. I've gone along with you because you work hard and I thought you deserved the chance. But commonsense has got to prevail. Expenses are piling up. If it's not the electricity, it's the registration on the vehicles or the medical insurance. Stick with George, at least you will get a raise. Go to a stable and you'll start at the bottom.'

Dusty tried to interrupt. 'Jen, it won't help sort this out if you get so worked up –'

'I have every right to get worked up. I'm the one who has to pay the bills. And that's not all. It's not long to Christmas, you know, and Rafe goes to school next year. That's another thing you don't seem to think about. Last week they had a dental check at school and Jem needs orthodontic work.' She sighed and stood up.

'Please, Jen. We'll work something out.'

But she wasn't to be brushed off that easily. 'Even with the $50 it's still not enough.' Her voice shook. She stared into the distance, brushing away tears with the back of her hand.

He took her in his arms, putting himself between her and the boys. Keeping his voice to a fierce whisper he said, 'I won't touch that money. I can't. I'll get a second job. But I won't touch it!'

She pushed him away. 'For God's sake, why do you have to be so difficult? Can't you think of anyone but yourself? You're a good man. I love you and I respect you, but there's only so much I can take. You don't have to face the people we owe money to, and I'm not prepared to risk the wellbeing of our boys.'

He tried to take her in his arms again. 'I'm sorry, Jen. I didn't mean to upset you.'

She pushed him away. 'For someone who didn't want to upset me you've done very well. Alright, get another job; get two for all I care. But I'm warning you, Dusty Rhodes, don't push me any further.'

She turned sharply and walked away in the direction of the

boys. She called to them and said something. They jumped in the air excitedly before heading back to the ute to scramble into the seat next to him. Jenny got in after them. 'Drop us off at Mum's. The boys and I are staying there for the night.'

◆

After he'd taken them to his mother-in-law's, Dusty drove slowly home. For a long time, he sat in the ute, staring at the back wall of the garage.

Everything she'd said made sense. He could hardly blame her, yet there was something which stood between him and commonsense.

His mind rolled back over their argument. She was smart. She could have done nothing more astute to concentrate his thinking than to leave him to his own devices. He could neither reassure himself what she said was right, nor find a reason to satisfy himself that she was wrong. The lack of resolution left an overwhelming sense of frustration.

He got out and went into the house, where he turned on the television to catch the news; political upheaval in Canberra and floods somewhere in the United States. In the back of his mind something stirred. The next story was about fighting in Iraq and Syria and another terrorist attack in France. He stood up, switched the television off and walked into the kitchen to make a pot of tea, then cut thick slices of bread and made a couple of doorstop sandwiches with cold meat, tomato, lettuce and mustard pickle.

Munching on his sandwiches he tried to focus his thoughts. Objective: to train racehorses. A dream? Perhaps, but a dream meant something unrealistic. Jenny called it an obsession, but an obsession was something removed from rational thought. To him it was his destiny: it couldn't be avoided.

His mind drifted back to when he was a kid, walking up from the lower paddocks towards the stable yard, taking two steps for every one of his dad's.

It meant everything to help with the afternoon feed. He loved his father's stories; they shared time and secrets. Jack Rhodes, the horse whisperer, trained horses for old man Jefferies who owned the sprawling property called Mowbray Park.

He remembered the afternoon as if it were only yesterday. 'Dad,' he'd said. 'How'll Razzle Dazzle go on Thursday?'

'Let's wait and see, son.' His dad was always cautious. 'But if he wins, it'll be because of the help you give me.'

He loved his dad, the strong, softly spoken man with the gentle touch, more than anyone or anything else in the world.

They walked on, both deep in thought. Then his dad said, 'Tell you what, son, if she wins on Thursday, how about we train a Melbourne Cup winner together?'

A week later his father was dead, caught by rapidly rising flood waters, helping the animals he loved so much.

'How about we train a Melbourne Cup winner together.' Those words had shaped Dusty's destiny, giving his life purpose and validity, for if they couldn't do it together, he'd do it for the man he loved so much.

His mother had walked out on him when he was twelve. He never understood why. He had withdrawn into himself and never told anyone of his silent pledge. But now he would tell Jenny the childhood story he'd shared with no one.

He found a writing pad and wrote her a note. In it he said he would take George's offer. He said he hoped it would make her happy. He also said he would try for a job at the club, but that he was determined to maintain the horse account. He was prepared to wait for another opportunity. And if it didn't come, there'd be a nice nest egg for later. He sealed the letter in an envelope, propped it against the bowl of fruit on the dresser and went to bed. The next morning, he got up at five as usual, dressed and was gone by a quarter to six. Jenny wouldn't be home until after she'd dropped Jem off at school. He hoped when she read the note she would be pleased. He'd ring Murphy and tell him he didn't want the job and return the thousand dollars.

3

Murphy wasn't so easily put off. He had asked Dusty to reconsider, hinting at the possibility of some extra money, and stressed the value of working for such a large operation, suggesting he should come to Mowbray Park to talk it over.

Dusty had managed to get the morning off and pushing his negative feelings to the back of his mind, drove up the long oak-lined drive of Mowbray Park. It was as impressive as he remembered it from childhood visits with his father. Around the first bend, hidden from the road by huge trees, the elegant Queen Anne style house was surrounded by magnificent gardens and manicured lawns. He drove slowly, taking in the landscape. About two hundred metres further on from the house stood a much newer construction, a massive stable complex, hub of the Park's racing enterprise.

Following the signs, he arrived at a neatly marked bitumen parking lot. Murphy had said eight sharp. He had plenty of time. Though summer was still a month away, it was already hot. A few wispy clouds, low on the horizon, were evaporating by the minute. Below him were neat paddocks with white painted fences and beyond them the training tracks. After a dry winter the emerald green pastures of Mowbray Park were in strong contrast to the brown landscape of other properties.

A tap on the roof of his ute broke his reverie. A foxy face appeared at the window.

'What are you doing here?'

'Got an appointment with Murphy at eight.'

'Said nuthin' to me about it.'

Dusty shrugged. 'That's his business, I suppose. Who are you?'

'Larry Grimes, stable foreman. Who are you?'

'Rhodes, Dusty Rhodes. Is he down at the track?'

'No. He was called up to the house about an hour ago.' He glanced at his watch. 'Should be back soon. Said he'd catch me about 8.30.'

The man walked back to a long wheelbase Land Rover utility, got in, reversed and drove off.

Dusty thought he should find Murphy's office.

From first sight, the stable complex took his breath away. Built in a style that complemented the house, there was a huge rectangular courtyard with a long line of stable doors on either side. Towers at each corner embodied features of the Queen Anne style. Everything reeked of money.

Though a working area, it was clean and well ordered. Each horse stall bore the occupant's name. In the four corners were probably the tack rooms, storage areas and Murphy's office.

The sound of a vehicle broke the silence. Murphy's black utility rolled into the yard, followed by a dark blue Mercedes E Class saloon with heavily tinted windows.

Shading his eyes from the glare, Dusty watched Murphy get out, walk back to the Mercedes and open the left rear door. A heavily built man alighted, about middle height, unseasonably dressed in a dark grey three-piece suit. They exchanged a few words, then walked together to the door of Murphy's office. Murphy was about to follow the suit inside when he glanced across to where Dusty was waiting. He stared for a couple of seconds then went in.

Dusty took his hands out of his pockets and started to walk over.

Metres from the office, the front doors of the Mercedes swung open, spilling out two men in bulging black suits and dark shades who moved with surprising speed to block his way.

One of them put up his hand. 'Where do you think you're going?'

'I'm here to see Max Murphy.'

'He's busy and doesn't want to be disturbed.'

'If you don't mind, I'll just let him know I'm here. I am happy to wait but he asked me to see him at eight, and it's just on eight.'

'I said he's busy.'

'But surely –'

'Busy, busy, busy. Don't you get it? Shove off and amuse yourself somewhere else.'

The bloke was getting up his nose. 'Who the hell do you think you are?'

Behind the men he heard a voice. 'Yuri.' Murphy had appeared at the office door. The second man stepped back, turned sharply on his heel and crossed to the office. Murphy seemed to be issuing an instruction, but the words didn't carry. Then he disappeared and the man returned.

'Mr Murphy said he will see you in his office in half an hour.'

The two muscle men went back to the car, probably to enjoy its air-conditioned comfort, while Dusty sat down on a pile of feedbags nearby.

His wait was, however, much shorter. Within ten minutes the grey suited man walked out of the office, the Mercedes took off and Murphy stood at the door waving him over.

'Sorry to keep you waiting. I've discussed your special talents with the boss, and he's agreed to you joining us.'

Dusty opened his mouth and then closed it.

'I need you to start training some of the younger horses,

including the fellow we bought the other day. More importantly, I want you to prepare a horse for the autumn campaign. Reckon you're just the man for the job.'

The euphoria of this prospect pushed aside any lingering reservations. He struggled to keep the excitement from his voice.

'Sure, sounds great. When do I start?'

'I'll ring you. Welcome to Mowbray Park, it's good to have you on the payroll.'

The big man turned on his heel and walked back to his office.

◆

Driving back along the avenue of trees, Dusty marvelled at how life could suddenly change. Now he only had to break the news to Jenny.

I'll take her to dinner at the club and tell her then, he decided.

The spiel of a shock jock on the radio talking to some bloke from the Registered Clubs Association grabbed his attention. 'So, if the government goes ahead with this new tax, many of the smaller clubs will struggle to survive.'

Before he realised it, he was turning into their street as the shock jock was saying, 'Perhaps the Minister will talk to us tomorrow. That's all for now folks. It's 8:59 at the top of the dial on this bright and sunny day – the news is next.'

He pulled into their driveway and parked as a newsreader began the day's diet of disaster.

Unlocking the back door he yelled out, 'I'm back.'

His voice echoed hollowly through the house. Jenny must have been held up at the school.

On the kitchen dresser among a pile of mail, a glossy brochure announcing the opening of a new restaurant, Il Giusto Posto, caught his eye. Customers bringing the flyer in would receive a complimentary bottle of wine.

His eyes lit up. Better still, do it in style. He'd book a table at the restaurant, and then, when she was relaxed, tell her the news. The small voice of conscience whispered its warning: she's bound to be suspicious if you suddenly splurge on an expensive dinner. You'd better think up something plausible.

◆

Friday turned out to be another stinker of a day, so Dusty and Jenny found Il Giusto Posto refreshingly cool. Lit only by discreet back lighting and the flickering flame of green candles, the large, framed prints of lakes nestling between hilly green slopes, snow-capped mountains and Renaissance architecture gave the restaurant a pleasing ambience. Dusty and Jenny peered at each other through the gloom.

A well-groomed waitress greeted them, cooing, 'And do we have a reservation?'

Dusty nodded. 'Rhodes, booking for two.'

With a pretentious flourish she crossed his name off her list, swept up two menus and with a, 'This way please', led them to a table against the far wall. With a flick of her lighter she lit the green candle. 'Can I get you a pre-dinner drink?'

'A sweet sherry for my wife, and I'll have a Crown Lager.'

The waitress nodded and glided off.

They held their menus up to the light of the candle. 'Should have brought a torch,' Dusty muttered.

After a brief perusal of her menu Jenny placed it neatly in front of her. 'Dusty! We can't afford this!'

'It's okay. Dropped in at the club on the way home and had a bit of a win on the pokies. I thought we'd have a little treat.'

'It could have paid some bills.'

He wondered whether he should say something about the thousand dollars, which remained untouched. No. Better to wait until he knew how Jenny would take his news. Thankfully she seemed resigned to making the most of a rare treat.

After a glass of complimentary red, Jenny's humour had improved considerably and by the time they were into their chicken with mascarpone and pesto, they were both in a mellow mood. The restaurant's ambience and the medley of Neapolitan folk songs playing in the background worked their subtle magic.

When the Campari jelly with citrus salad arrived, Dusty felt this was his best chance to break the news. He'd wracked his brain for a suitable opening, but his mind was blank. He stared into the ruby glow of his wine.

'Penny for your thoughts,' Jenny said.

'Nothing,' he lied. 'No, that's not right. I was thinking how much I love you.'

Jenny smiled. 'That's very sweet. I love you too.'

He plunged his spoon into his jelly. That wasn't exactly the right approach. He contemplated leaving it until tomorrow.

'Lovely, sweet,' Jenny said. 'Refreshingly tangy.'

Dusty agreed a little too enthusiastically. He was on a precipice – push on or blow the opportunity. He looked down into the remains of his jelly then up into her steady gaze. No, he'd grasp the opportunity. Some things he couldn't tell her, but the bit about the job he certainly could. With the extra money coming in regularly, they could pay their bills and enjoy these luxuries a bit more often. Surely, he'd done the right thing.

He looked across at Jenny but the words 'I have some exciting news' died on his lips. Even in the dim light he could see a change come over her face. Her lips pursed in a thin line and she seemed to have withdrawn into herself. Her eyes were fixed on a point somewhere beyond his right shoulder. Conscious of a presence behind him, he turned and looked up into the burly face of Max Murphy. What the hell was he doing here?

'Glad to see you celebrating,' said Murphy. 'Mrs Rhodes?'

She nodded an acknowledgement, but the grim look never left her face.

'I don't think we've met. Max Murphy.' He extended his hand.

'I don't shake hands with men,' said Jenny. 'They always crush my fingers.'

Unfazed, Murphy nodded. 'You must be pleased.' Dusty felt a hand on his shoulder. 'And once again, welcome on board. Mr Malek sends his regards. Enjoy your dinner.' He turned and walked away.

Dusty felt a knot in the pit of his stomach.

Jenny looked at him without blinking. 'What was that about?'

'Ah, that's what I was about to tell you.'

Jenny's intuition was uncanny. 'Something I won't like?'

'Well, you were saying how tight things were financially and I said, "I could get a second job", and you didn't seem to think that was a good idea …'

A spoonful of the jelly remained suspended somewhere between Jenny's plate and her mouth. 'Get to the point,' she said. 'What are you trying to say?'

'I – I've accepted the job with Mowbray Park.'

Jenny put her spoon down. Her eyes closed and she took a deep breath.

'Well?' He paused a moment, then measured out his words. 'They made me a great offer.'

There was no ignoring the edge to her voice. 'Did they now?'

The magic of the evening had gone, but he rambled on. 'And he wants me to get The Conqueror ready for the Autumn Carnival. He's the best potential stayer in the stable.'

She breathed deeply, her eyes looking straight through him.

He squirmed in his seat. 'It's worth an extra eight hundred a week.'

She snapped her fingers. 'And just like that you accepted?'

'It's what I've always wanted. I thought you'd be pleased with the extra money.'

'You don't understand, do you? It's not the money, it's what you've done.'

'Me?'

'Yes you, you dunderhead. I don't like the idea of you working for that Malek man. It can only lead to trouble.' Her voice rose steadily. 'The whole town knows something about that place isn't right.'

The couple at the next table turned towards them.

'I know there are rumours, but that's all they are,' Dusty said. 'You know how the locals always resent outsiders. They offered me a job on very good money, that's all. And if they want me that much, well, they'll have to let me do it my way, or not at all.'

Jenny was determined to have her say. 'Good old Jen, she'll understand. Take her out, sling her a few dollars, she's easily bought.' She let her words sink in. 'Well, I'm not.'

Some other patrons turned in their direction.

'For God's sake, keep your voice down. We don't want the whole town knowing our business. I accepted his offer because I thought I was doing what was best for us. Why are you so angry? You said –'

She dropped her voice to a fierce whisper. 'Yes, I am angry, you idiot. And I have every right to be angry. You didn't even have the courtesy to tell me before taking the job.'

A deep pit opened up before him. 'I'm sorry.'

'Sorry won't do. Thank you for spoiling what has been up until now a lovely evening. I was impressed when you suggested we come out tonight, but now I know it was just a bribe.' She pushed her chair back. 'I'll have the keys, thank you. I'm leaving. You can walk home.'

◆

Despite getting home later than his usual bedtime, he was still up at five. Why of all nights did Murphy have to come to that restaurant? Jenny had every right to be indignant and he had no defence. When he got home, she had dispatched him to the spare bedroom.

He went through his normal early morning ritual as quietly as possible to avoid annoying her even more, but when he was almost ready to leave, she appeared with a grim face.

'Dusty, I don't want you working for Mowbray Park. I've heard the rumours that are going the rounds and I do not want you to be associated with them. Just tell them you've changed your mind. Isn't the fact that I don't want you to take the job a sufficient reason?'

'No! I can't do that so soon after I have accepted the job. And besides, the racing world is a male dominated one, at least in Warrianderra, and changing my mind because my wife asked me to would make me a laughing stock throughout the district. Just give me the month and the time to think up a reasonable explanation.'

He took a deep breath. 'Sweetheart, I would like to tell you something I have never told anyone and then, perhaps, you might understand.'

'Alright, try me. And it better be good.'

'I've told you how much I loved my dad. Well, a few days before he died he said to me, 'If the horse we've got running on Thursday wins, how about we train a Melbourne Cup winner together?' I've never forgotten what he said. And …' Dusty started to choke on his words. 'Well, if we couldn't do it together, I wanted to try to do it for him. That's why I'm trying to break through. I know about the rumours, but honouring Dad's memory is so very important to me.'

Jenny looked at him thoughtfully. 'I don't know why you haven't told me before, but I'm glad you've told me now. I still don't like what you're doing but take the job. I love you and I trust you. See how it goes, but if there is any truth in the rumours, promise me you'll quit.'

4

On an impulse, Dusty decided to take himself off to the races. The races were generally held on weekdays, but twice a year they were held on a Saturday. He'd promised Jenny he wouldn't bet, but there was nothing to stop him pitting his judgement against the eight-race program.

The sun beat down relentlessly, driving race patrons to whatever shade they could find. Dusty purchased a race book and found a quiet corner to mark it up.

A horse he favoured, Justaminit, was showing eights. He touched the wad of notes in his pocket. He knew he should've given them to Jen to pay their bills, but that would've made things worse. She wouldn't have understood. He wasn't certain he did either.

Ticking the last of his selections, he picked his way through the crowd, across the concrete apron that fronted the TAB windows, and on to the mounting yard where he jostled for a spot against the fence.

The horses, led by their strappers, were beginning to enter the yard. Justaminit, with the No. 4 saddlecloth, looked superb, head high, ears pricked, coat gleaming and ready to take on anything. He thought about Jenny's words, 'Alright, go to the races, but mind you don't bet.'

He fingered the notes again. She'd never know. He could lose the lot and she'd still not know. Not that there was any chance of that; he had plans for the money.

One by one the horses filed onto the track. After a short and fruitless struggle with his conscience, Dusty hurried back to a bookie, bet $10 on four and then crossed quickly to the TAB to take a trifecta with three and seven. From the stand he watched Justaminit win by four lengths.

The first three races netted a modest profit. Feeling hungry and thirsty, he headed off to the Horseshoe Bar for a pie and a schooner of Old. From the far corner an arm frantically waved him over.

A good-natured chorus welcomed him. 'Come and join us, Dusty. Howya goin'? Winning or losing?'

He put his beer down and dragged a chair across with his free hand. 'Not bad.' He sat down, biting into the pie, careful not to let the hot gravy drip over his fingers.

One of them grinned expansively. 'We've had a couple of good wins. We were just debating whether we should quit now or keep going.'

'Keep going!' an optimist chimed in. 'After all, we're using bookies' money.'

A pragmatist offered his opinion, 'Yeah, so they can get it back.'

'Chance it, I say,' the optimist said. 'I'm feeling lucky. We'll clean up in the next.'

'What are you looking at?' Dusty said.

'Snakecharmer.'

The race was a maiden and Snakecharmer was a Malek horse. Dusty was quick to caution them. 'I dunno, only two runs in seven weeks for a fifth and a seventh.'

The optimist winked and tapped the side of his nose. 'Straight from the jockey. Says he's been set-up for it. Wanted to make sure they got a good price. Get the drift.'

Dusty was only half listening. It was a very open race and he knew Snakecharmer didn't have a show. He'd seen him race a few weeks ago. He was going nowhere, not today anyway.

'I think I'll give it a miss.' He drained his beer and got up. 'Good luck. Whatever you back, I hope it wins.'

'Cheers, Dusty, see you round, mate.' They raised their glasses.

To his great surprise, Snakecharmer won. It didn't make sense. The horse had never shown much promise. He shrugged. The rest of the field probably wasn't much either.

A successful quinella on Race 6 restored some of his self-esteem, netting $658.

Flush with the cash, he reconsidered Race 7, the feature race. Fashion Plate had a great chance: well-bred, right distance, comfortable weight. She'd relish the firm track and with a clever jockey he reckoned she was a winner.

He glanced at the other entries. Mixed Blessing seemed the main danger. The Mowbray Park horse, Blaza Trail, was out of its class. Why they bothered running the horse was beyond him.

For a few minutes, Dusty again wrestled with his conscience. His thousand had grown to over eighteen hundred. That'd pay their immediate debts, leave a bit over and get Jenny off his back – if she forgave him breaking another promise. Finally, he compromised. He'd bet eight hundred, leaving the thousand intact. When Dusty had given George his resignation, George had wished him luck. But with Christmas coming up, he'd tell Jenny that George had still given him his end-of-year bonus. Satisfied, he went back to the bookmaker. The board showed twelve to one.

'Eight hundred on Fashion Plate.'

The bookmaker punched his computer. 'Twelve to one, Fashion Plate.'

Another punter pushed him away. 'Five grand on Mixed Blessing.'

The favourite showed five to two. Dusty dropped back a few paces, staring first at the board then at the betting slip. He'd risk another two. He crossed to the TAB, took a banker quinella and made his way to the stand.

In the far distance he watched the bright splash of racing colours as the horses milled behind the barrier. He looked around and was glad not to see anyone he knew. He'd staked much more on this race than he normally would, and for now, preferred his own company.

The horses had moved into the stalls, the race caller picking up the action.

'The line's steady … and they're away in the Warrianderra Cup. It's a clean start with Ironsides going quickly to the lead, half a length from Sky's the Limit, followed by Wildflower who also jumped well, tucked in just behind Lucky Star, who has gone out three wide, looking for some clear air. Mixed Blessing has settled just off the pace, then comes Fashion Plate, followed by Pioneer Spirit, with Blaza Trail well out of it.'

Through his binoculars Dusty followed the string of horses as they passed the eight hundred mark. His heart was beginning to pound. Mixed Blessing had hit the front, pulling out a length on Ironsides. Fashion Plate had moved up to fourth, running one out from the rail and now three lengths from the leader.

The roar from the crowd was beginning to swell. His palms sweated. Fashion Plate was nicely placed but couldn't afford to lose touch with the leaders.

The caller's voice broke over the cheers of the crowd around him. 'At the five hundred Mixed Blessing still leads and is travelling well. His jockey's trying to steady the pace. Ironsides still second, Wildflower third; Fashion Plate's starting to challenge, Sky's the Limit's dropped back, then Lucky Star, Pioneer Spirit, with Blaza Trail four lengths behind them and right out of it.'

Dusty's fist pumped the air. Out of the turn and into the straight, Fashion Plate's jockey picked an opening and ran inside Wildflower for a clear run on the rails.

'Come on, Fashion Plate, you little beauty,' Dusty yelled, jumping to his feet. 'You can do it!'

The crowd rose as one around him, every punter roaring encouragement in an incoherent cacophony.

The caller fed the hysteria. 'Three hundred to go and it's Mixed Blessing, hard ridden under the whip, hanging on by half a length. Fashion Plate surges past a tiring Ironsides. Fashion Plate catches Mixed Blessing to hit the front and looks unbeatable in the run to the post.'

A euphoric Dusty settled back in his seat, ticking his race book. With every stride Fashion Plate increased her lead over Mixed Blessing, who was hanging on grimly for second. Then from nowhere, Blaza Trail surged through the pack. Back on his feet, Dusty could see the horse run out wide, and under the whip the horse was rocketing along like something possessed.

'With a hundred to go, Fashion Plate has pulled out a couple of lengths on Mixed Blessing, but – crikey! Look at this! – Blaza Trail has come from nowhere in an astonishing burst and is belting down the far side of the track … and folks, it's all over. Blaza Trail takes out the Cup, a short half head from Fashion Plate, three lengths back to Mixed Blessing …'

Dusty didn't hear the rest. He sank into his seat, dumbfounded, head in his hands. Unbelievable. Fashion Plate should have won. Frustration clouded his mind. There was no logical explanation for Blaza Trail's extraordinary run. But there it was, the result posted on the big board on the other side of the track. He screwed his race book into a tight ball. He knew the horse well; it was a roughie. It couldn't have won, shouldn't have won, but it had.

He began to shake. Something was desperately wrong; the notion tore at his nerve endings. Distractedly, he watched the horses returning. From a long way past the post, he saw Blaza Trail's jockey struggling with his mount. He trained his binoculars on the troubled horse, its head jerking from side to side. Deep in thought, Dusty left the stand.

5

With so many questions running through his head, Dusty decided he'd pay the local vet, Leigh Woodward, a visit on his way home. They'd met at the Pony Club and got on well enough for Dusty to run some questions past him. He drove along River Ridge Road towards the surgery, several kilometres north of the town.

Shadows were lengthening by the time he swung his ute into the forecourt of the concrete building. The location was a wise choice, with ample flood-free land for buildings and yards and about six hectares of river flats, lush with rich, year-round pasture. Unlike most land in the Warrianderra district, a spur of the Great Dividing Range had endowed this pocket of country with a generous balance of high and low ground, and above average rainfall. But Dusty gave such considerations only fleeting regard. His mind was on other things.

A magnificent, deep bay thoroughbred stallion occupied a small yard next to the vet's surgery. Dusty walked across, shielding his eyes from the setting sun. The horse could at full stretch reach a velocity of nearly twenty-three metres per second. He conjured up visions of the track, thundering hoofs, jockeys crouched low over their horses' necks. A thrill ran through him.

Behind him a refined voice broke his reverie. 'Admiring the patient?'

Dusty turned and extended a hand to Woodward.

'Got a few spare minutes?' Dusty asked.

'Depends on what you want me to do with them.'

'This may be presumptuous, but I'd like to ask what you thought about Blaza Trail's astonishing win yesterday.'

'Why?'

Briefly Dusty explained the chain of events that had brought him to this point. 'I lost the lot on Fashion Plate.' He grinned. 'I've got a theory, but it's so far-fetched I thought you might be the only person I could talk to about it.'

The vet allowed himself a small smile. 'You weren't the only one to lose a motza on Fashion Plate. What makes you a special case?'

Dusty began to regret his rashness. 'Don't suppose I am.' He looked back to the stallion. 'Beautiful horse!'

'Yes,' Woodward said. Dusty sensed the vet was sizing him up. 'If we talk, perhaps you'd do me a favour in return.'

'What sort of favour?'

'All my staff are off for the weekend and the stallion has come in unexpectedly. He's a very valuable horse and I will have to operate first thing in the morning. I could use an extra pair of hands. Interested?'

'Sure am.'

'Be here at seven. It'll take a couple of hours. I've got a pair of overalls that should fit you. While you're here, I'll show you around.'

The tour of the complex confirmed Dusty's first impression. Woodward knew his business, so much so he was puzzled why the man had asked for his assistance. The story about all the staff being off seemed odd, but he dismissed the thought. Here was a heaven-sent opportunity to gain Woodward's confidence.

6

THE NEXT MORNING DUSTY entered the surgery building where the vet was waiting for him. At one end, double doors opened onto the yard where the horse was waiting. A short race led to a crush adjacent to the operating table. Here the horse would be anaesthetised and then gently moved against the table, which was in a perpendicular position. At the right moment, horse and table would swing into a horizontal position for the operation.

Following Woodward's direction, Dusty selected a lead rope from a number hanging on the double doors. The horse quivered at the sight of a stranger and backed away, pawing the ground. Once again, Dusty experienced the thrill of the day before. Yet he felt at ease, at one with this beautiful animal. Nothing else existed.

He sensed the vet eyeing him intently. By a fusion of voice, eye and hand, he slowly but confidently closed the gap between himself and the horse. It wasn't just a matter of bringing the horse into the surgery; Woodward needed the horse to be calm and relaxed.

Talking softly, Dusty led it into the crush, the anaesthetic was administered and soon the vet was patiently and skilfully performing the procedure. Dusty, fascinated by the almost serene manner in which the work was performed, could only be impressed.

In slightly less than forty-five minutes the wound was being stitched. Quiet words of instruction made Dusty feel more like a partner than a new recruit.

'The anaesthetic will wear off in about twenty minutes. Can you stay for a while? It'd be good to have you here when he recovers.'

'No problem. Happy to help.'

He cleaned up while Woodward went into the small kitchen next to the surgery. A few minutes later he heard the vet call out, 'Come and have this while it's hot. You've earned it.'

Like everything else in the surgery, the kitchen was immaculate. Perched on a stool Dusty sipped steaming coffee.

'I'm impressed,' Woodward said.

'I'd like to do more, if that's possible?'

Ignoring the comment, Woodward asked, 'Why the interest in a horse from Mowbray Park?'

Dusty detected a cautious edge to his voice.

'I've just accepted a job with them. Start on Monday.' The vet's eyes took on a steely glint. 'You're not impressed?'

Woodward seemed to consider his reply. 'Let's just say I'm not overly keen on Donovan Malek or Max Murphy. When I first started my practice here, I thought I might get them as clients but they made it very clear I wasn't wanted.'

'I'm not so keen on Murphy either. Dunno about Malek, never met him,' Dusty said.

'Few people have. He keeps to himself. Murphy does the legwork.' The vet seemed to draw within himself.

'I took the job because I wanted to work for a racing stable and, out of the blue, they made me a great offer, and they do have a very impressive set-up,' Dusty explained. 'I'm not particularly wedded to working there, but I need the money. I'd gladly take a job with another stable if they'd make the same sort of offer.'

Woodward glanced at his watch. 'Let's get this horse sorted.'

◆

A little later they returned to the office. The vet took a springback folder from one of his filing cabinets, opened it and flicked through the four or five pages it held.

Dusty waited, scanning the impressive row of certificates on the opposite wall. He thought about the care and skill he'd witnessed.

Woodward closed the file and looked up. 'So, you didn't come here looking for a job?'

'No.'

'Grimes send you?'

'No.'

'Murphy?'

'No.'

'Then who?'

'Nobody. I just wanted to know what you thought about Blaza's win. For my money, there was something odd about it. The win was so inconsistent with his form. And the way he took off over the last four hundred was ... well, unnatural. Am I right?'

The other man's eyes bore into him, as if weighing how far he could be trusted. Then, in a measured tone Woodward said, 'I don't need to tell you Malek owns a lot of horses. He has some excellent bloodstock, but most are just average. I've only met him a few times, but I know he's not in racing because he loves horses. He's in it for the money and the status.'

'Not unusual. We mightn't like it, but that doesn't make it illegal.'

The vet nodded. 'But here's what's interesting. Four times in nine months a two-year-old horse has broken down and been destroyed. In each case it was attributed to a virus that attacks the animal's balance. All were insured.'

'Of course.'

'Yes but insured well above their value. But even that's not uncommon. A mediocre performer of good breeding has its value inflated. When it breaks down, there's a windfall gain. But that's not all. Like Blaza Trail, a couple of them had unexpectedly good runs just before the virus took hold. My PhD was on equine viruses, but I've never seen anything like it. So, I'm wondering if insurance isn't the only scam.'

Dusty studied the fine layer of dust patterning the toes of his boots. Looking up, he caught the vet watching him, his right arm resting on the arm of his spacious swivel chair and his chin resting on a partly clenched fist. It was impossible to fathom what was going on behind his grey-blue eyes.

The red numbers on the digital clock above the desk read 9:26.

The vet picked up the file. 'Six months and this is all I've got. I need to get closer. I tried to cultivate Larry Grimes, no dice.'

Dusty laughed. 'He's probably wary of getting on the wrong side of Murphy.'

Woodward gave a bleak smile, while Dusty resumed the study of his boots.

The red numbers flicked to 9:28.

They showed 9:29 before the vet finally asked, 'Any thoughts on why you were recruited? Surely that's a bit odd.'

The bluntness of the question startled him. Jenny had said much the same, but coming from Woodward it carried more weight. Even so, her comment had nagged him for days. He'd pushed it away, his excitement blinding him from the obvious.

Why had Murphy been so keen to bring him in?

He gazed out the window contemplating an answer. On the far side of the river, the high sandstone cliffs glowed brightly in the morning sun. Horses grazed and a gentle breeze stirred the eucalypts. He wanted Woodward's confidence, but he also needed to be sure he could trust the vet.

'I dunno. When he made the offer, I couldn't see a downside. Perhaps I should've been more sceptical.'

Woodward opened the file again and studied it for a few moments. Then suddenly he said, 'Do you know anything about a horse called Arctic Gale?'

'No. Why?'

'The first horse destroyed – on the 14th of May. Cavalier Lad?'

Dusty shook his head.

'Pop the Question?'

'Yep. Someone told me Murphy'd sold him on.'

'Afraid not. Who told you?'

'Can't remember. I think I just sort of got the impression that's what happened.'

'Grimes?'

'No. I think someone just mentioned it in general conversation.'

The vet sighed as he closed the file, returning it to the cabinet. The silence was heavy. Woodward was obviously disappointed with Dusty's answers, but it was the truth.

If the horses had been put down, it had been kept very quiet. While rumours circulated around the district, very little was known about what went on at Mowbray Park. The locals who worked there were tight-lipped.

Woodward nodded thoughtfully and said, 'They probably wanted to keep it quiet to avoid the place being quarantined. That'd certainly wreck their racing schedule.'

Dusty got to his feet. He didn't know whether the vet believed him, but he felt a sudden need to reconsider where he stood. He needed time to think. Woodward had told him a little, but not everything.

But then, Dusty hadn't been completely forthcoming either.

'I'd better be off. Told the wife I'd be back by 10:30.'

The vet nodded. 'Thanks for the help. I appreciate it.'

The grey-blue eyes held him for a moment, Dusty thought Woodward was about to say something more, but he didn't. Instead, he abruptly turned his back on Dusty. Returning to his desk, he sat down and opened a large blue diary, its pages crammed with detailed notes.

Dusty's eyes flicked from the diary to the filing cabinets. A startling thought came to him. He hesitated.

Woodward looked up. 'I thought you'd gone.' The vet glanced at his watch. 'I really must get onto these calls.'

But Dusty wasn't ready to leave.

'One quick question and then I'm off. If it wasn't general knowledge the horses were destroyed, and I don't think it was, how do you know?'

Woodward closed the diary with a snap. 'That's my business.'

Did Dusty glimpse a sudden spark in those grey-blue eyes?

It's a two-way street. If he wants my help, he'll have to take me into his confidence.

The vet turned away to look out the window. 'I'm not at liberty to tell you.'

'As long as I know where I stand. See you later.'

Dusty closed the door with a slam. He'd given his ultimatum. If the vet couldn't be frank with him, he could shove his concerns where it hurt most. From now on he'd just concentrate on his new job.

He went over to the holding yard for one last look at the stallion. The horse appeared none the worse for his operation, having polished off the lucerne hay Dusty had left in the string bag hanging from one of the posts. He called softly. Without hesitation, the stallion came across to nuzzle his outstretched hand. He stroked its head and was rewarded with a soft whinny. Horses, he concluded, are easier to understand than people. After a few more words and a final stroke of its magnificent head, Dusty went back to his ute.

Reversing to face the gate, he caught sight of Woodward waving frantically.

What the heck! What's he want now?

He braked, got out and they met halfway.

Woodward looked apologetic. 'I'm sorry, I was a bit abrupt just now. There are things I've been told in confidence. I can't tell you just yet, but I didn't want you to leave with any hard feelings. Sorry.'

Instinctively, Dusty decided on one last throw of the dice. 'I don't know what it's all about, but frankly I'm not sure I want to get mixed up with Mowbray Park. Reckon I'll quit now. Make the wife happy.'

Woodward looked him in the eye. 'Hang on a sec, don't be too hasty. I can't tell you more at the moment, but it would suit me to have someone I can trust at Mowbray Park.'

It was exactly what Dusty expected, but he wouldn't show his hand too quickly.

'I'll think it over and let you know.'

◆

Later that afternoon, Blaza Trail collapsed and died. As soon as he could, Dusty rang Woodward.

'Why am I not surprised,' the vet said. 'If you're willing to help me, we might be able to find out what's going on at Mowbray Park.' There was a pause before he continued. 'It would great if you could go back tonight to get me some samples before they get rid of Blaza Trail's carcass. Just be very careful though and then get yourself over here as quickly as possible. Then I'll tell you all you need to know.'

7

Dusty pulled off the road into a grove of gum trees just short of the float entrance to Mowbray Park. The low under-scrub would give his ute some protection from curious eyes.

A restless wind sent dark clouds scurrying across the inky blue sky. One moment the moonlight was quite bright and the next, he had to strain to see a few footsteps in front of him. He dared not use his torch.

Keeping clear of the drive, he climbed through the fence that separated Mowbray Park from its neighbouring paddocks. He used the fence line to guide him but made slow progress, stumbling a few times until his eyes became more accustomed to the dark.

He climbed through another fence towards the end of the tree line until he reached the edge of the broad open space that separated him from the rear of the stable complex. The space was lit by a floodlight. He recalled Woodward's advice: 'Just be very careful.'

To his right, a thick hedge offered some cover. Dropping back, he detoured behind it. Ground-hugging blackthorn shrubs tore at his trousers, its clinging tendrils preventing his passage. How the hell was he going to get through? Dusty moved further along until, at last, he found a spot where he hoped he could cross to the stable without being seen. He knew a security guard patrolled each night. If security showed up, he hoped he would see the guard before the guard saw him.

Conscious of his vulnerability, Dusty wasted no time in getting to the first stable, where he waited until his breathing steadied. The quietness of the night was broken only by the occasional snuffle and snort, and the stamping of the more restless horses. His heart thumped. He couldn't suppress the feeling that at any moment someone would show up.

Keeping close to the walls, ready to duck into the nearest stall, if necessary, Dusty moved silently and swiftly to Blaza's stall, opening the door and stepping into pitch darkness. Heart pounding, he put down the bag he had brought with him and switched on his torch. Its sudden brightness startled him. Cupping the torch's beam with his free hand, he wondered how he could dim it. The body of the horse lay before him, the head angled awkwardly to the chest. Leaning down, he pushed the torch up against the throat latch. Good, just enough light to work. Reaching back for the bag, Dusty took out the bundle Woodward had given him and unwrapped its contents: a cloth, a needle, vial, catheter and bottle. Using the cloth to keep them off the damp floor, he laid them out and checked his watch, 6:50. With any luck, he would be through and gone within fifteen minutes.

A quick inspection showed the chest thickly encrusted with sawdust. Tearing the piece of cloth in half, he spent precious time cleaning, as best he could, the spot where he had to place the needle. He carefully inserted it, then, attaching the vial, checked the angle and thrust hard until the full six inches disappeared. He was about to draw the blood when he saw the arcing beam of a vehicle's headlights. With pulse racing, he rewrapped the catheter and bottle, turned off the torch and shoved them into his bag. Half crouching, Dusty retreated to the front corner of Blaza's stall, tucking himself into a tight ball. There was no escape. He hoped it was the security patrol and that any inspection would be cursory.

Swearing silently, he remembered the needle and vial still inserted in Blaza's chest. His only hope was that the weight of the vial had made it drop below the line of the shoulder.

Vehicle doors slammed. The murmur of voices reached him. It didn't take long to recognise one as Murphy's, but he couldn't place the other, well-spoken with a slight accent.

He held his breath, as if that might give him away.

The voices came closer. He closed his eyes and called on a neglected God. The voices were now distinct.

'I'll show you the horse first,' he heard Murphy say.

'I'm really not interested. I trust your judgement. Just tell me what happened and what we do now,' the voice said irritably.

'I can explain it better in the office. I've got Callaghan's spreadsheets there.'

The voices receded. Dusty caught a brief glimpse of the men before the office light was partially extinguished by the door closing.

Praying that whatever Murphy had to explain would take some minutes, Dusty quickly turned on the torch, drew the blood sample and stowed it in the bag. Then he took up the catheter and took a deep breath. He hadn't come this far to leave empty handed, but ten minutes had already gone.

Alert for any noise, he threaded the catheter up the penis. With his adrenaline sky-high he heard every sound of the night, even his own repressed breathing. Every second, he expected to hear voices. What the hell would he do if they came back? He was beginning to lose track of time, but he couldn't risk pausing to check his watch. Finally, it was done.

He mopped his brow with his sleeve, packed the catheter and bottle in the bag and switched off the torch.

It was 7:10, so far so good. Another couple of minutes and he'd be safe. He slipped out.

He'd barely walked ten metres when the office door opened, spilling a shaft of light across the yard. He glanced towards the stable entrance, then sideways to the nearest stable door. He bolted into the stall. Its occupant snorted and stamped.

'Steady, steady on there,' Dusty said soothingly. Soon, the horse calmed.

The sound of the office door shutting came clearly to him. Peering out, he watched the two figures move towards the vehicle, Murphy's torch probing the darkness. Alarm caught at Dusty's throat. They were passing the vehicle, passing Blaza's stall and were heading straight towards him. The sound of their voices grew louder as he ducked down. Shit.

Murphy's voice sounded uncharacteristically troubled. 'I don't like it.'

'It cannot be helped. Spetcevic says we can't stop now.'

'Well, it's all going pear-shaped. Today's been a disaster.'

'Nonetheless, we must press on. We're playing for high stakes, my dear Maxwell.'

'Well, I'll be glad when we know exactly what we're doing. We can't afford to lose too many more. The insurance company will start screaming,' Murphy said.

'Don't worry. I have that contingency covered. I'm returning to Sydney for an important meeting first thing tomorrow. So, let's have a quick look at this horse. The things I do to humour you.'

'He's called Bold Challenger,' Murphy said.

Dusty tried to remember the name on the stall he was in. Crouching down, he hoped desperately it wasn't Bold Challenger dozing behind him. The light from Murphy's torch reflected on the roof above him. He could see the hairs on the back of his hands. They couldn't be more than two stalls away.

The torch flashed brighter before being eclipsed by the overhead light in the neighbouring stall. Murphy gave his companion a rundown.

'Magnificent! Now I must go,' his companion said.

The door closed, the bolt shot home and the light went out. A few steps more and they would be outside Dusty's stall. The torch beam split the darkness above his head, illuminating the horse's bulk and the rear of the stall. The horse didn't move.

Dusty curled into a ball. It was all over. The beam focused on the horse's head for a few seconds.

'Come on, that's enough. You fuss too much.' The man's voice flared with irritation.

The beam swung away, leaving the stall in darkness. The men moved off a few paces.

Murphy said something that Dusty couldn't quite catch, but the other voice carried distinctly. 'I've just said I trust your judgment, but let's not be too hasty, Maxwell. We can wait a little longer. Make it look all the more – what's the word? – Authentic? Genuine? Bona fide, that's it.'

'How long?' Murphy said.

'A couple of weeks, not too long, and then we'll start with Bold Challenger. In any case, it'll take Callaghan that long to get organised.'

'Right.'

The unknown voice took on a tone of silken menace. 'Put Rhodes in charge of the horse. Then if anything does go wrong.' He laughed mirthlessly. 'We will know the horse went down with the best of attention. The bona fide touch.'

'Is that wise? Rhodes might've tried to persuade Grimes to call in Woodward.'

'But he didn't?'

'No. Grimes was too scared.'

'It pays to have insurance.'

'Perhaps that's what we need for Rhodes?'

'A first-class idea, Maxwell. Has he, as they say, a skeleton in the closet?'

'I doubt it. According to all reports, he's as clean as a whistle, a good country lad. That's why I thought of him. That's what you wanted.'

'Yes, but I like your suggestion. We should – er – broker an insurance policy.' The voice hardened. 'If there is nothing in his past, then set-up something in his present.'

The voices were fading. Dusty strained to catch their words.

'Like what?'

The voices were getting fainter.

'Maxwell, my … fellow, that's what I pay … for … wanted him on the team … a good team player means compromising … what we want him to …'

The voices faded completely. Dusty tried to move, but the shock of what he'd heard numbed his limbs. He waited until his eyes readjusted to the dark and his heartbeat returned to normal. The vehicle doors opened and slammed shut. The engine started, the headlights came on and again, the arcing sweep of their beam momentarily lit the stall. Then the sound of the engine faded. A silence soon settled.

Dusty drew air into grateful lungs, conscious of how much he had restricted his breathing over the last ten minutes. He got up and stretched his cramped muscles, shivering despite the thick coat Woodward had given him. So that was Malek. What a cold, callous bastard. He would need to be very careful from now on, watchful for any trap Murphy might set for him.

He felt a sudden urge to be rid of the place. The first part of their plan was to put him in charge of Bold Challenger. Whatever else they had in store he hoped what he'd just heard might keep him one step ahead.

Letting himself out, he bolted the door and quickly crossed to the front entrance, deciding to gamble on the shorter route. He couldn't get away quickly enough.

Emerging through the arch, he broke into a jog and soon reached the shadow of the trees. The front gates loomed ahead of him. He was about to cross the road, when headlights punctured the darkness and lit the trees lining the drive. He'd barely time to scramble back to the sanctuary of one of the great oaks before the car roared past. Dusty recognised Malek's Mercedes and beyond it, a flash of colour where he'd left his ute. He waited for the car to slow, reverse and investigate, but it roared out of sight.

8

Dusty's image in the mirror revealed the strain of the last few days – dark shadows under his eyes, tension at the corners of his mouth. With a sigh, he scraped the last of the shaving cream off his chin.

Jenny's voice came clearly from the kitchen, 'Hurry up, boys! Breakfast! The bus will be along soon!'

The scamper of feet down the hallway brought home how little he'd seen of the boys lately. His long hours had wrought a subtle change in their attitude towards him – they were much more focused on Jenny.

After towelling his face and shrugging on his shirt, Dusty hurried to the kitchen, anxious to spend what precious time he had with them.

He found two very excited boys gulping down their cereal.

'Hey – slow down, fellas. What's this place you're going to today?' he asked.

'An alpaca farm,' Jem said, cramming mouthfuls of toast and Vegemite. 'Mum, c'n you ride alpacas?'

'No, they shear them for their fleece.'

'Like sheep?'

'Yes, like sheep. They make jumpers and rugs and things. You'll see when you get there.'

Feeling left out, Dusty shared his two bits worth of knowledge.

'They're very environmentally friendly. They've got soft, padded feet that don't cut into the soil like cattle, sheep and horses. They're even less damaging than some of our native animals. They browse on all sorts of grasses, so they don't eat out any one particular grass, which means quicker re-growth and less soil erosion.'

But the boys' attention had strayed.

'And there ith wallabies and wombats,' Rafe explained to the world in general, rolling the 'w's with relish as he made short work of his toast.

Jem threw in more information. 'And there are emus and a baby animal farm.'

'Sounds great,' Dusty broke in.

'And Mum, c'n I have pathionfwuit cordial?' asked Rafe.

'Not if you ask like that, young man.'

'Pleath, pleath Mum.'

'Of course. I've already packed it. You love your passionfruit cordial don't you, Rafe?'

'Yeth, I do.'

'And I've put in a couple of oranges.'

'Thank you, Mum,' Jem said rather pompously, demonstrating his superior manners. 'They're really beaut, Dad. Mum peels them a special way, then puts 'em back in the peel and wraps 'em in foil so they stay fresh.'

'Gee, I'll have to get her to do some for me,' he said, spooning cereal into his mouth. 'You kids like some more toast?'

They shook their heads and quickly left the table.

Dusty glanced across to Jenny at the kitchen bench, who was packing their lunches carefully into the boys' backpacks. She ate her breakfast while she worked. He admired her trim figure, set off by a slimming, blue skirt and simple white blouse, her blonde hair drawn back in a ponytail.

After putting the boys on the bus, she would be off to her new job as admin officer for the biggest doctors' practice in the district.

'Hurry up, boys,' she called out, lifting their backpacks from the bench and taking them through to the hall. 'Clean your teeth, brush your hair and out to the front gate. You don't want the bus to go without you.'

A couple of minutes later they hurried down the hall.

'Say goodbye to your father.'

Jem yelled back, 'See you, Dad!'

Rafe's voice echoed, 'Bye, Daddy.'

Soon they were gone. Dusty started to get up then sat down. He wanted to join them but felt shut out.

He reflected on the chain of events that had unfolded since the day of the auction, and he wondered, not for the first time, what the hell he'd got himself into. It had seemed simple enough to accept Murphy's offer, then Woodward had placed a large question mark over Malek and his operation. Now he'd witnessed a conspiracy to defraud insurance companies of millions of dollars. He hadn't slept well since.

He vividly recalled huddling in the corner of the stall, tasting the salt of fresh sweat, straining to follow what was said outside. He remembered the chill of hearing his name and the menace in their words, the dimly lit scene, the arcing headlights, but above all, he recalled the fear he had felt. He wanted desperately to turn back the clock and start again, but there was no turning back. From now on, he'd need to be more careful, smarter, taking every advantage he could from the unintentional warning.

Or should he just forget Woodward's crusade? Nobody could force him to do anything against his will. No more clandestine ventures, no more interfering. The next time a horse got sick, he'd look the other way, simple. Yet somehow, he doubted that's how it would go. Recent events had changed everything. His world had become a dangerous place.

He heard Jenny's footsteps in the hall.

'You should have come out. They're so excited, so cute.' She glanced at her watch. 'I don't have to leave for another ten minutes. I think I'll have another cuppa, how about you?'

'Thanks.'

'Why didn't you come out?'

'I dunno, I feel shut out. The boys almost ignore me.'

'What can you expect? They've hardly seen you since you went to Mowbray Park.'

'And you?'

'I feel shut out too. Two months into my new job and not once have you asked me how I'm doing.'

A wave of guilt swept over him. It was true. Absorbed with his own problems he'd thought about little else. He tried to catch her eye, but she had turned away to make the tea.

'Sorry, how's it going?' he asked.

'Good. The work's interesting, everyone's friendly. They're installing a new computer system so that'll be a bit of a challenge. It's helping money wise and with you away so much, well, frankly I don't know what I'd have done without it.'

She brought the teapot to the table and began to pour. When she'd finished, she looked at him in a way that seemed to penetrate his thoughts. 'I don't suppose I've asked how you're going either. Everything okay?'

'Full on. Enjoying it. Can't say they're all that friendly. Murphy's a funny guy – most times like a bear with a sore head, but sometimes he's almost human.'

There was an awkward pause. They sipped their tea.

Again, Jenny gave him that penetrating look and when she

spoke there was a sharp edge to her voice. 'Why were you so late getting back last night?'

'The vet, Woodward, wanted help with an urgent job.'

She slammed her cup down spilling tea into the saucer. 'That's rich. Whenever someone else asks you for help, you're there like a shot. We deserve your time too. I've tried to be patient, to give you time to settle in, but it's wearing thin. And you're a bad liar. What's really going on?'

He stared down at the table for a few moments, pushing the spoon around his bowl. Then he looked up and sighed.

'Woodward thinks something funny's going on at Mowbray Park. A number of horses have died. He thinks it may be an insurance scam.'

'So?'

Seeing the look on her face he added hastily, 'Not that I'm involved.'

'I should think not. If he wants to get involved, that's his business – he's got no right to drag you in.'

'I'm not doing anything.'

Jenny pushed her chair back, picked up the cups and went to the sink.

'They talk about Murphy in the office,' she said over her shoulder. 'No one likes him.'

'What do they say?'

'Well, for one thing, he makes no attempt to get involved in the town. They spend very little money locally, and even the locals they've employed only stay there because the pay is so good – which, if I may say so, is exactly why you're there.'

She was right. Jenny was always bluntly honest.

Another wave of guilt swept over him. Guilt for betraying Woodward's confidence. Guilt for causing her worry.

The cups clattered in the sink. She swung around. 'Just make sure you don't get involved. You've got the job you've always wanted; be content with that. But I know you – don't start playing detectives, it's not your scene.' She laughed with a touch of bitterness. 'For goodness' sake, you sound like someone from The Famous Five.'

'Leigh Woodward's a decent bloke.'

'Then leave it at that. I told you right from the start, and I'm telling you again, working for Mowbray Park will only lead to trouble.'

Then suddenly, for the first time in a while, their eyes met without hostility, mutual concern the dominant emotion. She came over to him, put her arms around his shoulders and kissed his forehead.

'Are you sure you're telling me everything? If there is anything else, please share it with me.'

'Nothing else, honestly,' he said.

'Dusty, I want you to be happy. That's why I've gone along with it, but Jem and Rafe need more of you. I need more. Can't you see that?'

He stood up, took her in his arms and kissed her tenderly on the cheek. Their mouths came together and he kissed her fully, fiercely, hungrily. My God, how he missed her. He pulled her blouse out, running his hands up her bare back. The skin was smooth and tantalising. He fumbled with the clasp of her bra. She pulled away gently, laughing.

'Naughty, naughty! I said ten minutes.' She looked at her watch. 'Get home early tonight. I'll make it worth your while.'

'Jenny, I really love you.'

'And I love you too, you blithering idiot.'

9

Dusty stared at the bedroom ceiling, studying the faint dapple of light filtering through the curtains from a street lamp. Jenny lay asleep, cradled in his arms.

Rekindling the passion of their earlier years, they'd made love for the first time in weeks.

That afternoon, he had kept his bargain. He got home in good time, early enough to be there when Jem and Rafe arrived back from their excursion. They were so tired; they'd almost fallen asleep over dinner.

Jenny had tucked the boys into bed early, so they could enjoy their own dinner, quietly. Then they'd snuggled up on the lounge with just the side lamp on to watch a film on the television. Before the movie was halfway through, they went to bed.

His arm was beginning to ache as the night wore on. Gently he eased it from under her. She stirred but didn't wake. Turning on his side he stared into space. She was right to ask him to give it up, he was out of his depth and it wasn't his responsibility. He'd taken a big risk the other night and got away with it, but next time, if there was a next time, he mightn't be so lucky. Again and again, he tried to think of a way to broach it with Woodward. He didn't like going back on his word, but he had just made a more important promise to Jenny. After what seemed like hours, he drifted into a fitful sleep with the questions unresolved.

◆

By Sunday, the questions were still unresolved. They were watching yet another replay of Jenny's favourite movie, *The Sound of Music*, when the phone in the hall rang. Dusty got up to answer it.

The voice at the other end said, 'It's Leigh Woodward.'

'Hi, I've been meaning to call you.'

'Anything urgent?'

'It can wait. What can I do for you?'

Woodward paused, then said, 'Could you meet me tomorrow, at four, at the Commercial Hotel?'

'Why? What's up?'

'I'll tell you when I see you. It's very important. Can you make it?'

'Sure, see you then.'

He put the phone down and gazed blankly at the wall. Why would Woodward want to meet him, and at the Commercial of all places?

'That was Leigh Woodward. I've arranged to see him tomorrow after work,' Dusty said. He returned to the couch.

'Just make sure you do.'

◆

The following day, he parked his ute across the road from the Commercial. The old pub's glory days had ended when the rail service stopped forty years ago, and the business centre shifted to the other end of town. Its once legendary accommodation for commercial travellers had been reduced to a handful of permanents taking advantage of the cheap rates.

Walking across the street, Dusty could see rust pushing through the wrought-iron railings on the upper floor verandahs. Wall tiles were missing. An old dog slumbered on the pavement, waiting for its master.

Dusty pushed open the door. The Seppelt's clock above the bar showed a few minutes after four. From their stools at the bar, a dozen or so patrons watched the replay of a boxing match on TV, while others sat around Formica-topped tables, mumbling into their beer. Dusty spied Woodward astride a stool in a distant corner. He raised an arm to wave him over and Dusty slid onto the next stool.

'What are you drinking?' asked Woodward.

'I'll have what you're having.'

Woodward called to the woman behind the bar. 'Schooner of Old, please.'

They exchanged comments on the weather and the Sheffield Shield results until the bartender brought their beer. Dusty dropped the level in his glass a couple of inches in one thirsty gulp. The beer had the sharp, clean taste of good management – the main reason the hotel survived.

'What's all this about?'

Woodward sipped his beer before answering. 'There are a couple of guys I'd like you to meet. They're upstairs. We're expected at 4:15 so when you've finished your drink, we'll wander up.'

Several minutes later, Woodward tapped discreetly on the door of a second-floor room and it opened almost at once.

Inside, a heavily built man in shirtsleeves said, 'Come in. Good to see you again, Dr Woodward.'

The room was warm and stuffy, with the musty smell of age and cheap cleaning products. To Dusty, it looked clean enough, but its dreary colours hadn't seen an update for years. The afternoon sun slanted through the window onto one of the two single beds with faded blue and white coverlets. Dust particles danced tirelessly in its brightness.

On the other bed, an expensive looking briefcase lay open, exposing several files, a calculator, dictaphone, tapes, pens and highlighters. There were no suitcases, no clothes, no sign of overnight occupancy. Through the window, he caught a glimpse of the old railway yard, the weeds thriving among piles of debris and litter, its derelict sheds covered in graffiti.

The heavily built man introduced himself as Len Carmody and his companion as Gus Becker. Becker was younger, of a slimmer build – handsome in a rugged way.

Woodward introduced Dusty. They nodded in greeting and shook hands.

Carmody, acting as spokesman, waved them to the chairs they'd placed in the centre of the room around a small table. On the table were two six-packs of beer, one torn open, and four glasses. Four bottles had gone from the opened pack and two of the glasses were stained with spent froth.

'Beer?' Carmody asked.

Woodward and Dusty shook their heads. Dusty felt uncomfortable. The room had an almost surreal quality, like a scene from an old American B-grade movie.

Woodward must have felt the same because he said, 'Is this really necessary? It all seems rather melodramatic.'

Carmody looked around the room. 'We believe it is. We'll be gone in a couple of hours and hopefully no one will know we've been here.'

'The publican, surely, or am I naïve?' Dusty said, shaking his head.

'The room's in someone else's name. That person picked up the key and passed it on to us. He'll be back later to stay the night and make sure anyone who's interested remembers him.'

Carmody looked at his watch. 'I'll come straight to the point. The sooner we're out of here the better.' He turned to Dusty. 'Our company has retained Dr Woodward for three reasons: his exceptional knowledge of horses, his unquestionable integrity and he's local.'

'And me?' asked Dusty.

'You're Dr Woodward's suggestion. We trust his judgement. Before I start, I must ask that you treat what we tell you with the utmost confidence. Okay?'

Dusty nodded. Carmody went over to the bed and picked up the top file. He sat down again and turned to Dusty.

'We're from Stock and Station Property Insurance, amongst other things. We are large insurers for the racing industry. Over the last five months, we've paid out on four hefty claims from Mowbray Park. That of itself may not be exceptional, such things do happen –'

Woodward broke in. 'In each case, the horse suffered a severe respiratory collapse brought on, so we are told, by a virus.'

'Their vet, a fellow called Callaghan,' Becker put in, 'certified it as a virus, but the exact nature of the virus is obscure.'

Woodward nodded. 'In each case, only one horse was affected and significantly, there've been no reported cases elsewhere.'

Carmody gave a short, harsh laugh. 'For which, I must add, we are very grateful.'

He paused and looked to Dusty, as if expecting some comment. With none forthcoming, he consulted the file. Dusty got the impression Carmody was using it as a prop, the man's seemingly steel-trap mind was sure to know every detail.

'At first, we put it down to good management and a rapid, yet effective quarantine. But none of the horses recovered. When the third claim arrived, however, we advised Murphy we'd require an independent autopsy before settling a further claim.' Carmody smiled thinly as if even the mildest attempt at humour came at a cost. 'After all, insurance companies don't like paying out. When the fourth one came, we called in Dr Woodward.'

Dusty turned to Woodward. 'What did you find?'

'As you probably know, viruses can cause problems in many ways. From the symptoms, I thought it could be encephalitis; however, the results were inconclusive. I could neither rule out nor confirm the virus theory.'

Carmody leaned towards Woodward. 'Getting into Mowbray Park with your vet practice has failed. Any idea why?'

'Not really. I don't think they're suspicious, just very cautious.'

While they talked, Dusty watched Becker's face. It gave nothing away.

'Whatever the reason,' continued Carmody, 'we can't get what we need.' He nodded to Becker, who rose, went to the briefcase and picked up a file and a pen before returning to his seat.

While Becker balanced the file on his knees, he put on a pair of reading glasses and peered at the top page.

'It's hard getting information, but we do have a list of employees. Among the more dubious names on the list is that vet, Callaghan.' Becker turned to the next page. 'He is somehow connected to a firm called Riekevic Laboratories.'

He turned another page, his pen stabbing the points he was making. 'Riekevic is a small concern. Sixteen employees, registered in Victoria with three shareholders: Boris Spetcevic, Browmay Holdings and ...' He paused. 'The Lim Wah Mercantile and Shipping Group, registered in Hong Kong.'

'Spetcevic?' Dusty broke in. 'I've heard that name.'

Becker shot a glance at Dusty and raised his eyebrows. He

drummed the pen on the file several times. 'And here's another interesting bit … Browmay's a subsidiary of Morgsmith Industries … and the largest shareholder in Morgsmith is Donovan Malek.'

Woodward looked puzzled. 'Do you know how Lim Wah fits in?'

'Not yet, but we're working on it.'

Dusty and Woodward exchanged glances.

'What does this Riekevic crowd do?' Woodward asked.

Becker looked at the file, his pen running down the page. 'Produces pharmaceuticals for the canine industry, particularly greyhounds.'

Dusty frowned. 'Why would a lab that makes dog products be involved in anything like a complex equine virus?'

Becker shrugged. 'Fair question. It'd be great to have an answer.' He turned to the last page. 'Three years ago, Callaghan was involved in allegations of administering illegal steroids and fronted the Veterinarian Disciplinary Board. Despite a strong case, some expensive brief got him off. We applied for further and better particulars and, surprise, surprise, the transcripts have gone missing.'

'Missing?' Woodward asked.

'Who knows?' Becker tossed the file back on the bed.

'You see, there are enough loose ends to be a major worry for the claims adjusters.' Carmody fingered his collar as tiny beads of perspiration trickled down his florid features. 'We looked closely at the claims. Three of the horses put in exceptional performances just before any evidence of the virus appeared.'

'So that's why you wanted to check Blaza Trail?' Dusty said to Woodward.

Woodward nodded. 'It seemed just too much of a coincidence,' he said. 'It was important to understand why he ran so much better than his form suggested. Perhaps they just let him run dead in his previous races to raise the odds, it happens. There can be legitimate reasons and you can usually uncover them after the race, but when I spoke to Grimes, he was very tight-lipped.'

Becker looked across to Dusty. 'Independently, you raised the matter with Dr Woodward. Why?'

'He mentioned the pattern,' said Dusty. 'Surprise win, hit by a virus.'

'And?' Becker shot back at him.

'When they couldn't get Callaghan in a hurry, and given the situation, the horse was in urgent need of attention. It seemed a great chance for Woodward.'

'And?' barked Carmody.

'No go,' said Dusty.

'How's the horse?' asked Becker.

'Dead.'

Becker looked thoughtful. 'When was this?'

'Last Wednesday.'

'Have we a claim?' Carmody asked Becker.

'Not yet.'

Carmody gave Woodward a puzzled look. 'Any thoughts?'

Woodward shook his head. 'Nothing for certain; however, that night, Dusty managed to sneak back to Mowbray Park to get blood and urine samples for me.'

Becker looked to Woodward. 'What'd they tell us?'

'Results aren't back; I'll keep you posted.'

For a few seconds, no one spoke. Carmody scraped his chair back and went to the window. He looked across the railway yard, arms clasped behind his broad back, head sunk between his shoulders.

Becker stood up, stretched and picked up another beer. 'Help yourself.'

Again, Woodward and Dusty shook their heads. Becker sat on

the bed and drank straight from the bottle.

Eventually, Carmody turned round, his head and shoulders silhouetted against the light. Still, no one spoke. Finally, he grunted, 'We're really up against it. But if my instinct's right, something really nasty is going on.'

Becker took another swig. Dusty and Woodward waited.

'In three months, we've got nowhere,' said Carmody. 'Police aren't interested. They say there isn't sufficient evidence of criminal conspiracy. They say it's between us and our client, but Malek has powerful friends. Money buys immunity. The club looks after its members.'

Another pause. It seemed to Dusty that Carmody was weighing carefully what he would say next. Abruptly he turned to Woodward. 'We need someone on the inside. We thought it could be you, but that hasn't worked. Now we're desperate. At best, it's costing us a packet. At worst ...' He sighed. 'Who knows.'

Easing forward from the window, Carmody went to the small table and tore open the second six-pack. 'Sure, you won't have one?'

'No, thanks.' Dusty felt his skin tingle. A large piece of the jigsaw had dropped into place. He shot a glance at Woodward but couldn't catch his eye. He looked to the door, wishing he was on the other side heading down the stairs. The stuffiness was oppressive.

Becker drained his beer and picked up another. Carmody circled the room liked a caged animal.

Dusty shifted uncomfortably and stared at the ceiling.

Suddenly, Carmody stopped his circling, swinging round to face Dusty. 'Rhodes, we need your help.'

Dusty knew it was coming, but the man's gruff pleading took him by surprise. Aware they were all looking at him, he stared back at them in turn. Time seemed to stand still.

He thought of Jenny. Of how, in the peace and serenity of his home, he'd agreed to quit playing detective.

'It's not your problem,' she had said. 'You want to train – be content with that.'

Looking Carmody straight in the eye, Dusty said, 'I can't. You're asking too much. I'd be out of my league.'

'We'll pay well,' said Carmody, again with that almost pleading tone.

Fair dinkum. Dusty wanted to say he'd promised Jenny, but that was passing the buck. He had to have the guts to say no. A simple, straightforward no.

Before he could frame the word, Woodward leaned forward. 'You were fantastic the other night, sharp and resourceful. If we plant someone, they'll be suspicious in no time. You're there already, and remember, they recruited you.'

Dusty avoided their gaze, instead watching the shaft of sunlight that had crept across the bed and up the wall. The dust particles still danced. He shook his head. 'No, sorry.'

He rose and walked to the door. His hand twisted the knob and it squeaked in the silence. Outside, he could hear the sound of cars, children's voices, a dog barking.

Carmody's voice, urgent and authoritative, cut the silence. 'Wait, hear us out.'

Dusty let the doorknob roll back. Turning around, he leant against the door, surveying three faces that were now fiercely animated.

'We know it's risky,' said Carmody. 'If there was any other way, we'd take it. We'll pay you a thousand bucks a week on retainer for eight weeks. If you get nothing, that's it. If you do, there's five thousand for every bit of useful information. If you help get us a good result, that's another fifty thousand.'

Dusty was dumbfounded. He wrestled between Jenny's stern

demand and a windfall that would otherwise take years to accumulate. 'If I did, how would I contact you?'

Carmody pointed to Woodward. 'He's the contact. The fewer involved, the better.'

For what seemed a few minutes, Dusty grappled with the consequence of what they were asking. It was easy for them; all they had to do was put up the cash. He would be taking all the risk.

And yet, if he did nothing, he could be eight grand better off. He'd already risked his neck. He might as well get paid for it. If it got too risky, he'd just walk away. It had a horrible fascination. He struggled with his conscience, his heart pounding. He saw Jenny's sweet face, Jem and Rafe's cheeky grins.

He sighed. 'No. I'm just an ordinary bloke. You're asking something extraordinary.'

'The Doc said you wouldn't do it for the money,' said Carmody.

Dusty felt a wave of relief.

'And that was why we wanted you, a man of principle. Too bad, it was such a good idea. We'll just have to chuck it in the rubbish bin, where all the rest of the good ideas in this godforsaken world finish up.'

Carmody walked to the bed, returning the files to the briefcase.

'A pity though,' he said, snapping it shut. 'Our connections in the racing game could have opened some great doors for you.' He extended a hand to Woodward. 'Thanks for your help, Doc, we'll be in touch.'

Dusty closed his eyes. In that instance, he saw all that was wrong with working for Mowbray Park, yet here was a chance to redeem himself, to do some good, to follow his dream without the baggage. To earn Jenny's respect.

'You mean that?'

'Sure, but forget it,' Carmody said. 'In my book, no means no.

Come on, Gus, let's get out of this dump.'

Something clicked in Dusty's head.

'Can I have some time to think it over?' he asked quietly but firmly.

Carmody extended his hand. 'Take a week – a couple of weeks. I know we're asking a lot. Let the Doc know when you've made a decision.'

10

WHILE DUSTY WAITED for a place at the wash bay, he reflected for the umpteenth time on his meeting with the insurance investigators: tough, hard men who only wanted a result. He'd told Jenny part of the truth – the meeting, their proposal to put him on a retainer as an informer and that he had knocked it back. What he hadn't told her about was the substantial reward he'd been offered for playing a part in exposing the fraud. She'd not raised the matter again.

In the meantime, the stable followed its normal, busy routine. Murphy had mentioned nothing about taking on Bold Challenger, nor had Dusty heard or seen anything of interest. The calm was unsettling.

The clatter of hoofs on concrete jerked him back to the present.

'It's all yours,' said Vicky Mifsud. She started to lead her horse away when she stopped. 'Oh, jeez, I almost forgot. Murphy asked me to tell you, he wants to see you when you're finished.'

'Urgent?'

'No, just when you've finished.'

Dusty liked Vicky. She stood out in the predominantly male group as a capable, efficient, no-nonsense person who genuinely cared about her horses. She stayed aloof from the backbiting, squabbling and pettiness that festered among the men. They didn't see her as a rival, nor was she. She liked her job, seemed to have no great expectations and she loved working around horses.

Without planning it, they often teamed up together, chatting about their work, helping each other out, giving that extra care and attention to the horses that set them apart from the others.

Dusty was convinced she was not aware of Mowbray Park's dubious side. Open and honest, he guessed that Vicky took life at face value. During their more recent chats, he'd learned a lot about the routine and personalities of their work mates, but nothing of value to his investigation. On the spur of the moment, he fired off a question about Callaghan.

She paused and turned, her horse gently nudging her in the back.

'I don't see much of him,' she said. 'Never had a conversation with him. In fact, I'd doubt any of the boys have. Suppose he's okay, but now you ask, there is something funny about him.'

'What do you mean funny? Funny ha-ha or funny strange?'

'Funny strange. He's a loner. He always seems, I don't know …' She searched for the right word. 'Furtive? Apprehensive? Guarded? It's hard to explain … he's sort of, uncomfortable.'

'Is he a good vet?'

'Must be. Murphy wouldn't keep him on if he wasn't, but I don't have much to do with him. See yah.'

She took her horse off and Dusty turned the hose on his horse.

When Dusty saw Vicky a little later, she came across to him.

'I've been thinking about Callaghan … about what's disconcerting.' She dropped her voice, put her head close to Dusty and whispered, 'I think he hits the booze a bit too hard.'

After he'd finished, he walked across the yard to the stable office, knocked and waited.

A voice called, 'Come in.'

He entered and saw a woman who he guessed was Murphy's secretary.

'Yes?' she said.

'I'm Dan Rhodes. I got a message the boss wanted to see me.'

She picked up the telephone and pressed a button. 'Dan Rhodes, says you want to see him.' She put the phone down and nodded towards a door. 'Through that door, second on the left.'

Murphy opened the door for him, waving to a chair in front of his desk. 'Sit down.' His voice was almost genial.

The desk was covered in large ledger sheets. Murphy had briefly shown them to Dusty in a previous meeting; said he recorded the progress of each horse, entering his notes from every training session. For such a big man, he had a remarkably neat and precise hand. He obviously took great pride in his records.

'Thank you for your sterling effort with Blaza the other day. Pity the result wasn't better. Not your fault though. Mr Malek was impressed.'

Dusty opened his mouth, then shut it.

'He'd like you to take on a bit more responsibility.'

'I don't know if I can handle much more, I've a full string.'

'Don't worry about that. I'll do a bit of a switch. It's a horse we picked up recently. Lots of promise and I don't want anything to go wrong.'

'Wrong?'

'Still haven't got a lead on this bloody virus, or whatever it is. You're horse smart. You could be of great assistance to Callaghan – a sharp pair of eyes and ears on the ground.'

Dusty said nothing, trying to look doubtful. If Callaghan took as long next time to get to a stricken horse, they'd be none the wiser.

'I wasn't too pleased about the other day,' said Murphy. 'So, I want you to look after Bold Challenger for a while.'

So, this was it, the move Dusty had been waiting for. He feigned ignorance. 'Eh?'

'The new horse.'

Dusty shook his head.

'I'm happy with what I'm doing.' He paused. 'But if that's what you want, you're the boss.'

'Good.'

'Just one thing though.' Dusty sensed it was time to press Murphy. 'Is this horse more likely to be affected by the virus than any other?'

'Good question. Knew you were horse smart. None of the horses who've had the virus are from our breeding program. Three of the five came from the same general area and the other two spent months in that area. We've only picked this up in the last week. When we checked Challenger's background, we learnt he had been in that area as well, but only for a month. It's the one possible link. That's why he needs special attention.'

'I'll need to work closely with Callaghan; understand where he's coming from so I know what to look out for.'

'I'm not sure I can go that far. It's hardly your field.'

Expecting a flat refusal, Dusty was encouraged. He decided to press home the advantage. 'If I can't be involved to that extent, you'd better get someone else. If I'm responsible, I need to know what I'm doing.'

'You'll be responsible for the horse's care and training, but you can't take on an area you know nothing about. It is a highly specialised field. Even Callaghan is working under instructions from the laboratory. I can't afford a repeat of the other day.'

Dusty couldn't recall Murphy being too agitated over Callaghan's tardiness. The plan had changed. He'd need to be wary, a little more conciliatory. 'You do see what I mean though, don't you?'

Murphy flashed irritation. 'What am I supposed to see?'

'That whoever is spending the most time with the horse is in the best position to observe what's happening. I'll keep a log, work out something with Callaghan. Got to be useful.'

'You're a bloody nuisance.' Murphy was getting restless. 'All I know is Mr Malek suggested you look after the bloody horse. I don't know why, and I don't particularly care. Whatever he wants, I deliver. I haven't the time to argue the toss.'

Dusty sensed he hadn't lost any ground. 'Then clear it with Mr Malek?'

'You're an insolent bugger.'

'If you can't clear it with him, get someone who doesn't care whether the horse lives or dies.'

Murphy shrugged. 'I'll see what I can do. Now, get the hell out of here.'

Dusty left Murphy fuming. He felt quite pleased with the way he had stood up to the manager, guessing correctly that he was under orders and not in a position to tell him he wasn't wanted. It might be different after Murphy had talked to Malek.

He decided to check out his new charge.

11

Two DAYS PASSED without any sign of Callaghan. Meanwhile, Dusty had plotted a chart to record Bold Challenger's performance, taking blood and urine samples, which he secretly conveyed to Woodward.

The next morning, when Dusty got to the track, Murphy called him over. 'I've spoken to Mr Malek. He's agreed. Get whatever you want from Callaghan. He'll be here the day after next.'

Dusty responded with as much enthusiasm as he could muster. They'd have ample time to decide what he should be told.

He'd ridden his first three horses and was switching gear from one to another when Murphy reappeared at his shoulder. 'Callaghan's arriving today.'

'What time?'

'Should be here by the time you get back up top. How's Challenger been going?'

'Great!'

'I'll tell Callaghan to give him a thorough check.'

'Right.'

Murphy made a note on the sheaf of papers he carried on his clipboard. 'I want you to take Challenger out now. Do a couple of circuits on the loam to warm him up, then bring him onto the turf. Do one and a half at a medium pace, then take him up to full speed around the bend. Let me know how he picks up. I'll clock him over the last four hundred.'

Dusty nodded. Murphy left.

He turned towards the horse's stable only to find Vicky Mifsud walking the horse towards him grinning. 'Here you are, Sir Galahad. Your steed awaits.' She handed him the reins and gave him a leg up.

'Gee, thanks,' he said.

Vicky called after him. 'Have fun!'

'I will.'

Challenger went well; his steady improvement giving Dusty immense satisfaction. They effortlessly covered the two laps on the loam before easing up to wait for a gap to get onto the turf. The horse danced with impatience. This one really loves racing, thought Dusty. You and I could go a long way.

A light touch of his heels took them onto the turf. Dusty revelled in the power under him, exhilarated by the rush of wind that drew the skin tight across his cheeks. Crouching low over the horse's neck, he said softly, 'Come on. Let's show that bugger Murphy what you can do.'

The horse responded without further prompting.

By the time they got back, Murphy was looking pleased. 'Thirty-five for the last two. Pretty good. How did he feel?'

'Very comfortable. Plenty there, just need to work him up steadily.'

He slid to the ground. Vicky came over to take the reins.

'Vicky'll look after him,' said Murphy. 'Callaghan's arrived.'

He pointed with the clipboard to a solitary figure in the stand. They walked over in silence. The man rose to greet them.

'Bryan, meet Dusty Rhodes. Dusty, Bryan Callaghan.'

Dusty took the man's hand and shook it – a cold, clammy hand with little strength in the grip.

Callaghan's eyes were pale blue, slightly bloodshot and with a hint of redness around the rims.

'Pleased to meet you,' Dusty said.

'And you. I'm told we need to talk.'

◆

Dusty caught up again with Callaghan in Mowbray Park's Stable Square at around eleven. The vet furtively scanned the bustling yard before grabbing his arm.

'Too crowded here,' he said, in a voice that sounded like gravel on tin. 'Let's go someplace else.'

Dusty shrugged. 'Wherever you want to talk's fine with me.'

'How about my wagon?'

'Sure.'

Leaving the noise and bustle behind, he followed Callaghan to a battered blue Volvo V70. It was completely out of character with the other vehicles driven by Malek's employees.

Callaghan wrenched open the off-side door, gesturing for Dusty to get in before walking around to the driver's side.

It smelt of stale cigarette smoke and another staleness Dusty couldn't identify.

Flopping into his seat, Callaghan leaned across to retrieve a pack of cigarettes and a lighter from the glove box. With hands that shook slightly, he expertly tapped out the cigarettes, extracted one with his mouth and flicked the lighter. He inhaled deeply before dropping the packet and lighter into the tray in front of the gear stick.

'That bloody Murphy won't let you smoke anywhere near the horses. He's a bloody fanatic. Hope you don't mind – desperate for a fag.'

Dusty did mind but thought it wiser not to object. Anyhow, it was a statement, not a question. Dusty took in the car's interior.

The back seat, a jumble of boxes and bags. The front, a litter of papers, empty food cartons and discarded cigarette packs.

The car quickly filled with smoke. Dusty coughed. 'Can I have the window down?'

'Sure.' He turned on the ignition and activated the window. 'What do you want to talk about?'

Dusty contemplated where to start. He peered through the grubby windscreen to the avenue of oaks, his gaze caught for a few moments by shafts of sunlight stabbing through the dense green canopy.

Before he could phrase his first question, Callaghan switched on the car radio. 'I like some background music when I'm talking around here.'

Dusty glanced out of his window. There wasn't a soul in sight.

Callaghan inhaled deeply again with obvious satisfaction. 'I said, what was it you wanted?' A note of irritation edged the gravelly voice.

'I've been told to take over Bold Challenger and I'm trying to get some background on this virus problem.'

'Background? What d'you mean? How much d'you know?'

Dusty briefly filled him in then said, 'Just before the virus showed up three of the horses ran well above their form. Any idea why?'

Callaghan stared steadfastly ahead. He frowned, as if displeased with something he saw. With an automatic reflex, he knocked ash from his cigarette into an already overflowing ashtray.

'Murphy plans his campaigns well. His job is to produce winners. In any case, there was no sign of the virus before those races. The virus could have been latent until stimulated by the pre-race preparation.'

'That hardly answers my question.'

'I don't know. Must there be a connection?'

'We're looking for common denominators,' said Dusty. 'I've been told all the horses had been kept in the same area for some time before they came here, so let's build on that. After the horses died, who did the autopsies?'

'I did the first two. Someone else did the third.'

'Right.' He wasn't making great progress. 'But surely they showed you that report?'

Callaghan fidgeted uneasily in his seat. He drew deeply again on his cigarette and licked his lips. 'How's about we go somewhere else?'

'What's wrong with here?'

'I dunno, but I need to get away from this place.'

He switched on the ignition and started the engine. 'Let's go into town and get a civilised cup of coffee. I'm thirsty.'

'I'll have to clear it with Murphy. He doesn't like any of us going off without telling him.'

'Ah, don't worry about that shit. If needs be, I'll square it with him when we get back. It's his bloody idea we talk. Dunno why? Can't see the point.'

They headed into town, Callaghan visibly relaxing the further he drove away from Mowbray Park.

Dusty tried again. 'The other day, the virus struck for the fourth time. These tests Riekevic are running, are they any closer to finding out the cause?'

Callaghan shook his head, lit another cigarette from the one he'd just finished and threw the butt out the window.

Dusty hung in there. 'Murphy talked to me yesterday about the geographic link.'

'Did he? News to me.'

The car topped a slight rise and started down the hill into Warrianderra, nestled picturesquely below. Beyond the town,

Dusty could see the river glistening in the sunlight and the steep tree-clad escarpment of the Great Dividing Range. He never tired of looking at it.

'Where else has the virus cropped up?' He knew the answer but wanted to test Callaghan's response.

'Nowhere that I know of. I call it the Malek virus, but only to myself.' His gravelly laugh set off a fit of coughing. When he recovered, he added. 'They don't appreciate my sense of humour.'

The vet avoided other questions Dusty put to him. Soon they pulled up outside one of the town's four hotels.

'Let's get a drink,' Callaghan said, switching off the engine.

'Wasn't it coffee?'

He winked, 'A handy euphemism.'

The Imperial was the second-best pub in town, with carpet on the floor, a pleasant blend of fake wooden panelling, bright, chrome furnishings, pictures of the local Rugby League team and country music playing softly in the background. A couple of men sat at the other end of the counter, while four older men played cards at one of the tables. In a room off the bar, Dusty could see a couple of women playing the pokies.

They breasted the counter. Without being asked, the barman placed a whiskey and a small jug of water in front of Callaghan and shot a questioning look at Dusty.

'A middy of Light, thanks.' He felt uncomfortable drinking at this time of day. He reached for his wallet, but Callaghan waved to the $20 notes he'd already placed on the bar next to his cigarettes and lighter.

'My shout.' He nodded towards the barman filling Dusty's glass. 'Anyway, that won't break the bank.'

Tossing down his drink, Callaghan gestured to the barman for another.

Cradling the fresh whiskey in cupped hands, he turned to Dusty and said in his gravelly voice, 'You don't seem a bad sort of bloke. How'd you get tied up with Malek and Murphy?'

'They offered me a job and they have the best set-up.'

'Be careful. They're not good people.'

Dusty sipped his beer, waiting for his companion to take the initiative. Suddenly, Callaghan raised his glass, looking up at an advertisement high on the wall behind the bar. 'Here's to you, Johnnie Walker, my one and only true friend.' He put down the glass and waved vaguely at the barman, who filled it without comment, taking money from the counter.

'Here, let me.' Dusty reached again for his wallet.

'Nah, forget it. Nothing else to spend it on.'

It was obvious Callaghan was not going to say anything, so he decided on a different tack. 'If Malek and Murphy aren't good people why stick with them?'

'No option, mate. No option.'

'How come?'

Callaghan lapsed into another long silence. Dusty studied his reflection in the mirror behind the bar and sipped his beer. It was so long before Callaghan spoke, he wasn't certain he'd still remember the thread of their conversation. Finally, Callaghan screwed up his face, closing his right eye.

'Some years ago, I had what you might term, a fall from grace. I needed money badly. Did something I shouldn't, got caught and was set for the high jump when a guy called Boris Spetcevic bankrolled an expensive brief to get me off. But mud sticks, I wasn't employable, so when he came up with a job offer, I took it. What else could I do? If it hadn't been for him, I'd have been struck off. Could've finished up in the slammer. Who knows.'

'What's his connection with Malek?'

'Old mates. Came here from Yugoslavia by the seat of their pants. They go back a long way.'

He drained his glass in another gulp, slamming it down onto the bar. 'Come on, I'd better get you back. I'm babbling too much. Let's talk again tomorrow.'

Dusty followed him out. Callaghan had to know exactly what was going on but was being tight-lipped. No doubt up to his neck in the scam, but either too scared or too cunning to talk. The drinking could be a front.

12

Leigh Woodward pushed off his reclining cane chair and crossed to Dusty, who sat with his feet dangling in the cool water of the Woodwards' swimming pool. 'You seem a bit preoccupied. You okay?'

'Yes and no,' Dusty said quietly. 'The last few weeks have been great, but I think I might have just been dropped right into it.'

'Right into what?'

'Whatever they've got planned for me.'

For a few moments, Dusty watched Jem and Rafe splashing happily in the water with the two Woodward boys, then glanced back to the house where Susan Woodward and Jenny were preparing salads for lunch.

'We'd better get the meat going,' said Dusty.

They walked over to a barbeque that looked like the bridge of a small cruiser.

Susan's voice floated from the kitchen with just the right hint of exasperation. 'I hope you've put the meat on, Leigh?'

'Women can see through brick walls,' Woodward pronounced solemnly. He raised his voice. 'Yes, dear.'

He forked steaks, chops and sausages onto the hot plate, which for a few moments claimed his attention. 'Dusty, fix me a wine while I get things going. And get yourself another beer.'

Satisfied with his efforts and with the sound of the now sizzling meat providing background noise, Woodward sipped the glass of chilled pinot grigio and said softly, 'Sure it's a trap?'

'Sure.'

'Want to tell me?'

Dusty described his meeting with Callaghan, the link between Callaghan and Spetcevic, and Spetcevic and Malek. 'Up until now it's been too bloody quiet. Now something's happening and I don't know which way it's going. I sense Callaghan wants to tell me something, but I'm not sure if he's too scared or part of the set-up. Who do you reckon the real brains are? Malek? Spetcevic? Jeezuz, it could even be Callaghan.'

Woodward turned the meat. 'What's your main worry?'

'I think a horse called Bold Challenger's the next mark. He's not great, slow out of the barrier, but once he gets going, he's got a strong burst for about three furlongs. After a lot of work with Vicky as pony rider, I've taken seconds off the first two hundred. If he's held steady for the next four, we can hopefully save something for the finish and he just might win the right race in the right field. Yesterday, I thought I'd test the waters, suggested to Murphy that we nominate him for a maiden over seven or eight furlongs.'

Jenny's voice startled them. 'Come on! Out! All of you. Lunch in five minutes.'

Dusty turned to see her pick up towels from a bench beside the pool.

'Dry yourselves and put your shirts and hats on, you don't want to get burnt.' She came across. 'How's the meat?'

'Ah.' Woodward peered down studiously. 'Ready in five minutes.'

He waited until she was safely out of earshot. 'What was Murphy's response?'

'Agreed,' said Dusty. 'He suggested the Matilda Plate – that's late April.'

Woodward pushed the sausages to the cooler part of the barbeque. 'Makes sense.'

'Then he said he's off to Hong Kong with Malek.'

'So?'

Condensation dribbled down the side of Dusty's beer. 'Grimes once told me Murphy's always dangerous when he's amenable.'

'And he was amenable?'

'For him. The question is what'll happen between now and race day? And if it is a trap, when will they will spring it?'

Dusty was interrupted by Jenny and Susan's arrival with the salads.

Woodward started to heap meat onto large platters. 'Damn it,' he said under his breath. 'Just as it gets interesting.'

They sat at the large outdoor table, enjoying the food, the wine and the conversation.

'Thanks for having us,' Jenny said when they were nearly finished. 'We do enjoy these days, and we actually get to see something of Dusty, don't we, honey?'

'I could say the same about Leigh. And if you're all finished,' said Susan to the boys, who were getting restless, 'you can go in and play video games while your lunch settles. Oh, by the way, Jenny, I must show you what I'm planning for the garden.'

Woodward watched them go. 'It may help if I fill you in on what Carmody's been doing since we spoke. He sent a couple of guys to Riekevic posing as reps from an overseas pharmaceutical company interested in funding new research. They have an experimental lab, but it's strictly off limits.'

'Did they learn anything?'

'Nothing – didn't get past the door.'

Woodward paused as their wives returned.

'I'll strike you some cuttings,' said Susan, sitting at the table.

'How about coffee, sweetheart?' Woodward suggested to Susan.

'I thought you might've made it for us,' she replied tartly. 'Jenny, would you like coffee?'

'Lovely.'

'Then, if you boys clear the table, we'll do coffee.'

'Fair enough, c'mon, Dusty.' Together, the two men scraped and stacked the plates.

In a voice that wouldn't carry to the kitchen, Woodward continued: 'So Carmody tried another tack, used some glamour girl to chat up one of the lab techs. She was a bit more successful. Found out they're developing a new type of drug to treat influenza in greyhounds, but there's also a top-secret project Spetcevic works on alone. Apparently, he's a brilliant chemist.'

Again, they were frustrated by the arrival of the coffee and strawberry tarts.

Woodward groaned. 'I'm glad we don't eat like this every day. I'd be as fat as a barrel.' He yawned. 'I think I need a sleep.'

'You need exercise,' Susan said with a laugh. 'Don't be so lazy. Show Dusty the Trakehner warmblood down in the bottom paddock. You'll love her, Dusty, she's gorgeous, well over sixteen hands.'

'Good idea. We need to settle lunch to make room for dinner.'

'Guts, don't be too long.'

The two men strolled to the bottom of the garden where a gate led to the run which serviced the lower paddocks.

Woodward turned back to latch the gate. 'By the way, the tests came up negative.'

'Tests?'

'The samples you took. Stuff in the vial was useless, probably exposed to the air for too long and the samples showed nothing. Not a bloody thing.'

'They took their time.'

'They tried growing cultures to identify the chemical elements, but it's not easy when you don't know what you're looking for.'

'Perhaps there's nothing to find.'

'No, I'm sure we're missing something. Blaza's reaction points to a side effect of something we can't pin.'

'Then what do we do?'

'That's where you come in. You've got to be on the spot next time they try something. If you're right, and Murphy is setting you up, then that's our best chance.'

Dusty gazed across the peaceful vista of paddocks stretching to the tree line and topping the riverbank beyond. The afternoon was hot and humid. Dark clouds were building beyond the range.

'Any theories?'

Woodward shook his head. 'For us to find out.'

Dusty thought it over. His voice carried a worried edge, 'I don't know. It's a big risk. I agreed to pick up what I could and to date that's been zilch, but how far am I expected to go?'

'Get a bit more proactive. Try to get closer to Callaghan or perhaps Grimes. He must know something. Drop a few hints you want a slice of the action.'

'Do you know what you're asking?'

'The stakes are high.'

By this time, they'd reached the lower paddock. The sight of the magnificent horse cropping the last vestiges of green pasture pushed Dusty's worries back.

He slipped through the fence and walked over to the grey mare.

'What a beauty.' He ran his hand down the deeply sloping shoulders and along her flank to the powerful hindquarters. 'When did you buy her?'

'Oh, she's not mine. Belongs to Mrs Seymour up the valley. She asked me to look after her while she's back in Germany buying another one. Her blood line includes the legendary Pythagoras. Trakehners go back nearly four hundred years, but they were almost wiped out in the Second World War.'

Dusty continued to run his hands over the mare, talking in a low, slightly sing-song tone. She responded by turning her finely chiselled head towards him and nuzzling his shoulder. He rubbed her nose and gazed into the large dark eyes.

Woodward called from the fence, 'Why would anyone want to destroy creatures like this?'

Dusty only partly heard the words, which were snatched away by the wind. He walked slowly back to the fence, turning for a last look.

'What was that?'

The other man looked at him intently for a few seconds, 'How can people like Malek destroy beautiful creatures like that?'

Dusty shook his head. 'Beyond my comprehension.'

They walked back to the house in silence.

Woodward's words troubled Dusty. He thought of Blaza dying in agony and the horses before that. When they reached the gate, he said softly but firmly, 'I suppose that's the best reason. They're evil bastards who've got to be stopped.'

13

Every Friday afternoon, a group of locals gathered in the Warrianderra Club for a drink and a postmortem of the past week. Although not a great drinker, Dusty liked the ritual of regularly catching up with his mates. Some he'd gone to school with, others he knew from the building trade. Most were interested in horses, or at least having a flutter on the TAB, so Dusty's advice was eagerly sought whenever they met.

'Going okay,' Dusty assured one of the guys. 'If you find a bookie who'll give you odds of ten to one or better on Bold Challenger, I'd stick $20 on him now. You'll get those odds because a horse called Red Sands is shaping up as the hot favourite and Bold Challenger's odds could shorten towards race day.'

'Youse guys want another round?' Sandy, the bartender, came over to collect their empty glasses.

'Sure, Sandy. Same again, everyone?'

They all nodded.

'Three schooners of New, one Old with a dash, two middies of Light.'

'Spot on, luv.'

As she filled the glasses, she spoke to Dusty in a quieter voice, 'How's that horse of yours goin'? When's he gunna race?'

'Matilda Stakes, late April.'

'Dusty says you can back your virginity on him, Sandy,' one of the men called to her.

'Goin' that bad, is he?' she replied with a laugh. 'Although, what you'd know about virginity'd go on the back of a postage stamp, Freddie.'

They all laughed at Freddie's expense.

She gathered the empties and nodded to Dusty to follow her down the bar where she stacked them in the dishwasher. 'I hear Red Sands is pretty hot.'

Dusty nodded. 'I reckon we'll give him a good run, so put a few dollars on as soon as you can, then on the day take the quinella on both. But if anyone asks, tell 'em you're putting your money on Red Sands.'

Sandy closed the dishwasher then turned back to the bar. 'Good luck. You deserve it. You're a nice man.'

After another round, Dusty was ready to leave. He'd promised Jenny he'd be home by five o'clock. 'Gotta go, fellas. See you next Friday?'

'Same time, same place,' came the answering chorus.

He headed towards the door that led onto a long narrow verandah overlooking the bowling green. Several older members were playing and the faint click of bowl on bowl came to Dusty's ears. It was a pleasant sound. He hoped one day he could be one of those players.

As he turned towards the path below, a slurred voice called out, 'Hey, Rhodes!'

He swung in its direction. At first, he saw only a group of bowlers, resplendent in their creams, having afternoon tea and analysing their games. Beyond their tables, he noticed an arm raised as if waving a salute, beckoning him over. Threading his way past the bowlers he recognised Bryan Callaghan, whiskey glass in one hand, cigarette in the other, a half-full ashtray in front.

'How's it going?' Callaghan's voice was thick but slow and deliberate. 'Have a seat, need to talk. Was going to talk to you tomorrow but saw you now and thought this'd be easier.'

Dusty glanced at his watch. He had neither the inclination nor the time to talk to the vet, even if the man were sober.

'Look, I'm late already. Can't it wait until tomorrow?'

'Thas the trouble with you eager young beavers, always in a hurry. No time to be sociable. Sid down. Only take a coupla minutes.'

Reluctantly Dusty sat.

'Drink?'

'No, thanks, I've had enough.'

'And you think I've had too much?'

'Perhaps.'

Callaghan stared intently at Dusty then caught sight of a roving steward in the background. He raised his glass to indicate he wanted another drink and drained what was left in his glass before replacing it on the table.

'I wanna give you a bit of advice.'

Dusty shrugged.

'You seem a decent young bloke and I like the way you handle horses. Take my advice – get out of Mowbray Park while you can. Malek and Murphy are setting you up, mark my words, and when they set their mind to it, there's no escape. I'm telling you, if you wanna finish up like me, just keep goin' as you are.'

He paused, frowning. 'Something else I should tell you, but if you've gotta go, it'll have to wait. Just remember what I said.'

He closed his eyes. Dusty got the distinct impression the vet was no longer aware of his presence. Quietly he got up and left.

14

On the day of the Matilda Cup, the last horse had been unloaded and Grimes and Vicky had gone up to the mounting yard for the first race. Warrianderra Race Club's annual Veterans Day had begun.

Dusty was glad to be on his own. For the last week he'd scarcely let Bold Challenger out of his sight. The last four nights he had slept at the stable to ensure there'd be no interference.

Jenny had been furious when he told her what he was doing. While she understood the significance of the race, believing the quicker he built his reputation, the quicker he'd quit Mowbray Park, she thought he was quite mad, not knowing the real reason for his concern. She'd even gone so far as to throw in the veiled suggestion that he might be having some sort of an affair. That really hurt.

Now at the track, he was keen to stay near his horse, glad his was in the second race.

A tiny electric shock ran through him when he saw Callaghan. The vet looked smarter than usual with neatly pressed trousers and shirt and a jaunty pork-pie hat, but Dusty detected an air of menace beneath the professional façade. When Callaghan saw Dusty, he seemed momentarily taken aback. 'Hi, Rhodes, beautiful day!'

'Sure is. What brings you down here?'

'Keeping an eye on things, earning my board and keep. Report that to Murphy, if you don't mind. Bugger accused me last time of spending all day at the bar. What's wrong with that? Not much else going on.'

'I'll tell him.'

'Thank you,' he said rather stiffly. 'Everything all right? Any need for my services?'

'No, everything's fine. Go back to the bar, then I'll know where to find you if I need you. And I won't tell Murphy.'

'A kind suggestion. Going to watch the race?'

Though casual, the question triggered another tiny jolt to Dusty's nerves. Keeping his voice equally casual he said, 'One last thing to check and I'm off.'

'Good lad. I'll take up your most excellent suggestion and repair to the Horseshoe Bar for some light refreshment.'

He turned on his heel and walked away. Dusty followed the pork-pie hat until it disappeared, but not in the direction of the Horseshoe Bar.

On a sudden impulse, Dusty wanted to know where Callaghan had gone. Reaching the end of the stalls, he walked towards the track to see if Callaghan might be watching. Continuing until he found himself behind a caterer's van, he veered off towards the grandstand to check the Horseshoe Bar. No surprise – Callaghan wasn't there. Certain that his hunch was right, Dusty doubled back through the crowd. Some twenty metres ahead he spied the pork-pie hat heading towards the stalls.

He'd closed half the distance before the man stopped and turned. The sight of a neatly trimmed beard created a surge of relief. Perhaps Callaghan had gone to watch the race after all, in which case there would be nothing to stop Bold Challenger racing on its merits. Quickening his pace, Dusty returned to Bold Challenger's stall.

He was four metres away when he saw a second pork-pie hat.

A few long strides covered the remaining distance. Callaghan was fumbling with the wrapping of a package.

'What d'you think you're doing?'

Callaghan swung around – a startled look, tinged with fear, flashed in his watery blue eyes. His left hand went under his jacket to hide what he was holding.

'Nothing! Can't a man move round here without being yelled at?'

'Not here. You know Murphy's instructions.'

'Yes,' he hissed. 'I know Murphy's instructions. I'm not sure you do.'

'What's that supposed to mean?'

'Look, son, I gave you advice once before, but you chose not to take it.'

'Did you really expect me to?'

'I thought you might. It's obvious you didn't, so let me try once more. Turn around, walk away, wait a couple of minutes. By the time you get back I'll be gone.'

'Why?'

'Because I know what Murphy's instructions are.'

This was the trap Murphy had set. He might be thousands of kilometres away in Hong Kong, but his evil influence was here on the ground. Dusty glanced at his watch. Grimes and Vicky would be back within fifteen minutes. He had to stall Callaghan from using the injection he knew was hidden under his jacket.

The vet licked his lips with fear.

Dusty glanced at his watch, then at Callaghan. 'What's in your hand?'

'Nothing.'

'Don't be pathetic.' Dusty stepped close to him, reaching forward to grab Callaghan's wrist.

The man took a step back, saliva dribbling from his mouth. 'Go to hell! Better still, take that walk.'

'Why?'

'For your good and mine.'

'Why should I worry about you?'

'No need.' His lips curled in a snarl. 'But I worry about me.'

'That's your problem. Get away from the horse.' Dusty roughly jabbed Callaghan's left shoulder, spinning him back against the rails that separated the stalls. Callaghan put out an arm to steady himself giving Dusty a glimpse of the packet.

'Nothing in your hand, huh? Then what's this?' Again, Dusty reached out, this time to grasp Callaghan's wrist, thrusting it high in the air and pulling him towards himself before turning to slam him against the solid back wall.

Callaghan gave a rasping gasp. 'Malek makes accidents happen,' he babbled. 'If … don't … dope … life not worth … living.' His eyes held a look of extreme anguish.

'What'll they do?' Dusty's voice was contemptuous. 'You're a weak, worthless drunk. If you'd any guts you'd be the one to walk away.'

Dusty pinned Callaghan against the wall, left hand high above his shoulder, his right clamped against the rail.

'If I don't,' the vet's voice dropped to a whisper, 'they'll kill me.'

'Come off it, this isn't the 1920s. Even the likes of Malek and Murphy don't go round killing people.'

Callaghan's legs gave way and he slowly slid down the wall. Dusty let him go. Callaghan dropped to his knees, whimpering. 'You don't know Malek … seen the things I've seen. I can't cross him.'

'How'll they know?' Dusty said. 'It's just between you and me. Hand over the stuff and get out or I'll report you to the stewards.'

'Jesus, Rhodes, you're more stupid than I thought.' Callaghan whimpered.

But Dusty's confidence was growing every minute. Grimes and Vicky must be back soon.

'Hand it over.'

Gaining some measure of control Callaghan returned the package to his pocket. 'You're not thinking straight. You're between a rock and a hard place. Go tell the stewards. For Christ's sake Malek and Murphy are in Hong Kong. Malek has connections. Who d'you think they'll believe? No mate, we're up to our necks in horse shit.'

'Okay. I won't tell them. I'll destroy the stuff. They'll never know.'

'Except Malek.'

'How? You've just reminded me he's in Hong Kong.'

'With this little package the horse can't lose. Without it, we don't rate a chance. They're clever. You're responsible. If the horse wins, it's been doped. If it loses, we've reneged. Believe me, they'll know. Both our lives won't be worth a pinch of shit.'

Dusty was growing impatient. 'No matter what you do, you can't be bloody certain the horse will win. You can improve its chances, but you can't be certain.'

'With this stuff you can. It's like shoving a rocket up its arse.'

'Given that sort of reaction the stewards will take a swab for sure.'

A sneaky look mixed with something close to pride crept across Callaghan's face. 'That's the beauty of it.'

'What d'you mean?'

'I've said too much.' Callaghan put his hand in his pocket and drew out the syringe then with unexpected swiftness kneed Dusty in the groin.

Dusty doubled up. 'You fuckin' old bastard.'

Through the tears in his eyes, he saw Callaghan fitting the

needle. Callaghan punctured the top of the vial. Dusty lurched forward, reaching the vet and pushing him once again back against the wall.

'Gimme the stuff,' he said, changing tack. Maybe this was his only chance to save the horse, save them both by giving Bold Challenger a reduced dose. 'I'll do it. Grimes and Vicky are due back any minute. Stall them until you see me step out on to the path.'

The look of surprise and relief in Callaghan's eyes said it all.

'Thank Christ, you've got the message.' He thrust the syringe at Dusty and pointed to a spot just above the breastbone. 'Here. And hurry, much later and it won't work.'

Behind them people were starting to drift back. 'Piss off. Keep Grimes and Vicky away for a couple of minutes.'

'Gotta stay here, to see you do it.'

'Get out there and stall them or nothing will happen, you bloody idiot.'

Callaghan left. A few seconds later Dusty heard him say, 'Just a moment, Larry Grimes, is that horse walking funny or am I seeing things?'

'Looks alright to me,' Grimes said. 'But be my guest. It was a pretty ordinary performance, so perhaps something's wrong.'

Dusty stared at the needle. Callaghan was right. Nothing could link Malek with anything that happened here; nothing to even link Callaghan. Callaghan was weak, frightened and untrustworthy. The dice was loaded, Dusty had no choice. He pressed the plunger, the contents dribbled to the ground.

Stepping onto the path, he caught Callaghan's eye and nodded.

Callaghan eased down the hoof. 'Looks okay. Bit of heat in the pastern and coronet, maybe a touch of laminitis. I'll check again tomorrow.'

Vicky came around Bold Challenger to where Dusty was standing.

'Ready?' she said. 'We need to start moving.'

'Ready as we'll ever be.'

'You've done a great job.'

'Have you seen Red Sands? Formidable.'

Vicky was irrepressibly cheerful. 'Gotta be an optimist in this godforsaken world.'

Callaghan chimed in, 'Just told him the same thing. He sure takes some convincing.'

Dusty untied the halter holding the horse's head and backed him slowly onto the path.

'Go ahead Vicky. I'll be with you in a minute.'

His stomach churned at the thought of what the drug could have done. He stood for a moment with his head pressed against the horse's shoulder.

He led Bold Challenger along the path to the mounting yard, handed him to Vicky just outside and found a place along the perimeter rail with a good view of the track. His heart thumped; his legs felt weak. He tried to act casual, but when he'd watched Red Sands enter the enclosure to be paraded, his heart sank. The horse looked every inch a winner. He tried to push away thoughts of the ugly consequences.

The horses were now out on the track, cantering in a strung-out line to the starting gate. For a couple of minutes, they milled around waiting their turn to be led into their stall.

Finally, 'The starter has them,' intoned the race caller. 'The line's steady. They're ready to break in Race 2, the Matilda Plate.'

'They're off. It's a clean start. Bold Challenger on the extreme outside has hit the front ahead of The Busker and Fast Lady, with the favourite Red Sands tucked on the rails. Come-by-Chance has settled just off the pace, then Dusky Rose, Loves-a-Luxury, Emancipist with Blue Sky last.

'Past the eight hundred and Bold Challenger leads narrowly from The Busker, who's pulling hard; with a length or so to Fast Lady; Red Sands jockey has put his foot down and is starting to close on the leaders. Come-by-Chance's found a gap and has moved up on the rails just behind the leaders, a length and a half back to Dusky Rose, Loves-a-Luxury and Emancipist bunched together with Blue Sky a length and a half away last.'

'Hold him steady,' Dusty muttered, hoping the jockey remembered his instructions.

'Bold Challenger's back to second at the four hundred, with Red Sands surging forward to take the lead. The Busker and Fast Lady are locked together, Come-by-Chance's still well placed on the rails. Dusky Rose is starting a strong run on the outside followed closely by Loves-a-Luxury. Two lengths back to The Busker with Blue Sky closing up fast, Emancipist dropping back to last.'

Caught up with the growing roar of the crowd, Dusty was yelling, 'Now! Now! Give him his head!'

The caller's voice had now reached a frenetic pitch. 'With two hundred to go, Red Sands still leads with Bold Challenger hanging on half a length back. Both have kicked clear of The Busker and Fast Lady, but it's a two-horse race – Dusky Rose fifth, Come-by-Chance dropping back, Loves-a-Luxury, Blue Sky and Emancipist well back.'

Dusty closed his eyes, but the commentary battered his ears.

'In the straight with a hundred to go, Bold Challenger has found some extra speed and has thrown down the gauntlet. They're on their own. It's all Bold Challenger and Red Sands. Bold Challenger hits the front and wins by a head. Three lengths back it's Fast Lady, The Busker ...'

Dusty didn't hear the rest. Instead, he offered up a silent prayer.

He became aware of Grimes standing beside him, obviously jubilant.

'I'm off to collect. How about you?'

'Didn't have a bet.'

'What! You're out of your cotton-pickin' mind!' Shaking his head he walked off to the betting ring to pick up a tidy bundle from the bookies. Dusty watched his departing figure. Grimes was in on the scam.

The four-sided tower clock on the Member's Stand ticked the minutes away to the next race. Punters and bookies alike would regroup, focusing their attention on Race 3, which was due to start at 2:55.

Dusty leant back against the rail and while his heart had slowed to a steady beat, the tension had moved to his head as his mind grappled with what might happen next. At least there was no immediate crisis on the Malek front, and Bold Challenger's finishing burst might have just been enough to satisfy Murphy.

Again, the loudspeaker crackled into life. The club secretary was introducing the club's chairman. On a sudden impulse, Dusty pushed off the rail and walked quickly towards the Member's Stand for the presentation.

Peering over the crowd gathered three deep against the fence, he heard the chairman thank the sponsors, the crowd and whoever sent the fine weather. He spoke of Bold Challenger's outstanding run and the strong support the Malek stable gave to local racing. Congratulating the stable on its win, he regretted Malek could not be present due to commitments overseas and welcomed Mr Clarence Keenan to accept the trophy. There was brief applause.

The secretary took the cut-glass trophy from the table, handing it to the chairman who in turn handed it to Keenan. The chairman was no stranger to the ritual.

Before stepping up to the microphone, Keenan took a sheet of paper from his jacket.

Keenan was Malek's accountant and, as the next in line after Malek, had got the job of accepting the prize.

Dusty soon lost interest. Idly he scanned the motley crowd, pausing to admire an attractive young woman standing by the fence to his left. A large brown leather bag hung from one shoulder, a camera from the other. She scribbled furiously in a notebook.

Dusty's gaze returned to Bold Challenger, who with ears pricked was enjoying the show and the attention. Then Keenan's words cut through his disengaged thoughts.

'Finally, we'd like to pay special tribute to one of our young trainers, Danny Rhodes, to whom all credit for this outstanding win must go. Without Danny's total commitment to preparing the horse, we may not have had the win. We look forward to his long and successful career at Mowbray Park.'

The words, simple and apparently unambiguous, carried a special and chilling message. Malek wouldn't let Dusty go. Troubled, he turned away, noticing again the attractive young woman. She looked in his general direction, her face lighting up with a smile. Dusty wondered who the lucky guy was, then joined Vicky who was leading Bold Challenger out.

'Keenan's gone to the Horseshoe Bar. Murphy said he was to shout you a drink if you won,' she told him.

Dusty pulled a long face.

'You'd better go,' she said. 'It's sort of expected.'

◆

Dusty pushed through the crowd in the bar to find Keenan holding court at the far end. A small, pasty-faced man, Keenan was neatly, almost fastidiously dressed. It was said that his much larger wife unmercifully bossed him around at home. Dusty could imagine him spending hours on Malek's ledgers to escape his wife.

Today though, he was enjoying a moment of glory and Dusty observed with amusement how success attracted hangers-on. Many glasses of champagne were consumed and the noise level threatened to break the work health and safety standard.

On the bar beside Keenan stood a silver-plated ice bucket, the neck of a magnum of champagne protruding. Perched on stools to his left and conspicuous in the male crowd were two flashily dressed young women.

Dusty, reluctant to plunge into the exuberant crowd, eyed the scene with distaste, like arriving at a party sober when everyone else was drunk.

The accountant caught sight of him and waved him over, pouring him a glass. Dusty smiled weakly when Keenan raised his glass. 'A toast!'

The acolytes dutifully followed suit. 'To our young trainer, Dusty Rhodes.'

A chorus of 'Dusty Rhodes' echoed around the bar. The two women giggled inanely. One grabbed Keenan's arm, drawing him to her in a big hug. Keenan flushed red but did nothing to break away. She kept her hold, clinging to him. The other patrons downed whatever they were drinking before slipping back into their previous conversations.

During the next five minutes Keenan's face became more flushed than ever, his voice taking on a distinctly raucous tone. Perspiring heavily, he waved again to Dusty. 'Come over here. Someone wants to meet you.'

The second woman held an arm out to Dusty. 'You're cute,' she said.

'I'd better get back to the horses,' Dusty replied, looking for an escape route.

'Can I come?'

'It's dirty down there. You'd spoil your clothes. Perhaps next time, if you come in jeans and a t-shirt.'

'Oooh, I couldn't come to the races dressed like that, could I?'

'No, I suppose not. Too bad. Nice meeting you.'

Detaching himself from the young woman, who turned her fluttering eyes elsewhere, he pushed his way across to Keenan who was laughing and joking with his companion. He had a smudge of lipstick on his cheek.

'I'm off, Mr Keenan. Thanks for the drink. Got to get back. I can't expect Grimes and Vicky to do everything.'

'Off you go then. Congratulations again.' The accountant put his index finger to the side of his nose. 'There'll be plenty more, if you get my drift.' He winked before turning back.

◆

From nowhere, a group of four men had materialised outside Bold Challenger's empty stall. One wore a white coat and carried a bag.

'One of the suited men addressed Dusty, who was busy in the next stall, 'Excuse me. Where's the horse?'

'At the wash bay, why?'

'Get him back here as quickly as you can. We want to take a swab.'

'A swab? Why, what's the matter?'

'None of your business.'

'It is my business, I'm his trainer.'

'Are you? That's interesting. So you would be …' The man in the white coat consulted the pad he carried. 'Daniel Rhodes?'

'That's right.'

'Then perhaps you ought to know, there'll be an inquiry into the running of Race 2.'

'Go right ahead. I am sure you will find everything's fine with us.'

Dusty looked down at a moist patch on the ground. The gods had smiled on him for his courage and his integrity.

15

After successfully negotiating the keyhole, the bay gelding knocked the top rail off the final triple bar jump. A ripple of polite applause from the small group of spectators greeted the rider as she crossed the finish line of the cross-country course.

The announcer's voice crackled over the loudspeaker, 'Number 27.' Leigh Woodward pushed his grey Arab mare up to the starting line.

The bell rang and Woodward, who liked to compete in the Equestrian Club's eventing days, headed towards the first jump. This was his release from the rigours imposed by his veterinary practice. He completed the round with only one jumping fault and a ten second time penalty. Woodward and his mare cantered over to where Dusty was waiting. Swinging down, he gave Dusty the reins and waved to Susan, Jenny and the children.

Jenny greeted him. 'Well done, Leigh. She handled the course like a veteran.'

'Do you want to eat now?' Susan asked.

'You go ahead. I'll help Dusty and we will be back that much quicker,' Woodward responded.

'You stay here. I can manage. I'll head over to the float with her and be back in no time,' Dusty said as he patted the horse's neck.

Woodward walked some way off with the women before he said to them, 'I think I had better go and help Dusty; can't expect him to do everything.' This would be a good opportunity to get a few minutes in which they could update each other on Mowbray Park.

◆

Dusty had the saddle off and was giving the mare a good rub down by the time Woodward came to the float. While he worked, he struck up a conversation with the young woman who had ridden the previous horse. She introduced herself as Kerry Suster, a journalist from the local newspaper.

As Woodward approached them, she greeted him enthusiastically. 'Hi, Mr Woodward. Your friend has been giving me some great advice.'

'Then listen carefully. He knows what he's talking about.'

She was in her mid-twenties and her large dark brown eyes sparkled mischievously.

'The girls will have lunch ready soon. Care to join us?' Woodward asked her.

'No, thanks all the same. That's very kind of you, but I'm with some friends.' She turned to Dusty. 'But I'd love it if you could demonstrate what you were saying … perhaps after lunch?'

Dusty checked his watch. 'The show jumping starts about 2:15 and you're Number 26, so it'll be at least 3:15 before you're on. I'll look you up, say about two. Where's your float?'

She pointed to a float painted in chartreuse and powder blue. 'Over there.'

Dusty smiled. 'See you at two.'

'Look forward to it.'

They watched her walk away.

'Just keep your mind on the horse, young fella,' Woodward said.

'Don't worry – she's in a different league.'

◆

After a pleasant lunch, Dusty lay on the bright tartan rug Jenny had brought, his head cradled in her lap. He closed his eyes and ran through his brief discussion with Woodward at the float.

Two weeks after the Veteran's Day meeting, there still hadn't been a result from the stewards' inquiry. Why hadn't Callaghan seemed concerned? And Woodward had said, 'It is unusual for Racing Analytical Services, the national drug testing agency, to take so long to submit their report.'

Dusty drifted into a light sleep, only to be woken by the laughter of the four boys playing a game.

'What were you dreaming?' Jenny said.

'Nothing much, why?'

'Your face was twitching, like a little dog when it's dreaming.'

'What's the time?'

'Ten to two.'

'Crikey. I'd better get moving. I promised one of the other competitors I'd show her how to get her horse to tuck his legs up more. The trailing leg keeps clipping the rails on the way through.'

He got to his feet and shook some crumbs off the front of his shirt.

'Help me up,' Jenny said. 'My leg's gone to sleep.'

He pulled her to her feet and held her steady for a few moments.

'That's better,' she said, stamping to get the circulation flowing. 'Off you go – mustn't keep your lady waiting.'

As Dusty started to walk away, he heard Susan call out, 'You can't help yourself, can you? Always got to be doing something for someone.'

◆

Kerry Suster was waiting beside her float, her horse saddled and ready.

'Nice horse, what do you call him?'

'Mister Darcy, after Darcy in *Pride and Prejudice*.'

'Looks like an ex-racehorse, where'd you get him?'

'Mowbray Park.'

Dusty raised his eyebrows.

'The Clarion runs a large commercial printing business as well as publishing the paper, and the Park's a good client. He who pays the piper calls the tune.' She laughed pleasantly. 'So, stories on their horses appear regularly. I cover the races, which brings me into contact with Max Murphy. I told him I was looking for a horse so he offered me Darcy at a good price.'

'Know Murphy well?'

'Oh, quite well. He often comes in with material. He knows I love horses, so we sometimes have a coffee at the Dew Drop Inn, and he talks about his work. Interesting man … and I think he enjoys talking to a pretty woman.'

'Bit of a ladies' man?'

'Not really. Anyway, he's not my type.'

Dusty sensed an opportunity. 'What does he talk about?'

'He's an organised sort of person, but you'd know that working for him. When he got me Darcy, he handed over all his papers. The detail was incredible. He says, "You can't know too much about a horse, from the time it foals to the time you've finished with it".'

'Finished with it?'

'You know what I mean. If it's no good for racing or for stud, it's not much use to them. As Murphy says, "They're running a business",' she finished rather lamely.

'I've never felt that he really loves horses.'

'I don't think that's quite right. Probably true of Malek. He pushes Murphy very hard.'

'The law of Mowbray Park,' Dusty murmured.

'What?'

'Nothing. Nothing at all. Now let me hop on. I'll show you what I was talking about, then you can have a go.'

He swung himself into the saddle. 'Now listen and watch carefully.'

He demonstrated the technique he'd explained earlier before handing her the reins. After several attempts, she cleared the triple bar with ease. She brought the horse back to Dusty, a smile lighting up her delicate features.

'That's absolutely fantastic. I can't believe the difference. You're a genius.'

'Don't know about that. With horses, it's a matter of understanding and working on the positives. Simple really, horses love to run and jump. They do it in the wild. If you encourage them to enjoy what they're doing, they'll always give more than if you force them. That's where so many trainers go wrong; they think they can punish a horse into performing well.'

She swung down and slackened the girth. 'Even Mister Darcy enjoyed it.'

'Because you collected him in a way that enabled him to clear the jump without striking it. Even if it doesn't hurt, and it can, they don't like knocking themselves. You'll seldom see a horse that's running free knock itself when it jumps.'

She pulled the saddle off and threw on a rug. 'We're going to enjoy the round aren't we, Mister Darcy?'

Mister Darcy shook his head up and down as if in agreement. She slipped the reins over her arm to lead him back to her float.

'Thanks again. Can't say how grateful I am.'

'Then don't. Glad to help.'

She started to walk off then turned back. 'Oh, by the way – off the record – is that how you got Bold Challenger to win last week?'

'What do you mean by "off the record"?'

'Journo's term for something they don't intend to report.'

Dusty looked thoughtful, taking a moment to consider if what he had just said would be off the record. Well, he had his version of the facts and he would stick to that. Satisfied it wouldn't matter either way, he explained how he'd been working on getting Bold Challenger out of the barrier quicker, then settling back in the middle of the race so that he still had a turn of speed at the finish.

'It was unexpected though, you've got to admit,' she said. 'Red Sands looked a sure thing at the five hundred.'

'Wouldn't be the first time that things turned out differently on the day.'

'There'd be a good story in your approach to training, particularly if you can repeat what you did with Bold Challenger.'

When they reached the float, she took the bridle off and slipped on a halter, tethering Mister Darcy to the side of the float.

'There's nothing special. It's knowing the horse, its temperament, its physical capabilities and taking it as far as you can, then in the race itself, getting the jockey to do exactly what you want – plus a little luck.'

She looked at him long and hard. 'I spoke to the jockey after the race. He was surprised he responded so well at the finish – said he had a real burst of speed.'

'Shouldn't have been. "Hold him steady," I said, then, "Two furlongs out, give him his head".'

'But he seemed to feel it was, shall we say, unusual, after being headed by a horse like Red Sands, to get up again so easily.'

'It was a tight race. Either horse could have won.'

By now Kerry had taken off her hard hat, running her hands through her hair and shaking it into a little tousled bob.

'Oh, by the way.' Her dark brown eyes fixed him with a steady gaze. 'I think I should tell you, off the record, the Race Club are about to launch an inquiry into the running of that race. They got an anonymous tip-off that Bold Challenger was doped. Know anything about that?'

16

Dusty arrived home from work with a headache and stress pains in his arms and legs. He'd been unable to shake the anxiety he'd felt since Kerry Suster had told him about the pending inquiry. He knew the test for drugging would be negative, but clearly suspicion was mounting about the training practices at Mowbray Park.

The boys rushed at him before he was properly in the door, grabbing him around the legs and gabbling together, 'Daddy, Daddy, there's an important letter for you.'

'It's got gowld on it,' Rafe said. 'Is it real gowld?'

'We'll have a look.' The envelope was prominently displayed on the kitchen dresser. It bore the gold crest of the Warrianderra Race Club.

'Looks like real gold,' Jem said.

Dusty carefully slit open the envelope, giving it to the boys who immediately rushed off to store it with their other treasures. He unfolded the letter. The heading read:

INQUIRY – SHOW CAUSE NOTICE

He read it quickly. The Race Club was instituting an inquiry into the running of Race 2 from the Veteran's Day meeting. As the trainer of the winner, he was summoned to appear before the club's committee. The inquiry related to the offence of 'Not letting a horse race on its merits'. In the event of a negative finding, his licence could be revoked. Dusty slumped in his chair. The letter gave no information and its officious tone was brutal.

◆

Dusty drove through the large ornamental gates of the Warrianderra Race Club and along the tree-lined driveway. Between the trees he caught glimpses of the immaculate gardens. One of the finest provincial race clubs in the country, it had been built on the legacy of the pioneer pastoralist and timber baron, Sir Charlton Matthews, whose passion was horse racing.

Matthews had created his own exclusive race club using part of his mansion as the club rooms. When his wife and only child were killed in a buggy accident, he'd become a recluse. A few years later, he transferred the house and racetrack, together with two hundred acres and a large settlement of money in public trust, to an independent club with the objective of maintaining a facility that would pursue excellence in the sport of kings.

Successive committees ensured his wishes were fulfilled. To maintain a cash flow, they'd established a large associate membership, although this did not include access to the clubhouse with its commanding view of the racetrack. Full membership of the club was limited under the terms of the trust to one hundred members. There was a long waiting list of hopefuls. It was rumoured Donovan Malek's nomination was still pending.

Dusty parked his ute in the red gravel parking area, noting the small group of expensive cars parked in spaces defined by their elegantly scripted signage. These, he presumed, belonged to the committee members who sat in judgement on the likes of him.

Crossing the neatly raked surface that crunched discreetly

underfoot, he stepped onto the wide, flagged verandah and into the coolness of the front hallway. A sign on a wooden pedestal directed him to the reception office, where he was greeted by an elegantly dressed woman sitting behind a large mahogany desk.

Her face betrayed no reaction. 'May I help you?'

He proffered his letter for her inspection. 'Dan Rhodes. I'm appearing before the committee.'

Waving it aside, she consulted a list on her desk. 'Rhodes. Yes, thank you.' She ticked his name. 'Would you come this way?'

He followed her along the hallway, the sound of their footsteps swallowed by the thick carpet. They passed a lounge on the right and a dining room on the left, before entering a large central lobby.

'Wait here. The secretary will call you when the committee is ready.'

Without further word, she turned on her heel and left him alone with his thoughts. Glancing around the lobby, with its dark wood panelling and austere portraits of past chairmen, Dusty felt like a schoolboy summoned to appear before the headmaster. From the high vaulted ceiling with its magnificent chandelier, to the red, studded leather chairs and the huge cedar cabinet displaying a collection of gold and silver trophies, it seemed as if everything was designed to intimidate. A grandfather clock ticked the seconds away in strong, even beats. The club was a remnant of an era of class and privilege now gone from everyday life.

He studied the trophies until he heard a door open. A thin bespectacled man appeared. He acknowledged Dusty with a nod. 'James Smythe, club secretary. The committee will see you now.'

His initial impression was of high ceilings, lots of light and an imposing portrait of a Victorian gentleman, who he assumed was the legendary Sir Charlton Matthews.

Beneath the portrait's stern and unfaltering gaze, the chairman sat at the end of the board table, flanked by his fellow committee men. The secretary directed Dusty to an uncomfortable upright chair at the near end before taking his place to the chairman's right. In front of each man lay an impressive pile of papers.

'Sit down, Mr Rhodes. Thank you for coming.'

Momentarily overcome by the grandeur of the room, Dusty nodded and took the seat.

The chairman looked down the length of the table, fixing Dusty with a steely glint.

Methodically selecting a file, he began to read. 'Following the running of Race 2 on April 23rd, the committee received an anonymous claim that Bold Challenger may not have run on its merits, but may have been under the influence of an introduced, banned substance. In accordance with our normal practices, swabs were taken of all horses in the race.'

He turned over the pages of the file. 'We now have the results of those tests.'

He perused them in an almost theatrical way before closing the file. 'At this time, we are not making any charges, but we wish to question you about the preparation of Bold Challenger.'

Dusty said nothing. His mouth had gone dry. He ran his tongue over his lips waiting for the chairman to continue.

'Would you agree that Bold Challenger performed better than expected?'

'Perhaps better than other people expected, not me. He suited the distance and was ridden exactly in accordance with instructions.'

The chairman nodded. The Secretary scribbled notes on the pad in front of him.

'Would you agree that having led early in the race, then dropping off the pace, the turn of speed he showed over the final three furlongs was, to say the least, unusual?'

'It would've been if Jacky, that's Jacky Deane, the jockey, hadn't steadied him in the middle stage. I was confident he would jump smartly, but I told Deane not to let him have his head too early – to leave something in the tank for the finish. He followed my instructions to the letter. We were lucky to get a clear run just when we needed it.'

'How much involvement did Max Murphy have in its preparation?'

'None really. In any case, he was overseas for the two weeks before the race. He arrived back the following weekend.'

'Yes, of course.'

For the next twenty minutes he was grilled on every aspect of the horse's preparation before the chairman abruptly switched back to the lead-up to the race. Dusty's steadily growing confidence began to falter. No way could he tell the complete truth.

After another few minutes the chairman brought the questioning to an abrupt conclusion by saying, 'And you were with the horse all the time?'

'Yes.'

The chairman whispered to the secretary who glanced at his watch, then at the door, and nodded. 'That will be all for the moment. Please wait outside. We may need to speak to you again.'

The secretary escorted Dusty from the room.

Jacky Deane, the jockey, was the next person to be interviewed. After the jockey had gone in, Dusty sat back down in one of the leather chairs to reflect on the interview. He imagined there'd be little Deane could tell them other than to confirm his riding instructions. Hopefully he wouldn't have too long to wait. The portraits seemed even more disapproving than before, as if resenting the presence of a humble trainer within the hallowed precinct. One by one, he recalled the questions he'd been asked and the answers he'd given. Apart from leaving out any reference to Callaghan, he hoped the truthfulness of his answers lent credibility.

Gradually he became aware of voices drifting in from the front office, with what seemed to be an increasing tone of confrontation. A gruff, angry male voice interposed on the softly modulated, but obviously agitated, voice of the receptionist. Was this another witness to the inquiry, or just a member upset about something? He tried to concentrate on his immediate concerns but was again interrupted by the sound of a couple of short buzzes and a change in the tone of the receptionist's voice, then, 'This way please.' A moment later, she walked into the lobby carrying several files, followed by Max Murphy.

'Please take a seat.' She gestured to a vacant chair before continuing to the closed door on which she knocked discreetly. After a short pause she entered the committee room.

Murphy turned to Dusty, a morose expression on his face. 'How long did they keep you waiting?'

'I waited about ten minutes, then went in. They questioned me for half an hour or so. Jacky Deane's in there now.'

Murphy jumped to his feet. 'Bloody hell, they've kept me waiting in that bloody lounge for the last two hours. What'd they want to know?'

Dusty tried to keep his voice non-committal. 'Mainly routine stuff – about the preparation, my instructions to Deane – that sort of thing.'

Murphy rose and walked across to look in the trophy cabinet for a few moments, then swung around and marched back snarling. 'Did they ask you about Callaghan?'

'His name never came up. Why?'

'He's started drinking heavily again, becoming unreliable. May have to get rid of him.'

Dusty offered no comment.

'What a bloody waste of time!' Murphy exploded. 'I don't know why they would want to talk to me. I wasn't even there. And I'm kept hanging around like a shag on a rock for two bloody hours.'

At that moment, a now quite flustered receptionist joined them. 'I'm sorry, Mr Murphy, Mr Rhodes. I wasn't supposed to leave you together. Mr Murphy, will you come this way?'

Murphy shot her a contemptuous glance. 'We've not tainted one another, if that's your concern. I've merely been admiring your magnificent trophies.'

'Still, if you would wait in the dining room.'

A few minutes later the secretary came out of the committee room with Deane, thanking the jockey for his attendance and his evidence. Turning to Dusty he said, 'The committee wants to see you again, Mr Rhodes.'

Dusty felt desolate and spent, with a confusion of questions in his mind.

'You may go now.' The flustered receptionist flung the words at Deane before escorting him from the premises.

The secretary stood outside the door fidgeting with his tie. 'They're having a private discussion. They'll let us know when they're ready.'

Ten minutes later, the door opened and for a second time he followed the secretary into the room. This time, the heavy brocade curtains and the large oil paintings of pastoral and forest scenes crowded in on him. The heavy gilded chandeliers hung over him like the sword of Damocles.

The chairman kept Dusty standing until the secretary was seated, then gestured for him to sit.

'Thank you for your patience. We wish to advise you that jockey Deane confirmed your riding instructions and that the horse responded in the manner you had predicted and, as you also pointed out, benefitted considerably from a clear run over the last few hundred metres. We now want to ask you some questions about a Bryan Callaghan who, we understand, is a veterinary surgeon employed by Mowbray Park.'

Dusty's stomach tightened. In truth he had little room to manoeuvre and wondered how he might steer through the Callaghan minefield.

The first question came from an unexpected quarter, a sandy haired man with a deeply tanned face lined by a life outdoors. His open, honest face only heightened Dusty's sense of foreboding.

'Is it common practice, in your opinion, for a stable, no matter how large, to have its own vet on staff?'

'I don't have much experience of such matters, but I wouldn't imagine it would be common practice.'

Further questions dealt with the nature of Callaghan's services, which seemed innocuous enough. Dusty began to relax a little.

Then the chairman intervened. 'Our inquiries reveal Callaghan was seen in the vicinity of the stalls before the running of Race 2. Is that correct?'

'Yes.'

'Why was he there?'

'He told me Mr Murphy likes to have him on hand on race days should he be needed. He told me he'd been criticised for spending too much time away from the horses. He was, as I remember him saying, "earning his money".'

'And did he, to your knowledge, perform any veterinary services on this particular day?'

'None that I observed. No, that's not right. He did briefly check the legs of the horse that ran in the first race. He thought the horse was favouring one leg and suggested it might have laminitis. Apart from that, no.'

'Have you ever faced an inquiry before?'

'Never.'

'Then you are probably not aware that the nature of this inquiry is a little different.'

Dusty waited for the chairman to continue.

'We are in possession of certain evidence that causes us considerable concern. We are determined to root out bad practices, if any, that could bring this club, or the industry at large, into disrepute. We will not tolerate malpractice in any shape or form and will deal harshly with anyone who has engaged in dishonest practices.'

The chairman looked around the table. There were nods and murmurs of concurrence from his fellow committee men who, with the one exception, had so far not spoken a word.

The chairman went on to advise Dusty that cooperation from anyone with useful information would not be forgotten in terms of any adverse findings. He stressed again the seriousness of the matter and the possibility of criminal prosecution arising from their investigation.

'If there is anything else you can tell us, now would be the best time to do so.' He let the words hang in the air.

They clearly knew nothing of the insurance investigation or the part he'd been recruited to play. This was a fishing exercise. If they had any concrete information, they would have acted more directly.

After a momentary pause, Dusty said, 'I know of nothing else that would help your inquiry.'

The chairman nodded and spoke to the secretary, who then left the room. Then the chairman pointed towards the man who had asked the questions about Callaghan earlier.

'Mr Loftus heads up the subcommittee which has carriage of

this matter between meetings. He has something to say. Tom!'

'Thank you, chairman. Mr Rhodes, at this stage we are taking no action to suspend your licence.'

Dusty could hardly believe what he was hearing. That they should leave him under a cloud of suspicion, make him the scapegoat for something in which, at the very least, he was a minor player, seemed against all the rules of natural justice. But the nightmare continued.

'However, as the chairman has indicated, we believe something serious is happening and the evidence we have points in your direction. We will issue a public statement to the effect that the inquiry into the running of Race 2 will continue.'

◆

Dusty sat in his ute for a few minutes, allowing the heat in the cab to thaw the numbness he felt and quell the shivers that shook his frame. There had been no sign of Murphy when he came out. He wondered what might have transpired behind those thick walls and if they had, at some other stage, applied the heat to his manager.

He backed the ute out of its place and drove slowly down the drive, unable to shake off the worry that firmly gripped him.

It was too late to go back to Mowbray Park before the lunch break so he may as well duck into town and pay the rego on the ute.

He had gone no more than a kilometre when he saw a man standing next to a car with its hazard lights flashing. He slowed and the man waved him down.

He pulled in behind the car and stepped out onto the road. With a shock he realised it was Murphy.

With a flick of his head, Murphy gestured for him to sit in the front passenger's seat. 'Get in! I want to talk to you.'

Dusty got in.

Murphy was back behind the wheel, slamming the door. 'What the hell's going on?' he asked angrily.

'What do you mean?'

'What went on in there? What are you up to, you little jerk?'

'Nothing.'

'What I want to know is why they didn't call me. I've been hanging around all morning. You go in for a second session, while all I get is a message that they no longer want to talk to me, but they might want to later.'

Murphy, red in the face, was working himself up to a pitch of fury and shouting, 'What'd you say?'

Something snapped inside Dusty. He had been badgered all morning, had no idea what the hell was going on and, if anything, had protected Murphy. Now the bugger was tearing into him.

'It's no use getting stuck into me. I don't know or understand what's going on and you'll have to take my word that I didn't say anything that might be incriminating. All I know is, I'm the one under investigation and they could suspend my licence. Think I'm happy about that?'

For a few seconds Murphy said nothing. He seemed to struggle to regain his composure.

Dusty thought he'd ram home the message. 'If you want my opinion … I don't think they know what they're doing. It's a fishing exercise.'

He glanced across at Murphy, who clenched the steering wheel with white knuckles then exhaled a deep breath as if he'd been holding it for a long time.

'There's something odd about it. I don't like it when things are happening that I don't understand.' Murphy glared straight ahead for another few moments before turning to look at Dusty. His brows furrowed and he slowly stroked his chin.

'We're a team, Rhodes.' His words were deliberate and loaded with menace. 'And teamwork doesn't mean doing your own thing. Now, get back to work. You've wasted enough of our time today.'

Dusty got out and stood to one side as Murphy gunned his car, leaving a cloud of dust to drift over him. He shaded his eyes, watching the car disappear around a bend before returning to his ute. He waited a couple of minutes, then drove off.

Bugger it. No way was he going straight back to work. He was fed up with being manipulated. He'd go into town as planned, pay the rego on the ute and have a 'Callaghan coffee'.

17

After paying the rego, Dusty's route took him past the Imperial Hotel. Recognising Callaghan's battered Volvo outside, he did a U-turn and drove back, parking behind it. He knew exactly where Callaghan would be. On his own at the far end of the bar. Nothing had changed since they'd sat there before, a half-empty glass and a pile of change on the counter. Dusty joined him.

'Hi!'

Callaghan didn't look at him, continuing to stare morosely ahead, no doubt picking up the newcomer's image in the mirror behind the bar. Dusty ordered a middy of Light and then in turn, looked at the vet's image in the mirror. Not the prettiest of sights. His face was flushed and he'd loosened his tie. His clothes looked like they'd been slept in.

The barman deposited the beer in front of Dusty and walked to the other end of the bar to serve another customer.

Callaghan finally turned to him, a baleful stare from bloodshot eyes. 'What are you so bloody cheerful about?'

'Buggered if I know,' Dusty admitted. 'I've just done a few rounds with those old farts up at the Race Club. I'm under investigation. Apparently, someone says we doctored Challenger.'

Callaghan said nothing, picked up his glass and drained its contents in a single gulp. The well-trained bartender returned with another. Dusty slowly sipped his beer.

When it was evident Callaghan would say nothing in response, he tried again. 'As far as I know, the only people who knew about the doping were Malek and Murphy, maybe Grimes.'

Dusty paused to give his next words greater emphasis. 'You and me. Malek and Murphy were overseas. I can't see why Grimes would kill the golden goose and I certainly didn't tell them, so that leaves you. Why did you do it?'

'Whatdayamean? Why did I do it? Haven't said anything.'

'Then why would anyone suspect Challenger was doped?'

'Dunno.'

Dusty took a pull on his beer and addressed the image in the mirror. 'You been questioned by the Race Club?'

'No.'

'They asked me what you were doing around the stalls that day.'

'Doing what I was told.'

'That's what I said. On call if anything went wrong.'

'Who else did they bring in?'

'Deane, the jockey, went in after me, and Murphy, but for some reason, after making him hang around all morning, they didn't call him.' He laughed. 'He was really shitty about that.'

Callaghan downed half his glass in another gulp. He ran his hand through his untidy hair. 'There's something you need to know. Something big has come out of the trip to Hong Kong and I'm feeling bloody jittery. We shouldn't be seen together too much. You know that little reserve about three k's up the Valley Road?'

'Yes.'

'Meet you there at eight tonight. Now piss off.'

Dusty drove back to Mowbray Park feeling decidedly uneasy. What Callaghan had just told him fuelled the fears plaguing him since he'd left the Race Club. It was now too late for him to walk away. He had to clear his name. But Callaghan was worried, his willingness to talk a sign of desperation. It also confirmed Murphy's comment that he was drinking heavily again and becoming … What was it he'd said? Unreliable. And there was something else?

He thought for a few moments before the recall cut in. Murphy's comment when they were waiting to be called, 'We may have to get rid of him.' What the hell did that mean? Despite the heat of the day, he shivered – his dad once described it as like someone walking over your grave.

◆

Although he kept himself busy throughout the afternoon, working horses in one of the round yards, his meeting with Callaghan that night was never far from his mind. During the afternoon he had seen no one, even when he took the horses back to the stables. He wondered if the other staff were giving him a wide berth. Perhaps the news of his morning at the Race Club had filtered back?

Was he now under such a cloud of suspicion that he was being ostracised? Late in the afternoon he ran into Vicky Mifsud.

She eyed him sympathetically. 'Heard you had a rough morning.'

'Oh, it wasn't so bad. Whatever's being said I'm sure I'll be cleared in the long run.'

'That's not Murphy's impression. He came back in a foul temper. Said something about turning his back for five minutes and everything going haywire.'

'Well, I'll just hang in there …'

Vicky popped the 64-dollar question. 'Do you think Bold Challenger was doped?'

Knowing it was an easy question to answer he said, 'No.'

18

AFTER HE'D KNOCKED OFF WORK, Dusty drove up the Valley Road to Tom Loftus' property. To say he'd been surprised when Loftus had rung, declaring he wanted to see him urgently, was an understatement. With some reluctance he'd agreed to meet him at five.

At 4:45 he pulled up at a gate carrying the name Gloucester Hall. Although he knew the district well, he hadn't been able to place the property, but now realised he knew it as Boulder Farm, named after the rocky terrain. Basalt upthrusts millions of years ago had created a distinctive landscape. Between the rocky outcrops, the ground was reasonably fertile but unproductive for cropping. The scattering of small rocks made it unsuitable for grazing, particularly for horses. Dusty wondered why Loftus had purchased such a property.

The gravel drive wound up through the outcrops. Cresting the hill, he was surprised to see a secluded valley. Selective clearing and a series of dams created a picturesque landscape, with the homestead nestled in a grove of pine trees. He had to admit it was a shrewd buy, although there'd been a big investment to get it to this standard.

Seeing the stable complex from the hilltop, Dusty drove round the house to reach it. He parked alongside what seemed to be an office, got out and looked around. It was a property he could only dream about. More modest than Mowbray Park, it made Dusty feel that humanity and kindness had taken root here – his first impressions of Loftus seemed spot on.

He knocked on the office door with no response. As he could see no one around, he walked to the house, pushing through a picket gate. He was halfway up the path when a plumpish woman in her fifties came out to meet him.

'May I help you?'

'Dan Rhodes, but everyone calls me Dusty.'

'Can't think why. I saw your ute coming down the hill.' She laughed with a warmth that instantly put him at ease. 'I've called Tom. He's down in one of the far paddocks. He'll be here in fifteen minutes. Cup of tea? I just happen to have some fresh baked scones and homemade strawberry jam.'

'Great, thank you.'

'You're welcome. Tom has told me a little about you.'

'That's a worry.'

'Not really, he is looking forward to showing you his horses. From what he's heard, you're something special in that department.'

'Who told him that?'

'George Mitchell for one, and Leigh Woodward.'

Good old George, he was Dusty's one-man PR machine.

'Leigh's very good.'

'Yes, he is. Now for that cup of tea. Sit here on the verandah and I'll bring it out.'

He settled himself into a finely woven cane chair, one of a set that matched the table and took in the vista of an immaculate garden and the distant hills. Despite the fact his troubles had brought him here, this secluded place made them seem remote. Events had somehow just got out of hand and what he needed was an objective friend. Woodward was a good friend but was too caught up in his veterinary practice to fulfill such a role. He wondered how much the vet had told Loftus.

Idly he watched half a dozen tiny honeyeaters fly in and out of the nearby shrubs, tiny perfect creatures not troubled by anything. As he drank his tea and sunk his teeth into a jam-topped scone Mrs Loftus had given him, he heard the sound of a one-tonner in the yard. Soon, Loftus came through the picket gate. Settling into a chair beside Dusty, he reached for a scone while his wife poured tea.

'Thanks for coming. I'm impressed with your promptness.'

Dusty nodded, his mouth full of scone and jam.

'Now before you start talking business, Tom, you're going to drink your tea without gulping it down. You know the doctor told you not to bolt your food. He's impossible,' Mrs Loftus said, directing the comment to Dusty. 'Always on the go. He's no sooner back from the club than he's into the truck and off doing something. You're not getting any younger, Tom. You really should slow down.'

He smiled indulgently at his wife. 'Wonderful to have someone who nags you for your own good.'

'My wife's the same,' Dusty said.

'Dorothy's an expert – she's had thirty-five years practice.'

They chatted about the weather, the phantom storms that never amounted to much, horses and how to handle them. Mrs Loftus asked about his family. She seemed genuinely interested in the boys, telling Dusty they had five grandchildren.

'We are very much into boys. We had two sons, and they have five boys between them. Perhaps I might get a granddaughter one day,' she added wistfully.

By now they'd finished the tea and scones.

Loftus rose and stretched. 'It's a curse getting old. When Bradman retired, someone suggested he could play a bit longer.

He told them only he knew the creaks and groans he felt every time he went onto the field. I know exactly what he meant. Come on, there's someone I want you to meet.'

They walked to the yard and across to the stoutly constructed stables. Inside there was a centre alley, giving access to stalls either side. A system of races fanned out to the paddocks beyond.

'How many horses do you have?'

'Nineteen. I'm mainly a breeder – that's my real love. Two stallions, five brood mares, three yearlings, four two-year olds, two three-year olds and three four-year olds.'

Each stall was neatly labelled with the name of its occupant. Dusty was immediately taken with their names: Firefly, Fire Dancer, Firestar, Fire Storm, Fire King.

Beyond the stable, standing in a yard with high railings, was a magnificent deep bay stallion. As they approached, it snorted, tossing its head imperiously and pawing the ground, before circling the yard and coming over to Loftus.

'This is my pride and joy, Ring of Fire. You might have noticed most of my horses have fire in their name. My little quirk – a dynasty of fire.

'I'm the only one who can really manage him. Bit of a handful, but he throws a great foal and that's what's important.'

'What a beauty!' Dusty said, walking to the rails.

He began talking in a soft tone – speaking a jumble of words, but with a distinct rhythm. Loftus stepped back.

After a few minutes the stallion made his way warily towards Dusty, who started to walk slowly along the rails. When he reached the end, he turned and without looking at the horse, started to walk back, all the while keeping up the rhythmic monologue. Back and forth he walked, slowly, deliberately. Each time, the horse followed him. They'd done this a dozen or so times until finally, he swung his leg over the lower rail and climbed through. He began walking around the yard, the horse following. When he stopped, Ring of Fire halted behind him. Dusty slowly turned and patted the horse, running his hands up and down the smoothness of its neck, over its coat, with the confidence of someone totally at home. He walked through the race that led into the stable until he was standing inside. The stallion followed him all the way.

Loftus walked back into the stable and flipped up the latch on the door that bore the horse's name.

'He's just a pussy cat,' Dusty said as he stepped out to join Loftus.

Loftus shook his head in amazement. 'If I hadn't seen it, I wouldn't have believed it. Simply amazing.'

After the stable door was latched, they walked to the small office near the entrance. Loftus sat behind the desk and gestured to Dusty to take the other chair.

'I was impressed with you this morning, I'd like you to come back and help me with the horses. I've also had the benefit of some useful input from George Mitchell and Leigh Woodward.' After a pause, he said, 'The chairman's a good man – straight as a die with the interests of racing at heart. The rest of the committee ... well, they're good fellows, but they tend to just go along with the chairman. He wants to send a message that we won't tolerate any shady practices and he was prepared, on the evidence we had, to make an example of you.'

'What evidence?'

'You'd be surprised what we have, but when it's all boiled down, it's largely circumstantial. Our inquiries aren't like a court of law's. We're not bound by the rules of evidence. We suspect something's going on and we suspect it's serious. The chairman was hoping that by making an example of someone, he could stop it progressing.'

Dusty shook his head in disbelief. 'I can only repeat, what have you got on me?'

'I'm not at liberty to tell you, but there's damning stuff and it points in your direction. Two things trouble me, though. Firstly, and with all due respect, you are a small fish. There's got to be someone bigger in the background and that's the person we have to nail.'

Dusty looked intently into his face, which had become very serious. 'And the second?'

'No one can handle a horse like you just did and be involved in doping. Call it instinct if you will, but I believed everything you said, so I persuaded the chairman to let me handle the matter.'

'Head up the subcommittee.'

'Which was formed five minutes before you came back. Dusty, I'm putting my faith in you and in turn you must have faith in me. I'm sure there are things you didn't tell us this morning so let's have a frank talk about what you know.'

19

Dusty drove through the white posts that marked the entrance to Lookout Reserve, his headlights picking up a cream Ford Falcon parked at the edge of the escarpment, certainly not Callaghan. He discreetly parked on the other side.

The reserve was a popular picnic spot by day and a lovers' trysting place by night. Below him in the distance, he could see strings of lights marking the streets of Warrianderra, splashes of colour from advertising signs and the scattered lights of houses – his town, a good town. From the corner of his eye, he noticed a movement. Two heads appeared in the car, and after a few minutes it left.

Five past eight, no sign of Callaghan. Typical.

Though the vet had been anxious to talk, Dusty wondered what he might learn of value. Tom Loftus had given him a little more of Callaghan's background – he'd graduated with honours from university, was employed by a large veterinary product company and rapidly promoted until he became involved with a senior partner's wife. One night they were driving together and had a serious car accident; the woman was left a paraplegic and Callaghan was sacked. The embittered husband spread the word that Callaghan was unstable. The vet started drinking and became entangled in a few dubious situations until a scam landed him in court. Dusty knew the rest.

Callaghan's notoriety had triggered the Race Club's suspicions, yet their inquiries had produced little. Malek had friends in high places, hence the need for confidentiality.

It was 8:15, and still no Callaghan. The drunken sod had probably forgotten. Getting out his mobile phone, he rang Callaghan's number. After a few short rings a recorded message said, 'Your call could not be connected. Please call again later.'

The chorus of crickets, a dog barking and the distant bellow of a calf, probably separated from its mother, frayed Dusty's nerves.

From time to time, he caught the reflection of headlights in the rear-view mirror followed by the roar of an engine accelerating up the hill. Each time, he expected the vehicle to turn into the reserve, but none did. Minutes passed – 8:20, 8:25. Damn it. He isn't coming – time to go.

In the quietness, the sound of his engine seemed alarmingly loud. He'd be glad to get away. He switched on his headlights, reversed and drove back to the entrance of the reserve. A couple of cars passed before he could nose his ute onto the road. He pictured Jenny, probably watching telly and catching up with the ironing.

Why'd Woodward drag me into this? He should not have allowed himself to be influenced by those jokers from the insurance company.

Since leaving the Race Club he'd speculated on a possible connection between Woodward and the Club, and now the coincidence of again being asked to act as an informant struck him as odd. He felt he'd been sucked into a vortex by forces beyond his control. But more worrying was the growing realisation that his job at Mowbray Park was driving a deeper rift between Jenny and himself.

Halfway down the hill the sudden glare of headlights on high beam blinded him. As the car wove dangerously toward him, he swerved, hitting the verge.

'Bloody idiot,' he swore.

As the car flew by, Dusty recognised the battered blue Volvo. That'd be right. Callaghan. In his state, time would mean nothing.

Damn him, no point talking when he's like that. It can wait another day.

But as he approached the township, he thought of Callaghan waiting at the reserve, the importance of what he might learn struck home. A quick U-turn took him back.

Nearing the reserve, he slowed to allow an oncoming semi-trailer to grind past. A black Holden Commodore blocked the entrance. He drove round the next bend, parking a few hundred metres further on.

His skin prickled. He wound down the window and listened – nothing but the wind sighing in the gums. After he got out, he closed the door quietly. Every nerve telegraphed alarm.

Nearing the reserve, he stepped off the road. Working his way through the bush that grew to the edge of the reserve, his eyes gradually adjusting to the moonlight. As he got closer to the reserve, he caught the murmur of voices. A twig snapped under his foot. The voices fell silent. He froze.

A voice said, 'What was that?'

The powerful beam of a torch flashed to his left. He flattened himself behind a gum, holding his breath. The beam moved past the tree.

Another voice. 'It's nothing. Let's get on with it and get out of here.'

The torch swung away and the voices resumed. Dusty was now certain something was very wrong. Leaving the protection of the tree, he moved stealthily to another, closer to the reserve. He could make out three figures – two standing, one on his knees as if looking for something in the grass.

One of the men yanked the kneeling figure up. 'On your feet, creep.'

'Please don't.'

'Mr Malek said to teach you a lesson … make sure you don't disobey orders again.'

'Whadayamean? I've done everything he wanted. Whad else do ya expect me to do?' The man's shrill voice lifted slightly, carrying clearly.

Shit, it's him.

'He told you to stay off the booze – that's what – and look at you … you're disgusting, you slob.'

Callaghan whimpered. 'Whad I do in my own time's my business. Gotta get through some'ow.'

'Not when it interferes with business. You're so stinking drunk you can hardly stand up.'

One of the men swung a solid punch catching Callaghan just below the heart.

Shit!

The vet staggered back, coughing and retching. The second man shot out his foot, Callaghan stumbled. Before he could regain his balance, another blow tumbled him onto his back. A kick in the ribs. He tried to roll away. More kicks. For a few moments Callaghan didn't move, then he rolled on to his face, drew himself to his knees and vomited.

'Disgusting!' the first man repeated. 'This's your last warning, dead shit. You're making too many mistakes and the boss don't like mistakes.'

Another kick sent the moaning vet sprawling.

With a last desultory kick at the prostrate Callaghan, the men went back to their car. In a matter of seconds they were gone.

Dusty watched its tail-lights disappear; a cloud obscured the moon. Silence.

Running from the trees, he knelt beside Callaghan, who was softly moaning. He had blood around his mouth and smelt of vomit.

'Callaghan.'

Callaghan's eyes fluttered. 'Rhodes?'

'What's happened?'

'Didn't tell 'em anything – you gotta believe me.'

'I do, don't worry. Got to get you to a doctor.'

In a hoarse whisper so faint, Dusty could barely hear, Callaghan said, 'No. No doctor … be alright, just an awful pain in me gut.'

'My ute is down the road. Hang in there.'

'Hurry.'

Dusty ran from the reserve to his ute. He dropped his keys and had to scratch around on the ground to find them. He turned the ute around and swung it into the reserve, pulling up where Callaghan lay crumpled on the ground.

'Come on,' said Dusty. 'I'll help you up. Get you home.'

He bent to get Callaghan's arm around his shoulder. The beam from the ute's headlights caught his pallid face. Fresh blood trickled from his mouth; eyes stared sightlessly. Gingerly, Dusty checked him for signs of a pulse. Nothing.

He staggered back, turning away as his stomach heaved. With a violent convulsion, he vomited – tears stinging his eyes – a corrosive taste in his mouth. He stumbled to the ute, wiping the bile from his face with his sleeve before pressing it against the cool of the metal roof. He could only think of one thing: to get away from this place of death.

20

On the short drive to the police station, Dusty barely registered the road. He was now much later than he'd expected. Jenny would be anxious, cranky or both. On the outskirts of town, he was stopped by an RBT check.

'Random breath testing, sir. Have you been drinking this evening?'

His heart raced. 'Middy of Light about one o'clock this afternoon.'

Should he tell them?

'Shouldn't be a worry. Just count to ten.'

The constable checked the meter. 'Fine … doesn't even show. Thank you, sir. Have a pleasant evening.'

Dusty drove on. He'd barely gone a block before he pulled over. The significance of walking into the station to say he'd just witnessed a murder jolted him into reality. How would he explain why he was there, why he hadn't gone to Callaghan's aid? While he couldn't identify the men obviously acting under Malek's instructions; giving them information could put himself in grave danger. He diverted to the post office and made a phone call.

◆

The kitchen was neat and tidy. The television, audible from the lounge room. Jenny was knitting and watching an American crime show.

'Sorry I'm late.' He leant over to kiss her.

'Hello,' she said, but didn't look up.

Dusty knew the signs.

'A load of new horses came in … took longer than I expected.'

'I hope you've had dinner because the kitchen's closed.'

'Yes, I have. One of the boys went down to Macca's.'

'Not very healthy.'

'No, but it filled a hole.'

'Everything okay?'

'Fine. Boys been in bed long?'

'Of course, they're always in bed by 7:30.'

Dusty sat in his chair, pushing a hand wearily through his hair. It was hard to be normal. The vision of Callaghan's face, eyes staring, with blood trickling from his mouth was beginning to get to him.

'I'll have a shower.'

'A good idea … you look terrible.'

'It's been a long day.'

'Well, don't expect sympathy from me. You wanted the wretched job. I wish you would give it away for something more family friendly.'

'Don't start that again. I'm not in the mood.'

'You're not in the mood? Well, I am. You were gone at daylight. What's the time now?'

He looked at his watch. 'A quarter to nine.'

'Are they paying you overtime?'

'No … goes with the territory.'

'Get out of those things before you leave marks on the chair.'

◆

The hot water steamed up the glass, shutting Dusty off from the outside world. For a few moments he could be alone with his thoughts. By now the police would've found Callaghan. They'd see the tyre tracks, the footmarks and presumably, the signs of a scuffle. They'd identify Callaghan's car. He closed his eyes, letting the water run over his tired limbs. Damn. Should've gone to the police. He turned off the taps and reached for his towel. Now he could only wait and see how it played out. In the meantime, he'd need to look out for himself. Malek's men played it rough.

He finished his shower, put on pyjamas and a dressing gown, and joined Jenny again.

'You took your time.' She continued to knit and watch.

The program started to irritate him.

He yawned. 'I'm off to bed … been a long day.'

'So you have said already. Well, it's been a long day for me too, so I'd appreciate you sitting here for a while to keep me company.'

'Alright, alright. I thought you weren't particularly interested in my company.'

'There was a time when your family counted for something.'

'Oh, for God's sake, you're more important to me than anything.'

'Don't bring God's name into it – I'm not sure he would approve.'

'What's bothering you, apart from me getting home late?'

'Is there any reason why something might be bothering me?' she said.

'How do I know? You're the one that's bothered.'

'I am not bothered, thank you very much.'

Dusty sighed. When Jenny was in this mood, he just had to cop it sweet.

'I know you're cranky, but I couldn't help it,' he said. 'I know you don't like me working at Mowbray Park, but for the moment, that's my job, and when something crops up, I just have to be there.'

'Can't you … just once … tell them you can't stay back?'

'We were shorthanded.'

'Heard of mobile phones?'

'Sorry.' He rubbed his hand over his face and sighed.

'Who else was there?'

'Vicky, Paul and David.'

'Grimes?'

'No, he went early.'

'Oh, I see.'

What the hell, why is she asking so many questions?

With relief, he watched the credits roll. Perhaps now they could go to bed. But Jenny sat there as the next program started. For the next ten minutes they watched in silence.

Suddenly, Jenny got up to switch the television off. She stood for several moments staring at the blank screen, breathing heavily but evenly.

'Dusty, have you any idea what you've just done?'

'What do you mean?'

'Are you so stupid you don't understand?'

'I …'

'I know you weren't working tonight.'

The room started to cave in on him. He felt his scalp prickle and his face flush deep red. They both continued to stare at the blank screen as if it were their only conduit of communication.

'When you were so late, I called Mowbray Park to see how long you might be … I was worried.' A bitter edge crept into her voice. 'By chance someone answered the phone. They didn't know what I was talking about.'

She stopped for a breath. She was shaking and close to tears.

'I'm sorry,' Dusty responded lamely. 'I didn't mean to hurt you.'

'Didn't mean to hurt me? Marriages are made on trust, on honesty. I've put up with your ridiculous ideas to be supportive. I've looked after the children, scrimped and saved, gone back to work to give us a bit more money and this is all the thanks I get?'

'I'm grateful for all you've done. I am proud of you,' he said, looking at her.

'Then be proud of the fact that my job has just been made permanent and I have got a raise. I wanted to celebrate tonight. I planned a surprise dinner, but you're so self-centred you just went off and did whatever it is you were doing tonight.'

'I'm sorry,' he mumbled.

'Stop saying you are sorry when you're obviously not. Why were you so late?'

'I can't say.'

'Can't say! I'm sure you weren't with some floozy the way you looked when you came in. So, what was it? At least you owe me an explanation.'

'I … I can't tell you. I'd like to, but I can't.'

'I have a right to know.'

'I'm sorry,' he said miserably. 'I know it doesn't make sense, but I can't.'

'Have you done something wrong?'

'No.' He stood up and reached for Jenny's hand, but she stepped away.

'Then you've been with another woman … that's the only explanation. It's that stuck-up bitch of a reporter you were so chummy with at the eventing day. What's her name … Kerry something? Helping her with the finer points of her technique, were you?' Jenny's voice was heavy with sarcasm.

'No, of course not. I haven't seen her since that day.'

'Dusty, I don't believe anything you tell me. I can't trust you anymore.'

'Please … as soon as I can, I will, but for now, you just have to bear with me.'

'Why? What's so extraordinary you can't tell me?'

'I can't, that's all.'

'Then as far as I am concerned, you and I are finished. What has always attracted me to you is your decency and honesty. If that's gone, there's nothing left.'

'What do you mean?'

'I don't know what I mean except that you're forcing me to consider a life without you.'

'But –'

'No buts about it. This is my ultimatum. While you stay at Mowbray Park, we live separate lives. Do your thing, but don't expect me to be the compliant, docile wife at home. I'm enjoying work – I'm good and appreciated. So, unless you've given Murphy your resignation, don't come home tomorrow. If I'm forced to make a life for myself and the children, I'll do it on my terms. You can pack your bags and get out. Go and sleep with those precious horses of yours.'

He could think of nothing to say. This was the final disaster of a day that had transformed his life.

Jenny rose and walked to the door. 'And you can sleep in the spare room. I can't bear to be in the same bed as you.'

She switched off the light and left him in darkness.

21

EVEN WITHOUT AN ALARM, Dusty woke as usual at five. After a quick wash and shave, he dragged on yesterday's clothes, so as not to disturb Jenny. He spooned out cereal, poured on milk and ate standing up before he grabbed some fruit from the bowl on the table and stuffed it into his carry-all, vowing to get home at a reasonable time.

'Don't I even rate a goodbye?' Jenny's sharp voice brought him to an abrupt halt – his hand on the doorknob.

'I thought you were asleep; I didn't want to wake you.'

'For goodness' sake, you haven't even put on a clean shirt. Hang on, I'll get you one.'

She went into the lounge room to the basket of freshly ironed clothes.

Dusty shrugged. For all her complaints, she still worried about him having a clean shirt. As if anyone at Mowbray Park cared a damn.

'Thanks,' he said. 'How are you feeling?'

'Lousy, thanks to you. What were you doing last night?'

He took her by the arms and looked sadly into her troubled face. 'Sweetheart, whatever you're thinking, it's way off the mark. Something has come up at work that's making life a bit difficult. I know it's only right to tell you, but for the moment I can't. Trust me until I have sorted it out. Then I'll tell you.'

She pulled her dressing gown tightly around her and pulled away from him. 'I don't see why. I'm not a child. I'm capable of taking my fair share of responsibility.'

'I can't argue with that.'

'Then tell me.'

'I can't and that's all there is to it. I can only ask you not to keep going over and over it. It's not doing you any good … and it is certainly not helping me.'

'That's rich, that is. Do you mean to say I've just got to play the dumb wife because your all-important "secret men's business" is beyond my feeble comprehension?'

'You never have been and never will be a dumb wife.'

'Then don't treat me like one.'

'I am not treating you like one. I've never treated you like that and you know it. It's because I care for you that, for the moment, I can't tell you.'

'Just tell me what you were doing last night.'

Dusty's shoulders slumped. 'How many times do I have to say I can't? Just leave it be … it's not that important anyway.'

'If it's not important, why can't you tell me?'

'You're impossible.'

'I'm impossible now, am I?'

Dusty felt the rising anger ricocheting around them with an intensity that seemed claustrophobic in the small kitchen.

Suddenly, he froze. Beyond Jenny, he caught a glimpse of two small anxious faces peering around the door. Jenny registered the change in his expression and the direction of his gaze. She turned quickly.

'Hello boys, you're up early.'

Jem stared back, his eyes wide and questioning. 'Why are you and Daddy shouting?'

Their anger collapsed.
'We weren't really shouting,' she said.
'I'll be off,' Dusty said quietly. 'Be good for Mummy.'
His eyes misted over as he left.

22

VICKY MIFSUD WAS CHECKING each set of harness to see if any needed repairing when Paul, one of the other strappers, poked his head around the door of the tack room.

'You two coming down for a cuppa?'

Dusty glanced at him but could only shake his head and focus again on putting the last of the saddles on their posts.

'Yep. Won't be a minute ... just about finished,' said Vicky.

She took up the small pile of harnesses she had put to one side. 'I reckon these will need repairing. Can you run them down to the saddler after morning tea?'

Paul walked into the room and said in a whisper, 'If Grimes lets me. He is like a bear with a sore head.'

'What's wrong with him?'

'The whole place is buzzing with the news about Callaghan. Murphy left yesterday and Grimes has been saddled with the lot. Not a happy chappy. What do you make of it all?'

'Heck if I know. Heard any details?'

'Not really. There was a brief mention on the news late last night that he was found dead at Lookout Reserve ... goodness knows what he was doing there. We might get some more news in the tearoom.'

She put the last halter back on its peg. 'Well, that's me finished for the moment. Let's go and see what we can find out. Come on,

Dusty, don't you want to know what is happening?'

He was about to say he was too busy, then thought he should find out what others in the stables were saying about it all.

For most people, violent death holds a powerful but morbid attraction, and the staff in the tearoom were no exception. The level of chatter, the rattle of mugs and plates, and the radio playing pop music gave the room a macabre, yet festive tone.

He joined Vicky and Paul as they pushed their way past the large table in the centre of the room.

Turning to an older man seated at the end, Paul said, 'What's the news on Callaghan?'

There was a definite pecking order at Mowbray Park. The younger ones didn't get seats if there was a full crowd. Today it seemed just about everyone was there.

'Waiting to see if there's anything on the ten o'clock news.' The man looked at his watch. 'Only be a couple of minutes.'

Dusty listened impatiently through the national stuff before leaning forward to catch the local news.

'The district has been stunned by the callous murder of a thirty-eight-year-old man at Lookout Reserve, five kilometres out of Warrianderra on Valley Road. In a statement released this morning, police say they believe the man, identified as Bryan Patrick Callaghan, was a veterinary surgeon employed at Mowbray Park. He died as the result of a brutal bashing. Police are anxious to hear from anyone who was in the vicinity of Lookout Reserve that night, between the hours of 7:30 and 9 pm. They are trying to establish what the victim was doing in the reserve at that hour and what may have occurred in the lead up to the attack. Anyone with information should contact the local police as soon as possible … the price of fat lambs dropped at this week's sales.' The radio was switched off.

◆

Meanwhile Jan Keaton, Murphy's secretary, was swamped in paperwork. At the sound of a car pulling up, she glanced up in time to see two men get out of a dark blue Holden Commodore. She sighed. As if there had not been enough interruptions already, and with Murphy away for the day, she was steadily falling further behind. The younger man extended an arm towards the car. She heard a blip and the hazard lights flashed.

Moments later, the door opened and they entered.

'May I help you?' she said.

They held up their ID cards. 'Detective Sergeant Lenski and Detective Constable Bryant. Who is in charge around here?'

'Mr Murphy is the manager, but he's not here at the moment.'

'When will he be back?'

'Not until tomorrow.'

'I expect we will still be here then.' He showed her his warrant card. 'As soon as he arrives, let me know. My mobile number's there.'

'Of course, certainly.'

'In the meantime, we would like to have a look around. I am sure you are aware that an employee of yours was beaten to death two nights ago.'

She nodded. 'So sad.'

'So, you will appreciate that we need to see his work environment and interview his colleagues.'

'Of course ... so awful.'

'So let us start with you. How well did you know Bryan Callaghan?'

'Not very well. He seldom came in here and I don't mix much with the people from the stable.'

Lenski looked at Bryant, just the touch of a wry smile lightening his habitually impassive face.

'Not quite your type, huh?'

'I didn't mean that exactly … just that I have no reason to go to the stable area and they have no reason to come here. My job is to look after Mr Murphy and Mr Malek.' She waved her hand at the pile of papers on her desk. 'And try to keep up with the paperwork.'

Lenski's eyes swept the neat office, the tidy trays of work and her smart, somewhat severe appearance. 'I'm sure you do that very well.'

Bryant cut in abruptly, almost rudely. 'Where would we find most of the men at this time of the day?'

Jan consulted her gold watch. 'At this time, I expect they'll be scattered around the property, but I'll ring the foreman, Larry Grimes – he'd know better.' She gave a nervous giggle. 'Thank goodness for mobile phones.'

Bryant gave a curt nod. 'As you say, thank goodness for mobile phones.'

◆

DS Lenski looked down at his notes with a sigh. His meticulous approach to evidence normally uncovered some vital pieces of information, but into a second day, nothing. Just information about the Mowbray Park routine, which was tedious, but necessary. The detectives had taken over two rooms in the main office building for their interviews, and separately he and Bryant had interviewed eight of the men. Bit by bit, they were establishing a picture of the dead man, who had been with Mowbray Park about three years. He was capable but moody – the foreman confirmed he had a drinking habit that sometimes got the better of him. Management had been supportive, but lately he had become a liability. Hardly reason enough to give him a bashing, but who knows. The pathologist had suggested whoever attacked him probably had not meant to kill him.

He flipped back the pages of his notebook. All the men had accounted for their movements at the time the victim had died.

A light knock on the door made him look up. He brightened a little. The next employee was a reasonably attractive girl although, after the men, any half-attractive bird would be a pleasant change.

'Name?'

'Victoria Mifsud … everyone calls me Vicky.'

He smiled at her. 'How long have you been here, Vicky?'

'Almost a year.'

'Nice place to work?'

'Fair enough. The men are a bunch of male chauvinist pigs, but if you want to work with horses you have to put up with that.'

'You like horses?'

'I love horses.'

For the ninth time since he had arrived, he asked, 'How well did you know Bryan Callaghan?'

The answer came like an echo. 'Not very well … tried to steer clear of him. Shouldn't speak ill of the dead, but he smelt of drink and was a bit of a groper.'

Lenski's mobile rang. 'Excuse me.' He walked outside before returning after a minute or so. 'We will have to continue this later. The manager's back and we need to talk to him.'

Five minutes later they were in Murphy's office.

Murphy handed a folder to Bryant. 'These are Callaghan's employment records. Keep them as long as you need … as long as we get them back.'

Lenski ran through the usual questions while Bryant made notes. The picture that emerged confirmed what they already knew. 'Enemies?'

Max Murphy thought for a moment. 'Wouldn't think so. He pretty much kept to himself. His main companion was the bottle. He could get argumentative when he'd drunk a bit too much … I suppose he could have got on the wrong side of someone.'

'Enough to bash him?'

'Seems a bit drastic doesn't it, but you read about such things these days … road rage, trolley rage … people are getting more and more aggressive.'

'Anyone he was close to at Mowbray Park?'

Murphy shook his head. 'Well perhaps one. Chap called Rhodes. He and Callaghan have been talking a bit lately … part of the job. If there is anyone who might know something it'd be him.'

The two policemen exchanged glances.

'Interviewed him?' Lenski's question to his companion was casual.

'No.'

Lenski turned back to Murphy. 'Where'd we find him?'

'Be round somewhere, but this is a big property. How about you come with me?'

◆

They drove to Stable Square where Murphy's ute was parked. Getting out they stopped to ask a couple of strappers if they had seen Dusty. The men shook their heads. Murphy drove the two policemen out of the square, continuing down to the training track then turning off into a lane that led to the lower paddocks. Lenski noted the well laid out paddocks, plentiful shade trees and the still reasonably green pastures. In the distance the trees along the riverbank shimmered in the heat. He was glad the Range Rover was air-conditioned.

'He could be down the bottom shifting irrigation lines,' Murphy said as they dipped on to the flats. 'If I just follow the circuit, we're bound to find him.'

The track now followed the willows along the riverbank. Lenski spotted a ute a bit further along. 'Perhaps that's him.'

'Could be.'

They drove on, a trail of dust marking the path they'd travelled. The ute was empty. Murphy got out and walked down a short track through the willows to the river. Minutes later he returned. 'He went downtown to the saddlers with some harnesses that needed repair. About thirty minutes ago.'

They drove back to the office.

'When he gets back tell him we would like to see him. In the meantime, we will continue interviewing the others.'

After Murphy left them, Lenski turned to Bryant. 'Think he's avoiding us?'

23

Dusty walked into Murphy's office; the police had by now taken it over for their interviews. The walls were lined with shelves of box files, which he knew were the records of horses that had passed through Mowbray Park.

A youngish man looked up from the spiral-bound notebook he had been writing in. He nodded and gestured to the chair on the other side of the table.

'I'm DC Bryant … and you're …?'

'Dan Rhodes.'

Bryant wrote the name on a fresh page in his notebook then put his pen down.

'Ah,' he said, looking at what he had written. 'Would you mind waiting a moment?'

Leaving the room, he returned a few minutes later with an older man he introduced as Detective Sergeant Lenski.

The slightly overweight and greying Lenski had a steely glint in his eye that made Dusty feel decidedly uncomfortable. Dusty knew that this was the detective who had interviewed Vicky and the others.

'Worked here long?' Lenski asked.

'Few months.'

'What do you do?'

'Assistant trainer.'

Lenski nodded, rubbing his chin thoughtfully. 'Going alright?'

'Had a win recently.'

Lenski exchanged a glance with his partner before asking, 'Know Callaghan well?'

'No.'

'Your boss says you've been working together lately.'

Dusty looked down at the table, trying to fathom what game Murphy was playing.

'We have had trouble with a virus. I talked to him about that.'

'Strictly professional, huh?'

'Strictly. What else?'

'You tell me.' The detective walked to the window. Dusty waited. Seconds ticked by. Finally, Lenski turned to fix him with a baleful glare. His voice took on a harsher note. 'A man was brutally bashed and left to die. We take that seriously.'

'Me too,' Dusty said.

'We are trying to build a picture of Callaghan. He drank a bit, right?'

'Too much for his own good. I told him he should cut down.'

'You a doctor?'

'No.'

Lenski walked from one side of the room to the other. He swung around and crossed to the table in two long strides.

'Psychiatrist? Counsellor? Welfare worker?'

The rapid-fire questions rattled him. 'Of course not. You wouldn't need to be any of those to see he was drinking too much,' Dusty stammered.

'You said your relationship was strictly professional. Sounds like something more to me.'

The animation that existed a few moments before in Lenski's face slipped behind a mask of impassivity. The detective's sharp perception rocked Dusty. His thoughts raced. He would need to be careful.

'Where were you that evening?' Lenski said.

'I went up the valley to see someone about a horse. You can check that.'

'We will.'

'I came back into town, had a bite and then went home.'

'What time was that?'

Dusty knew there was a time gap he could not explain. 'Can't remember exactly.'

'Where did you eat?'

'George's Café.'

'See anyone you knew?'

Dusty palms were getting sweaty. 'Angelo, the owner. It was a quiet night.'

Bryant flipped back a couple of pages of his notebook. 'Callaghan, the belligerent type?'

'I wouldn't have thought so.'

'Wouldn't pick a fight?'

'I don't know, but he never struck me as the fighting type,' Dusty said.

'Why would anyone want to bash him?'

'I wouldn't know.'

Lenski strode restlessly around the room again. 'Like a cup of coffee … tea?'

Nonplussed, Dusty nodded, grateful for the break. 'Tea, thanks … white and one.'

Bryant got to his feet, closing his notebook. 'I'll get it.'

'No, I'll get it,' Lenski snapped. 'I need to stretch my legs and have a pee.'

Bryant watched his senior officer leave then pushed back his chair. It made a scraping sound on the wooden floor. He stretched his legs.

'Don't let him get to you. He can be a bit in-your-face at times. The job does that to you.' He sighed. 'Not sure I can stick it much longer. It is so depressing the things people do to one another. Take this case … from all reports the guy's harmless, drinks too much, but is more likely to hurt himself than anyone else. Yet someone bashed him to death. Not fair, you know. Just in the wrong place at the wrong time.'

'Is that how it happened?'

'Probably, we may never know. Where do you start when there is no apparent motive … nothing that connects the killer to the crime? That is something else that depresses me: the pressure to get a result. If we fitted up one of the local hoodlums, would it matter if he went down for something he didn't do, instead of something we don't know about? See what I mean?'

Dusty's stomach churned. He wanted to tell Bryant what he knew, but he had seen the brutality of Malek's men. Deep down he was scared.

Bryant looked towards the door. 'I think Lenski's lost. While we are waiting, help me speculate. Say it was not a random attack. Say it was an old grudge. Did you know Callaghan had been in trouble?'

'He mentioned it, in passing.'

Bryant nodded, flipping back in his notebook. 'Got off on a technicality … banned from practising on his own … the Registration Board's heard nothing more of him until a few weeks ago when they learned he was employed by a firm called Riekevic and attached to Mowbray Park. We also know the transcripts of his disciplinary hearing have disappeared.'

My God. They have been doing their homework.

Bryant went on, 'That suggests he may've struck trouble.'

He looked across to Dusty with a disarming smile. 'Know anything about that?'

'No.' Again Dusty was racked by the temptation to say something, but instinct said he had better keep what he knew to himself for the moment. With nothing much to connect him to the dead man, it seemed wiser not to get involved.

The door opened. Lenski walked in with a manila folder tucked under one arm and a small plastic tray with three steaming mugs of tea. He kicked the door shut with his heel.

'Sorry it took so long.'

Lenski sat across the table from Dusty, handing him a mug. He passed another to Bryant before drinking from his own. 'Ah, I needed that. Now where were we?'

Bryant consulted his notebook. 'Did you know why anyone would want to assault the victim? Answer: no.'

'Of course, I remember now.' Lenski opened the manila folder. 'According to our inquiries, Callaghan's been in trouble before. You know about that?'

'Yes, he mentioned something, and Detective Bryant's given me some details.'

Lenski glowered at Bryant, then back to Dusty. 'A good vet?'

'I think so, but his heart wasn't in it … sort of went through the motions, if you know what I mean.'

'Seen anything around here that's not quite … right?'

Dusty pretended to think for a few moments. 'No.'

'Sure? Think hard, it could be important.'

Dusty let his mind go over the facts he knew. They didn't amount to much and he had no conclusive proof. What he did know, however, could incriminate him or at least make it very awkward.

He sensed he was taking too long to answer. 'I can't think of anything.'

Lenski's eyes narrowed. Bryant jotted a note in his book.

'Withholding information or obstructing police, in the course of an investigation, is a serious offence. Think carefully. I put it to you that this man may have been involved in something not quite kosher. Have you at any time observed anything suspicious involving Callaghan?'

There was no turning back. Dusty had committed himself. He would not make the mistake of hesitating again. 'No, I haven't,' he said firmly.

Lenski then said something so quietly Dusty had to lean forward to catch his words.

'You know, Rhodes, I don't believe you.'

Bryant looked up from his notebook expectantly. Dusty said nothing. The tension in the air had become palpable. In the stillness, he heard the chattering of birds outside. His skin felt hot and clammy. He could see small beads of perspiration on Lenski's fleshy face. Bryant's expression was fixedly neutral.

Dusty thought over everything he had said, wondering how he might've fallen into a trap. Nothing came. Slowly he said, 'I don't understand.'

Lenski paced the room again. He went to the window and looked out. The stale air was oppressive. Lenski circled behind Dusty. Dusty felt the closeness of the man but ignored him, staring stolidly ahead.

Suddenly, Lenski hissed. 'You know more than you are telling us. Maybe you are not directly involved, maybe you're shit scared, but we can't help you unless you tell us everything.'

Startled by the new line of questioning, Dusty's mind went into paralysis. An abyss yawned in front of him.

Lenski came round to face him. 'Want to know how I know you're lying?'

Dusty said nothing.

Lenski leaned in so close Dusty could smell the sourness of his breath. 'Your ute was seen near the reserve the night of the murder.'

24

IT HAD NOT BEEN the best of days for Jenny. The heat and high humidity had taxed the air conditioning so much it had given up the ghost just after lunch. The service people were flat out coping with similar problems everywhere and the earliest they could come would be some time tomorrow. She felt like a limp rag.

She went to the bathroom to freshen up. Staring at herself in the mirror, she saw weariness etched in the lines of her face. Guilt had robbed her of a good night's sleep but really, Dusty was impossible. Something was worrying him and his reluctance to confide in her was concerning and frustrating.

Ever since he had gone to work for Murphy, he'd changed. She knew it was partly her fault. She had to admit her hostility towards Malek and Murphy was only based on gossip around town.

After washing her face, she felt a little better. She dabbed on some powder, freshened her lipstick and combed her hair. Satisfied, she stepped out into the corridor to head back to her office. On the way there, she saw Dr Carter, the head of the practice.

He called out, 'Jenny, can you spare a moment?'

Her heart gave a little jump. 'Of course.' She was pleased she had freshened up.

'Have you finished those financial projections for next quarter? I need to present them to the directors tomorrow. They are a great improvement on what we've had in the past.'

'Thank you. I had intended to give them to you in the morning, but if you want them tonight, I can stay and print them off.'

'Don't bother, the morning will be fine.' He gave her a big grin. 'You're doing a great job; we really appreciate it.'

He came around the desk. Jenny felt excited by his proximity. Their eyes locked in a moment of intimacy. She had a sudden urge to give him a big hug, but the open door and the presence of others stopped the thought dead in its tracks.

Thank goodness. If she had been alone, she might've done something silly. The moment passed, but she was conscious of his constant looks.

'Okay?' he said.

'Yes. Why?'

'I … it doesn't matter.'

'Good night, then. See you tomorrow.'

'Yes, see you tomorrow.'

She went back to her office, collected her bag, and left the building.

Her car was a few blocks away in a side lane. Walking briskly along the pavement, she passed the post office, crossing the road to head along Campbell Street. As she was about to turn into the lane, she saw Dusty's ute pull up outside the police station half a block further on. Transfixed, she watched him get out and without glancing around, walk into the building.

A cold hand gripped her heart. When he got home, she would insist he tell her, plead with him. With a flush of remorse, she remembered he probably would not be home. At that moment she regretted her harsh words and rash decision.

25

DUSTY WALKED INTO THE POLICE STATION at two minutes past five. The constable at the desk looked up.

'Can I help you?'

'I have an appointment to see Detective Sergeant Lenski. My name's Dan Rhodes.'

The constable nodded. 'I'll let him know you're here.' He picked up the phone and relayed the message.

The austere office smelt of a mixture of floor polish and unwashed people. On a hard wooden bench in one corner, a thin, crumpled young woman with untidy hair sat rocking a stroller with a sleepy baby sucking a dummy. Two toddlers clutched her skirt fearfully, disconnected from the world. He looked away, pretending to study the posters on the walls.

Bryant's head poked around the corner. 'Would you mind coming through?'

Dusty followed him along a covered verandah to a small room with a desk, four chairs and recording equipment. A venetian blind screened the window.

Lenski motioned Dusty to a chair. He sat and waited while Bryant settled himself. Dusty watched the clock that adorned the otherwise bare light green walls. Lenski switched on the tape recorder.

'Interview with Daniel Rhodes, commencing 5:12 pm, DS

Lenski and DC Bryant in attendance. We want to question you further about your movements on the night of the 19th. This interview is being recorded. If at any time you feel the need for legal representation, please say so and we will terminate the interview until you get a solicitor; however, you are not under arrest and are free to leave at any time. We would be grateful for your full cooperation. Where were you on the night in question?'

He knew he could no longer hide his presence at Lookout Reserve.

'I went to the Valley to see Tom Loftus about a horse. I came back, had some dinner, then went to the reserve.'

'Why?'

'Callaghan asked me to meet him there at eight o'clock.'

'And?'

'I waited for about thirty minutes. He didn't show up. I left … thought he'd got drunk and forgotten.'

'Did you ring him to find out why he was late?'

'I did but I got his voicemail.'

'Any idea why he wanted to see you?'

'None whatsoever.'

'Didn't you think it strange?'

'I did.'

'Why you?'

'Since our discussions about the virus, he seemed to latch on to me a bit. Maybe thought I was sympathetic, or perhaps I was the only one who had patience with him. Earlier that day, we ran into each other, he said he wanted to tell me something but didn't want to talk where we might be overheard.'

'But he didn't give you any idea what he wanted to talk about?'

'No.'

'Interview suspended at 5:18.' Lenski switched off the machine and got to his feet. 'We'd like you to come with us to the reserve. Perhaps being there might jog your memory. Even the smallest detail is important.'

They made the trip in silence. Driving through the white posted entrance, Bryant stopped the car and they all got out.

'Where'd you park?' Lenski said.

'Over there. I noticed a car – a Ford Falcon – I think … over there.' He pointed to the other side. 'I knew it wasn't Callaghan; he drove an old Volvo. Then I realised the occupants were … well, you know the place is a bit of a lovers' lane. I didn't want them to think I was perving so I drove out and parked down the road a bit where I could watch for Callaghan. A few minutes later the Ford left. I rang again, got the same message, waited a bit longer, then I left and went home. I was pretty cranky. Thought if he couldn't be bothered turning up, I wasn't interested.'

Lenski strode across to a spot about forty metres from where Callaghan had been bashed. 'He was found here.'

They joined him.

'Good spot,' Lenski continued. 'Hidden from the road by the bushes. Makes us think it wasn't random.'

Dusty forced himself not to look at the actual spot. Sounds and vision of the savage attack swept over him. The violence of the two assailants, the vet's desperate pleading, his struggle to breathe during those last seconds. Did his shock register with the detectives? Their faces betrayed no emotion.

'It looks so ordinary. Hard to imagine someone died here a few nights ago,' Lenski said.

Bryant chipped in. 'Unfortunately, with the drought, the ground's hard. It doesn't tell us much'.

'Okay,' Lenski said. 'Let's go.'

As they passed the place where Callaghan had died, Dusty tried to see if there were any telltale signs of his presence – nothing except two patches of what looked like dried vomit. Bile rose up in his throat. He swallowed. The bile burnt his larynx.

Back in the interview room, Lenski switched on the tape recorder and took him through the facts again. Again and again, he asked Dusty why he thought Callaghan would have been attacked. Several times he returned to whether he had noticed anything suspicious going on at Mowbray Park.

Finally, the detective seemed satisfied. He leant over, switched off the recorder.

With a note of weariness he said, 'That will do for today. You have been very helpful.' He checked the recording device and left the room. Bryant remained. Dusty waited. He looked up at the clock. It was only 6:30; it seemed hours since he had walked in.

Tired and hungry, with the prospect of having to find somewhere to stay for the night before him, he thought he might ask them if they had a spare cell. Perhaps Leigh and Susan could help him out? If push came to shove, he would take Jenny's advice and sleep with one of the horses or bunk down in the hay shed. At least it would be warm.

Minutes passed before Lenski returned. 'I can't get this transcribed until the morning, so come in tomorrow … anytime after lunch. Read it and, if you are satisfied it's an accurate account of the interview, sign it. We may want to interview you again so stick around. You are what we regard as a "person of interest".'

'I wasn't intending to go anywhere.'

'Good,' Lenski said. 'And if you do remember anything, contact us immediately.'

'Right. Can I go now?'

'Yes. You have a vehicle? Otherwise, we could arrange a lift.'

He had seen more than enough of them for one day. 'I'll be fine.'

Dusty walked outside, shivering in the night air. The temperature had dropped and the finest of drizzles drifted down. As he stepped between his ute and a car behind, the car's headlights came on, flicking from high to low beam several times. Dazzled by the glare, he thought it looked like a sports car, but he wasn't certain.

A soft voice called out, 'Glad to see they let you go. Kerry Suster, we met at the one-day event.'

'Of course, I should have recognised the Alfa.'

'No worries. Can I talk to you?'

He squatted on his heels, next to the driver's seat. 'What about?'

'The Callaghan business.'

'Nothing to talk about.'

'Off the record.'

He hesitated. He needed to talk to someone, but a reporter wouldn't have been his first choice.

She switched on the interior light. Her blouse was unbuttoned enough to show cleavage and her skirt had rucked up to reveal enough of her upper thighs to be interesting. On the passenger seat were her tools of the trade, notebooks and a camera.

Her voice was gentle and inviting, 'Please? I'll shout coffee. You look like you need it.'

At that moment he felt as if he didn't have a friend in the world. A cup of coffee was hardly compromising, but he was becoming adept at dodging questions.

'Sorry, nothing personal, I'm through talking for today.'

'Pity. If you change your mind, here's my card.' She gave him a look that would've sent any bloke into meltdown. 'This is a big story, and I need the break.'

He took the card and stuck it in his shirt pocket. With a sigh he said, 'If I change my mind, I'll call you.'

The cab of his ute felt cold and uninviting. He wished he had taken up her offer. He started the engine and pulled out, heading slowly towards the main street where he turned left. In the rear-view mirror he saw the Alfa follow.

He had to find a bed for the night, but first he had to resolve something that rankled him.

26

HE'D CIRCLED THE BLOCK three times, wracked by indecision, before he parked thirty metres from the Imperial Hotel.

Although the bar was reasonably full and noisy, he had no difficulty finding the spot where Callaghan always drank. The barman came over, wiped the counter in front of him and took his order. He thought the barman looked at him with just a hint of curiosity. He felt strangely conspicuous.

Sipping his beer, he surveyed his fellow drinkers. No one seemed to be taking the slightest notice of him.

He downed the schooner too quickly, but he was thirsty.

The barman returned on his patrol of the long bar.

'Same again?'

Dusty nodded. 'Thanks.'

He waited for the barman to return with his beer before plunging in. 'Pretty crook, that guy getting bashed at Lookout Reserve What's the town coming to?'

'Yeah. Mate of yours, wasn't he?'

'Not really.'

'Remember you drinking with him a few times.'

A good barman does not miss much.

'We work … worked together. Bit of a sad case. Did he drink here a lot?'

'Too much for his own good, but good for business.'

'How full was he the night he died?'

'Pretty bad. Mind you, he held his drink well.'

'Any different to usual?' Dusty asked.

'Come to think of it, he was … sort of uptight. Normally, he'd be pretty relaxed.'

'On his own?'

'Most of the time, but then two guys came in, foreign looking guys.' He pointed to a table in a quiet corner. 'The three of them sat over there. I remember because he always drank at the bar.'

'Hear anything they said?'

The barman shook his head. 'Got the impression it wasn't too friendly but no, not really. After they left, he came back to the bar in a foul mood … talking to himself … saying something about "bloody slopes" and "Think they can push you around." Later I heard him say, "I won't do it, enough's enough".'

Dusty absorbed the information. 'When did he leave?'

'Not until after eight.'

'Sure, you didn't hear anything they said?' Dusty asked with forlorn hope.

'Look, mate, that's my busiest time. I went over once to see if they wanted more drinks. The two guys left me in no doubt I wasn't welcome.'

He moved down the bar to serve a group of new customers. Dusty took himself over to the table where Callaghan and the two men had sat. He tried to visualise the situation. They objected to the vet's drinking, that much he knew. But surely not enough to beat him? Dusty pondered the significance of Callaghan's words: 'I won't do it.' Perhaps Malek and Murphy had demanded too much, even by Callaghan's standards.

He finished his beer, feeling a little light-headed. He'd eaten nothing since breakfast. He needed a feed and somewhere to stay.

He would go to the truckies' rest stop on the outskirts of town, then try the Woodwards.

Leaving the hotel, he walked quickly back to where he was parked. The drizzle had stopped, the road drying in patches. Thunder rumbled in the distance, another dry storm.

The door of a car parked on the other side of the road opened. A young woman alighted. She walked towards him. It was Kerry Suster.

'What a coincidence,' she said. 'I was heading for the bottle shop.' Her voice carried a hint of amusement – tantalisingly attractive. It was no coincidence.

'Can't you just spare me a few minutes?' she said.

'Sorry, I've got to get something to eat. I haven't had anything since breakfast.'

'Nor have I. I'll shout you dinner? There's a new place that's opened in the old station master's cottage. The food's excellent and there are four separate rooms so if you want to be discreet … we might get a room to ourselves. How about it? I'm famished.'

Dusty took in her pleasant open smile, contemplating for a moment the warmth of what seemed a genuine invitation. Why not? Streets ahead of the truckies' stop.

After one last struggle with his conscience, he said, 'Sounds good. You lead; I'll follow.'

He waited for her return to the Alfa. The engine came to life, the car's headlights slashed the darkness and the right blinker flicked. She waited while two cars cruised by before pulling out behind them. He checked the rear-view mirror then joined the short cavalcade.

27

Dinner was great. The restaurant was tastefully decorated, preserving the ambience of the ninety-year-old cottage. Framed photographs of scenes from the grand old days of steam hung on the walls. Kerry knew the owner. They had a room to themselves.

After enjoying a roast dinner and a bottle of cabernet shiraz, Dusty waited for Kerry to probe him about Callaghan's death and his interview with the police. Someone had tipped her off that he was … what was it? A person of interest. She'd waited outside the police station and, after the first rebuff, had followed him to the Imperial and waited there; so she must have wanted to find out more.

But she didn't. For now, she seemed content to enjoy a nice dinner and a glass of red, talk about the weather, horses, eventing – in fact, anything but Callaghan.

His hunger sated – mellowed by the wine – he should have felt relaxed, but the coiled spring within him refused to unwind. As he sipped his third glass of red, she'd grown increasingly attractive – beautiful, he thought. The owner popped his head in the door for an opinion on the food and service, both of which they pronounced as excellent.

'Would you and your friend like a glass of port or liqueur?'

'That'd be lovely,' Kerry said. 'I'll have a Cointreau. What about you, Dusty?'

'I really should be going. I've got to do something rather urgently.'

'Go on, just a quick one and then we'll be off.'

'Okay, I'll have what you're having.'

The owner left.

'What's the hurry this time of night? It's after 9:30.'

'The truth is, I've got to find a place to stay. My wife chucked me out this morning.'

'Stay at my place. I've got a spare room.'

Desperate though he was to find a bed for the night, the suggestion seemed preposterous.

'I've enjoyed dinner, don't get me wrong, but it wouldn't be right.'

'Don't be silly. Can't see you stuck; tomorrow you can sort yourself out. Now, relax and enjoy the Cointreau.'

They left the station master's cottage just after ten. A vivid flash of lightning split the sky with brilliant effect. A few seconds later, thunder cracked.

'Let's get home before it rains,' Kerry said.

'Wishful thinking.'

'I'll lead the way. You okay to drive?'

'If you are, I am.'

28

TEN MINUTES LATER they walked into Kerry's place.

'Make yourself comfortable. I'll put coffee on.'

Dusty slumped into a large armchair. Two schooners, three glasses of red and the Cointreau had taken its toll. He heard the clatter of cups from the kitchen and was conscious of soft music.

His thoughts ran over the events that now gripped him like a vice. How many times had he said to himself to be more cautious? How many times when the signpost had said, 'Wrong way' – 'Right way' had he taken the wrong way? If he'd gone straight to the police and told them everything he would not be where he was now. But Lenski and Bryant's battering questions had been the last straw. Lenski might have described him as a person of interest, but he'd settle for dull and boring.

Jenny's face materialised and with it, embarrassment. This was another case of 'going the wrong way'. He'd have a coffee and leave. It was too late to try Woodward, so the hay shed beckoned. Tomorrow, he'd see Jenny and beg her forgiveness.

The next thing he knew, his shoulder was being shaken.

'Not a great compliment to a girl to fall asleep on her.'

Dusty jerked upright in the armchair. 'Sorry, I wasn't asleep. I was thinking with my eyes closed.'

'Only joking.'

They drank coffee. Kerry talked about her life, her career

prospects, how she'd like to get back to the city, but loved the country and her horse. 'I suppose I could stable him at Centennial Park, but it wouldn't be the same.'

Dusty talked about Jenny and the argument of the previous night. 'Can't say I blame her.'

'Still, chucking you out,' Kerry said. 'It's a bit rich.'

He laughed. 'I've bags of faults.'

'Haven't we all? But really, you're the nicest person. I knew it straight away when you helped me with Mister Darcy.'

He put his coffee mug down. The need to talk, to unburden his soul became overwhelming. 'Just lately, I've been really stuffing things up.'

'Want to talk about it?'

'Off the record.'

'Yep.'

It flooded out – his meeting with Callaghan, how he'd seen the beating, that someone had seen Dusty's ute and had reported it to the police, that he was certain a scam was going on at Mowbray Park and that Callaghan's death was probably linked to it somehow.

She listened in silence. When he finished, the look in her eyes was deeply troubled.

'I sensed a story some months ago, talked to the boss about it, but he told me to back off. So, I've pursued it in my own time. I'm getting nowhere though. Too many questions, not enough answers.'

He tried to read her mind and decided to play it safe. 'I'm not sure I want to know the answers.'

She got to her feet. 'Of course you do. You're just feeling down. I'll brew some more coffee; let's pool what we know.'

Before he could protest, she'd gone to the kitchen.

Misgivings kicked in. Taking her into his confidence was not the smartest thing. Although he'd not told her everything, he sensed she understood more than she let on. She might be a bloody good sort, but first and foremost she was a journalist. It occurred to him that it might all be a set-up. He was a fool to have come. She was too attractive, too smart and he didn't know how far he could trust her.

He got up and went to the kitchen. 'Look, I really think I ought to go. I don't think being here is such a good idea.'

'Nonsense. No one knows you're here.'

'The ute is parked outside. Someone could recognise it.'

'Park it down the end of the drive. No one will see it.'

His misgivings grew.

'It's really decent of you, but I think it's best if I went.'

He started to head for the door.

'If you want to go that's up to you, but for heaven's sake, two heads are better than one. We might have different reasons for wanting to crack this wide open, but the objective's the same. Pour another coffee while I get my stuff. We'll see what we can work out.'

With a sigh, he poured the coffee. Another few minutes wouldn't hurt. The hay shed wasn't going anywhere.

She produced a large pad of drawing paper, some pens and fluorescent markers, and set them out in front of her.

Patting the cushion beside her she said, 'I want you to help me with this.'

As they sat together on the lounge, she fired questions at Dusty, postulated theories, made notes, circled some and finally drew arrows between the circles.

At last, she sat back. 'That's about it.'

'What does it all mean?' Dusty said.

'These things stand out,' she said, highlighting five circles in orange: wealth, power, ambition, recognition and horses.

'And this,' she pointed to the orange arrows, 'is how they seem to link up.'

She pursed her lips and traced the vivid orange lines. 'These connections show us the horses are the key. It sounds so bleeding obvious that it could also be a red herring.'

Dusty shook his head. 'It surely can't be the insurance – too many dead horses are not a good look for Mowbray Park.'

Kerry nodded.

For a minute she seemed to be deep in thought. 'There's something in the puzzle we're not seeing,' she said at last.

Dusty fidgeted, checking his watch. 'I've got to go.'

Kerry didn't appear to hear him. 'I'm sure you're right. For Malek to take the risk, there's got to be mega bucks involved and he craves recognition. He's been trying to buy his way into the Race Club for months. So, he has the wealth … that sort of person craves power. All we need to know is what and why.'

Dusty sighed heavily. It was making less sense by the minute.

'I don't know. Anyway, I really do have to go. Think it over and let's talk again in a week.'

Kerry flopped back in the lounge. 'You're right. We've hit a blank wall.'

She leant towards him, gripping his arm. 'Thanks for trusting me.'

His doubts returned. He wished to hell he could trust her. 'You did say this was off the record.'

'If the boss knew what I was doing, there'd be hell to pay.'

He went to get up, but with the sweetest of smiles, her arms went around his neck, drawing him towards her.

'Which means I can do this.'

Dusty found the brush of her lips on his cheek intoxicating.

He tried to pull away, but Kerry drew him closer, this time kissing him gently on the mouth, but then more hungrily, passionately. She pushed him back against the lounge, stroking his cheek.

'Don't say anything you may regret,' she said with emphasis. 'This is absolutely off the record.'

He backed up to the corner of the couch. She followed him, kissing him and undoing the top buttons of his shirt.

He closed his eyes. How the hell do I get out of this?

Forcing his mind back to the notes and circles on the paper, something Kerry had said at the eventing day popped up. Of course!

He pushed her away as he jumped to his feet. 'That's the key! You're a genius.'

Caught by surprise, she almost slipped to the floor. 'Why, what've I done?'

'Murphy keeps a record on every horse.'

'What about it?'

Dusty pointed to the circle around the name Blaza Trail.

'Remember the record he showed you for Mister Darcy?'

Kerry stood up, giving him a bewildered look.

'You said you were impressed that Murphy put down even the minutest detail,' he said.

'Oh, yes. I remember. How does that help?'

'All those records are sitting in his office.'

'So?'

'I'll bet London to a brick he's documented everything that happened to the horses that died. We've got to get to those records,' Dusty said, running his hand through his hair.

'We? How, when?'

'Tonight.'

She screwed up her face, 'How do we get them?'

'We break in. You game?'

Kerry stared down at the jumble of lines on the paper. When she looked up, her eyes were shining with excitement.

'Count me in.'

Dusty took a deep breath. He'd just bought another ticket on the roller-coaster.

29

THEY DROVE TO MOWBRAY PARK in silence. Dusty thought through the chain of events that had brought him to this situation. His passion for horses and his ambition to win the Holy Grail of Australian racing were the spiritual temples of his imagination. Now the arguments with Jenny and his ephemeral obsession had brought him to the point of breaking into Murphy's office, with a reporter dressed in black.

They were about a kilometre from Mowbray Park when Kerry broke the silence.

'You're quiet. Want to turn back?'

'I was just wondering how I got myself into this. Tell me, what makes you so keen?'

For a moment Kerry didn't answer. Dusty kept his eyes fixed on the road. A slight spatter of rain marked the windscreen; the headlights' beams turned into sparkling pinpoints. A flash of lightning exposed the landscape. Seconds later, thunder cracked above. The atmosphere had become oppressive, but still the rain didn't come.

Kerry twisted to face him. 'Three things, I suppose. I hate horses being ill-treated, and I'm sure that's happening, I don't like dishonesty, and breaking this story is my ticket back to the city.'

They lapsed into silence again. He drove through the float entrance, along the avenue of trees and parked behind a small clump of trees fifty metres from the western end of the stables.

'Let's go hunting.'

They entered the stable yard by the back entrance; night lights shed pale illumination on a peaceful scene. It wasn't unusual for Dusty to come at this hour if he was concerned about one of his horses, yet the knowledge of what he was about to do fuelled a menace beyond anything he'd ever experienced. Sometime during the night, the security guard would be patrolling. Logic and rationality stood at odds with the task ahead.

The smell of rain in the air and the rising wind, moaning through the mighty oaks along the driveway, warned that the storm would be overhead any moment. His heart thumped as waves of excitement and doubt fought for control of his head. Adrenaline battled with tiredness. He looked at Kerry and gave her hand a squeeze. She responded.

He checked the stalls, his powerful torch shining a critical beam over their interiors. The horses were quiet, while the storm above was growing in intensity along with the turmoil in his head. He couldn't shake a sense of foreboding, an underlying pressure trough, with him at its epicentre. He gestured across the yard to Murphy's office. He was sure the answers, or at least some of them, lay inside. Cautiously, he tracked the perimeter of the stalls, keeping to the shadows. Kerry followed.

They reached the office, Dusty gripping his torch tightly. He had switched it off – darkness was safer, but at the door, he briefly turned it on, shielding its glare to examine the lock. Lockwood double latch security – there was no chance of picking it. The windows to each side were also securely fastened, but not, as he could remember, fitted with security locks. He could knock out a pane, undo the latch and be inside in seconds. But that'd leave evidence. Too risky – they may not find anything.

Another spectacular flash of lightning lit the yard, followed by a clap of thunder. Seconds later, the rain started.

He pushed Kerry into the stall next to the office.

'What now?' she said.

Dusty didn't reply. Then, in that strange way the mind has of ordering information, he remembered the hopper windows high on the back and side walls. He could tackle them, but at about two and a half metres from the floor they were out of reach.

He flashed his torch around the stall. The beam revealed several large drums.

'That's our way in. Keep your eyes peeled.'

Rolling a barrel under the windows, he clambered up, shining his torch on the catch. It was not properly fastened. Slipping the blade of his pocketknife under the ridge of the window, he managed to push the latch across. He gave silent thanks for someone's carelessness. He poked his head in and saw a cupboard below. He wriggled in, easing one leg and then the other through the narrow space. He perched on the cupboard for a moment, crouched under the ceiling.

Behind him, he heard Kerry's voice. 'Hey, wait for me.'

'I thought you were keeping lookout.'

'No, damn fear, I'm coming in. You're not leaving me here while you have all the fun.'

Fun be buggered.

He swivelled around and extended a hand. Kerry grabbed it and pulled herself up.

They angled the torch beam away from the windows and took stock. The room was familiar to Dusty – desk, chair, filing cabinets, tall wooden cupboards and a white board. Within a grid of black lines on the board, the names of horses in work were listed in the left column. The right column detailed the daily schedule and what the employees needed to know. Dusty's gaze went back to a side desk with its computer, printer and photocopier.

He pointed to one of the cabinets.

'Take that one. I'll keep an eye out for security. He may've been round already; then again, he may be due any minute.'

'What if he shows up?'

'Back through the window. Let's hope he's not so keen on coming out on a wet night.'

Rain lashed the windows for a moment before easing off.

'Can't we switch on the light?' Kerry grumbled. 'My torch is not so good for this sort of thing.'

'We can't risk it. If he comes around, it will stand out like the proverbial. Let's just get on with it.'

They worked while straining for any sound of a vehicle, or the glare of headlights. To get back through the window at short notice would be almost impossible. The quicker they were gone, the better.

Their search of Murphy's office revealed nothing. Blaza Trail's file made brief reference to the virus and recorded the date and time the horse died. Nothing else.

Strange, very strange.

If there was something funny going on, the details would have to be in separate files. By the time Dusty had finished checking the last cabinet, Kerry had turned her attention to the drawers on the left side of the desk. He moved to the drawers on the right.

A search of the oak desk revealed nothing. Moving from left to right across the top row of drawers were the blank foolscap notebooks Murphy used at the track, a couple of reams of Reflex A4 paper and some graph paper. The drawers below held the usual office paraphernalia.

Murphy was tidy, which made their task easier. Other drawers contained racing magazines, sorted in chronological order, and telephone directories for New South Wales regional areas and interstate capitals.

Suddenly, the room was brilliantly lit, brighter than daylight. Dusty spun towards the door. A crash of thunder fractured his already jangled nerves. Involuntarily, he switched off the torch, leaving them in darkness, except for the feeble beam of Kerry's torch. He reached out, sweeping his hand in a wide arc until it contacted the desk. Leaning against it, he waited for his nerves to settle. Rain beat heavily against the door and windows, blocking out all other sound.

After what seemed ages, he switched the torch on again. With increasing frustration, he stooped to open the last drawer. It revealed folders containing photographs of horses, trophy presentations and newspaper cuttings, including several from the local paper under Kerry's by-line.

'This is useless. Let's get out of here while the going's good.'

He was about to close the drawer when a tiny detail caught his attention. The drawer seemed shorter than the others. Pulling it out, he found it was only two-thirds the depth of the desk, which left a space of at least thirty centimetres behind.

Pulling out the drawer he shone his torch into the cavity. With a grunt of satisfaction, he spied a small brass plate in the top half of the back panel with a hole big enough to take the end of a finger. He reached in and pulled down. The catch moved smoothly and with it came a second drawer. Inside the drawer were six blue folders, each containing two or three sheets of ruled paper marked in columns. The top file was labelled 'Riekevic Laboratories' – the others bore a similar label neatly printed with the name of a horse. One file bore the name 'Blaza Trail'.

'I think this is what we've been looking for.'

Dusty opened Blaza's file, passing Kerry the remaining folders.

'Have a look at these.'

She quickly shuffled through the files. 'The horses that died from the virus.'

They opened two of the files, spreading the contents on the desk. The columns on each page were filled with Murphy's neat printing and figures. The words were cryptic and the figures meaningless, except for a date in the last column.

'Makes no sense to me,' Dusty said. 'What do you think?'

'Lend me your torch – mine's fading fast.'

She examined each page. 'No idea. They're not much good if we can't work out what they mean. What do we do now? I know; I'll copy them and we can show them to Leigh Woodward. Perhaps he can decipher them.'

'How?'

'With this.' While Kerry started photographing the pages with her phone, Dusty looked anxiously towards the window, blurred by the torrential rain that hammered down. It was getting all too complicated and the prospect of the security guard arriving seemed to increase with every passing minute.

He shone the torch on his watch. They'd been there almost half an hour.

'I'll copy a couple of pages from Blaza's file and some of the others,' Kerry said. 'Surely that'll give Leigh some idea.'

'Okay, but please be quick. This is starting to give me the heebie-jeebies.'

'Where's your sense of adventure?'

'I left it back at your place, so hurry up.'

'Don't be such an old fusspot.' she said. 'As soon as I'm done, we can go.'

Dusty went to the window and checked the yard; nothing but blackness and the teeming rain.

Kerry was well under way, but it was taking too long to photograph all the pages. However, unless they could take away enough material to give Woodward, their mission would be useless. Dusty looked at his watch, another fifteen minutes gone.

The rain had eased a little and in the quietness that followed, he thought he could hear the sound of a vehicle. As if in response to his doubts, a kaleidoscope of light flashed. Someone was driving into the yard.

Diving for the torch, he doused its light.

'What the hell?' Kerry said. 'What did you do that for?'

'Someone's coming.'

'Bugger! What do we do now?'

The vehicle came to a halt in the middle of the yard, the illuminated 'Security' sign starkly visible.

Luckily the guard started work on the other side of the yard. To Dusty, the check appeared methodical but cursory. As he paused at the door of each stall, he flashed his torch around the interior, then moved to the next.

Another flash of lightning illuminated the yard with startling definition, followed by thunder. The rain increased again in its intensity. Another flash of lightning caught the guard, who pulled his collar up as rain streamed off his yellow slicker.

Dusty followed the progress of the guard's torch. Each inspection was becoming briefer as the man was obviously anxious to get back to the shelter of his van. Soon he could no longer see the guard, who was now probably working down their side of the yard.

Desperately, they tried to tidy the office to remove any signs of activity.

'We've got to find somewhere to hide,' Dusty said.

'Why don't we go back the way we came?' Kerry suggested.

'We're not going to get away before he gets here,' Dusty insisted.

'There's nowhere to hide if he checks next door and we can't risk a dash. We should have gone sooner!'

Kerry crossed to the window. 'I think he's leaving. He's gone to the van. Phew, that was close.'

'Probably had enough,' Dusty said. 'Wouldn't blame him.'

'Now I can do a few more pages.'

'Haven't we got enough?'

'The more the better.' Kerry bent down to pick up the sheets they'd thrust under the desk. She looked across at the computer on the side desk. 'I don't suppose these would be on the computer?'

'I wouldn't even know how to get into it.'

'I would.'

Dusty groaned. The woman was bloody mad.

But before he could voice his thoughts, a beam of light hit the windows. A flash of lightning silhouetted the approaching guard. Dusty fell back against the wall and squatted down, pulling Kerry down with him.

'Behind the desk.'

They crouched behind the far end of the desk – knees drawn under their chins, heads bowed, mesmerised by the patch of light showing brighter on the far wall. Dusty was glad he'd not broken the window.

The light on the wall grew startlingly bright. They held their breath. The door handle rattled. The beam swung across the room, right to left, then left to right. With alarm, Dusty remembered the open hopper window. He twisted his head to look. It hovered just beyond the arc of light. The torch moved away for a few seconds, plunging them into darkness. Seconds later, it flashed briefly into the room before darkness again enveloped them.

They stayed behind the desk, giving the guard time to get back to his van. Through the sound of the rain, they heard the van's engine come to life. The swinging arc of the headlights pierced the rain-soaked night to briefly light the window.

Dusty waited a minute or so to let his taut nerves unwind and his breathing return to normal. Only then did they clamber to their feet to stretch their cramped limbs.

'I don't care what you say we're getting out of here and fast.'

Kerry didn't argue. Even in the torchlight her face was pale, visibly shaken. What had seemed a great adventure had rapidly verged on catastrophe.

'As soon as we put everything back, we're out of here,' she said.

Completing their tasks, Dusty gave the office a final once-over before legging Kerry onto the cupboard and hauling himself up. He waited impatiently for her to wriggle backwards through the window, steadying her until her feet rested on the drum below. It was more difficult for him. Grunting with exertion, he struggled to get the leverage he needed to push through the narrow opening, one leg at a time. For one dreadful moment, he felt himself stuck halfway, unable to push forward or back. Then he felt Kerry's hand grasp his ankle, guiding his foot to the drum. With a final desperate wriggle, he was through.

They saw no signs of movement. The only sound was the incessant drumming of the rain. The building's guttering above, blocked by debris, cascaded a sheet of water over the entrance.

With heads bent against the buffeting wind, they splashed through the puddles that flooded the yard. The water squelched in Dusty's boots, the rain soaking him to the skin.

They'd almost made it to the back entrance when headlights cut through the darkness and rain. Dusty glimpsed the sign 'Security' before it was blotted out by the intense beam of a spotlight.

Time stood still. Then with a roar, the van accelerated towards them.

An amplified voice broke through the rain, 'Stop! You can't escape.'

Dusty knew the van would be on top of them before they could clear the stable.

Grabbing Kerry's arm he yelled, 'Follow me!'

'Where are we going?'

'Come on.'

They cut across to their right, the van sliding wildly through the mud in pursuit.

Dusty headed for the tearoom. Pushing the door open he shoved Kerry inside.

'What are you doing? We'll be trapped in here.'

'Stop talking.'

Slamming the door, he grabbed a chair and jammed it under the knob. The beam of his torch picked up the couple of lead ropes he'd seen lying there that afternoon. Knotting them together, he tied one end around a rung of the chair. The door handle rattled and was followed by the thud of the guard throwing his weight against it.

Pushing Kerry across the room, Dusty jumped up on the kitchen sink to open the window.

'Hop through and wait outside.'

This time, Kerry obeyed without question. Dusty followed her through then turned back, waiting to hear the guard's weight thud into the door again. Counting the seconds he estimated would elapse before the next thud, he jerked the rope.

The guard tumbled into the room with a bellowed oath, his torch skidding across the floor. Dusty knew they'd gained only seconds at best.

'Go back to the ute. Here's the keys. I'll draw him off. Come round the front. Pick me up at the start of the avenue.'

Kerry ran to the right, following the wall. Dusty watched her disappear before moving away towards a clump of trees nearby.

By now the security guard was clambering through the window.

Dusty stayed in the open, long enough for the guard's torch to pick him up.

'Hey, you! Stop! Stop or I'll shoot.'

He wasn't sure if the guard had a gun but had no intention of waiting to find out. Zigzagging, he ran towards the protective darkness of the trees, his lighter build and fitness giving him an edge over the bulkier security guard. He knew Kerry needed time to reach the ute and bring it to the front.

He slowed to pinpoint the guard's position – about twenty metres away. The wildly swinging beam of the man's torch steadied.

A shot rang out. A bullet zinged high above his head. Shit! This is getting serious.

Reaching the cover of the trees, Dusty paused, his ears straining to catch the sound of the ute. Nothing. Moving deeper into the grove, he tried to keep some sense of direction and distance. He needed to stay close to the pickup point. Although the guard's torch showed he was getting closer, Dusty doubted the man knew exactly where he was. As if in confirmation, another couple of random shots rang out well away from him.

Moving as stealthily as the mud permitted, he worked his way through the undergrowth, hoping to double back on the far side to where Kerry would be waiting.

How long since she'd gone? He couldn't tell.

The undergrowth became thicker, making his movement more difficult. He risked turning on his torch to find his way.

The guard fired, the bullet ricocheting off a tree that was uncomfortably close. Dusty changed direction, moving deeper into the grove. To his right, he caught the rapid blink of the ute's lights – once then again.

He moved quickly in its direction. Too quickly. His foot caught some fallen branches and pitched him forward on his face.

Before he could scramble to his feet, the beam from the guard's torch fixed him.

'Got you.'

Dusty lifted one hand to shield the blinding glare of the beam. Leaning back to steady himself, his hand closed on a thick branch. He dropped his head with an air of defeat and waited for the guard's legs to come within range. Then, with every ounce of strength he could muster, he swung the heavy branch in a low arc.

A sharp cry of pain – he'd found his mark.

Leaping to his feet, he stumbled out of the undergrowth and ran the few yards towards the gate, waving his arms. The ute accelerated to meet him with its headlights blazing and its passenger door swinging open. Half-running, half-stumbling over the last few slippery steps, Dusty barely had time to scramble in before Kerry reversed in a sickening slide as the wheels skidded on the muddy surface. Dumping the lights, she threw the vehicle into forward and drove off.

Looking back, Dusty could see the guard making a stumbling run towards the stable.

'Get a bloody move on.'

In the darkness, Dusty caught the lilt in her voice. 'He's not going anywhere. I let the front tyres down.'

Reaching the road, she switched on the headlights.

The faint glow from the dashboard lit her face to reveal the sweetest of smiles. He grinned back, tension easing for the first time in what seemed ages.

'Kerry, we're quite a team.'

30

Kerry turned the corner at the end of her street. 'Are you staying?'

'I'll sleep in the ute.'

'No, you've earned a bed for the night.'

Dusty yawned. With relief had come fatigue.

'When that guy started shooting, I thought it was all over. Never thought we'd pull it off.'

'Nor did I,' she said, swinging the ute into the driveway. 'Let's get inside.'

Shutting the door behind them she said, 'I'm going to change. How about you? You look rather soggy.'

While she went to change, he sat on a kitchen stool in wet clothes.

She came back with a flannelette sheet.

'Get out of those things before you catch pneumonia.'

He started to protest.

'Don't argue. There's the spare room. Stop being stupid and do as I say.'

He returned with his clothes in a bundle and the sheet wrapped round him like a toga.

Kerry went to the laundry. Moments later, he heard the hum of the dryer.

She came back looking stressed. 'Before we call it a night, let's recap. Apart from break and enter, larceny, assault and wilful damage to property, we've been quite successful. But what if you'd been shot or someone'd recognised your ute? What if tomorrow morning they realise someone's broken into the office? They could call the police and your mates, Lenski and Bryant, put two and two together. This is dangerous stuff.'

A bit late for regrets.

'There's nothing to connect you,' said Dusty. 'As for me, I can only offer up a prayer to St Dismas.'

'Who's St Dismas?'

'Legend has it he was one of the thieves crucified with Christ. The two thieves held up the Holy Family on the way to Egypt. Dismas bought off the other thief to leave them unmolested. Jesus predicted they would be crucified with him in Jerusalem and that Dismas would accompany him to Paradise. He is often referred to as the Good Thief.'

'Dusty, you astound me.'

'About the only thing I remember from school scripture class.'

'Before we call it a night,' she said. 'I want to have a quick look at some of those photos I took.'

'Why? Look at them tomorrow.'

'Something's nagging away in the back of my mind.'

'You're a glutton for punishment. Leave it until the morning. We couldn't make much sense of them when we looked at them earlier. Why should they look any different now?'

She smiled ruefully. 'I have no idea. You're right. Things always look better in the morning.'

He cocked an ear towards the laundry. 'Does silence mean my clothes are dry?'

She went to the laundry and rescued his clothes. Walking back, she stopped dead in the middle of the room.

'What's the matter?' Dusty said.

'Just a thought … the computer in Murphy's office.'

'What about it?'

'Is Murphy a computer freak?'

Dusty shrugged. 'I doubt it. Never seen him use it.'

'I thought as much.'

'What do you mean?'

'If a person uses a computer regularly, they'd have it on their own desk. It looked to me as if Murphy rarely used it.'

'I hadn't even noticed it in his office until tonight. He's the old-fashioned, pen and paper type. That's how he keeps his records. You've seen that for yourself.'

'Then what's it doing there? More precisely, if Murphy doesn't use it, who does? And what for?'

'I don't see how we can get an answer to that tonight. Perhaps I can find out tomorrow. Come on let's turn in. Look at the time. It's after 11:30 … well past my bedtime.'

'I suppose you're right.' She handed Dusty the bundle of clothes. 'They're pretty dry. Just hang them up – there's a bit of space in the wardrobe. I'll see you in the morning.'

Kerry walked across to the door of her room. 'Goodnight.'

'Night.' Dusty closed the door behind him, thankful that at least he could get some sleep.

He pulled off the sheet he'd wrapped around his body and slipped into bed naked, pulling the light blanket over himself. The air was still cool from the rain, which had now stopped. For the sake of the countryside, he wished it was still teeming. It would take a week of rain to fill the local dams, get the river running again and bring green pasture to the paddocks.

But tonight the rain, particularly the storm at its height, had been their protector.

He was sure he'd drop off instantly, but the combination of an eventful evening, sleeping in a strange bed, and the thought of Kerry in the next room banished his sleep.

Was he imagining it or was that a soft knock at the door? He listened, eyes wide open staring at the ceiling.

No, he must've been mistaken.

He closed his eyes again. Then again, this time a little louder and unmistakable.

'Dusty, you awake?'

He wished he wasn't but answered, 'Yes, what do you want?'

'Can I come in?'

'I suppose so, it's your house.'

He didn't think she heard the last comment. She came in and sat on the edge of the bed. He pulled the sheet up around him.

'What is it?'

'Something is nagging me. I've been thinking. I was only able to copy a few sheets, probably not enough to really give Woodward all the information he needs.'

He groaned inwardly. Already, he'd got to know Kerry well enough to be worried about her.

'Well, what about it?'

'The computer – you're sure Murphy doesn't use it?'

'Ninety-nine percent.'

'Then who would? Think carefully, this could be important.'

'How the hell would I know?'

'Who on Malek's staff might use it? Someone, say, with a professional background?'

It came to Dusty in a flash. 'Callaghan! He told me they were using computer modelling to track the virus. What he meant was, he was tracking whatever they were experimenting with.'

'That's got to be it. It is the only thing that makes sense.'

'Suppose you're right, how does that help?'

'Don't you see? If we access the computer, we can locate all the files. I can download them to a stick and Woodward will have the whole shebang. That would be a real breakthrough.'

'One little point.'

'What?'

'How do you access it? And even if you can get into it, don't you need passwords and that sort of thing?'

'Heard of hackers?'

'Yes, but how does that help? We can't involve anyone else.'

'Don't worry, once I'm in, it wouldn't take long to load the files and leave no trace of us being there.'

Dusty could sense another crisis bearing down on him. 'That means getting into the office again?'

'Of course.'

'Why don't you think up some reason to come over to Mowbray Park to do a story. Ask Murphy if you can use the computer to take your notes and then when he's not looking do your stuff?'

It sounded like a good idea.

'No, that wouldn't work,' she said. 'In any case, if they have any suspicion that someone's been in the office, they'll get rid of the computer quick smart, especially if the person who used it no longer needs it. No, we go back tonight!'

'Tonight!' Even in a night of shocks and surprises, the very thought left him weak. 'We can't … too dangerous. Security will be everywhere.'

'That's just it. He won't. No one will expect, whoever the intruder was, to come back the same night. Come on, Dusty, there's no time to lose. And if the place is crawling with police and security, we can always abort.'

Dusty looked at his watch. It was ten minutes past midnight.

◆

Kerry was right – everything was in darkness. Sheets of water left from the downpour reflected an indifferent moon. The van sat in the yard, settled on its front rims. They crossed to the storeroom. Once inside, they risked turning on Kerry's phone, now recharged. Nothing seemed different.

'Better take our boots off. Otherwise, we'll leave mud all over the place. If they haven't worked out that someone's been in the office, they will tomorrow.' They pulled off their boots and clambered up to the window, which yielded to Dusty's push. The security guard hadn't bothered to check.

Inside, Kerry went straight to the computer and turned it on. The screen glowed brightly in the darkness of the room.

'That's a dead giveaway,' Dusty said. 'We need to screen the windows.'

'That's your department. I'll get started,' she said, tapping the keys, soon lost in concentration.

Dusty flashed his torch around the office. He could see nothing to help cover the windows. 'I'll duck back out and see what I can find.'

In the storeroom, Dusty found some horse rugs that had been repaired. Rolling them lengthwise, he was able to push two through to the office. Draped over the window, they'd provide a shield.

He switched on the light.

'Great,' Kerry said. 'That's much better.'

The next ten minutes dragged interminably as frustration gave way to impatience.

'Got anything yet?' Dusty asked.

'Keep your hair on. I'm into the program, but the files are password protected. What kind of password would he use? I've tried variations of Callaghan, Mowbray Park, research and equine. What's the name of that laboratory?'

'Riekevic.'

Kerry tapped out several variations. 'Something else?'

Dusty gave her a few more suggestions. Kerry's nimble fingers explored the possibilities.

He looked at his watch. Twenty minutes had gone. The threat of detection weighed heavily.

'Forget it, let's get out of here. If that security bloke comes back, it's all over, red rover.'

'Stop talking and let me concentrate,' Kerry said. 'If I keep trying ones that don't work, the computer will freeze.'

She tapped her head lightly with her fist. 'Mostly people pick uncomplicated passwords because they're easy to remember. That's why hackers are so successful. Think, Dusty, think. What sort of password would Callaghan use.'

'For God's sake, how would I know?'

'Get into his head. What sort of man was he?'

'Loner, didn't talk much. He spent most of his time talking into his glass.'

'What'd he drink?'

'Whisky.'

'Brand?'

'Johnnie Walker, Red Label'

Kerry tapped in several combinations before typing in 'JayWalker'. With a gleeful smile she watched the screen blink and then reveal a list of files titled, 'Experiment 1' up to 'Experiment 8'.

'Bingo,' Kerry whooped. 'Quite clever really, devious old bugger.'

She put the cursor on one of the files and clicked.

'Which makes you even cleverer,' Dusty said in genuine admiration.

'Oh no! Another password! Blast and damnation! Have a look at this and help me make some sense of it.'

Reluctantly he peered over her shoulder to study the file names. 'What do you need to know?'

'Each file has its own password.'

Dusty stared for a moment, trying to get his head around the problem. 'You're pretty sure these files relate to the horses they've been experimenting on?'

'Yes.'

'Using your theory, simply connect each file to the name of each horse.'

'A reasonable assumption.'

'And let's assume they're in chronological order.'

She nodded.

'That makes the last one Blaza Trail.'

She tapped in the letters. Nothing happened. She tapped in variations of the horse's name.

'How about …' Kerry tried B-1-1-z-1. Like magic, a spreadsheet appeared for Blaza Trail. Five familiar columns, a sixth containing dates, then five more columns of information.

Using the same formula of capitals and substitute numbers for vowels, she brought up another file.

'Fantastic.' She sounded ecstatic. 'Give me the names of the other horses and I'll load them onto the stick.'

'Ah, let me think. How long will all this take?'

'A few minutes. Then we're out of here.'

'Ah, Arctic Gale, Cavalier Lad, Pop the Question. But we're stretching our luck. I'll go outside for a mosey. If he turns up maybe I can draw him off.'

'Whatever,' Kerry replied, her mind engaged on downloading the files.

Dusty shook his head, amazed she could be so detached.

Once again, he exited through the window and stepped out into the fresh night air.

Rain now came in a gentle drift. He moved noiselessly around the perimeter of the yard, listening intently.

Reaching the front entrance, he scanned the driveway for any sign of a vehicle. Nothing. On a slow circuit of the outer perimeter of the stables, he found the window of the tearoom shut. Continuing his inspection, he reached the rear entrance. It was then his straining ears caught the sound of a vehicle in the distance. Doubling back to front corner of the stable yard, he saw headlights coming from the direction of the house. The security guard had got another vehicle and was back on the job. There was no time to warn Kerry. He could only hope she would hear the vehicle and douse the light.

He racked his brain for a diversion, but nothing came before a tow truck – its amber roof bar flashing – backed into the yard and stopped just short of the van.

The doors opened and two men alighted. One, he recognised as the guard, was limping.

From fragments of the men's conversation, he realised the guard was only back to tow the crippled van away. He'd had enough for one night.

'Nah,' the guard answered to the other man – a question Dusty hadn't heard. 'I checked earlier, nothing disturbed. Probably a couple of hoods looking for a quiet spot to smoke dope. One of the bastards whacked me on the shin. Let's get this damn thing away before they find out I've stuffed up.'

The clatter of chains and the scream of the winch blotted out their conversation. Finally, they climbed in and drove off.

Silence descended. Dusty returned to Murphy's office.

'That was a close shave,' he said to Kerry.

'What was?'

'The security bloke coming back for his van.'

'I didn't hear a thing.'

'You didn't? Never mind. Finished?'

'On the last one. One more minute.'

'Let's get out of here. I've had enough for one night.'

Kerry grinned. 'You've got to admit though, it's been fun, and we've got great stuff. It's a huge break.'

'If you're happy, I'm happy,' Dusty said without much conviction.

31

The whistle of the kettle pierced the air.

Dusty looked up from pouring boiling water into a mug as Kerry came to the kitchen door wrapped in a dressing gown and yawning. 'Tea or coffee?'

Kerry shielded her eyes from the brightness of the light. 'How in the hell are you so awake at this hour of the morning?'

'It's the time I always get up. I start work at 6:30. I saw bacon and eggs in the fridge, how's that for brekkie?'

She groaned. 'Coffee and toast will be fine.' She waved a limp hand towards the refrigerator. 'But feel free.'

'I'll fix breakfast. You check that USB stick.'

'Good idea.' Stifling an involuntary yawn, she crossed to her desk, sat down and switched on the computer.

He glanced across to watch as Kerry pushed in the stick, tapped a few keys and a spreadsheet materialised.

Kerry gave a sigh of satisfaction, 'Clear as a bell. The great thing is no one knows we've got it … only need to make sense of it.'

She brought up Blaza's file. Dusty carried a mug of coffee and a plate of toast over to her as his bacon and eggs sizzled in the pan. Starting with the dates, he pointed to the date of the last race and the date when Blaza contracted the so-called virus. Some of the figures he recognised were routine TPR readings and some of the observations were clear. There were notes about the horse's 'recovery', but the limited information didn't provide clues. The little they knew about chemistry made the rest of the spreadsheet impossible to interpret.

She nibbled absent-mindedly at her toast while he went back to prepare his own breakfast and sat down to three eggs and a pile of crispy bacon.

After ten minutes of futility, Kerry sighed and said, 'We need an expert.'

'How about I check with Woodward. Perhaps he'll see us tonight.'

'Is that wise? I like Leigh, but this is getting murky. How do we know who to trust?'

'I'll vouch for him. Who else is there?'

'My editor could engage an independent firm of chemists.'

'But can we trust him? Remember, he told you back off. What's different?'

'This'll whet his appetite. An old journo like Tom can't resist a scoop and this one's sensational.'

Dusty was quiet for a moment before he said, 'No, we take it to Woodward. Trust me, he's the best.'

He thought she would argue, but after a pause, she exhaled. 'Alright, but I'm sticking with this all the way.'

32

Work next day proved uneventful for Dusty. Nothing seemed different, and his fear that someone would raise something, gradually subsided. Late in the afternoon, he met with Kerry at her unit and rang Woodward.

Susan answered. 'Dusty, nice to hear from you. I ran into Jenny today. She was quite upset … said if we heard from you, to tell you to contact her urgently. She also said to say nothing about her being upset, but I thought you ought to know. It's obviously something important. Just don't tell her I told you. But that's not why you rang – how can I help?'

Dusty was hit by a wave of guilt. So much had happened in the last thirty-six hours, he'd hardly thought of Jenny. 'Right, I will, thanks. Ah, is Leigh there?'

'Still out. Should be back about six. Great drop of rain.'

'Yes, badly needed, that's for sure, but we need plenty more. If I call about quarter past, he'd be back by then?'

'Probably, but, well, not for sure.'

'We'll leave it until 6:30.'

'We?' There was a note of surprise in her voice.

'Ah, yes. I'm bringing someone else. See you then.'

He hung up before she could ask any more questions.

'What was all that about?' asked Kerry.

'Nothing. Just that Susan and Jenny are good friends.'

'I hope that doesn't make it difficult.'

'Of course not, why should it?'

'There's nothing between us, but I don't want a jealous wife interfering with my work. What time did you say we'd be there?'

'Around 6.30.'

'Then let's work out what we need to know and get a move on. I've haven't been able to concentrate all day for wondering.'

They compiled a few notes, which Kerry slipped into a large manila envelope with the USB stick. 'You lead the way. I'll follow in the Alfa.'

Taking the long way round, they arrived at Woodward's and saw his vehicle was outside and the lights in the surgery were on.

Woodward raised his eyebrows when Kerry followed Dusty through the door.

'Susan said you were bringing someone, but this is a surprise. Don't misunderstand me, it's a pleasant one. I just didn't realise you knew one another so well. Is Dusty helping you with Mister Darcy?'

'No. This is strictly professional. We need your help.'

'How?'

'It's quite a story.'

Beginning with her suspicions about Mowbray Park and her editor's reluctance to run on the story, Kerry said she'd met Dusty at a local cafe and after remembering he worked at Mowbray Park, she started pushing him for information. One thing led to another and resulted in their nocturnal trip to Murphy's office.

Dusty was fascinated by the way she told the story leaving out any compromising details. When Kerry, with a magician's flourish, produced the USB storage stick, Woodward gave a sigh of satisfaction. Taking it delicately between finger and thumb he slipped it into his computer.

'If this is what I think it is, you've done more in one night than the rest of us have achieved in months.'

Kerry looked startled. 'Who else is involved?'

'Doesn't matter. But there are a few people interested in Mowbray Park.'

'What do you mean it doesn't matter? My whole career's riding on this and no one's going to cheat me out of my story.'

'No one will cheat you out of anything; first we've got to make sure you have something.'

By now Woodward had brought up the three files they'd previously examined. As he printed the spreadsheets out, he laid them out across the desk and wrote down names, numbers, chemical formulas and equations onto a note pad. From time to time he checked a textbook, adding a note to the growing matrix of information. Finally, he sat back and shook his head in disbelief.

'Incredible. We were so far off the mark.'

'What is it?' Kerry stared across the desk at him. 'What do you mean?'

Woodward gestured to the spreadsheets, leafed through his notes and shook his head before he answered her in slow and measured words.

'From the beginning we've been working on the premise that it involved an insurance scam of some magnitude. Malek has recently made five claims for a payout of just over two million, enough to spook the industry and bring in the Fraud Squad. But despite autopsies on the last three horses and numerous inquiries, there's no evidence to show the horses died from anything other than natural causes – a virus, heart attack, whatever ... leaving no option but to pay up.'

He gestured again to the spreadsheets. 'Evidence here suggests otherwise; that the deaths were caused by a drug overdose. My bet is the drugs were performance enhancing and on these five occasions, something misfired with the dosage. If I'm right, the ramifications are mind-blowing and could turn the racing industry on its head.'

Dusty sat in silence, waiting for more.

'Know what I think this is?' said Woodward.

'Never know unless you tell us?' Kerry said testily.

'This is a "win at will" scheme.'

'What's that?'

'What I suspect is that Malek, through Riekevic Laboratories, has been developing a cocktail of chemicals that stimulates a horse to perform well above its normal level. Over the past eighteen months, they've been experimenting with dosages to get the balance right – too much and the horse over-reacts, causing a fatality; not enough and the horse isn't guaranteed to perform. The timeline of effectiveness appears critical. There have been many tests to trace the progress of the drug through the horse's system. There's a period of short-term effectiveness before its absorbed by the horse's metabolism.'

'Surely that would leave detectable traces in a routine swab,' Dusty said.

'That's the clever bit. I also suspect they're using another drug to act as a masking agent.'

'A masking agent?'

'Masking the presence of the first drug by neutralising it against test protocols. In a routine test, nothing shows up that contravenes the list of banned substances.'

Woodward looked at Kerry then at Dusty, who said, 'They pick their race, dope the horse to win against the odds … and if a swab is taken, nothing shows.'

Woodward nodded. 'That's the general idea. There's just one snag.'

'And that is?' said Kerry.

'This information has been illegally obtained, and it would require rigorous testing to verify my theory.'

'Which means?' Dusty asked.

'More work before you can break your story, Kerry, and we can put an end to Malek's scheme.'

Woodward explained the areas where he needed confirmation and the consequences for the racing industry if the scheme ever gathered momentum. Finally, he drew their attention to the fatal bashing of Callaghan.

'Callaghan must have been brilliant in his day. Malek picked him out of the gutter and in exchange exploited his knowledge. Either Callaghan's drinking was making him unreliable or perhaps he'd become dispensable.'

'Or both,' said Kerry.

'You could be right,' Dusty said. 'The pressure was getting to him. He told me he drank to get through the day.'

Woodward went on, 'If the final development of the drugs is close, the chance of a breakthrough becomes more difficult. We can't request the RAS to widen its testing program without revealing our source of information, and that gets you two into deep trouble.'

'What have the Royal Agricultural Society got to do with it?'

'Not that RAS, Kerry,' Woodward said with a laugh. 'The national drug testing agency, Racing Analytical Services. It's based in Melbourne. They process all blood samples and urine tests taken at race meetings throughout the country.'

'Then surely they have all the resources to do the necessary research,' Dusty said.

'Not necessarily. It is a major problem keeping test protocols up to date. For example, there's been little research on the time it takes for certain drugs to be excreted from the system, let alone the precise amounts that affect a horse's performance. They develop a list of suspect substances, and each substance has a threshold which must not be exceeded. The list also contains a number of therapeutic products as well as chemical drugs, although the tolerance levels for many of those are higher and more flexible.'

'So, if a substance is not listed or isn't registering above the legal limit, it doesn't contravene the rules?' Dusty asked.

'Correct. If a substance is not listed, then it slips through the net and if it relates to a therapeutic product, the levels may not attract a sanction. That's what's so diabolically clever.'

'Where to from here?' said Kerry.

'I'll start working on it, but I'm afraid I need to know more. Which means, Dusty, we still need you on the inside.'

Dusty was startled by Woodward's last remark.

'With what happened to Callaghan, I want out. If they take a tumble to what I've been up to, I'm dead meat.'

'You can't pull out now,' said Kerry. 'Think of what Leigh's just said. If they succeed, it'll turn the racing industry on its head.'

'I'm not the industry's keeper. I'm a little bloke who wants to train horses and be left in peace. I'm already in more trouble than my nerves can stand. No, I want out.'

'What about my story? Dusty, you're my hero, you can't let me down.'

'I'm not anyone's hero. You're a journalist after a story. Woodward, you're a vet – it's within your professional field. Me? I've already taken more risks than I care to think about. My wife's thrown me out. I've got to get my priorities straight.'

'I'm not sure Jenny's really thrown you out,' Woodward said. 'She rang Susan today very worried about you. I'm sure everything will be alright.'

'It's all very well for you; you're not in the dog house.'

Woodward handed the USB stick to Kerry. 'Better hold onto

this. It still might prove useful.'

'That's it?' said Kerry. 'You're both going to leave it there? After all we've risked? You're both wimps.'

Woodward seemed to lose all interest. 'Sorry, Kerry. Without Dusty I don't see how I can pursue it. The evidence is all at Mowbray Park.'

He turned to Dusty.

'By the way, I was talking to Tom Loftus the other day, a great guy and the horses he's breeding are something else. He just mentioned, in passing, that he wished he could get your help in preparing Fire King for the Melbourne Cup. And together, you know, you could do it. But what if … no, it doesn't matter,' he said gruffly.

'What do you mean, "what if"? And why doesn't it matter?'

'I just thought … what if Fire King could win the Cup, everything is set and then you're beaten by a Malek horse, full of an undetectable drug. Tragedy.'

The phone rang, a harsh intrusion. Woodward lifted the receiver.

'Yes … Oh … right.' He ended the call and stood up from the desk.

'That was Susan. She called to see if you would like to come over to the house; she's made coffee. But I don't want to spring any surprises, so I should say, Jenny's dropped over.'

'I'd better go,' Kerry said hurriedly.

'I'm sure there's no need,' said Woodward.

'Be for the best. Anyway, I've got to get back to the office. See you.' She tucked the USB stick into her bag and walked to the door. 'Thanks for nothing, you guys.'

A void filled the room after she'd gone. They heard the Alfa's engine roar to life, then the sound of spraying gravel.

Woodward turned to Dusty. 'Are you going to tell Jenny about this Mowbray Park stuff?'

'No, it's better she doesn't know, especially now that I'm pulling out.'

'Won't she be surprised you're leaving Malek?'

'She'll be delighted. That's her terms for taking me back.'

'Surely you should tell her something. At least then she'll understand the strain you've been under.'

'It'll only worry her.'

'She's been worried ever since you walked out. She didn't think you'd take her literally.'

33

They left the vet's surgery, walking in silence to the house, up the steps and along the timbered verandah.

'Sure, you don't want to tell her something? I think you owe her.'

Dusty shook his head.

They stepped into the brightly lit kitchen. Jenny's eyes grew wide at the sight of Dusty's scruffy appearance. She jumped up and rushed to him, throwing her arms around him and hugging him tight.

'Twenty-four hours away from home and you look like something the cat's dragged in. Where've you been?'

'You told me to get out, so I got out. Slept in the ute last night. I was coming round tomorrow afternoon.'

'I have missed you so much,' she said. 'You look all in.'

'Didn't sleep too well.'

'Danny Rhodes, you can be the most exasperating person. Let me take you home.'

He nodded wearily; grateful she'd not questioned him further.

'Susan,' Jenny called out. 'We're going.'

'Not before you eat.' Susan frowned a little. 'Where's the other person?'

Woodward jumped in. 'Went back to the office – an urgent deadline.'

'What other person?' asked Jenny.

'Kerry Suster,' Woodward explained. 'You met her at that event the other day.'

'Oh,' said Jenny.

◆

Dinner passed in a spirit of companionship, though Dusty sensed their problem was never far from Woodward's mind.

'I have freshly picked berries for dessert,' Susan said. 'I won't be a minute.'

'Sounds delicious. I'll help you,' said Jenny.

Sure enough, when they left the room, Woodward seized the opportunity, a hint of exasperation in his voice.

'You won't reconsider?'

Dusty shook his head and before Woodward could press him further, Jenny and Susan returned with bowls of berries and cream.

'What are you two looking so serious about?' Susan asked.

Dusty shot him a warning look. Woodward flushed beneath his tan.

'Don't keep us in the dark,' Jenny said. 'Are you two plotting something?'

Dusty saw Woodward's eyebrows raise a fraction. For a moment Dusty showed no reaction.

Woodward pursed his lips. 'I'd like Dusty to help me with something, but he says it's not fair on you, Jenny.'

She frowned. 'What is it?'

Dusty fiddled with the tablecloth.

'It's a bit more than just something,' he said. 'I'll explain.'

Dusty listened with mounting concern while Woodward methodically sketched out the events of the past few months. He was grateful that Woodward skirted around the more graphic details and with admirable discretion, touched only briefly on Kerry's role. He mentioned nothing about the brush with the police over Callaghan's death. Even so, the risks Dusty had taken were obvious. Jenny's face reflected her rising agitation.

Finally, Woodward sat back in his chair. 'That's it. We need his help.'

Jenny sat deep in thought.

Dusty fiddled again with the tablecloth.

Slowly and deliberately, she said, 'I agree with Dusty. It's not our fight.' She took her husband's hand. 'No wonder you've been acting strangely, but you should have told me.'

'I didn't want to worry you.'

'And worried me more.'

Dusty shrugged, looking ruefully across at Woodward, whose disappointment was obvious.

'Don't worry,' Woodward said. 'I'll think of something. Can't let the whole racing industry go down the gurgler.'

Jenny laughed a little shrilly. 'You're not implying the whole of the racing industry rests on Dusty's shoulders?'

Woodward looked at her, unable to hide the depth of his concern.

'He could be that important.'

Jenny frowned. 'Surely Malek's influence can't be that great?'

'If he only fielded horses in the major Group 1 races, he could shred the integrity of the industry. He's smart – he wouldn't overdo it. Guaranteeing the outcome of some of the biggest races would be enough.'

Jenny looked shaken.

'That's evil,' she said.

'Like sportsmen using performance enhancing drugs. They don't see any difference to using specialist running shoes, aerodynamic bikes or winged keels,' Woodward explained.

Silence fell over the four friends. From another room, Dusty heard the steady tick-tock of a clock. He reached eighty-three ticks before Woodward spoke.

'What is so really evil, is the fate of the horses trialling the damn stuff, that die in agony. And that won't stop.'

'Horrible. Those beautiful horses. How could anyone be so cruel?' Susan whispered.

Woodward smiled gently at his wife then said softly, 'But you're right, Jenny. It's not your problem.'

Jenny gave Dusty a distraught look. 'I know now why you felt you had to help. And why you wanted to keep it from me.'

Dusty slumped back in his chair, torn between helping Woodward, and the voice of reason telling him Jenny and the boys were more important. You clever bastard, Woodward. I don't care what you say – family comes first. But he sensed Jenny beginning to waver.

'Leigh is professionally involved. He's retained by the insurance company,' Dusty said to Jenny. 'And he's not the one taking the risks.'

Jenny nodded, then turned to Woodward. 'Why is Dusty so important?'

'He's on the inside, he cares, he can find out things about what is happening at Mowbray Park, and he's already found out things the rest of us never could.'

Dusty desperately sought a way out. 'You've forgotten something.'

Woodward frowned. 'What?'

'The Race Club.'

Jenny was startled. 'Oh no. What's that all about?'

Dusty glanced at Woodward, who smiled enigmatically, and

stared into his coffee cup.

'Dusty,' Jenny said sharply.

Reluctantly, he explained how they wanted to make an example of someone – that he was an easy target and how Tom Loftus had persuaded the club's committee to back off, suggesting instead that Dusty be there to report what was happening.

Dusty sighed heavily. 'But since then, things have become very heavy. I'll talk to Tom … tell him it's getting too nasty.'

Jenny's eyes grew wider by the minute.

'Coffee, anyone?' Susan said. 'I know I need something after hearing all of this.'

'Whisky?' said Woodward bemused, lightening the mood a fraction.

'No, thanks, Leigh,' Jenny said. 'I need a clear head, but coffee would be great. Thanks, Susan.' She turned to her husband. 'Dusty, you're saying you need to clear your name?'

Dusty nodded.

Jenny gripped his arm tightly. 'Of course, I don't want you to take any real risks, but surely helping Leigh is the best way to do that?'

Dusty groaned inwardly. *This is going from bad to worse. She does not understand the dangers.*

'A moment ago, you agreed I should walk away. What happened to you not wanting me to work for Malek?'

'Working for Malek led you to doping Bold Challenger, which led to the inquiry that compromised you. You could've gone to the stewards on the day. No one needed to know. It's time to set things right.'

'The swab was negative,' Dusty protested.

'But you knew what was going on.'

'There was no proof; my word against theirs. Who do you think they would have believed?'

Jenny looked at Woodward. 'If Dusty had come forward, would they have done more tests?'

'If the routine tests proved negative, I doubt it,' Woodward said. 'And while the horse did win against the odds, it wasn't such a big win to seem totally out of the ordinary.'

Dusty grew more exasperated. 'I'm telling you; they could have tested from now to Christmas. They wouldn't have found anything.'

'You can't be sure,' said Jenny.

Dusty slowly shook his head. 'Challenger wasn't doped.'

Susan came in and stood listening, holding the tray of coffee cups. 'Not doped, but you …' she broke off, as she put the tray down and passed the cups around.

'No, you all jumped to that conclusion. I told Callaghan I'd dope the horse, but I didn't. I gambled on him winning and he did. I did nothing wrong. I'm calling it quits.'

He turned to Jenny seeking support, but she sat rigidly upright, a picture of moral indignation.

'Perhaps so, but you knew what they intended to do. You have a moral obligation.'

Woodward stared at Dusty, perhaps sensing a narrow opening. 'I don't want to force either of you into anything, but by working with Loftus as well as the insurance company, we might really get somewhere.'

The room fell silent again, each immersed in their own thoughts.

'Dusty wants a career in racing.' Woodward turned to Jenny. 'And you have a high moral standard.'

Dusty could tell that Jenny was cautiously playing with the bait. 'What's your next move?'

Woodward weighed his words carefully. 'The evidence we have has been illegally obtained. It points us in the right direction, but we can't use it.' He looked at Dusty. 'We need someone to replace Callaghan.'

Dusty shook his head. 'That counts me out. I'm no vet.'

Jenny lips spread in a grim smile. In a quiet voice she said, 'Why can't you?'

Dusty stared at her, incredulous. 'Why can't I?'

His wife's eyes were shining. 'That's where you're wrong. You know what I think? You should tell Murphy you know about the scam and you've got the files. Say, Callaghan told you what was happening and gave you the files. He was scared and wanted someone else to know in case anything happened to him. Tell him they're in a secure place with instructions that if anything happens to you, they'll be immediately handed to the police.' She paused and took in a deep breath. 'Then tell them they have to bring you in,' she said, and reached for her coffee.

Woodward looked at Jenny with admiration. 'Pure genius.'

Dusty was not so sure. 'I don't believe it. I try to do the right thing, and you suggest a scheme that drops me in up to my neck? Not on, it's too dangerous. These are ruthless men, they …'

He wanted to tell her about the bashing, but he held back.

'I'm not saying you have to do it, but you could,' Jenny said. 'You could get enough information to bust their racket wide open.'

'No go! It's too dangerous.' His chest was tight with anxiety.

'You have the files. They wouldn't dare touch you.'

'I don't understand the files and …' He paused to deliver the clincher. 'I know nothing about computers.'

'I'll teach you,' she said. 'I want to help. Leigh can bring you up to speed with the science side. Go along with them, and as soon as Leigh and the others have the evidence, they need … bingo!'

Dusty shook his head. It might seem simple to Jenny, even Woodward, but he knew Malek better. He'd seen Callaghan beaten to death. Malek was ruthless. He couldn't match them.

'I'm not risking my neck or yours.' He drank his coffee, trying to give himself time to calm down.

'Mine?' Jenny said.

'If they sense I'm the rat in the ranks, you and the boys would be in danger.'

Woodward stood up, raising his hands in a wide supplicant gesture. 'I don't want to push you, but what Jenny's suggested is brilliant. And telling them you've got the files is powerful insurance. They wouldn't be game to touch you or Jenny.'

Dusty looked at Jenny. She carried a worried look, but her jaw was set in firm determination. 'You're as smart as they are.'

Maybe. But not as ruthless. With a deep sigh he got to his feet.

'Everything tells me this is about as stupid as it gets. Come on. It's time we went home.'

34

Dusty paused outside Murphy's office. A fortnight ago, he'd committed himself to their crazy plan. Two weeks in which every spare moment had been spent learning scientific names, formulas and their applications – to say nothing of the crash course Jenny had given him on computers. From newspaper articles, insurance reports and the stolen files, they'd assembled a bank of detail that he'd committed to memory.

'You're a natural with the computer,' Jenny told him, sounding excited to be involved.

Fascinated by veterinary science, he'd quickly absorbed all Woodward could tell him, even making a few shrewd observations that impressed his friend.

Over the weekend, he'd run through the material several times to satisfy himself and his teachers that he understood every aspect. Time to put it to the test.

Dusty squared his shoulders and took a deep breath. He'd seen Murphy enter the office a short while before. He followed him in.

Murphy's secretary looked up from her work. 'Can I help you?'

'I'd like a word with Mr Murphy.'

'He's very busy, but I'll check and see if it is convenient.'

She picked up the phone and pressed a button.

'Dan Rhodes would like to see you.' She paused, holding the phone away from her ear. 'Yes, I'll tell him.'

The woman looked up at Dusty. 'He said to give him ten minutes, and perhaps I should warn you, he's not in a very good mood.'

'I'll wait outside.'

Dusty stepped out of the office, closing the door behind him. On the one hand, he was glad for the short reprieve, on the other, unsettled by the delay. All morning he'd been psyching himself up. He walked the line of stables, the calm of the horses easing his heightened tension. He told himself this was what he wanted to protect: each horse a magnificent example of God's handiwork, and potentially the victim of a harsh and cruel plan that had already taken the lives of several of their stablemates. The end justified the means.

His paces measured distance as units of time. After what he deemed five minutes, he turned and walked back with the same measured strides. Reaching the door he hesitated. Did Murphy mean exactly ten minutes or about ten minutes? Should he go in or give him a few more minutes? He waited a while longer, turning his head skywards to watch feathery clouds drift over the horizon.

When he went back into the office, the secretary waved him towards the corridor leading to Murphy's office. He knocked on the door.

'Come in.' Murphy's voice didn't sound particularly irritable. He waved him to the only other seat. 'What do you want?'

'Boss, how much do you know about computers?'

Murphy was thrown by the unexpected question.

'Hell, nothing! Can't even turn the damn thing on.'

'Well, that's what I want to talk about,' Dusty said.

Murphy screwed up his face, obviously puzzled as to why anyone would walk into his office and ask him that. Dusty waited for the impact to sink in.

Staring at him, Murphy leaned forward with his right elbow on the desk, cradling his chin on his hand.

Dusty wanted to look around the familiar features of the office to see whether they'd left any tell-tale signs of their break-in. Instead, he steadily returned Murphy's gaze.

'Why should I want to talk about something I've absolutely no interest in?' Murphy asked.

Dusty cocked his head to one side, summoning up the hint of a lop-sided grin.

Softly, he said, 'Depends.'

Murphy jerked upright, pushing his chair back from the desk. He folded his arms across his chest.

'Get on with it,' he said, irritation creeping back into his voice. 'I'm busy. I don't have time to play games. Say what you have to say and get back to work.'

'It's about Callaghan.'

'What about him?'

'Before he died, he told me what's going on around here.'

'What do you mean, "going on around here"?'

'I always thought that virus stuff was bullshit.'

Murphy stared at a point just over Dusty's head, as if something on the wall had taken his interest.

'That time Blaza got sick, I checked a few websites,' said Dusty. 'Couldn't find anything that made sense, so I tackled Callaghan. He clammed up, so I dropped into the Imperial one night. Lonely fellow. Instead of treating him like shit, you might've been wiser to help him with his drinking problem.'

He paused, waiting for Murphy's reaction.

Except for the slightest furrowing of his brow, Murphy stared impassively.

'He opened up, couldn't stand it any longer, needed someone

to share the burden. I was there to listen.'

Silence hung like a blanket over the room. Dusty waited again.

Finally, Murphy broke the silence. 'What did he tell you?'

'Everything. Once he started, he couldn't stop. Sort of poured out.'

Murphy reached across the desk to pick up the phone, punched a button and waited. In an expressionless voice he said, 'Down here. Bring Yuri with you.'

He returned the handset to its cradle.

'That wasn't smart of Callaghan,' he snarled. 'He always was a mixed-up bastard. The grog dissolved his brain. I warned him, but he wouldn't listen. Got things mixed up. Started to fantasise.'

He leaned forward with studied malevolence. 'Don't believe anything he said.' He smiled a thin, mean smile. 'No one believes a drunk. Anyway, he's dead.'

'Convenient.'

'You insinuating something? He got into an argument with some hoodlums. Probably didn't mean to kill him. Couldn't have known how sick he was.'

'I don't think so. He wasn't the type. According to the Imperial's barman, there were no hoodlums – just two mean looking buggers with foreign accents.'

Murphy shrugged. 'I wouldn't know. Where's this leading?'

'I don't much care what happened to him, but I was interested in what he told me. He told me he was the only person around here who could access the computer files and process the information between Mowbray Park and Riekevic Laboratories.'

Murphy stiffened visibly. He glanced towards the door.

The look was not lost on Dusty. 'If you're in a hurry I can always talk to you later.'

A car pulled up.

Murphy visibly relaxed. 'No, it's alright. What about Riekevic?'

'I know what's in those files.'

'What files?'

'You know what files.'

The door opened and two men walked in. Dusty recognised them: Callaghan's killers. They stood either side of Murphy's office doorframe with hands clasped in front of them.

'You haven't met Goran Yanovic and Yuri Schokolov.' Murphy indicated each with a brief nod of his head.

Neither acknowledged the introduction. They stared at Dusty with studied detachment.

Murphy seemed to relax. 'A little knowledge can be dangerous. How much do you know?'

Dusty turned over in his mind whether he should play his trump card. He'd wait a little longer. 'These guys here to intimidate me?'

'Why'd you think that? Do you need intimidating?'

'I can't help thinking of Callaghan in that park, retching his life away.'

Murphy's eyes narrowed. 'Cut the crap. What's all this about?'

'Callaghan's death must have left a hole in your organisation.'

'There are plenty of vets.'

'I gathered he was more than just a vet. He was right under your thumb and good with computers, wasn't he?'

Murphy's gaze strayed to the computer on the corner table, its screen grey and lifeless.

Dusty pressed on. 'I was able to access a file or two.'

'Get to the point, or I might just suggest to Goran and Yuri that you need a little workout.'

Murphy nodded to them, and they moved quickly, surprisingly lightly for such big men.

Dusty felt a hand on each shoulder.

'Tell them to take their hands off.'

'Tell me what this is all about, or they'll do more than lay a hand on your shoulders.'

'Let me show you something.'

Dusty tried to rise but was held down. He shot Murphy a questioning look.

Murphy lifted his gaze. A quick nod of his head released the pressure from Dusty's shoulders.

Without a word, Dusty got up and walked across to the computer, dragging his chair after him. Entering the username and password, he selected a program.

Murphy watched, mesmerised. As the spreadsheets materialised, Murphy's jaw sagged. When a horse's name appeared at the top of the spreadsheet, his eyes widened.

'How'd you do that?'

'Simple.'

Murphy grasped a straw. 'You couldn't possibly understand what's in them.'

'Yep!'

'Callaghan told you.'

'No.'

'Then how the devil –'

'With the information I got from him, it was child's play to analyse the content.'

'Here?'

'No.'

'Where?'

'At home. Wonderful things, computers. You see, computers are designed to talk to each other. Systems are built on the premise of transferring information.'

'This is a secure system.'

'Heard of hackers? A good hacker can break through most security systems. This was easy.'

A couple of weeks ago, Dusty had known no more than Murphy. Now their exchange had a surreal quality. The hours spent with Jenny and Woodward were paying off.

Murphy seemed almost impressed. 'Who else has this information?'

'Just me.'

'So, if anything happened to you, it'd be just us.'

Time to play his trump. 'Don't get any wild ideas. I've taken out insurance.'

'What do you mean?'

'I've saved all the material on two USB sticks. Each is in very safe hands with instructions to hand them to the police should anything happen to me, or my family.'

This was the point at which their strategy succeeded or failed. With the two heavy men emphasising the potential danger, Dusty fought to hide the fear that gripped him.

Murphy frowned, flicked a quick glance at the heavies and then returned his gaze to the screen.

Dusty pressed on. 'If the shit hits the fan, you are history. Want to know what this is all about? I want a slice of the action. I want Callaghan's place. You need someone who knows the score, can feed info to Riekevic, carry out their instructions, and stay sober. The files tell me you're close to solving the last few problems but not quite. You may think you don't need me but you're wrong. Unlike Callaghan, I'm no fall guy. A slice of the action. A cut of the profits.'

Murphy nodded, almost imperceptibly rising to stare at the screen over Dusty's shoulder.

Dusty took the cue. He brought up each file, leaving it on

screen long enough for Murphy to read the names. Even though Woodward and Jenny had trained him well, he didn't want his new-found knowledge tested too closely. As Dusty went through the files, commenting from time to time, Murphy said little. For the most part, he just watched. The two heavies had again taken up their positions either side of the door. His confidence grew.

Finally, he shut down the files and swivelled to face Murphy. 'Want me to send a message to Spetcevic?'

Murphy's face flushed an angry red, the veins on his neck standing out like cords. His fists opened and closed. For a moment, Dusty thought his boss might hit him. Abruptly, Murphy swung away, crossed to his desk and leaned on it – his hands spread flat with his head down.

Eventually, he looked up and glared. 'Think you're pretty smart, don't you?'

'It's not hard when you know what you're doing,' Dusty said. 'The point is you need me. The ball is in your court, but I won't wait too long.'

'I'll need to discuss your proposition with Mr Malek. But before I do, you'll have to show me you've got the guts. Spetcevic says we still need to run a few more trials. I'll get him to set the next one up, a sort of make-or-break run. You up to it?'

'Try me.'

35

AT 6:45 THE FOLLOWING MORNING, Dusty was back in front of the computer in Murphy's office reading the latest email from Spetcevic. He forwarded it to Woodward, who'd analyse it and report back. He clicked on the spreadsheet. The name at the top was Bold Challenger. He studied the figures and instructions.

Murphy poked his head in the door. 'Make sense?'

'It will soon. Give me time to read it.'

Murphy's thin, cruel smile mocked Dusty. 'I'll be down at the track. Leave you to it. Bring Challenger down at about ten.'

After Murphy left, Dusty stared at the computer screen. The figures seemed odd; he checked several times, comparing them against past rates and results. He checked again. They didn't make sense. Was he missing or misreading something? It didn't add up.

He checked his email inbox – nothing from Woodward. Of course not, it was too soon. He pictured Woodward in his office, distracted by early morning calls. Perhaps he'd not even opened his emails.

Dusty eyes focused on the figures. He compared them with the pattern of past tests, noting the even but modest variations in rates and chemical balances. He checked the dose that had so gravely affected Blaza Trail. The dose he was to give Bold Challenger was a much larger dose, with a corresponding sharp increase in the performance boosting compound 'JX/82'. Surely, he was misreading it. Even Malek and Murphy couldn't be that ruthless.

He heard footsteps outside. Nervously he clicked onto another file, pulled a pad towards him and began jotting down random figures, absorbed in his task. One of the strappers knocked and entered; he crossed to one of the filing cabinets, extracted a file and left.

Dusty flicked back to the inbox. Woodward's answer had arrived. He opened it and read the words on the screen:

An excessive dose. This is a test of your commitment to Mowbray Park. Warn Murphy the dose for Bold Challenger is excessive. It may be a mistake. Suggest reducing JX/82 by half and the other by a third, which should bring Bold Challenger's dosage more in line with the pattern of earlier tests. I suspect he'll order you to stick with Riekevic's instructions. If he does this, you must do as you are told. If you don't, we may as well give up.

Dusty deleted the email abruptly and, to be sure it had gone, deleted it again from the trash folder. He'd been right. He wanted to just walk away, disappear. This was his test: to cold-bloodedly kill a horse. And not just any horse, but a horse that meant so much to him, a horse who'd helped him beat the odds. Just to prove his loyalty.

In despair he went to the office next door to access the refrigerator which housed the drugs. From his pocket he extracted the key Murphy had given him. He opened the refrigerator and scanned its contents – mostly the usual veterinary products; however, on a lower shelf he found what he was looking for. He took out two vials; one contained a clear fluid while the other was amber coloured. From another cabinet Dusty collected syringes and gauze pads. He wrapped the syringe and vials in the pads and walked to the door.

36

The morning sun was harsh on Dusty's face. Of all the times he'd questioned the path he had taken, in this moment, the weight of his decision was almost crushing him. Mouth set in a grim line, he walked to Bold Challenger's stall.

While still in the stall, he administered the masking agent JY/83, then put on the saddle and bridle. Woodward's words hammered in his brain. It was alright for him, sitting in his comfortable surgery. He didn't have to do the dirty work.

Dusty took the horse to the mounting block and was soon trotting out of the yard and down to the track.

Under Murphy's watchful eye, Dusty slipped off Challenger.

'We need to talk,' said Dusty. 'Something's wrong.'

Murphy waved for the last couple of horses to return to the stable. They were alone in the heat and the dust.

He moved close to Dusty. 'Wrong?'

'The dose – it's way too much. This dose isn't an experiment, it's an execution.'

Murphy's eyes were mean and cold. 'Riekevic calls the shots. You want to be part of the team, you follow orders. Got the stuff with you?'

'Yes.'

'Then get on with it.'

Frantically Dusty racked his brains for something that, even at this late stage, could avert the inevitable.

Turning his back on Murphy, he unwrapped the bundle he'd stowed inside his shirt and knelt down to spread out its contents. The second vial containing the stimulant JX/82 glinted evilly in the sun. He scribbled the time on the pad he'd brought with him. Timing was critical. The stimulant's effect would raise the horse's performance well above normal levels before being broken down by the masking agent, which should counteract the effect on the horse's heart. Half an hour later both drugs would be undetectable.

Under Murphy's scrutiny, Dusty picked up the JX/82 vial and pierced the end with a needle to draw out its contents.

As he steadied Bold Challenger, the horse snorted and rubbed his head with affection against Dusty's shoulder. The enormity of Malek's test put his stomach into spasm.

He twisted his body slightly to conceal the needle from Murphy, hoping to squirt out at least some of the drug before injecting the horse. His eyes flicked to Murphy. Murphy had shifted around to keep the syringe within his sight, watching his every movement with calculating eyes. Dusty had told Kerry that Murphy had no love for horses, and he'd been right.

For a brief second Dusty closed his eyes and, though not a churchgoer, offered up a silent prayer for forgiveness. If he was to save many horses in the future, this was a chance he'd have to take. Any further hesitation and he'd lose his nerve. He plunged the needle into the horse, attached the syringe and steadily depressed the plunger. Bold Challenger didn't move.

Dusty looked at Murphy with a sense of deep loathing.

'Done,' he said almost choking on the word.

Murphy showed no emotion.

'Trot the first eight hundred, extend to full gallop for the next five, ease off for another five, then flat out for the last eight.'

He legged Dusty up. He stared down into Murphy's heavy features.

Fighting back a sudden urge to spit in his face, Dusty took Bold Challenger onto the track.

Away from Murphy, he experienced some momentary relief. The horse showed no sign of a reaction to the drug. At the horse's greatest point of exertion, JX/82 would hit its target – the horse's pumping heart absorbing the full impact of the toxic cocktail.

Wind tugged at his face. The immense power of the magnificent thoroughbred, covering the ground with effortless ease, evoked happier days and memories of exhilaration and pleasure. His father's image flashed before him. What would he think? Dusty couldn't imagine. Crouched over the horse's neck with eyes on the track, memories of his father drifted through his head.

The eight hundred metre marker flashed by. Leaning his weight forward to urge the horse on, the response was immediate – the product of good training, not the drugs. Dusty trained his horses to enjoy racing. He reckoned this was logical; you did your best when you wanted to, not when you were forced.

They sped over the next 500 metres. Even without a stopwatch, Dusty knew it was quick. He eased up, keeping the rhythm for another five as they moved towards the moment he was dreading.

Again, he urged the horse on. Again, it responded. Then Dusty felt something else – the horse exploded beneath him, surging forward with a frightening, erratic turn of speed; its head flicking as if to shake something clear. Bold Challenger struggled with the unnatural energy coursing through its system, rasping tortured breaths from heavily pumping lungs. With superb balance, coordination and reflex, Dusty stayed with the horse's pitching back.

Eventually, on the far side of the track, the stressed horse slowed with exhaustion and a defeated energy. On the way back to the waiting Murphy, it stumbled.

The distress was obvious: chest heaving, coat lathered in sweat, blood-flecked foam around the nostrils. Still Murphy seemed unmoved.

'Stuff sure works. Get him back to the stable and clean him up. I'll talk to you later.'

By the time Dusty reached the stall, the after-effects of the drugs had begun to kick in – the side effects magnified. Frantically, he stripped off the saddle and bridle and fetched a bucket of warm water and a sponge to clean Bold Challenger's nostrils, the horse's breathing was laboured. Then he sponged off the sweat from the horse's dust-caked coat.

Challenger stood, head down and facing away from the light with its legs splayed and body strangely stiff. Dusty pinched the skin. It remained in the little pyramid his fingers had formed – massive dehydration. Blood flecks again formed around the nostrils; the eyes bulged in a vacant stare. Woodward's advice for dehydration had been a massive dose of Hartmans Fluid. If not checked, the muscles would go into meltdown, triggering kidney failure and agonising death. He needed the Hartmans quickly.

Racing back to the stable office, he heaved a sigh of relief to find it empty. He phoned Woodward and briefly described the reaction.

'I'll be at the front gate in ten minutes with twenty litres of Hartmans,' Woodward said.

Within fifteen minutes, Dusty was stringing up the first of the five four-litre packs Woodward had brought.

Bold Challenger had hardly moved, his frame rigid except for the heaving rise and fall of the rib cage. Its rasping breath characterised the torment it was suffering, with blood-flecked foam spewing from its nostrils and mouth, sending shivers of anguish through him. No time to lose. For the second time that day, he found a vein, rapidly inserted the catheter, then hooked up the drip and activated the flow. It was all he could do.

It was futile. Three hours later, Bold Challenger collapsed in a thrashing heap. Soon the thrashing stopped.

Dusty sank to his knees, buried his head in his hands and wept as he tried to absorb the consequence of his actions. His sadness fought with his anger, sadness for the loss of an equine mate and for the sacrifice that Challenger had to make, and anger at man's cruelty and heartlessness toward God's gentle creatures.

Now Dusty faced another challenge: to push back his grief, assume a mask of indifference and face the harsh reality of the world around him. He retraced the all too familiar path back to Murphy's office.

Murphy was at his desk, filling in the record of the training session. A glimpse of the neat columns and finely scripted notes evoked memories of the files in the secret drawer. No doubt Murphy would make the closing entry on Bold Challenger's file when there was no one to disturb him.

Dusty fought to hide the tremor in his voice. 'He's gone. What now?'

'Ring George Gavin; he'll collect it later. He knows the routine.'

Dead horses had become so common. Calling the man from the knackery had become just routine.

But Dusty wasn't quite finished. Somehow, he would bring these bastards to account.

'Is that wise?' he said.

'What d'you mean?'

'Can you risk another insurance claim so soon? Isn't it smarter to just bury the horse somewhere on the property? I'd reckon the fewer people who know the better. I'll do it after everyone's left.'

Murphy rubbed his chin thoughtfully. Then his eyes took on a crafty gleam.

'Smart thinking. You know, mate, I never thought you had it in you – had you down as one of those bleeding-heart horse lovers. Racing's a tough game. No room for sentiment.'

To hide his relief, Dusty went to the computer to send a short report to Riekevic, which he knew was Callaghan's practice.

Now he could fulfill Woodward's final bizarre instruction: 'Bring me the head. I have a theory I want to explore and I need to do an autopsy on the brain.'

He glanced over his shoulder. Murphy was absorbed in his record keeping. Just another day at the office. Dusty sent a brief email to Woodward before trudging wearily to the door.

Murphy called after him, 'Before you go.'

What in the bloody hell could the bastard want now? Dusty stared out the door, unable to face the man he now considered a monster.

'What is it?'

'Look at me when I'm speaking.'

Reluctantly Dusty turned.

'Mr Malek wants to see you. Six o'clock sharp, in the main office.'

37

Dusty walked along the far side of Stable Square from what was once Bold Challenger's stall. He could do no more; time to put space between what had been and what lay ahead. Why would Malek want to see him? They had tried to call his bluff, tested his mettle and forced him to act against his every instinct. Weariness of spirit weighed him down. The coldly calculated sacrifice of Bold Challenger sickened him, and the thought of Woodward's request compounded his misery.

He went to the tearoom, noticing the new lock on the door and when he topped up the electric jug, he saw a lock on the window. A sad smile crept onto his mouth. He drank his tea in solitude and nibbled on a couple of semi-stale biscuits. He wouldn't have minded company yet felt some relief in not having to make small talk or face awkward questions about the events of the day.

Later, after checking no one was around, he backed the tilt tray truck up to the door of the horse's stall and winched Bold Challenger's carcass on board. From the workshop he'd picked up the tools he needed plus a hessian bag and a chainsaw.

By 5:55 he had delivered the bag and its grisly contents to Woodward, washed away any traces of blood and changed his clothes, and was driving through the shadowy canopy of the mighty oaks back to Mowbray Park. The magnificent red-brick Queen Anne house, with its beautifully manicured gardens, was a picture of dignity and serenity, although its closed windows and drawn curtains created an ominous feeling. He'd soon learn what sort of welcome awaited him.

Outside the office building, Murphy's 4WD and Malek's dark blue Mercedes were parked side by side. As Dusty pushed open the door, the secretary, Jan Keaton, looked up. She peered over her glasses with an expression that didn't disappoint, looking as if she had sucked a lemon.

With a quick glance at the clock she said, 'They're expecting you.'

He walked down the corridor to the office and tapped on the door.

Murphy's gruff voice called, 'Come in.'

Murphy stood to one side of the room. Opposite him were the two men, Yanovic and Schokolov. Their woodenness reminded him of humanoid robots. At the window, a man of middle height and stocky build, stood with his back to the room. Dusty waited. No one spoke. The atmosphere was hot and heavy despite the air-conditioning.

After almost a minute the man turned. In a soft, modulated tone with the trace of an accent, he invited Dusty to take the seat facing the desk. The man was the mysterious Donovan Malek.

Whatever apprehensions Dusty might have entertained earlier, they were now supplanted by a sense of deep foreboding. Hopelessly outnumbered physically, he was disadvantaged in almost every way. Yet the anger and loathing he felt towards this man, Malek, and his henchmen empowered him with an inner steeliness that he knew would help him face whatever was to come.

Malek surveyed him with almost scientific curiosity, taking a leather case from the inside pocket of his coat to extract a cigar. He produced a gold clipper and neatly trimmed the end of the cigar before taking a gold lighter from his right waistcoat pocket. With the same care, Malek lit the cigar, turning it in his mouth and drawing down until it was properly lit. He exhaled a cloud of blue smoke and then examined the cigar's grand proportions. He let out a sigh of satisfaction.

'At my age, Mr Rhodes, there are so few genuine pleasures. Good of you to join us. Can we get you a drink? I am sure Mr Murphy can find something in his cupboard.'

Dusty shook his head. No one moved. They hadn't expected him to take up the offer.

Malek settled into the large leather chair behind the desk, swivelling it to the left so that both Dusty and Murphy were within his immediate sight.

'Mr Murphy tells me you are a person of wide and varied talents: horse breaker, trainer and …' He paused, raising his eyebrows as if a little incredulous. 'Computer whiz and veterinary expert, matched only by a singular sense of purpose. We are indeed fortunate to have the opportunity to avail ourselves of your talents, more so in light of the sudden and sad passing of our colleague Mr Callaghan.'

Malek's slight smile disappeared. His tone hardened. 'We now have to see whether your talents are compatible with our purposes.'

Dusty nodded, waiting for Malek to show his hand. Malek smiled. 'I like a good listener, so listen and listen well. I'm a tolerant man. I appreciate talent,' he snapped, 'but I don't like being threatened.'

Dusty felt he had to say something. His intuition told him remaining silent would weaken his position. 'I put a business proposition to Mr Murphy, that's all.'

'Ah, yes, a business proposition. You have information, which we would deem commercial-in-confidence, and you will respect that confidentiality for a price. Correct?'

Dusty nodded. 'I want to take over the training of certain horses, especially those being prepared for Group 1 races, including the Melbourne Cup, and I want it to be worthwhile financially. I'm not greedy but my knowledge is valuable. All I ask is a fair return.'

Another long silence while Malek continued to study him.

'Very well. This is my offer; it is not negotiable … now or in the future. I will not be trifled with – understand?'

'If it's fair, I'm happy. If not, that's your problem,' Dusty said. His outward confidence was at odds with his feelings.

Malek puffed on his cigar, eyes fixed on its glowing end. He seemed to be turning over in his mind what Dusty had said. Twice his eyes flicked towards Murphy. Dusty wished he could see the expression on the manager's face, but he kept his gaze fixed on Malek.

'You may train four horses of your choice and certain others we nominate. For every horse that wins you will receive the usual trainer's bonus plus twenty percent for your special skill and knowledge. For every Group 1 race you win, you will receive a further twenty percent. It goes without saying I expect every horse we nominate to win. You win – I win – everyone is happy. If there is any default on your side, the consequences will be grave. Remember your friend Callaghan. Is that a deal?'

Dusty nodded. 'It's a deal.'

He'd achieved his goal. A run on the inside rail of the conspiracy, the chance to set Malek up for a grand showdown. The choice of his own horses and races was more than he'd expected. Malek clearly understood the hold Dusty had over their enterprise and the need for someone on the ground who could deliver the on-course element without raising too much suspicion. For the first time Dusty felt some confidence. Their plan might just succeed. Now he needed to maintain the initiative he'd so dearly won.

'Let's celebrate our successful bargain,' said Malek. 'Maxwell, open your cabinet. I will have my usual and you, Mr Rhodes? Or should I call you Daniel now you are one of us? What will you have?'

Nobody had ever called him Daniel – not even his mother when he was in trouble.

Dusty merely smiled. 'Light beer.'

Murphy opened cabinet doors that revealed a well-stocked bar. Dusty glanced towards Yanovic and Schokolov.

Malek smiled bleakly. 'They are on duty.'

The faces of the two men remained impassive.

Dusty found it hard to believe the sinister deal he'd just struck. A sense of disquiet crept into his mind. Had it all been too easy? There seemed to be no loose threads. They'd accepted he would work with them in exchange for a solid financial bonus and a free hand. Of course, he had to deliver but much of that responsibility lay with Riekevic.

He desperately wanted to get away but couldn't think of a way out without upsetting Malek and Murphy's supposed goodwill. As if reading his thoughts, Malek suddenly turned to include him in their conversation.

'Another, Daniel? Or perhaps you'd like to get away? You've had a busy day. I'm sure you want to get home to your family.'

'If you don't mind, I would like to head off.'

'Of course. I envy you Daniel – a lovely wife and two great little boys. I have no family. You are indeed fortunate. Jennifer, isn't it? And Jeremy and Raphael?'

Malek knew about his family, even their names.

'That's right.'

'Then off you go. Give them my best wishes. You must take good care of them.'

'Thank you, Mr Malek. I will.'

'Just one final thing; I expect total loyalty. If you should try to take advantage of my generosity, it would not bode well for your lovely family.' His voice took on a sharper edge. 'I am not a sentimentalist. Business is business. Anyone who cheats on me pays a high penalty. Am I understood?'

Dusty felt a shiver. Malek was staking out his insurance, and in doing so, had raised the stakes even higher.

38

Early morning fog hung in the valley, with a hint of autumn coolness in the air. Grateful a week had passed without incident, Dusty settled into the new arrangement, taking on three promising two-year-olds and a four-year-old with potential as a stayer. His daily routine had been so normal and enjoyable he found it hard to retain focus on the events leading to his meeting with Malek, whom he'd not seen since. His daily scrutiny of the computer had not revealed anything from Riekevic.

Behind the scenes, Woodward was working feverishly to develop an antidote for the deadly stimulant compound JX/82.

It was the first race day since they'd struck the deal. Dusty had received no instructions and assumed the horses weren't ready to move. He didn't want to be hurried but thought to check his emails to see if any instructions had arrived from Riekevic, the mastermind behind the development of the drugs.

He went to the office where Murphy was going over his paperwork. As Dusty entered and headed for the computer, the manager grunted a greeting without looking up.

A message from Riekevic materialised: 'Joey's Girl – Race 4 – a Group 3 Handicap over 1300 metres.'

Malek and Murphy had taken precautions, giving Dusty minimal notice. The details were precise. He went to the fridge – the drugs were there – delivered overnight. He re-read the instructions.

This was not a repeat of Bold Challenger's situation. The carefully balanced doses would get Joey's Girl comfortably over the line without much risk.

In four starts she hadn't done better than fifth and the tipsters had her on the wrong side of twenty. While a win would be unexpected, stranger things had happened on the track. Horses performed better or worse for many reasons.

◆

At the Race Club meeting, Mowbray Park, as usual, had nominated horses in five races. Summer Dance, one of Dusty's horses, won the first race, confirming Dusty's hopes for the two-year-old, but it was important not to run her too often. Young horses, still growing in bone and sinew, could easily breakdown if overworked. It was a clean win for Summer Dance and he felt good about it.

The bustle around the stalls meant everyone was intent on their own business. An hour before the third race, Dusty had administered the masking agent to Joey's Girl, one of Malek's 'chosen' horses. The timing was critical and he needed to be careful. After forty minutes, he injected the horse with the stimulant, JX/82.

Dusty stowed the vials and needles before turning to see Grimes' leering grin behind him.

'Come on, lad. No slacking! Got to get this horse up to the mounting yard – can't keep the punters waiting.'

Dusty couldn't bring himself to watch, instead retreating to his truck to listen to the race on the radio. Joey's Girl missed the start and tailed the field for the first 500 metres.

Jacky Deane, a regular jockey for Mowbray Park's stable was up. At the eight hundred, Joey's Girl made up a couple of places, travelling two-wide from the rail. She was described by the commentator as 'bowling along'.

As the drugs took effect, the change in the horse was dramatic. Around the turn, she started to move up quickly. With four hundred to go, a gap opened on the rail as the leading bunch drifted out on the turn. Hanging in, with Deane riding hands and heels, Joey's Girl hit the front with 200 metres to go and pulled away to win by three lengths.

It was a good win – a well-judged ride by an experienced jockey who'd made the most of a burst of form on a horse from a successful stable.

Dusty felt no satisfaction in the win, only frustration and remorse. Without the drug, the horse would have been well back in the field. This was a classic demonstration of the danger Malek posed to the future of racing.

◆

The strappers took charge of the horses and the jockeys presented for the weigh-in. Dusty caught sight of Murphy, standing tall in the crowd. He was talking to Kerry Suster, who wore a wide-brimmed hat. A photographer hovered nearby.

At first glance, Joey's Girl looked reasonable, though sweating heavily. Dusty noted foam at the nostrils and a fleck or two of blood. Still, it'd been a hard run. He ran his hand down her fetlocks, feeling the swelling.

'Get her away as soon as you can,' he said quietly to Vicky. 'Clean her up; give her a good rub down and pay special attention to her legs – there's a bit of swelling. Not surprising – the track's as hard as buggery.'

Vicky nodded.

Joey's Girl tossed her head, but no one paid much attention. Few really cared. Horses were just one part of the equation.

The presentation rambled through its predictable format: courtesies indulged; platitudes uttered.

As the small knot of people began to disperse after the presentation, Murphy looked uneasy. 'The press is sniffing around and I don't want them near the horse,' he said to Dusty. 'Get her back to Mowbray Park as soon as you can. Take Vicky with you and stay with Joey's Girl. Vicky'll bring the truck back and look after the others. I'll stall that damn reporter.'

As Dusty hurried off to attend to Joey's Girl, he heard Murphy call out to Kerry with abundant geniality, 'Sorry about that. Now, what were you saying?'

39

Later that afternoon, Kerry Suster's editor called her in.

'I've told you before – I'm not keen on the Mowbray Park story. I've given you some latitude, but it's going nowhere. Don't waste my time. Here, I want you to have a look at this.'

He stubbed his cigarette into an overflowing ashtray before waving a folder of documents at her.

Kerry took the folder reluctantly. 'What is it?'

'A story that's got legs – Council's new industrial estate. They want us to promote it. It's good for the town's unemployment rate and economy. The Council's wanting to take up the government's new decentralisation package.'

Kerry couldn't hide her reaction.

'Don't look so down in the mouth. Find a human-interest angle – some poor blighter who's been out of work for months. Present it as an exciting opportunity to promote innovative new products. Get on with it.' He turned back to the papers he'd been editing. The discussion was over.

Sitting down at her desk, Kerry idly thumbed through the documents in the folder.

'Human interest!' She snorted.

As Kerry flicked to the last of the papers, she froze at the words 'Riekevic Laboratories – Manufacturer of Quality Veterinary Products'.

After reading the contents of the folder and searching the internet for information on the company, she grabbed her bag and headed for the door. On her way out, she looked into the editor's office. 'It's a good story, boss. I'm off to check out the Council's new industrial estate.'

The editor gave her a derisive look. 'You youngsters are a pain. Have to spoonfeed you stories all the time.'

◆

As Kerry drove out of town, she considered the implications of Riekevic Laboratories moving its operation to the new industrial estate. Her quick internet search of the company had shown a strong link to Malek and revealed a shareholding with the Lim Wah Mercantile and Shipping Group. A further search, of Lim Wah, had listed newspaper articles relating to drug trafficking, race fixing and Triad links. Malek was stepping up in the criminal world.

Kerry needed to see Dusty and Woodward; she had not spoken with either of them for several weeks. If the mountain would not come to Muhammad, Muhammad would go to the mountain. But before that, she needed to catch up with Dusty.

◆

Parking the Alfa outside the Stable Square at Mowbray Park, Kerry headed for the offices. Murphy was at his desk, but there was no sign of Dusty.

'Hi, Max. Hard at it I see.'

'A man's work's never done.' He looked bleakly at her. 'What do you want?'

'It's a sort of double assignment. Firstly, I'd like to do a story on Rhodes.'

Murphy's reaction was non-committal. 'And the other?'

'My boss wants me to do a story on firms relocating to the new industrial estate. I checked the list and found a Victorian company, Riekevic Laboratories. I'm sure I can get something out of that.'

Kerry could've sworn Murphy's jaw muscles twitched.

'When I did a routine check of its shareholding,' she continued, 'I saw Mr Malek's name. It'd make a great story – "Prominent businessman increases investment in local community" or "Malek shows confidence in town's future" – that sort of thing.'

Murphy relaxed. 'News to me. Mr Malek's not here this week. Sorry, I can't help.'

'That's alright, perhaps next week. There's no urgent deadline on the story. In the meantime, I'll just do a general good news story on Rhodes, with an interview and photo. The town likes to see its sons doing well.'

'Okay, pull up a chair then. I'll get someone to find him.'

She looked around the room – the desk with its secret drawer, the filing cabinets and the computer. Somehow, they looked different in daylight.

Minutes later, Murphy returned with Dusty. 'You can do your interview here. Don't mind me.'

'Thanks, but I'd like to get a photo of Rhodes with the winning horse. Our readers love pictures,' she said, grinning at Dusty. 'Anyway, animals are more photogenic. No offence.'

'None taken,' said Dusty. 'Take the picture without me, I don't mind. I hate having my photo taken.'

'I'll make it as painless as I can. I'll just duck back to the car and get my camera.'

Murphy closed the door after her. 'Can't let her see Joey's Girl in the condition she's in. Take her down to paddock nine. That's where I've put Last-Card-Lulu.'

Lulu was the half-sister of Joey's Girl and even the strappers found it hard to tell them apart.

Dusty shrugged. 'Sure.'

One glance at Joey's Girl would be enough even for a novice to know the horse was distressed.

A knock on the door. Murphy nodded and Dusty opened it.

'You guys having a private chat?' Kerry said with a disarming smile. 'I'm all set. Lead on, Mr Rhodes.'

◆

When the local paper came out, Dusty was embarrassed by the extent of the coverage. A full-page spread, three photos and a write up that made him blush. Kerry had made sure he received his full measure of credit. Jenny showed it to the boys, who were excited to see their father's picture splashed across the page.

Down at the pub, he was ribbed a bit about his new-found celebrity status, but most of his mates had good wins as a result of his advice and were too grateful to take the mickey out of him. He was popular and respected because he never hesitated to spread the luck whenever he could.

At Mowbray Park, the reaction to Dusty's fame was less friendly. Some, like Vicky, admired his ability and understanding of horses, but amongst the men were some who resented his rapid promotion.

'Self-opinionated little shit,' one man grumbled.

'Always suckin' up to Murphy,' another whined.

At their morning break, one pathetic individual put salt in his tea. Most of all, Dusty felt an increasing sense of isolation.

40

THE HORSE FLOAT ground to a halt inside Stable Square. Three more weeks and another successful race meeting had passed without incident. Dusty jumped down from the cab, feeling buoyed. Glancing towards the office, he hoped he could still catch Murphy. While Grimes went to check the stalls, Dusty walked to the back of the float, hauled down the ramp and swung the doors open. Vicky walked on and unhitched the first horse. Within minutes, the last horse was being bedded down for the night. They'd established a well-ordered routine.

Vicky bundled the lead ropes before returning them to the tack room.

'For a day when we didn't expect to win a race, I'd call two wins pretty successful.'

Dusty grinned. 'Thanks to Jacky. He's a good jockey – listens to what you tell him and shows initiative.'

Although the last few weeks had taken Dusty almost to the point of exhaustion, today had given him a lift – he didn't have to deliver on Murphy and Malek's demands. The wins took his tally to five from eleven starts.

The six wins he called 'Riekevic wins' gave him no satisfaction. But the drugged horses were still alive, giving him some source of satisfaction.

As Vicky took the last horse off she said, 'I'll finish up. Go home to Jenny and put your feet up in front of the telly.'

'Thanks, but I have to see Murphy before I leave.'

'He's not here – left last night.'

Dusty raised his eyebrows. 'I'll be home then. See you tomorrow and thanks again.'

'Don't mention it, happy to help.'

With a wave, he drove off. He needed to caution Murphy about the attention they were attracting from the stewards. By any standard, their winning streak was outstanding. He'd drop in at the office and ask Jan Keaton when he'd be back.

◆

Opening the office door, Dusty caught Murphy's personal assistant pouting into a small silver compact. When she saw him, she hurriedly put her lipstick away. 'What do you want?'

'Do you know when Murphy'll be back? I need to see him urgently,' said Dusty.

'Tuesday. Now if you don't mind, I've got to lock up.'

She picked up a large bunch of keys and hustled him out, turning back to lock the door.

Dusty had barely settled into his ute when a distant voice called to him, 'Hey, you.' In the rear-view mirror he caught sight of a man hurrying towards him waving his arms. Yanovic or Schokolov. He never could tell them apart.

Dusty got out of the ute. 'Do you mean me?'

'Mr Malek wants you,' Yanovic said. 'Now.'

Dusty heaved a sigh. Just when he thought he could be free of the place. Yanovic turned and headed towards the house, Dusty following a few paces behind. Then up the broad sandstone steps that led onto a verandah and through a pair of French doors.

The softly lit interior reminded Dusty of the Race Club. Panelled wood, thick carpet, glass-fronted cases with impressive trophies and walls decorated with framed photos of Malek's winners.

Malek stood in front of a huge marble fireplace.

Yanovic joined Schokolov, who was guarding the French doors.

Malek greeted Dusty genially. 'I saw you go to the office and thought I'd ask you over for a drink. You have done well.' He paused as if turning something over in his mind. 'And there was something I wanted to talk to you about.'

Dusty stood in silence while a woman came in with a tray of drinks, offered him a beer and then left. He took a sip. Knowing Malek, he reckoned this meeting meant trouble.

Malek gestured to a large armchair. After a few minutes of track talk, he crossed to the cedar sideboard, poured another drink, and then settled into an armchair opposite Dusty. He rolled the liquid around his mouth before he said, 'Happy with our arrangement?'

Dusty did his best to sound enthused. 'Yes.'

'Excellent. From our perspective it's working well. A number of our horses have been swabbed, some carrying the Riekevic compounds. No traces have been detected.'

Dusty sipped his drink again, deciding not to voice his concerns about the high percentage of wins. Malek wouldn't want to know; he was convinced the drugs were undetectable.

So, what Malek said caught Dusty by surprise.

'However, I am thinking we should scale back our program to avoid unwelcome attention, there has been an interesting development.' Malek raised his eyebrows and then said with a smile that carried no humour, 'We've been called on to produce something quite spectacular.'

Dusty tried to keep his voice steady. With a forced grin he said, 'How spectacular?'

Malek's eyes glistened as beads of perspiration trickled down his face.

'We've attracted the interest of a syndicate in Hong Kong; that is where the real money is.'

Dusty took the initiative. 'Lim Wah Mercantile and Shipping?'

Malek put his glass down on the table beside him. 'Lim Wah?'

'They're a shareholder in Riekevic Laboratories. They're suspected of involvement in drugs and race fixing.'

Malek eyes blazed. 'Then you'll know they're not to be trifled with. They're considering a very large investment with Mowbray Park. Maxwell's there now, checking it out. They want proof of the drug's efficacy.'

Dusty stared at the floor, trying to imagine what the something spectacular might be.

'The Race Club's Golden Guineas will be the seminal event, but they want more than a win – that would be too easy. To place our claim beyond any shadow of doubt, they want six wins including the main race.'

'Six races? That's ridiculous. The stewards would be down on us like a tonne of bricks.'

Malek nodded soberly. 'Undoubtedly, but that's the beauty of it – we will survive investigation, and no matter how suspicious it seems, they can only be, suspicious. Maxwell did his best to persuade them to set their threshold a little lower but they were adamant. They have a right to protect their investment.'

Dusty glared at Malek, struggling to find words. 'It can't be done. It's an impossible ask under any circumstances. Just tell them it can't be done. It'll blow the whole thing, and you'll have nothing.'

Malek rose and moved to the fireplace. He nodded towards Yanovic and Schokolov.

'I don't need your advice. It means a fortune for us.'

Dusty jumped to his feet, slamming his glass heavily on the side table. 'Count me out. It's madness. I didn't sign up to commit suicide.'

'Sit down.'

Heavy hands pushed him back into the chair.

'You're in no position to walk away. You know too much and you play an important role. Maxwell tells me we need the right horses. It'll be your task to select them – horses that'll attract good odds, but with the necessary winning potential. If we're successful, Lim Wah Mercantile and Shipping will close the deal and you will get a very significant commission. We value your talent.'

Dusty shook his head. 'Bloody madness.'

'But you'll do it. If you have any second thoughts, you and your family will regret it in the most unpleasant way.'

Rage and frustration welled up. He struggled to come to terms with the absurdity of the proposition and the menace of Malek's threat. They'd raised the stakes too high. He had to find a way out. They needed Dusty's skill to deliver the impossible. The gift he hoped would take him to the top had now taken him to the edge of a precipice.

Malek's eyes shone with the glow of the fanatic. 'Murphy is capable; but he doesn't have your talent. I'll give him some credit though – he found you, but that's as far as it goes.'

For Dusty, the room took on a surreal quality. Malek, flushed and perspiring, stood posed in front of the fireplace. Yanovic and Schokolov were now standing impassively on either side of him.

Dusty sipped his drink, buying time to think through the ultimatum. He and Woodward would have to accelerate their plans.

But the meeting had at least exposed Malek's number one weakness: greed. And greed had blinded his objectivity. If they could exploit that, they might still avert a monumental disaster.

41

DUSTY DROVE THE LONG WAY HOME. The afternoons were shorter without daylight saving so by the time he pulled into his driveway it was almost dark. The questions buzzing in his mind remained unresolved. Malek's greed-driven venture was bad enough, but it was the threat to his family that most unsettled him.

He had been persuaded by Woodward into believing they could control the situation. Now he wasn't so sure.

Jenny came out to meet him. 'I've been trying to keep your dinner hot for the last half hour. Where've you been?'

'Malek called me in for a drink – wanted to discuss something.'

'That's unusual.'

'Sure is. Murphy's in Hong Kong negotiating some sort of deal.'

They went inside. The boys had already eaten and were watching cartoons on the TV. Jenny served dinner.

'Not hungry?' Jenny asked as he pushed the food round his plate.

'It's just this deal of Malek's. He tells me I'm essential to its success, but it has every potential for a major disaster.'

'Why are you essential?'

He shrugged. 'It seems that my increasing visibility as a trainer is essential to giving this deal a reasonable level of credibility.'

'Surely there are others with the knowhow?'

He shook his head.

'They need someone to pick horses that can win races with the lowest dosage of the stimulant. That's where Callaghan started making mistakes. Since I've taken over, we haven't lost a single horse. And having a local reputation for being good with horses lends credibility to Malek's stable – I make the wins look possible. After all, I've had five wins from eleven with my own horses.'

Jenny looked grim. 'What about Malek's deal?'

He shared vague details based on his conversation with Malek.

Jenny ran her hands through her hair. 'I'm glad you took a stand. When will all this end? It's becoming a nightmare. You're so tired and stressed. I know I said I'd go along with what you're doing but now, well I'm not sure I can.'

She was right.

'I'll talk to Woodward and Loftus again. We need to bring it to a head soon. With this new deal, I'm even more certain.'

'Well, make sure you do. I'll do the washing up; you get the boys into bed.'

When he returned from the boys' bedroom, he found Jenny still sitting at the table, holding a buff-coloured envelope.

'I forgot – this arrived,' she said, handing it to him.

The envelope bore the name 'Carisbrooke Ellis Management Group' and a Caulfield postal address.

The letter inside had a green embossed letterhead, which was underscored with 'Victorian Racing Division'. As he read the letter, his eyes widened with astonishment, and he gave a low whistle.

Jenny watched anxiously. 'What is it?'

'It's a letter from one of Victoria's top racing stables – Carisbrooke Ellis. They want me to work for them. Someone's noticed me, that's for sure.'

He handed her the letter.

'They want to know if I'll take up a position with their stables at Werribee. They want to talk to me. They'll pay travel and accommodation for five days.'

Her face lit up. 'This is fantastic. Contact the racing manager – they've given you his name and telephone number.' She looked at Dusty and frowned. 'What's the matter? You don't seem too excited.'

Dusty knew his reputation had not been won honestly. He could get results but not the dazzling performance of the last few weeks.

'I can't do it.'

'Why?'

How could he tell her such an action would bring unimaginable disaster to their family. Malek would exact a savage revenge.

'It wouldn't be honest.'

She looked into his face. 'Sweetheart, please. This is a chance to get out of all this mess.'

Dusty reached out and pulled Jenny towards him. He gave her a hug and kissed her on the forehead.

'I wish it was that easy. Malek won't let go. He plays very hard.'

'How can they stop you?'

I can't tell her the extent of Malek's threat, Dusty thought, all I can do is stall.

'Well, I can't do anything until after the Guineas, but tomorrow I'll ring Carisbrooke Ellis and explain my commitments. I'll tell them I can work for them as soon as my commitments here are fulfilled. If they really want me, they'll wait.'

42

THE NEXT MORNING at Mowbray Park, Dusty received a comprehensive calendar for the period leading up to the Golden Guineas. As he read Malek's detailed instructions, he realised why Grimes had been in such a bad temper. It was a gruelling schedule by any standard. Malek was well under the thumb of his Lim Wah masters.

It was Dusty's task to make the final list of the six horses to be drugged, thus ensuring six wins. Lim Wah had set an impossible target from the day's program: to deliver six winners.

Later that afternoon, he caught up with Murphy who seemed distracted.

'What do you want? I'm busy.'

'We need to talk,' said Dusty. 'Do you know what the target is for the Guineas Day? Nine races and six winners, including the Golden Guineas. This is ridiculous. It can't be done.'

Murphy heaved a sigh. 'I know, but it's our job to follow instructions, not to give advice. Leave me alone. I've enough problems without you adding to them.'

Dusty wasn't put off that easily. 'There's more than one person curious about us. We're still in the clear, but they're not likely to give up. I'll make a list of the best horses; but some of them will have to be so pumped up with drugs, they're likely to have a heart attack at the finishing post. It's asking too much. Either we need a less ambitious target, or we need more time to get the horses up to the mark.'

Murphy rose to return a bundle of files to a cabinet. He closed the drawer before he turned to Dusty. He leant against the cabinet with his arms folded. 'I hear what you say. I've warned the boss, but he won't listen.'

'You mean Lim Wah won't listen.'

Murphy pushed away from the cabinet. 'Lim Wah – what about them?'

'I know enough.'

Murphy thumped the desk, anger and frustration boiling over. 'Then you'll know their passion for gambling is matched only by their entrepreneurial zeal and ruthlessness towards anyone who gets in their way. They're prepared to put up more than enough capital to float a joint venture with us, but they want a high return and fast.'

He flopped into his chair and sank his head in his hands. 'In Hong Kong they wined, dined and entertained me in grand style. I made a fool of myself. Boy, they suck you in. By the time I woke up to what was happening, we were locked into their offer on their terms. I tried to win back some negotiating space – said we needed time to make sure the formula was perfect – but they wouldn't listen. By the end of the week, I felt shredded. I was so relieved to be on that Qantas plane heading home.'

Dusty had never heard Murphy say so much at once. Murphy's unity ticket with Malek was showing signs of wear and tear.

◆

The following day, Dusty was summoned to the Malek mansion for a second time. No drinks were offered. There was no invitation to sit. Yanovic and Schokolov stood at their usual place by the door. Gone was any semblance of geniality on Malek's part. Even his attitude to Murphy was different. Dusty suspected they'd been arguing.

Malek stared angrily at Dusty before speaking with slow deliberation, 'I have been thinking over our recent discussion, and now I believe letting you prepare horses of your own selection has placed our enterprise in jeopardy.'

'I don't understand,' Dusty said.

'Maxwell agrees you've been too successful, so the blame rests with you.'

'What am I supposed to have done? I've followed orders. The other night you said you were pleased.'

'I know, but now I have changed my mind. I think you have been too successful.'

Dusty was dumbfounded.

'Since we engaged with our program, you have produced eleven winners, the six we nominated and five others of your selection. If you had not been so successful we would not have attracted so much attention. From now on you will field only the horses we nominate. Understood?'

Unwilling to let it go he said, 'I've followed instructions. Anyway, it adds to my credibility.'

'Perhaps, but none the less it has attracted unwanted attention. The Race Club has demanded an explanation. We told them you were an excellent trainer, one of the best, but from now on, at meetings between now and the Guineas we will field fewer horses, and only the ones we nominate. You will follow my instructions, to the letter.'

Dusty turned away so Malek couldn't see his face. Through the windows he saw gardens with manicured lawns and flower beds full of blooming dahlias, zinnias and poppies. He looked across to Murphy, trying to gauge his reaction. His eyes, tired and tense, peered from under hooded lids in an otherwise impassive face. He sensed all was not right between Malek and Murphy.

Dusty decided to push it a little further. 'Why the sudden change of mind?'

'Just do as you're told.'

Murphy broke his silence. 'He needs to know.'

Dusty caught the morose look Malek shot Murphy but had missed Murphy's response. His words had a positive impact. Finally, Malek nodded thoughtfully. 'Hong Kong has just advised me they want a higher level of proof. They now want a clean sweep of the meeting.'

Dusty shrugged. 'That's beyond any level of credibility, but if we have to, so be it. But if it all goes pear shaped remember you were warned. Anyway, why is Hong Kong so important?'

Malek's eyes gleamed with the same touch of madness Dusty had seen before. 'That's the golden door to the rest of the world. The Chinese have the best networks. Dominance of world racing is within our grasp. You can be the most famous trainer in the world.'

With the tension that was making the room hum Dusty thought it wise, though seething inwardly, to mask his anger. 'I'll see it through. Then I'm off. From then on you can manage on your own. Someone else can take the glory.'

43

Dusty and his family ate dinner in silence. For once, the boys were subdued, feeling the tension between their parents. Dusty stared gloomily into space, realising how far he'd pushed himself out on a limb.

The strong winds of the day had not died down. Wind always disturbed him. It had howled the night his mother had not returned home, leaving him to fend for himself. For Dusty, wind was an omen of disaster.

He and Jenny washed up in silence. The silence continued until the boys had gone to bed and Jenny had read them a story. When she came back, she placed the buff envelope from Carisbrooke Ellis on the table.

'I want you to accept their offer,' she said. 'Ring them tomorrow and say you're accepting it, and you'll start as soon as they want you to.'

'You know I can't do that. I am stuck with Mowbray Park until after the Guineas – perhaps even after that.'

'Dusty, I'm frantic with worry.'

'Malek won't let go.'

'He can't stop you from resigning. The last time I looked, Australia was a still a free country.'

The vision of Callaghan's dying moments flashed before Dusty – Callaghan's battered body, the tortured breathing, the vomit, but most of all the life leaving his eyes.

Dusty shook his head. 'Malek is ruthless.'

◆

Despite a stormy and restless night, Dusty woke at 5:30. He lay in bed for a moment before stumbling to the bathroom to splash cold water over his face. The mirror reflected red and sore eyes, as if the night wind had peppered them with dust.

After last night's long and emotional discussion with Jenny, he'd finally given in. The job offer with Carisbrooke Ellis was everything he'd dreamed of. He'd come to bitterly regret the events that had led him to conceal so much from those around him. He hadn't been totally honest with anyone, least of all Jenny. She mightn't have been so insistent if she knew the whole truth.

He skipped breakfast, not wanting to wake his family, and was about to let himself out the back door when he sensed someone behind him. Jenny leant against the hall door. She had dark circles under her eyes and her hands clenched the front of her dressing gown.

'You will ring, won't you?'

So often he'd done what he'd wanted; so often he'd gone against her wishes. And so often he'd been wrong. This time he'd do what she wanted. He put down his bag, put his arms around her and hugged her tight.

◆

At lunch time, he left work and drove into town. After parking near the Clarion, he made a phone call to Carisbrooke Ellis to accept their job offer. The racing manager's reaction to his prompt reply was in sharp contrast to his present situation. They'd agreed he could start immediately after the Golden Guineas. Dusty would see it that far with Malek and then he'd be off. The reference from Tom Loftus had carried a lot of weight; he would ring tonight to thank him.

Dusty slipped into the Clarion to ask Kerry to type up his letter of resignation.

She stared at him. 'Sure about this?'

'I've got to for Jenny's sake.'

'I understand, but is it wise?'

Seeing the deep concern in her eyes he swallowed hard and said, 'Just do it.'

◆

When Dusty returned to work, he found Murphy in his office and handed him the letter.

'What's this?'

'It's self-explanatory.'

Murphy quickly read the few typed lines. His eyes flicked to Dusty. The grey eyes held only a mixture of curiosity and pity. It did nothing to relax Dusty's tautly strung nerves.

'Sure you don't want to think this over?'

Dusty shook his head. He left the office feeling ragged at the edges.

He finished work in a haze of unreality, expecting a tap on the shoulder at any minute, but nothing happened. Throwing his bag onto the passenger seat of the ute, he hoped he'd called their bluff. He wouldn't relax until he was out of Mowbray Park's gate and on his way home. Reversing out of the carpark, he reflected on how pleased Jenny would be. He'd taken the plunge somehow and pulled it off.

Dusty swung his ute onto the main drive and drove down the avenue of trees now deep in shadow. The open gate beckoned.

Thirty metres short of the gate, a dark blue Commodore eased out from between the trees, blocking the exit. Dusty slowed to a halt.

This was what Dusty had been dreading. He slammed the ute into reverse, sending it back along the drive and into a single, slewing turn. Twisting the wheel to the opposite lock, he accelerated, sending the ute lurching in an arc that took him within centimetres of the nearest oak.

He passed the office building in a blur and gave his rear-view mirror a quick glance, catching sight of the Commodore close behind him.

He turned left and pressed on towards the float gate. It was never closed but today was different. He screeched to a halt, his heart thumping. The gate had been padlocked. He reversed and headed back down the drive. Nearing the corner, he saw the Commodore in front of him. It crunched to a halt.

Wrenching at the wheel, Dusty swung wide and swept around the Commodore, speeding past the office building again. If he could reach the back entrance on the other side of the property and make it to the open road he had a chance. He took the last turn at speed, the squealing tyres throwing up a shower of gravel.

But the wooden gate at this entrance was also closed. For a moment, he contemplated smashing through but braked with inches to spare. He jumped out, hoping it wasn't locked. A fleeting glance took in yet another padlock. Before Dusty could get back in his ute, the Commodore pulled up behind him, jamming him in. Its front doors swung open to reveal Yanovic and Schokolov. They walked towards him.

'Mr Malek wants to see you.'

44

Dusty was frog marched by Yanovic and Schokolov around the side of Malek's house to a small, solid door set low and deep in the wall. Panic surged in Dusty as visions of Callaghan flooded his mind. Damn it. Why hadn't he told the police all he knew?

Thrust into a stone passageway, he was bundled down a narrow flight of stairs to a bare, narrow room, then through another door before being shoved into a larger room lit by a single light bulb.

Several large iron hooks hung from the thick ceiling beams, probably once used to hang meat; Dusty had no doubts about their more sinister use.

Yanovic pushed him onto the single wooden chair. Schokolov left the room.

Dusty tried to keep his voice calm, but his stomach tightened, and his heart thumped. 'What's all this about?'

'We wait for Mr Malek.'

Nothing more was said.

Eventually, the door opened and Malek entered. He said nothing, merely nodding to Schokolov who'd followed him in. Yanovic and Schokolov closed in on Dusty. Grasping him by the arms, they hoisted him off the chair, his feet several inches from the ground. Effortlessly, they carried him across the room and flung him heavily against the wall. His feet hit the floor and his legs buckled, jarring his whole body and forcing the air from his lungs. He staggered a few steps, trying to get his balance, but heavy punches caught him just below the heart. The men kicked his legs from under him, sending him sprawling to the floor.

Malek's voice cut the air. 'Enough.'

Dusty struggled for breath. From the corner of his eye, he saw Malek's heavy, expressionless features. He struggled to sit up, panting heavily. Yanovic and Schokolov loomed behind him.

Malek pulled the chair away from the centre of the room and sat down with his back to the light, his face in shadow. His words were matter of fact: 'You've been very, very foolish. Foolish people must be taught a lesson.'

Dusty caught the slight nod of Malek's head. He heard Yanovic and Schokolov behind him. He was yanked to his feet. Twisting around, he tried to protect himself but to no avail. A heavy blow hit him behind the head just below the skull; a fist crashed into his stomach. Coughing, Dusty gulped air. He stumbled sideways but they closed in again, laughing. They caught him and twisted his arms painfully behind his back.

Malek's voice was hard and cold, 'I don't play games. You will move with your family to live at Mowbray Park where I can keep an eye on you. The cottage has been vacant for a couple of months so you'll move in there. If not, neither you nor any of your family will be safe. I know everything there is to know about them. We will strike in the most unexpected places. Perhaps the bus that takes Jem to his football matches will crash.'

Through a red mist of pain, Dusty stared into Malek's cruel face.

'I have laid down my terms,' said Malek. 'This is the only warning you will get. When you sign on with me, it's until death do us part.'

Dusty nodded, seething inwardly. One day he'd get the bastard.

45

They'd just finished the washing up; the boys were asleep, and the house was quiet.

'No option. It'll only be until after the Golden Guineas event. We can move back when it's all over.'

Jenny paced the floor angrily. Several times she went to speak but didn't. He knew exactly how she felt. He waited for calm before pressing the issue again.

'No! No! No! I won't do it. We won't do it. No, it's just not on. Why should we disrupt our lives? How do I explain this to the boys? To Mum and Dad? Tell Murphy we won't move into Mowbray Park. You've agreed to their demands. What more can they want?'

'Malek and Murphy are not your average bosses.'

'Tell Murphy I won't agree. Blame me.'

Dusty shook his head. 'I don't think it will be any use. I know Malek. When he makes up his mind, he won't budge. He's used to getting what he wants.'

'I'll ring Murphy and tell him myself. Does he know you've told me what's going on?'

'I've told him nothing.'

'Then don't you see? It's logical that your wife would object to the move. We'll see what he says.'

'Worth a try.'

◆

Murphy and Dusty were sitting in the stand watching the morning workout. They'd finally agreed on the horses they would run in the Golden Guineas. Dusty had to admit, the horses looked the part. In less time than he needed, his job was to bring their form within a winning envelope for a drug dose that wouldn't kill them.

Murphy looked up from his clipboard and said, 'That wife of yours is a feisty woman.'

Dusty pretended he didn't understand. 'What do you mean?'

'She rang me this morning to give me a piece of her mind. Said she wasn't moving house for anyone. Asked me to give her one good reason why she should.'

'What'd you say?'

Murphy shrugged. 'I gather you haven't told her anything?'

'Think I'm stupid? She'd go ballistic.'

Murphy clicked the stopwatch in his left hand and noted a time on his pad. 'I think it'd be wise to take the risk. I told her it was a generous offer from Mr Malek. That he wanted you all here because your workload was heavy and he thought living in the cottage rent free could save you some money. It sounded a bit thin, but it was all I could think of on the spur of the moment.'

'And she said?'

'She didn't want charity and hung up.'

'So that's it? We're not moving?'

Murphy shook his head. 'You're moving all right. I wouldn't cross him any further.'

Dusty stared across the racetrack to the mountain range beyond. He sensed Murphy watching for his reaction.

Murphy clicked the stopwatch again and noted another time. He got up and turned to leave, letting the watch hang from the lanyard around his neck.

'I'm off. You can handle the rest. By the way, Malek said to remind you.' He paused and swallowed hard. 'If you value your family, don't step out of line. I don't care how you explain it to your wife, but you're expected to move by the weekend.'

46

Malek perused the immaculate gardens through the French doors. After swirling the golden liquid long enough to melt the ice cubes, he sipped his drink appreciatively.

His plans were going well. He had negotiated the Hong Kong deal and his purchase of a local agricultural chemical business would facilitate the development of the doping package, now being handled by the plant in Victoria.

A few unwelcome visitors had necessitated changing the location of Riekevic Laboratories. In Warrianderra they could continue manufacturing the existing and highly profitable proprietary lines while setting up a small experimental lab to develop new products.

A glance at the clock told him his old friend Boris Spetcevic would arrive any moment.

He recalled their school days in Belgrade. Spetcevic was the clever one, but even then, they had worked as a team. If trouble arose, Spetcevic would sort it out.

After a brilliant university career, Spetcevic landed a plum job with an international pharmaceutical company, while Malek struggled with an economics degree. The day the conscription papers arrived; their world collapsed. Armies on all sides were suffering heavy casualties. Young men were called up as cannon fodder.

One night in a wet and miserable trench, choked by the smell of decaying bodies, Malek and Spetcevic decided they'd had enough. They broke camp and headed west – avoiding towns, travelling at night and sleeping by day in squalid shelters. They made it to Slovenia and a few weeks later arrived in Gorizia, Italy, where they joined a group of refugees.

Four days later, they reached Venice, where they signed onto a Liberian freighter that would eventually sail to Australia. In Sydney, they were lucky to find an organisation that helped refugees and after a few years, they received permanent residency. Malek and Spetcevic had learned to fight and that only the ruthless survived.

Malek swirled the remaining contents and drained the glass. A car pulled up. The door opened behind him and Boris Spetcevic entered. Malek raised his glass with a questioning look.

'Thank you,' said Spetcevic.

The two men settled into chairs that faced the grey marble fireplace. The clock chimed the hour. Spetcevic sipped his whiskey. 'Very good, my dear Don.'

'Only the best for you.'

They exchanged pleasantries before getting down to business.

'You did well to secure the chemical business,' said Spetcevic. 'I didn't think he'd sell.'

'I offered him a good price.'

'He told me he wouldn't sell at any price. You must have offered considerably more.'

'Less, but I threw in an incentive.' He pointed to Spetcevic's empty glass. 'Another?'

He nodded. 'An incentive?'

Malek poured them both another drink and settled back in his chair with a wolfish grin on his face.

'Fortunately for us there aren't too many good people in this world. Keenan did some digging and found the owner – a pillar of his church – was having an affair with an employee. He wasn't happy, but he saw the value of my silence. We signed the contract two weeks ago. You can inspect the plant tomorrow.'

Spetcevic nodded. 'Then I'd like to meet Rhodes – his performance is remarkable.'

'He's not to be underestimated; but I have taken precautions.'

Spetcevic smiled. 'Insurance?'

'There are still concerns. Rhodes is shrewd and thinks too much.'

'I am a fresh face. Tomorrow I will talk to him. We'll test his knowledge, and his loyalty.'

They talked late into the night. The level of the Glenfiddich dropped considerably.

◆

As Spetcevic drove up the avenue into Mowbray Park, he passed a white ute. Its driver waved to him, which he acknowledged by lifting his right hand above the steering wheel.

Swinging into Stable Square he parked outside Murphy's office.

'You've just missed Rhodes,' Murphy said. 'I sent him into town to pick up some printing. You probably passed him on the way here.'

Spetcevic smiled and said, 'Let me know when he returns.'

47

OVER THE WEEKEND, Dusty and his family moved into the cottage at Mowbray Park. Although Jenny remained cranky about being forced to move, she had to admit the cottage was quite nice and now they would see a bit more of Dusty. Surprisingly, the boys had taken the change well, perhaps seeing it as an adventure. And at least they could all look forward to going home after the Golden Guineas.

When Dusty returned from working the morning session, he saw a figure standing on the hill above the track.

The man waved and called out in a casual, almost affable tone. 'Hello, Dusty, I'm Boris Spetcevic. Go well this morning?'

'Quite well, thank you.'

Dusty felt an immediate uneasiness. So, this was Spetcevic.

Spetcevic continued expansively. 'We're lucky to have you. Where did you study veterinary science?'

'A part-time interest, I've found it useful in the job.'

'That explains it. You seemed a little lost at times but no matter, it's not important. The main thing is you're interested.'

'I certainly am,' Dusty said, a little too quickly.

'Then you'll be interested in a new drug formula I'm keen to trial.'

'How's it different?'

'From time to time, your reports have expressed concern about the after-effect of the masking agent. I admit it's a problem. You've shown considerable skill judging the level of the dosage and in managing the recovery of the horses. Better than Callaghan. Anyway, I've taken heed, and I believe I've found something more effective that can be administered the day before.'

Dusty nodded. 'Sounds good.'

Spetcevic looked thoughtfully at the string of horses walking back to the stables.

'The drug takes longer to assimilate into the horse's system, which lessens the impact on the circulatory system. But I need to assess its efficacy in masking the stimulant. Tomorrow at five, I want you to inject the drug into the horse, Scottish Realm. We'll give it twenty-four hours before running the horse, then swab at regular intervals to monitor its recovery.'

◆

That evening, Dusty met Woodward at the surgery. He pointed to the whiteboard covered in scientific equations, circles, arrows and asterisks. 'My head looks like that.'

'Mine too. I've been trying to get it around these formulae. It's not coming together.'

'I need your help.'

They left the stark brightness of the surgery for Woodward's dimly lit office. A sole light shone on papers piled high on his desk. In the kitchenette, Woodward made coffee.

'You look worried. Malek making your life hell?'

Dusty sat on the far side of the desk, angling his chair so the shaft of bright light shining through the open door wasn't in his eyes.

Woodward dropped wearily into a big leather chair and sipped his coffee. 'Fire away.'

'Spetcevic's turned up. Malek's establishing a local laboratory.'

Woodward whistled softly. 'Where?'

'Bought out Mallesons.'

'Interesting, but what brings you here at this hour?'

'Spetcevic put me through the third degree. I'm not sure I impressed him.'

'You're here to criticise my teaching?' Woodward said and grinned.

'Of course not. He's trying a new masking agent. We need to know what we're dealing with.'

Woodward leaned forward, his chair creaking in the quietness of the office. 'Get me a sample. I'll give you a harmless saline solution to swap for the injection, then bring me whatever they want you to inject.'

'A tough call.'

'But not beyond your ingenuity.'

'Thanks for nothing.'

◆

Dusty checked his watch, 5:15 am. Except for Murphy's ute and the dark blue Commodore, Stable Square was deserted.

Switching the drug sounded easy, but nothing was simple any longer. He patted the packet in his pocket – the saline solution Woodward had given him.

As Dusty passed the Commodore on the way to Murphy's office, he gave it a quick glance, but the heavily tinted windows prevented him from seeing inside.

He entered the office building and saw a light on in Murphy's office. Dusty walked down the corridor and momentarily stopped outside the door; he knocked.

'Come in,' Murphy called out. As Dusty entered, he continued, 'The stuff's in the frig in a white polystyrene box. Got your instructions?'

'Inject at 5:30.'

Murphy nodded and stood up. 'I'm off. Got to be in town by six. Yanovic and Schokolov will check everything goes smoothly.'

'How would they know?'

'You'll see.'

After Dusty collected the box, he took it back to Murphy's office where he opened it to check its contents. Nodding his head, as if to affirm it was what he needed, he left and began walking towards the stable of the horse called Scottish Realm.

Behind him, he heard car doors open and close. He was being followed. By the time he reached the horse's stall, they were right behind him.

'What're you doing here?' Dusty said.

Yanovic grunted, pointing to the box. 'See you do the job.'

'Be my guest.'

Dusty whistled and a horse's head poked over the top of the door. Scottish Realm, who went by the stable name, Scotty, was a dark bay, seventeen hand gelding.

Dusty patted the majestic head. 'Isn't he great?'

Yanovic and Schokolov said nothing but Yanovic approached tentatively. Without warning, Scotty jerked his head up and let out a piercing squeal. Yanovic jumped back.

Good old Scotty, Dusty thought. Like dogs, they smell fear.

'They're in training, full of feed and exercise – temperamental.'

In that moment Dusty saw a glimmer of hope. 'Hold this.'

Passing the box to Yanovic, Dusty entered the stall and took Scotty to the rear, allowing Yanovic to venture a little closer. Slipping on a halter, Dusty clipped on a lead rope and began circling the horse. Each time Scotty approached, Yanovic stepped back.

Out of Yanovic's line of sight, Dusty flicked the lead rope against Scotty's rump. The horse began pawing the ground, laying the odd kick into the walls. Dusty slipped out and latched the door.

'I'll need your help to hold him.'

'Not fuckin' likely,' Schokolov snarled. 'Give it the injection.'

'Right,' Dusty paused, and frowned. 'But I'll need someone to hold him. When I open the door, hop in quick.'

The heavies exchanged a look, shaking their heads.

'Alright, don't worry, I'll hold the horse, you give the injection,' said Dusty. 'I'll show you where to put the needle.'

Schokolov shook his head while Yanovic's face went pallid.

'No fuckin' way,' said Yanovic. 'Give the injection or we'll thump the hell outta you.'

Dusty shrugged. 'Okay, have it your way then.' Grabbing the box from Yanovic, he entered the stall.

Yanovic sidled closer, checking the door was latched.

Dusty randomly indicated a spot on the horse's rump. 'It goes here.'

Yanovic eyes widened. 'Do it.'

Dusty prepared the needle, holding it out for Yanovic to see. 'Wicked, isn't it?'

Yanovic's eyes grew wider.

Dusty took out the ampoule.

Yanovic watched closely. 'Turn him around … wanna see you do it. Murphy warned you might try some kinda stunt.'

Dusty felt in his pocket for Woodward's substitute, all the time easing Scotty closer to the door.

Yanovic yelled over his shoulder. 'Yuri, over here. Get in and hold the fuckin' horse.'

Schokolov's voice floated back. 'Do it your fuckin' self.'

Scotty, sensing the tension, was becoming genuinely agitated. He stamped his hoofs, sending up clouds of dust that made it difficult for Dusty. As the horse began to settle back on his haunches, ready to rear, Dusty leapt aside to avoid the hoofs.

Schokolov called out, 'Hurry up!'

'Stick the nag, or you'll get the dose yourself,' Yanovic said.

'Steady. Steady, old fella. It'll soon be over,' Dusty said gently.

Gradually the horse quietened. It was now or never. This time, when Dusty manoeuvred the animal, Yanovic didn't object.

Wiping the perspiration from his face, Dusty shook his head to clear the sweat from his eyes.

With Scotty's bulk momentarily blocking Yanovic's line of sight, he swapped the ampoules, then turned the horse around to show the needle in full view. He slowly depressed the plunger. Yanovic watched, mesmerised.

When it was done, Dusty barely got out of the stalls before Yanovic slammed the door firmly shut.

'Thank God that's over,' said Dusty.

Before he could react, his feet went from under him. Dusty felt the thud of boots against his ribs. A wave of pain exploded through him.

Yanovic towered over him. 'That's for being a bloody nuisance.'

Through the red mist swimming before his eyes, Dusty watched his feet retreat to the Commodore. Its engine revved hard before accelerating towards him in a wide arc. Dusty's eyes widened as its front wheel passed close to his head. The car braked.

Yanovic leaned out of the window. 'We'll tell Murphy you stuck him good.'

Dusty lay on the gravel for a minute, trying to read his pain. Broken bones or not, he had to get the sample to Woodward.

48

THE NEXT DAY, Dusty followed the usual routine at Mowbray Park. During the morning break in the tearoom, he felt increasingly isolated. As the workers were dispersing, Vicky came over.

'What's on?' she whispered to him. 'Murphy wants to see everyone in Stable Square at 3:45. Bit odd, isn't it?'

Dusty shrugged. 'Dunno, I just do as I'm told.'

'Like the rest of us.'

'Like the rest of you.'

At 4:15 Murphy addressed the staff. 'Mr Malek wants to send horses to Melbourne. We've arranged for them to be stabled with Martin and Charley until the Autumn Carnival is over. Grimes will take them tonight. Clark, these are the horses we need to load, so pick your men and get started.

Murphy handed the man a sheet of paper.

'Doherty, you'll supervise the loading and I'll need three volunteers to stay back and help him so that Grimes can be away by six at the latest. He'll pick up Gerry on the way. They'll travel in the cool of the evening. I don't want them on the road any longer than necessary.'

Jack Doherty looked around the crowd and nodded to three of his mates.

Dusty turned to Vicky as they walked away. 'Glad he didn't pick me. Place is going mad. I was talking to Murphy about our racing program a few days ago and Melbourne wasn't on the agenda.'

'He talked to you?'

'Well, not really … just wanted my opinion on the agenda for the next few months. Believe me, you're better off not talking to them.'

◆

Just before five, the last horse clattered up the ramp. Once they had been tethered, the last metal-mesh partition was swung into place and made fast; the ramp was raised and the doors were closed and locked down.

Murphy consulted his watch. 'Where in the hell's Grimes? Should've been here half an hour ago. I want this rig rolling as soon as possible.'

The four men who had stayed back to load the horses answered with shrugs and shaking heads.

With a look of disgust, Murphy fished his mobile phone from his trouser pocket and punched the speed dial.

'Jan,' he barked. 'Can you get onto Grimes' place and find out what's happened to him? No, he's not here … Yes, should've been here half an hour ago … Ring me as soon as you've got any news … Yes, I'll ring you if he turns up.'

He mopped his brow.

The men looked at each other, then at Murphy. Doherty spoke for them all, 'Want us for anything more or can we go? I expect Grimes'll turn up any minute.'

'And if he doesn't?'

Doherty looked non-plussed. 'I dunno.'

'We'll have to unload them, stupid.' He let out a sigh of frustration. 'Just hang on until we know what's happening. If there's any hitch, we'll have to take them off and try again tomorrow night. I've never had a good feeling about this from the start. Mr Malek has decided to establish a base in Melbourne, but I don't think we're ready. It doesn't make sense, but then, who cares about my opinion? I'm only the racing manager.'

Such open criticism of Malek was rare around Mowbray Park. Something had certainly upset him and Grimes' absence had done nothing to improve his temper.

The four men drifted over to the tearoom, grumbling about the delay.

Murphy returned to his office.

Ten minutes later, he appeared in the doorway of the tearoom and the chatter ceased.

'His landlady says he has come down with some sort of virus. Not fit to drive.'

'We take the horses off then.'

'No. I've rung Mr Malek and he insists they go tonight. Jack, drive up to the cottage and get Rhodes. He'll have to take over.'

'A bit rough at short notice, isn't it?' Doherty said.

'I didn't ask your opinion. Unless you want to do it, shut up and get on with it.'

'No bloody fear – gotta take the wife to bingo tonight.'

'Tell Rhodes to be ready to leave in an hour. The rest of you, stay here until he arrives.'

◆

By the time Dusty arrived, it was dark. The black semitrailer emblazoned with Mowbray Park livery stood like some huge monster, dwarfing the men standing beside it.

Murphy came straight to the point. 'Rhodes, I need you to drive these horses to Melbourne. Grimes has got some sort of virus. Pick up Gerry on the way; he'll share the driving with you. I'll ring him to tell him you'll be at his place about 7:20.'

Dusty nodded. He'd been cranky as hell when Doherty had arrived with the message. Inwardly, he seethed.

'Get there as soon as you can, but don't take any risks. You should be there by morning. I don't want the horses on board any longer than necessary.'

Murphy handed him an envelope. 'The details are here. Gerry will fill you in on anything else you need to know. No need to hurry once you've got them there. Take a day or two off, before you start back.'

Dusty nodded again. He opened the envelope and scanned its contents, noting with interest their destination – Charley and Martin Racing Stables, Werribee. It was not far from Carisbrooke Ellis.

He stuffed the papers into his back pocket and began checking the air pressurisation system.

Murphy watched impatiently. 'We've done that – hundred percent guarantee everything's in top working order.'

'If you don't mind, I'll do my own inspection. Not only is it the law, but it's my life on the line if they're not.'

Murphy shrugged. 'Well hurry up – we've lost enough time as it is.'

Dusty knew he was well within his rights. After a brief inspection, he swung up into the cab, threw the envelope into the tray beside him and settled behind the wheel. He was just as anxious as Murphy to get on the road. At least he'd be away from Mowbray Park for a few days. It'd be like a breath of fresh air.

The engine roared to life. 'See you,' he called to Murphy, who raised a hand in acknowledgement.

Slowly the rig rumbled out of the yard and along the drive. At the entrance he swung left, another kilometre a long left again, onto the winding road that climbed steadily to the top of Greens Ridge before starting the long descent to the highway. In the rear-view mirror he noticed headlights following. There'd be nowhere to pass the long rig until he reached the highway.

His thoughts turned to Jenny. It had taken all her persuasive power to stop him from telling Murphy exactly where he could shove his Melbourne trip, but he'd calmed down a bit when she'd said, 'At least it'll get you away from here for a little while. While you're down there, look in on Carisbrooke Ellis.'

'Good idea,' he'd said. But deep down he couldn't shake the foreboding feeling that had gripped him the moment Murphy ordered him to take a load of horses to Melbourne.

The rig ground up Greens Ridge; the headlights in Dusty's rear-view mirror appeared and disappeared with each bend. Cresting the ridge, he saw the valley off to his right; a tapestry of textured shadows, its undulating pastures dotted with majestic trees and giant granite outcrops. In the far distance he could just glimpse the thin line of the river sparkling in the moonlight. He loved this land – the countryside he'd grown up in. Much as he recognised the potential of the Carisbrooke Ellis offer, he would regret leaving it behind.

The calmness relaxed him. Soon he'd pick up Gerry. He got on well with Gerry – he was solid, dependable. Not blessed with any self-initiative, Gerry would do what he had to but no more.

By the time the rig began its descent, the moon was hidden behind heavy clouds. A pattern of misty rain settled on the windscreen. Within seconds, it was raining heavily. Dusty's view across the valley disappeared as the storm enveloped it.

He dropped down a couple of gears and touched the brakes to

take the corners. The car that had dropped back for a while, was now right behind him. He adjusted the rear-view mirror to avoid the glare of its headlights.

Dusty rang Gerry's number to let him know he'd be there soon. The phone rang for several seconds before a female voice answered.

'Hi there,' Dusty said. 'Tell Gerry I'll be there in fifteen minutes.'

'Gerry's not here. Can I give him a message?'

Disbelief almost made him drop the phone.

'What do you mean he's not there? Murphy's arranged for me to pick him up. We're delivering a load of horses to Victoria.'

'Gerry's been in Umina for the last week with his mother – she's not well. It's her heart, poor love.'

Dusty hung up. What the hell? Murphy's farewell wave flashed before him – the affable smile now a malicious grin. As soon as he could turn around, he was heading back. Damn them. He wasn't going any further.

Distracted by the call, he almost overshot the next bend. He touched the brakes. The rig slowed but not as much as it should. A glance at the air-pressure gauge told him everything was fine. In any case the prime mover's instrument panel was fitted with warning tones. He just needed to concentrate.

Driving down the steep eastern face of Greens Ridge, Dusty constantly checked his mirrors. The car following him still had its headlights on high beam. Inconsiderate bastard.

From there on, the way down had more than the usual quota of hairpin bends. He tested the brakes as he went into the next turn and did a routine check of the gauges – all okay.

On the next bend though he thought he felt the trailer brakes dragging. He eased the truck round the bend and into the steepest section. The rock face to his left rose sharply; miniature waterfalls cascading down its sides. Although he couldn't see it through the water streaming off the cab, he knew the offside took a sheer drop to the road below the next bend.

Reaching the next corner, he again detected drag from the trailer. The last thing he needed on this treacherous road was the braking system on the trailer to be out of sync with the prime mover.

By now, the truck was moving slowly and at each bend he swung across the double lines, sounding his horn. He lined up for the next bend. His world had shrunk to no more than the truck, the road ahead and nature's spectacular light show.

Another check of the gauges and mirrors. Jesus Christ! That bloody idiot behind him was trying to pass him on the inside of the looming bend.

He blew the horn furiously, the bugger backed off. Using every inch of width, he put the bend behind him. Five to go and he'd be finally onto the easy run to the highway. Then he would pull off until the storm blew itself out.

As he started to navigate the second last bend, he saw the headlights of an oncoming vehicle light up the rock face ahead of him. Instinctively, he braked harder than he should have to allow the vehicle room to clear the corner. The pedal was spongy – the air-pressure warning tone chimed and the gauge began to drop. Pumping the brakes would only release more air and drain the system quicker. Without enough air pressure the brakes would lock.

Fragmented pictures flashed before Dusty: Jenny, the boys, his father, his dreams and Malek's face, ugly and menacing. With horrifying clarity, he saw every step of Murphy's elaborate plan, knowing he'd have little use for the brakes until the descent to the highway; Grimes' sudden virus, out alone on the pretext of picking Gerry up. All devised with one intent – to kill the only person who could destroy their assault on the racing world.

Despite the montage of images, another part of his brain assessed the situation with remarkable clarity. If he could negotiate this bend and the next, he might just have a chance.

The oncoming vehicle curved into view. He glimpsed two terrified faces. He held his line. The vehicle accelerated past him and was gone. As he drifted to the right on the next corner, he prayed nothing was coming and steered wide. Somehow, he had managed it, but the emergency brakes on the trailer had been activated. The trailer had taken a life of its own.

With some relief, he saw the road was clear. The warning tone continued to chime. Under other circumstances, he'd try to stop, but the final bend was too close. He mustered up every ounce of concentration.

The bend rushed towards him; he could see now it was not as tight as the previous ones and his hopes lifted a fraction. He touched the brakes again and took stock of the best driving line.

But the corner was coming too fast. The warning tone gave one last wail, and he felt the brakes lock up. The prime mover rocked alarmingly as the trailer took control. Somehow the cab and trailer remained upright. A loud bang and a screech of tortured metal tore through the night as the side of the trailer hit the rock embankment on his left. Sweat streamed down his face, his eyes almost painful with the strain, knuckles white on the steering wheel. He fought to stay on the road. Behind him, the trailer began to fish tail, building a deadly energy of its own. He struggled desperately, trying to counter the twisting force. Inexorably, with every split second and against all his efforts, the prime mover and its trailer escaped his control.

His heart was thumping and rasping breaths tore at his lungs. He saw rocky outcrops pock-marked with stunted trees and beyond that, the river flats. For a moment, time stood still.

The truck lost traction. The trailer jack-knifed ahead in a hellish tympanic climax of metal, crashing through rocks and trees. The truck, dragged over by the trailer, reared on its back wheels and was flung onto its side.

For a moment there was deathly silence, broken only by the sickening sound of horses squealing in pain. The truck gave a final lurch, the seat belt crushing into Dusty's chest.

The last thing he saw was a silver shower of granulated glass before a light exploded in his head. A velvety blackness enveloped him like a shroud.

49

His eyes flickered open to unnaturally bright surroundings, almost ethereal. He closed them against the glare. By degrees, his recollection returned; the gathering speed of the truck, the speedometer dancing, the noise, the smell of burning rubber, the blackness. A soft, gentle hand touched his. He gripped it weakly.

A far-away voice said, 'I think he's coming round.'

Through slitted eyelids, he struggled to take in his surroundings. He'd never been a patient in a hospital, but his recollection of medical soapies on television told him where he was.

A doctor opened one of Dusty's eyes, then the other, peering into each pupil with a small torch.

'Amazing! Given what he's been through, he's in remarkably good shape.'

His eyes fluttered open again.

'How are you feeling?' the doctor said.

He worked his mouth, licked his lips to fashion a response. 'Don't really know. How long … have I been here? What's the time?'

'You came into casualty at about eight last night. It's now after five in the afternoon,' the doctor said, glancing at his watch. 'You've had a mighty crack on the head, but otherwise you're doing pretty well.'

The doctor turned to the nurse. 'He's to be transferred to a private room as soon as can be arranged.'

Dusty closed his eyes.

A short time later he felt the bed move out of casualty and along corridors, then into a room.

'We've rung your wife,' the nurse said. 'She'll be in shortly. She's organising someone to look after the children.'

'Thanks.'

The nurse turned away, speaking to someone beyond his vision. 'Tell your colleagues they can speak to him now, but only for fifteen minutes. Doctor's orders.'

He twisted his head painfully, catching sight of a person speaking on a mobile phone. 'You can talk to him now. The nurse says fifteen minutes.' The man grimaced in response to a comment from the other end before turning his back on Dusty.

Dusty realised the figure was in a police uniform. He frowned. Talk to him about what? He'd nothing to say to the police. He just wanted to sleep.

Before he closed his eyes again, he saw the constable sit on a chair in the corner near the door, looking as if he wished he was somewhere more interesting.

Dusty fell into a sleep filled with tortured dreams of horses squealing in fright, running free, crowding into a small corral, which seemed to get smaller and smaller. The corral fence collapsed and a deep crater appeared, the horses reared in panic. A sharp stab of pain shot through his head, a glittering shower of silver and with it, his memory came flooding back.

His eyes snapped open. Two men were standing beside the bed.

The older man indicated his companion. 'Detective Constable Bryant. I'm Detective Sergeant Lenski. Remember us?'

Dusty struggled with the question as another memory swam into focus. He nodded feebly.

'You've had a lucky escape. Can you tell us what happened?'

Dusty shook his head. He had trouble forming words. They came slowly.

'I remember … trying to get … the rig … through the corner … I guess I didn't … succeed.'

'Actually, you did a pretty good job,' Lenski said. 'It's a miracle you're alive. You gave a zero-blood alcohol reading.'

'Not a drink in days. What happened … the horses?'

'Not so lucky. We got a vet in to put the survivors down. Guy called Leigh Woodward. He recognised you – made our job easier. Sorry.'

Lenski paused, obviously taken aback by the look of horror on Dusty's face. Dusty looked away, struggling to hide his emotion.

Bryant waited before he said with surprising gentleness, 'It wasn't your fault. The trailer brakes failed, probably poor maintenance. Odd though – even with relatively low air pressure, you should've been able to stop. On first inspection, there are no obvious signs of tampering, though we can't rule out the possibility until the Crash Investigation Unit have gone over it thoroughly. Know anyone who would want to kill you?'

Dusty shook his head. 'Took the job, last minute. If anyone … target … be Grimes – the foreman at Mowbray Park.'

'We'll follow that up,' Bryant said. 'It certainly throws a different light on things. Who was there when the horses were loaded?'

Dusty gave them the names as he best remembered them but said he hadn't been there. Bryant scribbled them in his notebook.

'Oh, by the way, we're still investigating the death of Bryan Callaghan,' Lenski said as if it were an afterthought. 'The coroner found he died from a beating. His debilitated condition due to heavy drinking, made him vulnerable. You were at the reserve the night he was killed. You and he were sort of connected and you've more or less taken on his job. If someone did try to kill you, that may be the link.'

'Sorry, I can't help.'

'We think you can. It's a serious offence to hinder a police investigation and if we're right, you may need us as much as we need you. We're not saying you're directly involved, but you may not have told us all you know. We're treating you as a material witness, so we'll keep a guard here while you're in hospital. When you're ready to be discharged, we'll consider our next step. Think it over. It'd be better for you if you tell us everything. Things you don't see as important may be vital to us.'

The detective began to question him about events leading up to the drive to Melbourne.

The nurse interrupted. 'That's enough for now. The patient must rest.'

'Just another few minutes.'

'I said that's enough. Doctor's orders.'

Reluctantly, Lenski moved to the door. 'We'll talk again tomorrow.'

'I imagine I'll still be here,' Dusty said with an attempt at a grin.

A second nurse arrived, pushing a trolley of monitoring equipment.

The first nurse looked at Lenski with distinct hostility. 'Off you go. We have work to do.'

Lenski pulled a face behind her back. 'Yes, nurse. Thank you, nurse.'

'Don't be cheeky with me.'

50

Dusty slept fitfully, losing track of time. An annoyingly cheerful nurse came in. 'And how are we this morning?'

Dusty grunted. He struggled to wake up, tiredness and depression battling for domination of his brain.

He hoped Jenny would visit him soon. His thoughts drifted back to the police interrogation. His eyelids drooped. Within a few minutes he was fast asleep.

Later when he woke, he thought he noticed some movement in the room. He hoped it was Jenny. He opened his eyes. It was Woodward.

'Thought I'd come in before I do my rounds. How do you feel?' His friend's voice seemed cautious. 'You look better than last night.'

Slowly, Dusty spelt it out. 'They tell me I had a lucky escape; nothing broken, just severe concussion. They're keeping me here to do more tests.' He paused trying to think. 'Oh, yes, and a brain scan later this morning.'

'I spoke with the doctor,' Woodward said. 'He's confident about your recovery, but I'm very worried about the way things are going. I must confess; I took the danger you were in far too casually. This was undoubtedly an attack on your life. I told Loftus to fill the Race Club's chairman in on everything we know. He could pull some strings at the highest level in government. I'll tell you as soon as I hear anything. Also, as soon as I told Susan about you, she rang

Jenny's mobile – no answer. She has rung several times.'

After Woodward left, Vicky Mifsud dropped in.

'Murphy is like a bear with a sore head,' she reported. 'The whole schedule for the Guineas is coming unstuck.'

They talked briefly, then Vicky said she'd better go so he could rest.

Dusty pulled himself up and rang the buzzer. A nurse he'd not seen before entered.

'We'll be taking you for a scan shortly. We're just organising the paperwork. Do you need something?'

'One of the other nurses told me the hospital had contacted my wife. Could you check? My wife hasn't been in to see me yet. I don't understand it. The nurse said Jenny was coming in after she'd organised someone to look after our kids.'

'I'll check, but I'd be surprised if they didn't call her. It's standard procedure.'

'Thanks, I'm a bit worried.'

The nurse left and returned a few minutes later. 'Yes, they rang again at 7:45. Do you want us to ring her again?'

'Thanks. She works for Doctor Carter. If she's not at home, try the surgery.'

'While you go for your scan, we'll try your wife again.'

The nurses got Dusty up and into a wheelchair to take him to the imaging technician. The mystery of Jenny's disappearance troubled him. Why would she need someone to mind the boys? Why not just bring them in to see him?

He felt helpless, and more worried by the minute. Later, when he was back in bed, he pushed the buzzer to call a nurse.

'How do you feel after your little excursion?' the nurse asked.

'Quite good,' he lied. His head was still thumping. 'Were you able to contact my wife?'

'No. We've rung several times but got no answer. We also rang the surgery. She hasn't been there and they haven't heard from her either.'

◆

The faces of the two detectives gave no indication of what they were thinking. Bryant took the inevitable notepad from his pocket. The morning clouds had lifted. Lenski turned back to Dusty with a blank expression on his face.

'Beautiful day out there. Pity you're cooped up in here.'

Dusty looked out of the window to the cloudless blue sky and nodded his head.

A long silence ensued, broken finally by Lenski. 'You wanted to see us? Decided to tell us something?'

'Not exactly. I need your help.'

'That's our job. But why should we help you when you won't help us?' Lenski continued to look out of the window.

'I don't know that I can help you.'

Lenski sighed while Bryant looked down at the blank page of his notebook.

'Well, what do you want?'

'The hospital contacted my wife, Jenny. She told them she'd be in as soon as she could arrange someone to look after the children. She hasn't arrived. The hospital has rung several times, at home and at work. No one has seen her. I don't understand it. She couldn't have just disappeared. Something has happened to her and the boys. I know it.'

Lenski leaned forward with sudden interest. His whole demeanour changed. 'How do you know it?'

'If someone was trying to get me, why wouldn't they take it out on my family if they've realised I have survived?'

'So, you agree someone planned to kill you?' There was a steely edge to the detective's voice. 'Who are they?'

'Whoever fixed the truck's brake lines.'

'We don't have proof of that. I know you've been through a lot and I'm trying to be patient, but I suspect you know more than you're telling us.' Lenski paused. 'Suppose the brakes were sabotaged – no one does that without reason. Now, you claim your wife has disappeared and 'they' might be responsible, the same 'they' you suspect tampered with the brakes. That means you must have some idea who 'they' are.'

Dusty closed his eyes and took a deep breath. It had all got so hopelessly out of hand. Here he was, banged up in hospital while out there something was happening to Jenny, Jem and Rafe. He needed help and he needed it quickly.

'Donovan Malek.'

Neither detective reacted.

'He's been a person of interest to us for some time,' Bryant said. 'But he hardly seems the sort of bloke to be crawling under a truck tinkering with brake lines.'

'Not him personally … someone else … someone who works for him, or someone he's got to do his dirty work.'

'Whatever we may think of Malek, we just can't accuse him of attempted murder and kidnap without evidence. We've found nothing to link him, or anyone connected with him, to an accident in which eight valuable racehorses were killed. Surely there'd be easier and less costly ways to get rid of you?'

'Malek couldn't care less about the horses or the cost,' Dusty spat back. 'Please check. You will find they're all heavily insured, along with the rig.'

Lenski raised his eyebrows a fraction. Bryant scribbled a note.

'You seem to know him quite well – well enough to think he might be connected with your wife's disappearance?'

'Yes. Please, you've got to find her. I'm worried sick.'

'We'll find her, but you must tell us everything. If what you say is right, we'll need every bit of information you can give us.' Lenski's tone was emphatic. 'You can't expect us to work with our hands tied behind our back. Tell us all you know; we find your wife.'

Dusty gestured towards the door. 'Shut the door. I don't want anyone overhearing what I have to say. If I tell you all I know, promise me you'll do everything to make sure my wife and boys are safe.'

Bryant closed the door.

Lenski nodded. 'Promise. We'll put every available police resource onto it. Don't worry, we'll find them.'

Dusty took a deep breath. 'It's hard to know where to start. I just seemed to get gradually sucked in.'

'Start anywhere, we'll put it together. We already have a lot of information, but there's still too many loose ends.'

The door opened and a nurse came in. 'We don't like the door being shut,' she said.

Lenski flicked his badge under her startled eyes. 'Just give us half an hour or so, unless you've something urgent?'

'No, nothing that can't wait half an hour.'

'Thank you.'

The door closed again.

Lenski listened to Dusty while Bryant wrote furiously in his notebook.

Now and again, Lenski posed a question to clarify a detail. He took particular interest in Dusty's account of Callaghan's beating at the hands of Yanovic and Schokolov.

'Can you positively identify them?' Lenski asked.

'Not positively, but I know it was them; they mentioned Malek's name, referred to him as the boss.'

'I'm sure you're right, but we need hard evidence.' He turned to Bryant. 'Do a check on them – see if they have form.'

It was well over the half hour by the time Dusty finished his account.

Lenski stood up. 'We'll check with the wife of the guy you were supposed to pick up. And we will check on Grimes. Devious little bastard – had his arm broken a few years ago by some thugs in Sydney who thought he'd ratted on them.'

'He told me Murphy organised that,' Dusty said.

Lenski shook his head. 'Murphy wasn't even in the picture at that time. Just another one of his porkies, I'm afraid.'

Lenski gestured to Bryant to open the door.

'Thanks. We'll work on finding your wife immediately. I'll let you know as soon as we have any news.'

51

LATER, AS DUSTY POKED at his unappetising lunch, he was interrupted by another visitor: Max Murphy. Before Dusty could get over his surprise, Murphy launched into a short speech.

'Rhodes, Mr Malek and I were greatly distressed by your accident, but we were delighted to hear that you survived the crash. Mowbray Park will pick up any expenses you incur, arising from the accident and we hope you will soon be well enough to resume work. The Guineas is only a few weeks away and your expertise is greatly missed. I won't stay as I am very busy, but Mr Malek insisted I come personally to give you our best wishes. We look forward to seeing you back at work shortly.'

Before Dusty could respond, Murphy turned on his heels and left.

Dusty closed his eyes and shook his head. In no way could Murphy's visit be one of goodwill. It must have been almost humiliating for him to come to the hospital. Dusty mulled over Murphy's words to try to find some hidden message, but to no avail.

◆

Later that afternoon, he received a message from the constable on duty. 'DS Lenski says to tell you they've made some preliminary investigations but with no results. He said not to worry. He's sure they'll locate your wife soon.'

Dusty mumbled his thanks, but the constable's words did little to ease his anxiety. He knew they couldn't just roar in guns drawn. And if he was wrong, Malek would make lots of trouble and Lenski and Bryant could finish up being buried somewhere out the back of Bourke.

Still, he knew Malek better than they did and he certainly knew Jenny to be tough and resolute in her own way. No way would she have failed to come to the hospital once she'd got the message. A sudden thought flashed into his mind. Had someone else answered the phone? After all, the hospital could easily have assumed they were talking to Jenny. He had not even checked they'd rung the right number. Jenny could've walked straight into a trap. Had she gone to Mowbray Park to inquire about him when he hadn't rung her?

A rather pompous looking young man with all the shininess of a new resident doctor checked Dusty's vitals. 'Your blood pressure's still way too high. Something worrying you?'

Dusty shook his head.

On his way out the doctor turned and said, 'Try not to worry too much. I'm sure the police are doing all they can to locate your wife. I'll see you again later. A couple more days and you can go home.'

Dusty groaned inwardly. If they hadn't located Jenny before then, he'd go crazy.

◆

The doctor had prescribed Dusty something to help him sleep. He woke next morning at six and waited impatiently for news from Lenski and Bryant. After checking that the constable was still guarding the door to his room, Dusty soon drifted into a light doze. He dreamed of Jenny. She was coming into the hospital. Her footsteps were echoing down the corridor. He heard her voice.

'Hi, Dusty. When I got the news, I was so worried. I'm just back from Sydney.'

He blinked. Kerry Suster stood beside his bed, looking glamorous in a tight blue skirt and polka dot blouse. He couldn't hide his disappointment.

'I thought you were Jenny.'

'The nursing staff thought I was too. They seemed glad to see me. I didn't enlighten them. If I'd let on I was a reporter, they probably wouldn't have let me in.' Kerry paused. 'What's wrong? What's going on? It all sounds so ghastly.'

'Jenny and the boys have disappeared. I haven't seen them since the accident.'

'My god! That's awful.'

'The police are looking for them.'

Pulling a chair close to the bed, she sat beside him, taking his hand in hers. He caught the delicate scent of her perfume. Her hands were soft and warm; he squeezed them. There was a responsive pressure.

'I'm so, so sorry.'

'I am glad to see you. I felt like I'd lost every friend in the world. Thanks for coming.'

'I really wanted to come. What's going on? Why's the copper outside?'

The phone on the bedside table rang. Dusty grabbed the receiver. 'Jenny?'

A soft voice he didn't recognise echoed in his ear. 'I have a message from Mr Malek. Your wife and boys are in his care. Don't say anything to anyone or do anything foolish. If you do, you'll never see them again. You'll receive instructions later today.'

'Who are you? What do you mean?'

The phone went dead.

His look of alarm spurred on Kerry. 'Who was it?'

'I knew it. Malek's got them.'

'That's appalling. What can I do?'

'They told me not to tell anyone.'

'There must be something I can do. We make a pretty good team.'

Dusty smiled wanly. 'Seems so long ago – so much has happened.' He sighed heavily. 'I need time to think. They're going to ring back later today with instructions. Come back this evening. Tell the hospital you're not my wife, just a friend.'

Kerry looked at him pensively. 'Sure. See you tonight.'

After she'd gone, Dusty slipped into a sedated sleep. Eventually, he woke up, only to be harassed by the nurse. 'And how are we this afternoon?'

He gritted his teeth. He had to get out of this place. He wasn't well enough to cope with this relentless agenda of care. Putting on a bright front he said, 'Great! I reckon I'm ready to go home.'

The nurse briskly took his temperature, pulse, blood pressure and then stuck a needle in his leg for some inexplicable reason.

After the nurse left, he swung his legs over the side of the bed and stood up. Unsteady on his feet and with legs a little rubbery, he reached the door, leaning against its frame. Out of the corner of his eye he saw the police constable sitting on a chair with a crushed polystyrene coffee cup in his hand and a bored look on his face. Seeing Dusty, he got to his feet.

'The nurse says I've got to try walking,' Dusty said by way of explanation.

The constable nodded. As Dusty walked away, he followed him along the corridor.

After a full circuit of the floor, a plan started to form in his mind.

On the next circuit, Dusty pretended to rest. 'Still pretty groggy.'

The constable looked concerned. 'Take your time.'

After a few minutes, they moved off again. 'Got long to go to the end of your shift?'

The constable looked at his watch. 'Another half an hour. Change over at three.'

'Must be pretty boring.'

The constable yawned. 'All part of the job, but you're right, not exactly exciting.'

'Well, I'm going to go round this corridor for the next fifteen minutes. Why don't you get another cup of coffee while I'm doing it?'

'Okay, I think I will.'

52

LATER THAT EVENING Kerry was back at the hospital. 'How's the walking wounded?'

'A lot better. I've had a few trips around the corridor, and I think I'm well and truly on the mend. After you left, I had an idea.'

Kerry raised her eyebrows.

'I need you to do something.'

'Sure, what is it?'

'Help get me out of here.'

'Just discharge yourself.'

Dusty nodded towards the door. 'It's not that easy,' he said. 'And what's more, I haven't got any clothes.'

'Where are they?'

'They chucked out the clothes I was wearing. Jenny was supposed to bring in fresh stuff.'

'You want me to get you some?'

'Bring them in tomorrow morning? I want to get out as soon as possible. The police aren't having any success, so I think the search for Jenny needs a less orthodox approach.'

Again, Kerry raised her eyebrows.

'When you come back, I'll get you to distract the copper. I'll go for a walk around the corridor and slip down the fire escape. I've sussed out the lay of the land. I'll only need a few minutes.'

'What then?'

'That's where I need your help again. I'll head for the Golden Bell Cafe. Pick me up there. We'll go back to your place?'

Kerry looked a bit startled. 'My place?'

'Please, I have nowhere else to go.'

Kerry looked as if she was pondering his request. 'If you keep well out of sight, I suppose we can manage it.' She beamed conspiratorially. 'It'll be just like the spy movies.'

◆

About thirty minutes before the end of the hospital's visiting hours, Kerry returned with a small carry-all bag.

'Is our friend out there?' Dusty whispered.

She nodded.

'Bright eyed and bushy tailed?'

'Bored scratchless more like it,' she said. 'Looks half asleep.'

She opened the bag, producing jeans, a shirt, a jumper and a pair of socks.

Dusty got out of bed, a wave of dizziness sweeping over him. He slumped back down, shaking his head.

'Are you alright?' Kerry said.

He waited for the dizziness to pass. 'I'll be okay.'

Gingerly, he put on the shirt then the jeans, rolling them up to just below his knees before easing the jumper over his head. 'They fit well. You're a good judge of size.'

She winked and grinned. 'I sized you up some time ago.'

His face flushed. 'Right. Distract the copper. When the coast is clear, I'll slip out. If anything goes wrong, I'll come back. We'll try again later.'

'Nothing will go wrong, promise.'

He felt a surge of gratitude. 'What'd I do without you?' he said.

She smiled. 'Stay in here and recuperate. Now, for God's sake be careful,' she whispered. 'You're still a bit shaky.'

'Sure will. Golden Bell Cafe in fifteen minutes.'

On a nod from Dusty, Kerry stepped out into the corridor, her face lit by a radiant smile. In her skin-tight, lime green matador pants and bright orange tank top that hid nothing of her figure, he knew she would make a profound impact.

Her voice floated back to him. 'I'm so worried about him, poor dear. I'm so glad you're here to look after him. A lot of people don't realise how good you policemen are.'

'Kind of you to say so, ma'am. There are a lot of people who just don't appreciate what we have to do. How's he going?' The constable's voice was tinged with genuine concern. 'Poor bastard doesn't look too good.'

'Internal injuries. It was a bad accident. He'll be here for ages.'

Kerry turned away to put her head around the door to Dusty's room. 'I'm just gonna see if I can get a cup of coffee.'

'Machine's on the next floor,' Dusty called out. 'The constable'll show you where it is.'

He couldn't see them but imagined Kerry turning the full force of her vibrancy on the defenceless young constable.

'I really need a caffeine fix,' she cooed. 'Where's that coffee machine?'

'Downstairs, turn left, then halfway along the corridor.'

'Why not show me?' Her voice invited. 'I'm sure you could do with another.'

'I'm not supposed to leave.'

'He'll be safe for a few minutes. Come on, I get lost so easily.'

Their footsteps receded down the corridor.

Dusty slipped out of bed and stood for a moment to check his balance, waiting for the second hand on his watch to creep tediously around the dial twice. He got up, pocketing his mobile phone, which seemed to have miraculously survived his ordeal, and scanned the corridor, and soon was on his way along the corridor to the fire escape door. As he opened it, he gulped in a lungful of fresh air, instantly feeling better.

Gripping the rail, Dusty descended the stairs to the delivery dock. Emerging into a back lane, he turned left and walked to the street corner from where he could see the cafe's sign across the road.

Once in the street, he felt uncomfortably conspicuous and worried he'd run into someone he knew, but there were few people about. He waited for a couple of cars to clear the intersection before crossing the road.

In the cafe, he slipped into a cubicle with a clear view of the street. He took stock – a little breathless and light-headed, but mighty glad to be out of the hospital. He felt, in a small way, he'd regained some control over his life. But really, control over what?

Since he driven out of Mowbray Park three nights ago, nothing had gone right. He had no time to lose. Once they discovered he was gone, the police would be looking for him as well. Luckily, Kerry could not be linked to his disappearance. Finally, but more importantly, he was unsure of his next move.

All he could do was lie low until he could work something out. He wondered how long it would be before Malek got wind of his disappearing act.

His thoughts were interrupted by a gum-chewing waitress. 'Whatchawant, luv?'

'Waiting for a friend.'

'Give us a yell when you're ready.'

'Thanks, I will.'

She wandered to the back of the cafe, her thongs flip-flopping on the vinyl tiles.

He should try to get a message to Woodward but, for the moment, he suspected the fewer people who knew his movements, the better. The street was still empty. Where the hell was Kerry?

More than fifteen minutes passed before the powder blue Alfa pulled into the kerb. Kerry got out and walked into the cafe without looking at him. She bought a takeaway chicken and a carton of milk. Then she walked back to the door, looked right and left along the footpath, raised the carton of milk and scratched her chin: the all-clear signal.

He got to his feet, sauntered the few yards to the passenger side and got in. Kerry started the engine.

'How'd it go?'

'Like a dream. Sorry I was a bit long, but I had to pretend I was talking to you before I left. Our friend seemed quite happy.'

She drew away from the kerb, its engine throbbing quietly under the bonnet. She cruised down the street, turning right a couple of blocks further along.

'Just to be on the safe side, Dusty, I don't think we should go straight back to my place.'

He settled back, closing his eyes. 'Whatever.'

'I'll take her out onto the highway, show you how she performs.'

As the Alfa picked up speed, Dusty thought he noticed a black car pull out from the opposite kerb, do a U-turn and start to follow them. Three blocks later, when they turned right, the black car turned right.

Within a few minutes, they were on the highway heading north. Kerry planted her foot on the accelerator, sending the car surging forward. As the speedometer climbed rapidly, she flicked a switch to open the roof, letting in a stream of refreshing night air.

She pulled out to pass a car and caravan. Once past, she moved back into the left lane and put her foot down. Soon they caught up with a semitrailer loaded with cattle.

Again, she pulled out to pass. Frowning, she checked her mirrors.

'What's up?'

'The car behind seems to be tagging us.'

Dusty glanced over his shoulder. The car's headlights began to flash up and down. It drew closer.

'It's the police,' he yelled into the wind.

'Be damned,' she yelled back. 'We're in trouble. Hold tight.'

She accelerated, but the car matched her speed, flicking its headlights again.

She slowed and the Commodore came alongside them, easing past.

Braking hard, Kerry allowed the car to shoot ahead before swinging onto a patch of cleared gravel between the north and south bound lanes. Spinning the car in a U-turn, Kerry drove out onto the south bound lanes, narrowly missing a couple of cars and a furniture van.

'Well done.'

'My advanced driving course wasn't wasted after all,' she shot back.

The Alfa straightened up. Throwing the gear stick back a notch, Kerry powered ahead. Dusty looked behind in time to see the other car exiting the gravel patch and begin threading its way through the gaggle of vehicles they'd left in their wake.

Dusty groaned, 'Fuck.'

'What?'

'Those guys in the car – they're Malek's men.'

By now the speedometer was hovering around 180. Rocketing under an overpass, Dusty caught a glimpse of a highway patrol vehicle tucked behind the bridge's buttress. In the mirror, he saw the headlights of the police car come on, its lights flashing red and blue. Their pursuers swept passed the police car.

'This'll be interesting,' Dusty said.

In the split second before a bend shut out his view, he saw the police car closely tailing the Commodore. Dusty smiled. 'They've pulled them over.'

Kerry flashed a grin. 'Praise the Lord.'

Twenty minutes later, they arrived at her place.

Driving into the garage, the door clunked closed behind them.

'I have a couple of stories to file. Get some sleep. If you're hungry there's food in the fridge. I'll be gone for a couple of hours – now make sure you keep out of sight. Don't answer the door or the phone and don't turn on any lights. Remember, no one's supposed to be here.'

She gave him a peck on the cheek. 'See you later.'

The heavy stillness of Kerry's apartment closed in on him. He went to the spare room, took off his boots and lay down on the bed.

53

Dusty opened one eye. The room was dark. He lay still, collecting his thoughts, listening to the faint sounds around him – the hum of the fridge, a passing car.

He hoped Kerry would be back shortly. Getting up, he moved to the door and felt for the switch. He paused, remembering her caution.

The driveway light dimly lit the kitchen. Dusty found a glass and gulped down two glasses of cold water. Crossing to the couch, he stretched out, only to get up a few minutes later to restlessly pace the room. Sitting about doing nothing was getting to him, but there was nothing he could do but wait. He slumped back onto the couch, closed his eyes and played through everything that had happened: the accident, the telephone call with its curt ultimatum, the car chase.

Malek was obviously not finished with him. He'd been lucky to get out of hospital, to have Kerry's help in eluding the Commodore. But how much longer could his luck hold out?

His intentions may have been good, but it had brought his world crashing around him. Why did he ever think he could match Malek's ruthlessness?

The sound of a car outside interrupted his troubled thoughts.

Kerry came in with two plastic bags of groceries in one hand and a briefcase in the other.

Plonking the groceries on the kitchen bench and the briefcase beside her desk, she joined him on the couch. 'It's going to be alright. I talked to Lenski – said I needed an angle for the paper. He mentioned someone's been stirring things up at a senior level. They're sending a special team down from Sydney, then they'll move on Malek.'

She smiled. 'Oh, and you'll enjoy this. The highway patrol boys got a gold star for picking up Yanovic and Schokolov. There was an all-points alert for the car. They've taken the two in for questioning.'

While she talked, Dusty continued to study her. 'Lenski say anything about me? Or you? Make a connection?'

'If he did, he didn't let on. When I asked him how you were coping, he was non-committal. So, stop worrying. Stay here until you sort yourself out; give it another couple of days. You're in no shape to play urban commandos.'

He took her hand, giving it a squeeze. 'What'd I do without you?'

A phone rang. It was Dusty's phone. Before he could answer the call, it stopped ringing. He turned back to Kerry. 'Perhaps I should check the number – at least I'd know who's calling.'

'Forget it. If they really want you, they'll call again.'

He punched the buttons to bring up the missed call – a mobile number he didn't recognise. He shrugged and waited. After a few minutes the phone rang again. Dusty pressed the button to take the call. 'Hello.'

He nearly dropped the phone when he heard the strained voice at the other end.

'Dusty, it's Jenny. I only have a minute. Mr Malek is looking after us. We're all right, but he says to tell you if you don't cooperate, you'll make it hard for us. He knows you've left the hospital. He wants you to be at Murphy's office at midnight. Please do what he says, we're frightened. Also, please bring Jem's medicine. It's in the green cabinet.'

Stunned, Dusty tried to piece together what he was hearing. 'Jenny, where are you?'

Malek's cold voice answered him. 'Do what she says, Rhodes, or I'll start with the kids.'

The line went dead.

Dusty stared at the phone in disbelief. Slowly his head drooped until his chin rested on his chest. A wave of remorse sweeping over him. 'Oh, God! What a bloody selfish fool I am.'

He turned to Kerry, but words failed him.

Her eyes widened with concern. 'What was that all about?'

'It was Jenny. Malek's holding them hostage.'

'Who else was on the phone?'

'Malek. He's given me a deadline – midnight – to meet him at Murphy's office. Also, Jenny said something odd, "Bring Jem's medicine. It's in the green cabinet".'

'What's odd about that? He needs his medicine.'

'That's just it. He doesn't take any, and we don't have a green cabinet. She was trying to give me a message. What the hell could it be?'

'Ring Lenski straight away.'

'I can't risk it. It's me Malek wants. I'll go to Mowbray Park. I've got to try to find Jenny. At least I'll have more chance with Yanovic and Schokolov now in Lenski's care.'

'I'll come with you.'

'No. I can't risk anyone else. Especially you.'

Kerry gave him a gentle smile. 'Dusty, that phone call changes everything; you love Jenny and those gorgeous boys. They need you.'

'I'm sorry. I ...'

She raised a finger to his lips before hugging him tightly. 'I understand.'

Dusty stood up. 'You're wonderful.'

She shook her head. 'Just practical. I think you are a very special person, and I want you to come through in one piece.' Her voice broke a little.

As Dusty made his way to the front door, Kerry stood up with brisk efficiency.

'Hang on, I'll drive you up to Mowbray Park,' she said. 'But I'm warning you, if you don't ring me by 12:30, I'm contacting Lenski. I'll tell him you called me to say you'd be at Murphy's office. That's all he needs to know.'

Dusty insisted Kerry drive her conspicuous Alfa Romeo through the back streets until they were forced onto the main road that led to Mowbray Park. The night sky was dark; heavy clouds obscured the moon. With nerves on a knife-edge, Dusty was acutely aware of the smell of leather, the dull glow of the instrument panel and the sweet fragrance of Kerry's perfume. He had brought nothing but a torch. Ingenuity would serve him best.

'Drop me off at the dirt lane, just short of the float entrance,' he said.

Kerry swung the Alfa into the narrow lane, doused the headlights and, stopping just short of the corner said, 'This is as far as I go. No point in saying be careful, so good luck.'

He went to give her a hug, but she pushed him away. 'Go!' There was a catch in her voice.

Dusty got out, the darkness closing around him. At the gate to Mowbray Park, he turned back to watch the tail-lights of the Alfa disappear.

He waited, straining to hear anything that might signal an unwanted presence. The once familiar territory now seemed alien.

Satisfied, he struck off along the avenue of oaks, moving from one trunk to the next. At the end of the avenue, he contemplated the space between him and the stable yard. Though he had not heard or seen anything unusual, Dusty decided to go the long way round to avoid the open areas.

The stables were silent, except for the occasional snort of a horse. Murphy's office was in darkness.

Reassured Malek and Murphy weren't there, Dusty moved to the rear of the stables and cut across the garden towards the house.

Walking stealthily on the soft grass, he approached it making full use of the cover the garden provided. Every nerve ending tingled. Jenny and the boys had to be here. But with its many rooms and cellars, it would be a challenge to search in the dark.

Nothing moved. No vehicles were parked in the immediate vicinity. There was a garage but no way of checking what might be inside.

Reaching the house, Dusty decided to try the door that had once taken him to the cellar, but a brief flash of the torch revealed a pile of leaf debris against the bottom of the door that had built up over the last few days. Moving cautiously along the verandah he came to what he knew was the drawing room. Throwing caution to the wind, he peered through a gap in the curtains. The drawing room was as he remembered it. The room was brightly lit. As he went to move away, he saw the housekeeper shuffle in.

The housekeeper crossed to the bar, stopping to straighten some cushions, before she collected a tray of empty glasses, an empty bottle and switched off the lights as she left.

It was sign that at least the place was inhabited.

Continuing his reconnoitre, Dusty continued to move around the house, looking for any possible entry point, but found only small, barred windows and a door at the back that was securely locked. He continued his search, staying close to its shadowy walls. On the way, he saw lights in some of the upstairs rooms. That could be Jenny and the boys.

By now he had almost completed his reconnoitre when at last he saw light streaming from a ground floor window. He hoisted himself onto a narrow ledge below the windowsill and looked in. It was the kitchen. On a wooden table lay some knitting and a pattern book. Nearby, a small television set was playing loudly.

It took him a good ten minutes to complete his investigation of the house perimeter, finally returning to the French doors – all were locked. His only recourse would be to break in, but how?

It was then he remembered seeing a collection of paint tins and tarpaulins in the dark recess of a small portico at the back of the house. He then had his second stroke of luck. Returning to the portico for a closer inspection, he found an extendable step ladder.

He lifted the ladder and opened it, positioning it just under the edge of the upstairs balcony. The snapping clips echoed like rifle shots. Dusty held his breath, half expecting pounding feet. Gradually, his racing heart steadied. Luck stayed with him. He began to climb.

Balancing precariously on the top rung of the ladder, he reached out to grasp the rail and swung himself onto the balcony edge. From there he threw his legs over the railing.

Most of the rooms fronting the balcony were dark, but one of the windows had its curtains partly drawn. Peering in, Dusty could see the room was unoccupied; however, there was light coming in from a hallway. Wrapping his shirt around the torch he tapped the glass panel of a door that led onto the balcony with increasing force until it cracked. Prising out the broken pieces, he eased his hand in to unlock the door.

Once inside the room, Dusty checked the hallway. He stopped

and listened. He could hear nothing but noted a slit of light under one of the doors. He braced himself, then slowly turned the handle. A bedside lamp threw a pool of light over an unmade bed, but the room was empty.

Certain no one was upstairs, he moved to the staircase. Below, he could just see the entrance to a dimly lit hallway and as he slowly crept down the stairs, he saw what he presumed was the entrance to another more spacious hallway. He hesitated – there was no turning back. He was just a few steps from the bottom of the staircase when he heard a tread creak. He froze. All he could hear was the faint sound of the television in the kitchen.

Reaching the ground floor, he looked around to get his bearings. No light, no sound. Perhaps the housekeeper was the only person in the house. His heart sank. Were Jenny and the boys even here?

Then, in the stillness, he heard another faint creak – the kind a person makes when they transfer their weight on a wooden floorboard. His skin prickled. There was the creak again – closer, more distinct. From the hallway to his left a bulky shadow emerged from the darkness. Then he was blinded by a strong beam of light.

A guttural voice broke the silence. 'Don't move, creep. Yer not goin' anywhere.'

Dusty shielded his eyes from the glare. He instantly recognised the voice. Schokolov, what the hell was he doing here? He should be in a police cell.

Dusty stepped towards Schokolov and with all the strength he could muster, swung his torch up under the thug's light, sending it spinning away. Schokolov turned to retrieve it, but Dusty swung his torch again. The arc of the beam picked up a heavy vase on a table. Dusty lifted the vase and brought it crashing down on Schokolov's head. The man staggered back.

Dusty bounded back up the stairs, two steps at a time, intent on reaching the room that offered his only escape.

His heart sank.

Yanovic stood at the top of the stairs, a baseball bat in his hand. 'We reckoned you'd try something.' He sneered.

54

A cold dampness seeped into Dusty's soul. His eyes opened to darkness. Fighting the throbbing in his head, he checked his surroundings. His ankles and wrists were bound and his mouth was taped shut.

Dim moonlight filtered through small, high windows. He realised he was in the cellar again. Rolling over several times until he was close enough to a wall, he was able to push himself into a sitting position. He sat for a moment, catching his breath.

He tried to reach the knotted rope at his ankles but only succeeded in rolling onto his side. He grunted and squirmed until his fingers finally touched the knot. Closing his eyes, he probed the rope. A cramp shot up his legs, forcing him to straighten them.

Reality ebbed and flowed. Lights danced behind his tightly closed eyelids.

Images of Jenny, Malek and horses screaming in agony; headlights in his eyes and the crunch of metal and shattering glass. Was he dreaming or hallucinating? Nothing made sense.

A boot rolled Dusty onto his back. He lay still.

Then he heard Malek say, 'Is he dead?'

Fingers touched the side of Dusty's throat. 'Nah, he's still alive.'

He heard laughter and muttered words he couldn't catch.

Someone threw a bucket of cold water over him. He coughed and spluttered with shock. Rough hands dragged him to his feet.

The tape was ripped from his face.

Through half-closed lids he surveyed the room.

Malek stood in front of him, his face menacing. Schokolov and Yanovic stood behind him.

'You're a damn nuisance.' Any veneer of civility was gone from Malek's voice. 'The boys suggested I should get rid of you, but they tend to take the simple view.'

Dusty said nothing, returning only a sullen stare.

'Your blundering has brought us the unwelcome attention of the police. We have had several visits from them.'

Dusty heaved a deep sigh of despair.

'So, there's been a change of plan. You may yet prove useful,' Malek said. 'This time you will follow orders … or I will take the boys' advice.'

'What's the plan? What d'you want?'

'You'll be told only when you need to know. In the meantime, to guarantee your cooperation I'm holding your wife and boys. They're not happy, and if you doubt me, I have these.'

He held out his hand. In his palm were two rings. Dusty recognised the gold band with its heart and orange blossom pattern and the engagement ring, its small diamond set in a white gold coronet. Jenny would never part with them. A shiver ran through him.

Yanovic looked restless. 'It's nearly twelve, boss. Shouldn't we get moving?'

'Yes, since Rhodes has delivered himself a little earlier than expected, we should take advantage of it.'

Kerry's parting words came back to Dusty. If he hadn't rung her by 12:30, she'd call Lenski. He'd have to try to stall them.

'Wait a moment. Can we talk this over? What guarantee do I have that you'll leave my wife and kids alone?'

'Unlike you, I am a man of my word.'

'What d'you mean?'

Malek leaned in so close Dusty could smell the last cigar on his breath. He barked a short, mirthless laugh. 'Think you're clever? Thanks to Spetcevic, we traced your emails to Woodward, and given the police's questions, we know you've spilled your guts to them.'

Dusty's face took the full force of a blow from Malek's fist – his signet ring a knuckle duster – followed by another stinging blow from the back of Malek's hand.

'You worry over a few horses. I have much more at stake. You'll not spoil it.'

Dusty gritted his teeth, tasting the blood oozing from his lip. 'You've got a snowflake's chance in hell of getting away with this,' he said. 'D'you really think you're smart enough to fool the whole racing industry? You've been lucky so far, but your luck won't hold. And when they get you, they'll get you good, you murderous bastard.'

Malek raised his hand again. Dusty steeled himself. Malek's face had gone red, and his breathing sounded tight. He dropped his hand. 'Pah, you're not worth the effort. You're scum. Luck?' He shook his head. 'Luck doesn't come into it. Spetcevic and I have been working this operation together for two years. The racing industry is in our hands. They won't trace the drugs. Even if they think they know what we're doing, they will never be able to prove it.'

His eyes gleamed. 'You think I'm only interested in this country and a bit of racing in Hong Kong. Our plans are much bigger than that.'

Dusty looked at him contemptuously. 'You'll finish up like all bad bastards, sucked down the gurgle pipe with all the other refuse.'

He expected retaliation. Instead, Malek winced, sucking in

short, urgent gasps of breath. The redness in his face gave way to a dull grey pallor. Beads of perspiration ran down his pudgy face, moistening his collar. His hand went to his chest. Malek closed his eyes, stepped back and took in several deep breaths. No one spoke until he opened his eyes again.

Slowly, Malek walked to the door. Leaning against the frame for support he said, 'Goran, get Murphy to bring the car round. Yuri, watch Rhodes. I'll be back in ten minutes.' He walked out, followed by Yanovic.

Without a word, Schokolov checked Dusty's wrists and ankles, blindfolded his eyes and stuck fresh tape over his mouth.

Minutes ticked by before Dusty heard footsteps. Someone pulled at the rope that bound his ankles. Rough hands grabbed him and pulled him to his feet, then pushed him forward, but his stride was cut short. They'd freed his legs, but only enough for him to shuffle. He heard the door creak and felt a strong draught. Each time he stumbled, he was given a shove forward.

Soon Dusty felt the freshness of the night air. He drew in a deep breath.

Approaching cars broke the silence of the night.

For the first time, Dusty heard Murphy's voice. 'What the hell?'

'It's the cops,' said Schokolov.

Dusty's spirits lifted. Kerry hadn't wasted any time. He tried to shuffle forward, but the halter around his ankles sent him crashing. Hands grabbed at him, dragging him to his feet. Feeling their grip loosen, he dropped to his knees and rolled across damp grass only to find himself tangled in shrubbery.

A voice he recognised as DS Lenski rapped out orders. 'Okay, boys! Spread out, surround the place, make sure no one leaves. Bryant, around the front with me. If they won't open the door, we'll use the ram.'

Rough hands lifted Dusty up, holding him in a vice-like grip. He felt himself being dragged back down the cellar stairs. Twisting and arching his body to get free, he broke their grip. His head hit the wall with a solid thump. If only he could cry out.

He heard more shouts. Then he went limp.

A door slammed. He was back in the cellar. More rope encircled him and was cinched tight. Metal clanged. His new bonds took the strain as he was lowered into some sort of shaft. A dank odour assaulted his nostrils. His feet hit ground and his knees buckled. The rope went slack. Moisture soaked the bottom of his jeans. Metal clanged again before silence fell. Total, frightening silence.

Dusty imagined the police conducting their search, willing with all his might they find him, Jenny and their boys. Despair grew. He imagined Malek greeting Lenski with studied politeness, surprised at the late-night intrusion. Could he help? No, he knew nothing about Rhodes. Wasn't he still in hospital? If you must search, go right ahead.

Dusty was utterly on his own. Jenny's words floated through the deep gloom of his despair. 'Look for Jem's medicine - in the green cabinet.' What was she trying to tell him?

◆

Later, in Murphy's office, Malek sat behind the desk, cradling a whisky. Dusty was propped on a chair opposite him, Yanovic and Schokolov holding station. They had moved him from the cellar once the police had left.

Dusty looked at them. 'You guys ever relax?'

No reaction.

'No sense of humour either.'

Malek's eyes glittered with malevolence, but his face was sallow.

'I'd cut the smart comments since your clumsy attempt at ambush failed.' He studied a file on Murphy's desk, ignoring Dusty.

Dusty fought to stay awake. Malek was trying to break him.

When Malek finally looked up, his lips were a thin malicious line. 'You betrayed me.' He sighed heavily, his fingers drumming the desk. 'I should kill you.'

Dusty stared at him. 'You'll have to do better than last time, or get rid of these two yobbos,' he said, nodding at Yanovic and Schokolov, feeling some grim pleasure in at last provoking a reaction from them.

They stepped towards him, but Malek waved them back.

Dusty turned his attention to Malek. 'You've got me, how about letting my wife and kids go?'

Malek smiled vindictively. 'You don't deserve to live, but inspiration springs from adversity. I'll keep you alive but …'

He gestured towards Yanovic and Schokolov. 'Any more stunts and my boys will have a little fun with your wife and then the boys. You can watch.'

No matter what it costs, Dusty thought, I must save them.

'I can still be useful,' he said.

Malek relaxed a little, his voice taking on a silky tone. 'I think you can.' He gave an almost rueful smile. 'I hired you because of your gift with horses. I've invested in you and helped to build your reputation, but you've got greedy.' He shrugged. 'I thought I'd found a kindred spirit, but Spetcevic got suspicious. We have travelled a long way together. He's smart – I trust him completely. So, we tested you and you failed. It was Grimes' idea to fix the truck. Regrettably, you survived.' Shutting his eyes, Malek leant back in his chair.

After a moment, he opened them and stared at Dusty. 'Yes, I should kill you.'

He got to his feet, lumbered around the table and leaned into Dusty's face. 'But I have a use for you.'

Dusty forced a grin. 'I'm sure we can come to some arrangement.'

Malek's laugh cut through him like a knife.

'Well, while racing is important, we have another objective,' Malek said, leaning against the edge of the desk. 'Remember Murphy's trip to Hong Kong? We've locked in a deal to manufacture and distribute drugs – ecstasy, crystal meth and some other variations. We will be moving horses between here and Hong Kong, and you will be our courier. Your wife and children will guarantee that.'

The words hit Dusty like a hammer. Race fixing was one thing, drugs were quite another. 'I won't do it,' he said.

'You can and you will. We're working on a secure method to ship them. You're the ideal person.' Malek was enjoying himself. 'Rising young star takes champion horses to the east. Who would suspect? Attention will be on the horses and your spectacular success. And if anything goes wrong.' He pointed a finger close to Dusty's face. 'There will be a price to pay.'

Dusty clutched at a straw. 'You've forgotten something.'

'What?'

'The police know the truck was sabotaged and that you're involved in some sort of race fixing racket. It's beyond credibility that I should reappear as if nothing happened.'

Malek smiled. 'Convince them. They can't prove the brakes were tampered with. And as for the horses, there's no evidence. By this time next year, I'll retire, having taken out a Melbourne Cup. We do have that goal in common.'

'Then what happens to me?'

'If you play your cards right, you'll be rich enough to have your own stable.'

Disgust rose from the pit of Dusty's stomach. Fighting it back, he said through gritted teeth, 'That's what you want? Then that's what you'll get. If arseholes want to destroy their lives, that's their business.'

Malek nodded. 'Good. The weak destroy themselves. The strongest survive.' The corners of his mouth twisted as his words came out cold and hard. 'You've ignored my warnings before. This time don't try anything funny. Remember what is at stake.'

55

THREE WEEKS LATER and it was the day of the Golden Guineas. Floats rumbled along Mowbray Park's driveway with nine horses on board, turning left to head for the racecourse. Paul, one of the strappers, was driving a float that carried three of the horses. Vicky sat beside him. On Malek's instructions, Dusty and Grimes were in the back. Yanovic followed in the Commodore. It was the first time he had seen the duo split up.

Grimes, who'd barely given Dusty a glance, studied the form guide for the day's racing, removing the stub of a pencil from behind his ear to mark up his fancies.

'How did Murphy decide on this shit load?' he grumbled. 'None of 'em could win a race for three-legged donkeys.' He went back to writing on the form guide.

Dusty picked up the section of the paper Grimes had discarded. He thumbed through the pages. Nothing grabbed his attention. He only had two thoughts: rescue Jenny and the boys; get even with Malek. Over the past weeks, between snatches of fitful sleep, Dusty had run through a few hare-brained schemes and rescue plans. But Malek had been remarkably thorough. He had no clue as to their whereabouts and the clock was ticking. He was to take the first load of drugs to Hong Kong within a few weeks.

He looked at his watch. They'd be at the racetrack in less than ten minutes. Without a miracle, he would be stuck there for the next four or five hours. Anything could happen.

As he looked through the papers, an article with Kerry's by-line caught his eye. She was billed as their Industrial Reporter. The editor must've twisted her arm to get her to write this sort of crap. Then two words sent an electric shock through him: 'Riekevic Laboratories'. Under the heading, 'Victorian Capital Boosts Local Chemical Plant' were details of the unexpected takeover of Mallesons Chemicals, their plans for expansion and more employment.

Bloody Malek sticks his nose into everything.

Well, he hoped they would keep the same products. Dusty used them and they were good – he'd quite a collection in the green cupboard in the garage.

A shock of realisation hit him. Of course, not green cabinet, green cupboard! Jenny had said 'green cabinet' when she'd rung him. She'd been trying to send a message about the cupboard he stored his chemicals in – chemicals from Mallesons. For the first time his heart lifted.

The float eased into a parking spot near the stables. Through the side window, Dusty watched Yanovic pull up alongside and get out of the Commodore. He marvelled at the agility of such a big man. Shaking off the bastard wasn't going to be easy, yet he had to. He had to get to Jenny. Fast.

◆

After unloading the horses from the first float, Dusty watched Grimes follow Vicky and Paul towards the stalls, leaving him to handle the remaining horses on his own, typical of the bastard. Yanovic stood a few metres away, all bristle and menace. Malek's explicit instructions were to not let Rhodes out of his sight.

From nowhere, an idea began to take shape. Dusty jumped up into the float to unload the first horse, then the second. As they clattered down the ramp, he ran the first, then the second to the full length of their lead ropes, each time wheeling them past Yanovic before tethering them to the side of the float.

Each time, Yanovic jumped out of the way. 'Watch it buster.'

Watch it yourself, you useless bastard, Dusty thought as he tied up the second horse.

The third horse, a two-year old called Chukka, came off snorting and shaking his head.

'Here, hold him a moment,' Dusty said.

'That's your fuckin' job.'

Without wasting a second, Dusty led the horse close to Yanovic, using its bulk as a screen to flick its belly with the end of the rope. The horse snorted and reared. Yanovic backed off a few paces. 'Whaddya think you're doing?'

From the corner of his eye, Dusty watched the thug circle the horse with one fist poised to strike. Sensing Yanovic behind him, Dusty wheeled around. Yanovic lashed out, the blow missing Dusty's shoulder by inches. Yanovic stepped to Dusty's left, close to the float.

'Get the hell out of the way, you bloody nuisance,' Dusty said, running the horse to the opposite side of the float.

Yanovic moved to Dusty's right, a little closer to the ramp. Dusty smiled. This was like herding sheep, and what's more, the guy was shit scared. If anyone was watching, it'd be worth a laugh, but this was no laughing matter. He needed just one more manoeuvre to put Yanovic where he wanted him.

Dusty reverse circled the horse to force Yanovic against the ramp. He gave Chukka a good belt under the belly. The horse reared in protest.

'You're spooking the damned horse,' Dusty yelled. 'For Christ's sake, get out of the way!'

Yanovic scrambled halfway up the ramp. 'I don't know what you're doing, but I can see everything from up here.'

This was Dusty's chance. 'Look out!' he yelled, urging the agitated horse towards Yanovic.

Yanovic hesitated. 'One more crack like that and I'll belt the hell out of you.'

But as Dusty manoeuvred the horse closer, the thug backed further up the ramp. Dusty swung Chukka around to face the ramp, then ran him into the float. With a yelp, Yanovic stumbled back.

With the horse now inside the float, Dusty put his shoulder to Chukka's rump, turning him to block Yanovic from getting out. Chukka lashed out, his rear hoofs landing a crashing blow on the side of the float.

Dusty heard Yanovic's panic. 'Get it away, for Christ's sake! Get it away!'

By now, Chukka was thoroughly stirred up and even Dusty was wondering whether he'd pushed things too far. The horse half-reared with eyes bulging, its hoofs beating a rapid tattoo on the metal floor. Again, Chukka lashed out, missing Yanovic by centimetres.

'Steady there, steady, boy. There's a good fellow.'

Dusty calmed the horse, taking it further into the float, then secured the lead rope to a centre bay. Giving the rope a quick half hitch, Dusty strung up the partitioning rails, locking them into place. He ducked under the horse's neck.

Yanovic cringed in a front corner of the float – his face drained of colour, his mouth opening and shutting soundlessly. Dusty warily moved towards him. Sensing there was little resistance left, he stepped in close and punched him hard in the solar plexus. The big man went down in a crumpled heap.

Snatching up a spare lead rope, Dusty secured Yanovic's wrists and ankles. Then he grabbed a long length of bandage to use as a gag, winding the remaining length around Yanovic's face to blindfold him before tying it off. Picking up another lead rope, he fashioned a noose, slipped it over Yanovic's head, then passed the free end around the ankle rope and pulled it tight. The more Yanovic struggled, the more the noose would close on his windpipe.

Fishing Yanovic's car keys and mobile phone from his pocket, Dusty admired his handiwork. As an afterthought, he flung a horse rug over Yanovic. Satisfied, he untied Chukka and led him back down the ramp. He swung up the ramp and closed the float doors with a loud clang.

Dusty walked the horses down to the stalls and handed them over to Vicky.

'Yanovic's got the shits about something and we've got to take a quick run back to Mowbray Park. Hold the fort for me; I'll be back as soon as I can.'

Before Vicky could protest, Dusty walked away.

56

THE COMMODORE'S TYRES crunched over the soft gravel road in front of Mallesons Chemicals. Dusty stepped out of the car after dialling the police. If he needed help, he didn't want to waste time dialling.

Mallesons Chemicals stood several vacant lots from its nearest neighbour. Scanning the tall chain-wire fence enclosing the building, he saw the gates were shut.

Skirting around to reach the back fence, Dusty noticed the customer entrance had a 'Closed' sign on the door. Moving quickly through the long grass and piles of discarded building materials, he scouted the fence until he found a section where the wire looked rusted and weak.

With the help of a discarded steel rod, Dusty worked on the fence until it gave way. Peeling back the mesh, he wriggled through. He checked his watch – twenty minutes had passed.

Taking the steel rod with him, he moved quickly to the large asphalt apron fronting the delivery bay. From the previous times he'd shopped there, he recalled a door leading from the storage area into a corridor with rooms either side.

Jenny and the boys were probably in one of them. All he had to do was get in.

The windows and doors were tightly shut. He'd have to get Schokolov to open the shutter to the delivery bay.

Looking towards the main gate, his eyes lit up when he saw a sign with Mallesons phone number. He took out Yanovic's phone and rang the number. Perhaps Schokolov wouldn't answer.

Then a guttural voice echoed in his ear.

'Yuh.'

In a voice he hoped sounded something like Yanovic's, Dusty said, 'Yuri, open the roller door.'

'Yuh.'

'Check the front. Someone snooping round.'

'Yuh.'

The phone went dead, and the roller door rattled up. Dusty peered around the corner. No sign of Schokolov. He crept slowly towards the open door. Taking a deep breath, he gripped the steel rod and stepped into the building. A surge of relief swept through him. The storage area was empty.

Stacked against the walls were rows of 200-litre drums colour coded to identify their contents. In front of them was a line of pallets, each carrying a dozen red drums marked 'Highly Flammable'. A large forklift was stationed next to the pallets. Dusty noted the key in the forklift's ignition.

He had to get moving. He jogged to the door, which he presumed led to the corridor. His hand closed on the handle. He turned it and pulled. It was locked.

Somewhere behind him a voice grated. 'You're not going anywhere.'

He slowly turned around to face Schokolov.

'Think I'm stupid. Where's Goran?'

So much for fooling the bugger.

Schokolov moved closer. The next few minutes were make or break. Shuffling forward, Dusty narrowed the gap between them, the steel rod hanging loosely behind his leg.

'He wasn't feeling so good,' Dusty said. 'He's taken the day off.'

Schokolov rolled the matchstick in his mouth from one side to the other. 'What are you doing here?'

Dusty tried to keep calm. 'Just checking on the wife and kids.'

'You lie.' He reached into his trouser pocket and pulled out a phone.

As Schokolov glanced down to dial, Dusty leaped forward, swinging the steel rod viciously.

Before Schokolov could back away, Dusty caught him on the wrist. Schokolov stumbled as the phone flew from his hand. Dusty ground his heel onto it. He felt a satisfying crunch as the phone splintered under his weight.

Schokolov backed away, holding his hand and cursing. Dusty followed him, swinging the rod, trying to land a blow on the man's head. Schokolov flung up his good hand to block the blow, grasping the rod in a strong grip.

Dusty felt it twist out of his hand. Feeling helpless, he backed away towards the red drums.

Schokolov's hand groped under his jacket. Soon Dusty was staring into the muzzle of a revolver.

Gripping the upper rim of a red drum, he pulled it over on its side and with a swift kick, sent it rolling towards his adversary.

A bullet ricocheted off a drum close by with a sharp crack. Jumping behind another drum, Dusty rolled it towards Schokolov. He moved towards the forklift and scrambled into it. Turning the key, the engine roared to life. With the fork waist high, he pushed the throttle. It surged forward. Another shot rang out, the bullet going wild. He had Schokolov on the run.

Dusty tried to manoeuvre him towards the drums on the far wall, but Schokolov was too fast, working his way ever closer to the roller door. Dusty swerved towards him. Another shot, its vicious zing echoing around the delivery bay.

The forklift collided with one of the wayward drums. Swinging around, Dusty scooped it up with the forklift and charged at Schokolov. Out of the corner of his eye he could see fluid spreading rapidly across the floor. Another shot rang out.

Schokolov was now at the roller door feeling for the switch. Dusty swung hard towards him, trying to juggle the drum on the fork but it rolled off.

The red drums were spurting out their contents, flooding the floor. Dusty reversed, the tyres, throwing up a spray around him. He had to get out.

With horror, he watched the door start to roll down. Schokolov held up a cigarette lighter.

Dusty accelerated. The door was halfway down. Schokolov bent down and flicked the lighter before stooping to touch the liquid on the floor.

Dusty crashed the forklift into the door. A sheet of flame leaped into the air, encircling him. The flames spread rapidly.

Outside, Schokolov was waiting to pick him off.

With ominous finality, the roller door crunched onto the concrete apron. But Dusty hadn't come this far to die in a fiery hell. Somewhere in the building, beyond the locked door that led to the rest of the building, Jenny and their children needed him. He'd come here to get them and that bastard Schokolov wasn't going to stop him.

Pungent fumes stung his eyes and throat. He coughed, struggling for breath, his lungs afire. The heat of the metal wheel guards scorched his jeans. Gripping the hot steering wheel, Dusty reversed the forklift in a tight, swift arc to face the door that led to the interior of the building. He held his breath, bracing himself.

Engaging forward, he pushed the throttle to the floor. The

forklift lurched forward, gathering pace as it charged through the wall of flame – a shower of burning droplets rained down. Dusty squinted to avoid being blinded by the flaming particles swirling around him.

A short distance from the door, he dragged the wheel hard to the left. The full force of the forklift's right tine hit the door and rocked with the impact, almost jerking Dusty from his seat.

The door didn't budge. He rammed the forklift into reverse. The rising flames spread along the tyre tracks. He rammed the door a second time, then a third. He could barely breathe.

He rammed the door again before it splintered.

'C'mon! Once more, you little beauty.'

Flames licked the rear tyres. Dusty crunched the gears again. The forklift surged forward and pounded the door with the full thrust of both tines. The right tine embedded in the door. The door opened half a metre.

That was all Dusty needed. Clambering over the front of the machine, he ducked and squeezed through the narrow space. Clear of the door, he rolled on the floor and slapped at the glowing holes in his jeans.

From the storage bay came the deafening sound of an explosion. Hot air, carrying tiny tongues of fire, gusted through the partially open door. With each exploding drum, the fire intensified. Before long, the rest of the drums would join the cacophony.

Dusty hammered on doors yelling, 'Jenny! Jenny, where are you?'

Behind the third door he heard her scream, 'We're in here!'

Dusty threw his weight against the door and staggered back. He looked around for something to batter it down. The sound of three more explosions seemed to rock the building.

'What's that?' Jenny yelled.

'The drums – the place is on fire. We haven't got much time.'

Behind the door he could hear the boys crying.

Burning fluid had begun to ooze past the forklift and the jammed door into the corridor. The flames crept towards him like a malignant creature from a sci-fi film.

'I've got to find something to break the door down!' he yelled.

He ran blindly and flung himself at another closed door, sobbing with frustration as the seconds ticked away. He rattled the knob and to his astonishment, the door flew open. He stumbled into what he remembered as the company's showroom and office.

Dusty squinted in the glare of the afternoon sun reflected off the far wall. Looking around, he saw a glass-fronted showcase containing a collection of rural memorabilia. Hope spread within him. His frantic gaze swept the collection, settling on an adze, the chisel-like axe used by early settlers to dress timber.

He grabbed a chair and with all his strength, hurled it at the cabinet. The glass shattered, showering glittering shards in all directions.

He reached past and lifted the adze from its mounting.

Back in the corridor, the heat had become intense. The fire leapt at the doors nearest the storage area, their paintwork blistering. Dark brown fumes drifted above the flames. Dusty had only seconds to get them out.

'Stand back from the door!' he screamed, then swung the adze. The door yielded. Two more swings opened a hole in the door big enough for Jenny, Jem and Rafe to scramble through.

Jenny pushed the boys out first. Their faces were white with fear as they choked back tears. Dusty dropped the adze, grabbed them and gave them a quick hug.

'Wait there while I help Mum out.' He pointed to the safer end of the corridor.

They scuttled down there as Jenny climbed through the ragged gap and fell into his arms. 'Thank God,' she said as she hugged him.

He shut his eyes and muttered a silent prayer, calling on a strength he was not sure he'd find.

Fumes were filtering through the air-conditioning ducts, and the advancing river of flames attacked the shattered door. Retrieving the adze from where it had fallen, Dusty stumbled after Jenny as she ran to the boys. They raced down the corridor towards the front of the building.

'We've got to get out … don't know how long the building'll hold,' Dusty said. 'I'll have to smash the front door.' He looked around. 'Take the boys behind that counter. Keep your heads down.' He waited for Jenny's head to disappear behind the counter before turning around to the front door.

He stepped towards it, grasping the adze in both hands, and like an Olympic hammer thrower, he lifted it into a wide arc. With the momentum of the spin, he let the adze go.

It bounced off the glass door and hit the floor with a sharp crack. Dusty stared at the door in disbelief. It was unscathed.

Wearily he got to his feet. Picking up the adze, he swung it over his shoulder and stepped closer to the door. He smashed the adze into the door a second time. A hole the size of a soccer ball materialised. Several more swings opened the hole further. A large section hung precariously from the upper edge of the frame, like the blade of a guillotine. He knocked it away.

'C'mon!' he yelled. 'Let's get out of here.'

Jenny and the boys emerged wide-eyed and rushed over.

While Jenny cradled Rafe in her arms, Dusty swept up Jem, still carrying the adze for protection. They picked their way through the debris to fresh air and freedom.

The sun shone brightly. Dusty was stunned by the normality of the calm street scene. The other factories were closed for the weekend. He looked back through the shattered front door. Beyond it, the place seemed to disappear in flames. He glanced up. Smoke poured from under the eaves and the vents on the roof.

Jenny hugged Dusty; her eyes clouded by anxiety.

'Get back,' Dusty said.

Breaking from her embrace, he ran to the corner of the building and saw the large double entry gates were now wide open.

Jenny was at his elbow, the boys clinging to her skirt.

'Looks like Schokolov's gone.'

Jenny hesitated, 'Are you sure?'

Dusty nodded but could imagine the sadistic bastard sitting in his car, watching to make sure they didn't escape.

He gripped the adze.

'We can't go round the other side. If Schokolov is there, we won't stand a chance. We'll be like ducks in a shooting gallery.'

They retreated along the building.

'There's a hole in the fence over there, near that scrubby gum,' said Jenny.

'If I wave, make a dash for it and head along to the left,' said Dusty.

'No fear. We're coming with you.'

Jem tugged his arm. 'Hey, Dad,' he whispered. 'Feel the wall.'

Dusty touched the wall. It was hot. Several windows exploded in quick succession; brown smoke billowed from them.

'Stay back! Get clear of the wall,' Dusty said.

He saw the fear in Jenny's eyes.

After they made their way through the hole in the fence, Dusty hurried them back to the car, bundling them into the Commodore.

There was no sign of Schokolov. Thinking discretion was the better part of valour, Schokolov was probably putting as much distance as he could between himself and the building, believing

Dusty and his family would die in the fire.

As Dusty drove towards town, he glanced at Jenny in the passenger seat beside him. 'I'm taking you to the police station. They're the only ones who can provide you with proper protection. I'll brief them on what's happened, but then I've got to get back to the racecourse. There are a few loose ends I need to stitch up.'

57

Back at the race track, Dusty hurried through the throng of racegoers towards the mounting yard, hoping the excited crowd would lend him some anonymity.

A shower, a change of clothes and the knowledge that Jenny and the boys were safe with the police had lifted his mood. But it all still seemed unreal.

Looking back to the grandstand he could just pick out Malek at his usual table in the Rails Bar. Malek looked animated and cheerful. Not that it really mattered. The police were throwing a cordon around the racetrack, and he would get what was coming to him.

Yet somewhere deep inside Dusty, doubt kicked in. It all seemed too easy.

He turned his attention to the horses coming into the mounting yard for the start of the Golden Guineas. They were now parading around, led by their strappers.

Tom Loftus' horse, Fire King looked magnificent. The big chestnut gelding's coat gleamed like burnished copper, living up to all the expectations he carried with him.

On the far side of the yard, Vicky was leading Malek's horse, Flash Chance. Dusty had to admit the horse also looked good – head high, ears twitching, a dance in its step, excited by the crowd. Some horses were like that; they loved the atmosphere. Malek's jockey, Jacky Deane, walked over to Vicky and exchanged a few words with her. She nodded and gave him a leg up into the saddle.

Dusty's stomach tightened with fear. He'd come this far; what would the next few minutes hold? He scanned the sea of animated faces focused on the race.

But he was running on empty, powered by adrenaline alone. He grasped the iron railing to steady himself.

The fifteen runners filed onto the track, accompanied by the track marshals on their immaculate greys. By the time Flash Chance had cleared the gate onto the track, the first horses had gone about 400 metres along the track towards the starting gate.

The crowd pushed around and in front of Dusty, jostling for a view. He needed air. With some effort, he made his way back through the crowd, and moved quickly along the almost deserted colonnade behind the grandstand, hurrying towards the battery of televisions near the TAB windows. From there he could also keep an eye on the Rails Bar.

An announcement echoed. 'We apologise for the short delay in the start of the Guineas. There was a problem with the timing equipment, but it has now been remedied.'

The television screens showed the horses gathering on the far side of the starting gate and the barrier attendants beginning to lead the first of the horses into their stalls.

Out of the corner of his eye, Dusty saw a face he recognised: Detective Sergeant Lenski. He was moving purposefully towards the Rails Bar entrance. He breathed a sigh of relief. The police had acted with remarkable speed.

The race caller's voice punched the air. 'They're almost ready. Four horses still to go in: Bold Archer, Flash Chance, Crusader and Rich Kid. As soon as they're settled, they'll be away for the Golden Guineas over 2400 metres. The track's fast – it promises to be a ripper. Rich Kid's in now, but Flash Chance is playing up and unsettling Bold Archer. The stewards have taken them out of their stalls to be vetted for their fitness to start. Crusader's in. Two to go but, boy, they're really playing up. If they don't go in soon, they may well be scratched.'

On the television screens, Dusty saw Bold Archer start to rear. Jacky Deane was having difficulty staying on Flash Chance.

What the hell! What's happening? thought Dusty.

'Well, folks, that's one in and now the gate is closed behind Flash Chance, but the jockey is off Bold Archer and yes, there's the notification – he's been scratched. The line has settled and is in the starter's hands. They're off. Flash Chance is away quickly to take the lead a length and a half out from Cast-A-Spell, Cedar Ridge, Lucky Tarot and Bunbury Boy ...'

Dusty's instructions to Deane had been to hold Flash Chance back in the early part of the race, but the horse was clearly so fired up he couldn't hold him.

Dusty smiled grimly; the delay hadn't helped. The drug was kicking in too early. Fire King was running about eighth, two out from the rails and travelling comfortably.

'At the eighteen hundred, Flash Chance has the bit in his teeth and leads by five lengths from Cedar Ridge. Cast-A-Spell's third, strongly challenged by Lucky Tarot and Bunbury Boy, who are shoulder to shoulder ...'

Fire King had moved up another place. An old punter, sitting on a nearby bench lurched to his feet. 'Atta boy, you little beeeudy!'

Flash Chance still held the lead, but by any standard, a horse setting such a cracking pace would find it difficult to sustain it over the distance. The drug was taking effect and Dusty wondered how the horse would respond.

Cedar Ridge had gained a couple of lengths on its rivals and was now third. Dusty sensed Flash Chance was easing up. The jockey, Deane, seemed more in control. The pack behind Flash Chance was now a blur of colour, surging towards the long sweeping turn that would take them into the final straight, each rider striving for the best position in the dash to the post. Here, fortunes were made or lost.

'Come on, Fire King,' Dusty muttered. 'Get moving.'

As if in response, Fire King's jockey swung him wide on the turn to go around two horses into fifth place. The horse was beautifully positioned and ridden exactly to the instructions Dusty and Loftus had worked on weeks ago.

Fire King was in with a chance. Dusty held his breath and the caller's voice rose to near hysteria.

'With six hundred to go, Cedar Ridge's a length from Flash Chance. Lucky Tarot third, Cast-A-Spell's dropped back to fourth. Fire King is making a move, travelling wide to get past Cast-A-Spell. Bunbury Boy is sixth, followed by Rich Kid, Just-A-Chance and Flat Chat. Then comes …'

'Go for the whip, Jacky,' the old punter screamed, his pallid face flushing with excitement. 'Go, go, go.' The words came in raspy gasps.

Flash Chance, hugging the rail, was now labouring. With four hundred to go, Fire King made its run.

'Cedar Ridge's one out from the rails, perfectly placed half a length back from the leader, hanging on grimly under the whip. Fire King's challenging them with a withering run down the centre of the track …'

The roar of the crowd was deafening, the barracking rising like a tidal wave of sound. The three leading horses were now clear of the field by several lengths but after leading so early in the race, Flash Chance was running out of legs.

Then Dusty saw something that made his heart sink, Flash Chance was lunging across the track in front of Fire King. Moving into the gap on the rails, Cedar Ridge surged forward, only to be buffeted by Flash Chance suddenly veering back towards the rail.

Something was desperately wrong.

Dusty watched incredulously. Flash Chance collided with Cedar Ridge's rump and careered headlong into the rail, rearing and pigrooting. The hapless Deane was thrown headfirst over the rail. The riderless horse reared a couple of times more before its legs went from under it. The horses following swung wide to avoid the flailing hoofs.

The caller's voice hammered in Dusty's head. 'Flash Chance is down.'

Dusty held his breath. There was still a chance.

'Come on, Fire King. You can do it.'

The punters were in a frenzy. The race caller's voice hit the highest decibel of controlled hysteria.

'With two hundred to go, Cedar Ridge and Fire King are locked stride for stride. Four lengths back to Lucky Tarot. Half a length back, Pay the Piper and Bunbury Boy are bunched together. Fifty from the post, Fire King gets his nose in front and wins the Golden Guineas by a half head from Cedar Ridge. Lucky Tarot three lengths back third, then Bunbury Boy, Pay the Piper, Enchanted Forest, Gadfly …'

Dusty barely listened to the caller rattle through the rest. Over the heads of the milling crowd, he could just see Flash Chance writhing on the ground. Stewards were rushing to the stricken horse. The ambulance had arrived to attend to the injured jockey.

It was all over for Malek. He must have seen it unfold. Dusty pushed through the throng of punters. When he finally reached the entrance of the Rails Bar, he was alarmed to see Malek missing.

58

Dusty thrust his way through the crowd. He had to alert Lenski and Bryant. But as he struggled to make progress, he thought better of it. Malek would be quick to leave. He'd seen Malek's surprising mobility before. He had to intercept him.

Adrenaline pumping, he reached the back corner of the grandstand and looked along the colonnade. No sign of Malek. He hurried toward the grandstand exit, only to find his view blocked by punters returning to the betting ring, stepping further out, Dusty scanned the length of the colonnade and finally spotted a bulky figure emerging from a small doorway at the far end. It was Malek, in one hell of a hurry, trying to put the greatest possible distance between himself and the police. There was little doubt he would have an exit strategy. Once clear, he could flee in any direction.

Dusty pushed through the crowd, struggling to keep Malek's tweed jacket in sight.

As he broke clear of the throng of punters, he spotted Malek walking through the main exit and out of sight. He broke into a run, vaulting the turnstiles just in time to see Malek getting into his Mercedes.

Weaving his way through the parked vehicles, Dusty crouched behind the car next to the Mercedes. He watched Malek throw his phone onto the seat beside him and then lean across to retrieve something from the glove box.

In a crouching run, Dusty reached the rear of the Mercedes on the driver's side.

The engine roared into life.

He lunged forward and wrenched the driver's door open, looking directly into Malek's startled eyes.

Dusty could see the key ring dangling from the ignition. He quickly switched off the engine and pulled out the key.

'You're not going anywhere. You've got questions to answer.'

'I don't answer to you,' Malek said. 'What the hell do you think you're doing? Give me the keys.'

'Get out. It's the police who'll ask the questions.'

'Rhodes, you're in this as much as me. You need to get away. Be sensible, get in the car. I'll fill you in as we go.'

'Why me, when you've left the others behind?'

Dusty caught a note of exasperation in Malek's voice. 'They can look after themselves. Give me the blasted key.'

Dusty stepped back from the car, dangling the keys in his outstretched hand. 'Get out. You're not going anywhere.'

Suddenly, Malek grunted and clutched his right hand to his chest. A groan erupted from somewhere deep inside him. 'Tablets … got to get my tablets.' He leaned across to open the glove box. Seconds passed before, still clutching his chest, he swung back, pushed himself out of the seat and stood up.

Dusty froze. Pointed directly at his stomach was the barrel of a pistol.

'That's where you're wrong,' Malek snarled. 'We're going for a ride.'

Dusty saw Malek glance over his left shoulder, but the gun never wavered.

Malek grunted. 'It's your friends, Lenski and Bryant. They're with a couple of plods. Why must you always complicate things?

If you hadn't been so quick, I'd have been gone.'

Malek moved closer, the barrel of the gun pressing hard into Dusty's belly.

'Don't move,' Malek hissed. 'Don't say anything. Do exactly as I tell you. Otherwise, you'll finish up with a nasty hole in you.'

Malek stole a fleeting glance to his right and saw two uniformed policemen walking towards them. 'Good afternoon, officers, don't come any closer. And listen carefully to what I have to say.'

Then Dusty heard Lenski's voice behind him.

'Donovan Malek, I have a warrant for your arrest. We're here to question you in connection with a number of serious offences.'

Malek's voice was quiet and deadly. 'I have a gun pressed into this man's stomach. He's coming with me. He will be safe provided you do nothing to stop me leaving.'

Dusty risked a quick look around. No one else was in the car park.

Lenski continued, his voice calm and even, 'Don't do anything silly. You can't get away – it's all over. Yanovic and Schokolov are in custody. We know what was going on at the warehouse, and we know you ordered the bashing that killed Callaghan.'

'Then you know I mean business,' Malek said. He gestured towards Dusty with the gun. 'Get in and drive.'

Dusty looked towards Lenski, who nodded. 'Do as he says. The last thing I need is a dead hero.'

Malek got in the back seat of the Mercedes as Dusty scrambled into the driver's seat, the muzzle of the pistol pressed against the back of his head.

'Start the engine. I presume you still have the keys?'

Dusty grimaced. Why the hell didn't he throw them away?

The gun pressed a little harder. Dusty caught the sweet and sour tang of sweat and aftershave.

Malek's voice was low and steely. 'Get going. I'm in a hurry and you've cost me valuable time, so don't try any funny business.'

Dusty's shaking hand struggled to get the key into the ignition. He hit the starter. The engine throbbed to life. Behind him, he heard the purr of an electric motor as the rear window of the Mercedes went down.

'No one will get hurt if you don't try to stop me,' Malek called out to Lenski.

'You won't get away with this,' Lenski responded. 'Be sensible. Give yourself up. I've got the entrance blocked.'

'Then unblock it, fast.'

Malek closed the window. The gun dug into his temple. 'Move it.'

Perspiration trickled down Dusty's face and into his eyes. A slight touch on the accelerator sent the car smoothly along the gravel driveway. He took a sharp left, then right – the entrance fifty metres ahead.

Don't do anything to upset Malek, he told himself. He had visions of his brains splattered over the windscreen. It took only seconds to cover the short distance to the entrance, but not quick enough to get past the police van that was blocking the road.

Dusty heard Malek's muttered oath behind him. 'The damned fool.'

He braked hard, the muzzle of Malek's gun bumped against the back of his head. A hot prickly flush suffused his body. The Mercedes crunched to a halt. He held his breath, waiting.

Dusty could see a policeman crouched behind a parked vehicle. It looked as if he had a gun. Shit. I'm in the fuckin' crossfire.

'Don't switch the engine off,' Malek said. 'We're not staying long. Get out and put your hands behind your head.'

Dusty did as he was told. Malek backed out of the car.

With the gun rammed into Dusty's ribs, Malek ordered the policeman behind the car to throw down his gun and come out into the open.

The constable looked young and inexperienced. For a moment he hesitated, looking across to his companion for guidance. The second constable, an older man, nodded slightly.

'Don't waste my time.' Malek's voice cut the air like a whip. 'I won't hesitate to kill him.' The gun swung in Dusty's direction before swinging back to the constable.

Malek raised his voice. 'You, behind the van. Out here, where I can see you or I'll shoot your mate.'

The older constable emerged, gun in hand.

'Throw it down.'

He also dropped his gun.

Malek turned back to the younger constable. 'Turn around, put your hands on the roof of that car and spread your feet.'

The constable did as he was told.

Dusty stole a look at his watch. Less than a minute had passed since they'd left Lenski. Too little time for any counter measures.

He looked on helplessly, convinced Malek, with nothing to lose, would do whatever it took to get away. Lenski's words, 'The last thing I need is a dead hero,' echoed back to him.

Dusty closed his eyes. He should've stayed in the crowd and let the police find Malek. Now he was caught up in a chain of catastrophic events and he was the weakest link.

'Get the van out of the way, then get back here.' Malek's voice was harsh in Dusty's ear. 'And don't even think of doing anything clever because your colleague presents a very easy target. Ten seconds before I shoot. One …'

The senior constable scrambled into the van, slammed it into reverse and backed away from the entrance. Malek's gun fanned between Dusty and the police. 'Four … five,' he counted loudly, motioning for Dusty to get behind the wheel.

Dusty climbed back into the Mercedes. His hands gripped the wheel so tightly his knuckles showed white. The van had moved forward enough to allow the Mercedes to get through. 'Eight …'

Dusty closed his eyes, praying Malek wouldn't shoot. He stole another glance at his watch. What was Lenski doing? He heard the handbrake being hauled on and the van door open. He opened his eyes to see the constable get out.

'Around here with your mate. Hands on the car, feet spread.'

Malek scooped up the police guns, sidled back to the Mercedes and yanked open the rear door. He got in. The older constable started to turn around.

'Don't turn around. Better still, down on your knees.' The constable didn't move. 'I said down on your knees.'

Suddenly an explosion went off in Dusty's ear. The constable collapsed to his knees. Dusty's ears rang.

Faintly, he heard Malek saying, 'Face down on the ground and you won't get hurt.'

The two officers obeyed him. Two more shots. Christ. Bile rose in his throat.

Then Dusty saw the back of the van settle onto its rims. His whole body began to tremble. His ears rang and he had difficulty thinking straight. He seemed unable to take in what was happening.

With the police officers now prostrate on the ground, Malek prodded the gun against Dusty's right temple.

'Get moving. Put your foot down. I need to make up time.'

Dusty gunned the Mercedes past the police van. He turned right with a screech of tyres and drove the fifty metres that would take them to the highway, heading towards Sydney.

Dusty concentrated on his driving. When he'd settled down a

bit, he would have time to work out his next move. It would take hours to get to Sydney.

'Turn left up here,' Malek said. 'We're going to Mowbray Park. I have some important business to attend to.'

As the turn-off to Mowbray Park approached, Dusty put his foot down and got into the left lane to leave the highway. The Mercedes sped up the long, steep hill. The driving began to ease the coils of tension which, until now, had paralysed his thinking. His brain was slipping back into gear. They'd be there within six minutes. Time to plan a way out.

Halfway up the hill, Dusty almost ran into the back of a low-loader that was grinding its way up the hill with a DH9 on the back.

'Get past it,' Malek growled.

Dusty looked at the double, unbroken line. He felt the gun pressed up against his neck. Taking a deep breath, he stamped down on the accelerator. He had no vision ahead. The surge of power swept them alongside the truck. In seconds they were round the bend. The road was clear. He exhaled slowly. Despite the desperateness of his situation, the rush of adrenaline had pumped him up.

Malek had said little since they'd left the track. Dusty needed to know more if he was to have any advantage.

'Won't the cops have the place staked out?'

'They think we're on our way to Sydney. If we move fast, we might just get out before they realise we're not.'

'And if you're wrong?'

'I'll deal with that if I have to, but I have an appointment to keep and I need to collect something.'

At the top of the hill, Dusty braked hard to avoid a four-wheel drive towing a horse float. The car slid sideways onto the gravel edge, drifting close to the wire safety fence. He straightened just in time. Glancing in the rear-vision mirror, he caught Malek sitting back with his eyes half-closed. He couldn't see the gun, but now wasn't the time for anything stupid. He'd wait for a better opportunity.

Using the full width of the road, Dusty drove through the long bends on the run down to Mowbray Park. A sense of optimism filtered his thoughts. Jenny and the boys were safe. All he had to do was get out of this mess.

He broke the silence. 'The way you handled things back there was incredible. You out-witted Lenski and those two mug coppers at the gate.' He laughed. 'They looked bloody ridiculous lying on the ground. When you shot out their tyres, I thought they'd shit themselves.'

Malek said nothing.

Mowbray Park came into view.

'The main entrance?' Dusty said.

'This one, slow down. I need to check the lay of the land.'

Dusty swung the car in a wide arc through the float entrance and coasted along the tree-lined avenue towards the stables.

'Spetcevic sure stuffed things up,' Dusty said.

'How do you mean?'

Dusty sensed a fleeting opportunity. 'Told me he wanted to give Flash Chance a bit of extra juice, just to make sure. He made sure alright – made sure he fuckin' overdosed.'

Malek lapsed into silence again. Another fleeting look in the rear-vision mirror revealed a pensive face. Dusty took the plunge.

'I'm the only one left.'

Malek snorted from the back seat. 'You? Why trust you?'

'Because now I'll do what I'm told. I may not want to, but I can see how the cards fall. You hold all the aces.'

The car rolled into the stables. Everything seemed normal.

'What I'm trying to say is, whatever happened is in the past,' Dusty said. 'I'm on your side. I can help you. Two heads are better than one. After you've gone, I'll say you dumped me. Then when you're ready, contact me and I'll join you.'

He paused a moment for Malek's response. None came.

'I've got all the drug info,' Dusty continued. 'I'm no chemist, but I know the formulas and I know how to use them. You can easily get someone to make them up.'

Finally, Malek spoke, 'But can I trust you?'

Dusty picked up the slight change of inflection. 'Take the chance. You hold the aces and I'm all out of luck. Gimme a chance. I won't let you down.'

'You sure about the formulae?'

'Very sure,' Dusty said. 'But I'll tell you what, it'll only take a second to pick up all the info we need from Murphy's office. Then it's beyond a doubt. There you are, an act of good faith.'

Dusty eased the car to a halt outside the office.

'Well, what's it to be?'

'Get what you need and I'll see about it,' Malek said. 'But if you even think of double-crossing me …'

Dusty had no idea where this would go. He'd been in freefall since he'd left the hospital. With the engine still running, he jumped out of the Mercedes and headed towards Murphy's office. Malek followed, hard on his heels, still holding the gun at Dusty. One wrong move and the situation could rapidly change.

The office was deserted. Dusty wasted no time going through the motions of getting what he wanted. He passed the USB storage stick to Malek.

'Are you sure this is it?' asked Malek.

'Want to check?' Dusty said, nodding towards the computer.

He walked over to switch it on.

'I'll take your word for it. Let's go to the house.'

The mansion exuded an aura of peace. No police cars, no sign of life.

They moved towards the side of the house. Malek still had his gun at the ready, but for the moment he seemed to have accepted Dusty, perhaps concerned that more serious trouble might lie ahead. He motioned Dusty forward with a wave of the gun.

'Keep in front. Up those stairs,' he said, pointing to the steps that led onto the wide verandah.

Dusty's nerves tingled, his hair rising on the back of his neck.

Silently, Malek gestured him along the verandah. At the end, they came to a small door set deep in an ornate portico. Malek fished in his pocket and threw Dusty a bunch of keys.

'Open it and leave the keys in the lock.'

The door swung open. They were greeted with cool, but slightly musty air from the dim corridor beyond.

'There is a bank of switches to your right,' Malek said. 'Switch them all on.'

Dusty fumbled in the gloom and found the switches, but didn't switch them on.

'You sure?'

'Of course, I'm sure you bloody fool. Just feel around a bit – you can't miss them.'

Dusty pretended to fumble for a few more seconds before switching them on. Light revealed a long corridor with several doors on either side.

'First door on the right,' Malek instructed.

They entered the large drawing room, now lit by the soft glow of antique lamps. They moved silently over the carpet; the rhythmic tick of the grandfather clock the only sound.

Malek wasted no time. 'Get those horses on the mantelpiece down for me.'

Dusty shook his head in disbelief. This was taking sentimentality to an absurd degree. When he'd first visited the room, Malek had pointed with pride to the pair of magnificently cast bronze and enamel horses, their harness and saddles encrusted with rhinestones, replicas of the originals in the Sculpture Museum of the Serbian Academy of Arts and Science in Belgrade. They were a reminder of Malek's homeland.

Dusty lifted the horses down one by one and placed them carefully on the carpet, surprised by their weight.

Malek gestured to a cupboard. 'In there you will find two black leather cases – pack them up.'

Dusty did so and picked up the first statuette, running his hands over it and marvelling at the craftsmanship. He put it into the first bag, then slowly lifted the second horse.

'For Christ's sake, get a move on,' Malek said. 'They may be valuable, but they're not fragile. I can't rely on the police to stay away for too long.'

Dusty packed the second horse and weighed a bag in each hand. No one would travel very far or fast carrying these.

Since he'd been taken hostage, Malek's gun had relentlessly followed him, but time was running out. At any moment, Malek might think his usefulness was over. Somehow, he had to win Malek's confidence and get him to drop his guard.

'Where to now?' he said, trying to sound positive.

'I've got to get some documents. Over there.' He pointed to two impressive doors. Going through the doors, Dusty recognised the hallway and staircase that had played such a part in his last disastrous visit.

'Leave the bags here and come with me.' Malek pointed up

the stairs. They climbed the stairs and headed along a corridor. At the end, they entered a room which was obviously Malek's study. From the drawers of a large desk, Malek collected a passport, bank notes and a pile of thick files. From a cupboard, he took a heavy-duty torch and shoved it, the papers and money into a large leather briefcase and snapped it shut. The sound echoed along the corridor. Pushing Dusty before him, they returned to the stairway and began their descent. A few steps from the bottom they became aware of a noticeable creaking sound.

Was someone in the house? Malek's mysterious associate? Someone else? Dusty's heart leapt. Someone who was intent on not being heard.

'Hear that?' Malek said softly.

'What?'

'Floorboards creaking. Grab those bags. We're out of here.'

Malek moved swiftly into the drawing room. They were halfway towards the doors leading onto the verandah when he heard a man's voice to his left.

'You're not going anywhere. Hands up, both of you.'

Slowly, Dusty put down the bags. He turned around.

A uniformed policeman stood in the shadow of another doorway onto the verandah with his two hands steadying the service pistol pointed in their direction.

Dusty looked at Malek, who was raising his arms in surrender. There was no sign of his gun.

Dusty put down the bags and raised his arms.

The policeman took a step into the room, followed by a policewoman.

'What's the meaning of this?' Malek said.

'As if you don't know,' the policeman said sarcastically.

'No, I don't. How did you get in? I thought breaking and

entering was an offence.'

'Don't get smart with me,' the policeman said. 'DS Lenski will be here any minute. Argue the toss with him.'

Malek shrugged and sighed. 'Then we'd better give ourselves up, eh, Rhodes? Pity. So near, yet so far.' He thrust his arms forward with his wrists together. 'Shouldn't you handcuff me?'

The sergeant nodded towards the policewoman who moved forward, slipping handcuffs off her belt. In doing so, she stepped in front of Malek, momentarily blocking the sergeant's line of sight.

It was enough.

With a quick pace forward, Malek grabbed her wrists and yanked her off balance, twisting her round in a blur of movement. Using her as a shield he reached down to pull up the gun he'd concealed in the armchair beside him.

Startled, the policeman stood helpless.

Malek fired at point blank range, the sound deafening Dusty in the confined space.

For a second, the policeman's face froze with a startled look, then his features twisted, and the gun dropped from his hand. He crumpled to the floor.

Savagely, Malek pushed the policewoman away and sent her sprawling over a side table, shattering a vase and the figurines on it. She landed among the debris, her head hitting the floor with a sickening thump.

The sudden violence stunned Dusty. His legs felt like lead; his head spun from the sound of the shot. He should help the fallen man; he took a few stumbling steps.

Malek's voice was cold and hard. 'Leave him.'

Dusty turned to Malek, whose gun swung through a small arc from him to the policewoman. She was groggily trying to get to her feet, her hands bleeding from broken fragments.

'Slap the cuffs on her.'

The wail of sirens broke through the brief silence that had enveloped the house.

Malek laughed mirthlessly. 'I didn't think it would be long. This calls for a change of plan. Forget about the cuffs. Here's your chance to be useful, Rhodes.'

'You,' Malek said to the policewoman. 'Lie on the floor, face down. Spread your arms and legs.' Then he pointed the gun at Dusty. 'Get to the window. Tell me exactly what's happening.'

Dusty moved to the window, peering through the long drapes.

Three police vehicles, flashing red and blue, swept up the driveway and screeched to a halt.

Dusty fought back a surge of helplessness.

'I see two cars and one van … looks like a SWAT team, about eight officers in all. I can see Lenski. He's sending some of them around the other side of the house; the others have taken cover behind the vehicles. Lenski's got a loud hailer.'

The hollow sound of Lenski's voice filled the drawing room, 'Malek, the house is surrounded. You don't have a chance. Come out with your hands up.'

'What now?' Dusty said.

'I hold the aces, remember,' Malek said softly. 'Take two steps out onto the verandah with your hands up … act frightened.'

'What if they shoot?'

'They won't. They're hoping we'll do what they want.'

Far from convinced, Dusty stepped through the French doors.

'Someone's coming out,' an officer yelled.

Dusty held his hands high above his head. At any moment he expected to be hit by a hail of bullets. Nothing happened.

Behind him, Malek's voice was clear. 'Repeat what I say.'

Dusty nodded.

'Malek's shot an officer and disarmed another.'

Dusty's voice shook with genuine fear as he yelled Malek's words.

'Malek's got a gun at my back. He'll shoot me and the other officer if you attempt to storm the house.'

'Understood. How badly is the officer hurt?' Lenski said into the loud hailer.

'I don't know. Pretty bad, I think.'

Malek's voice, low and confident, said to Dusty, 'Now get back inside and lock the door.'

Dusty retreated, flicking the latch that locked the door.

'Pick up the bags.'

Dusty did as he was told. He'd seen enough of Malek's ingenuity to know he was still in control.

From across the room came a shuddering groan. The injured policeman clutched his stomach, his face contorting with pain. Blood was seeping through his shirt and his fingers onto the floor; a deep, red stain spread across the carpet.

He was alive, but for how long?

The policewoman pleaded with Malek. 'My colleague needs help. If not, he'll die.'

'Shut up.' Malek bent down and took her gun from its holster.

'Handcuff her, hands behind her back,' Malek said to Dusty.

Dusty handcuffed the woman. Above the sound of the cuffs snapping shut, the rhythmic tick of the grandfather clock measured the seconds and minutes of their lives. He heard the crackle of two-way radios and in the distance, the wail of another siren, hopefully an ambulance.

Malek nodded to him. 'Time to go.'

'Where?'

'You'll find out.'

'What about them?'

'He stays. She comes.'

Malek's orders were crisp. 'Over there and through that door, then keep going to the door at the far end of the corridor.'

The weight of the bags restricted Dusty's mobility, perhaps a tactic to stop him from doing anything unexpected.

Behind him, he heard Malek say to the policewoman, 'Follow him and make it snappy.'

Dusty stopped at a solid, wooden door.

Malek's voice boomed in the corridor. 'Open it, damn you! And keep going.'

Dusty put down the bags and opened the door; it was a short passage leading to a flight of stairs. With a bag in each hand, he had to twist sideways to negotiate the worn steps. One foot in the wrong spot would plunge him headlong to the bottom. The policewoman's footsteps padded behind him. They reached a room at the end of the stairs. Dusty heard Malek lock the door to the stairs, he seemed to be sealing off any chance of escape.

The room was large and windowless. Fluorescent tubes produced a flat, white light that drained whatever colour remained in the assortment of dilapidated furniture.

Dusty ran a quick eye over the jumble of broken chairs, old cupboards and discarded rolls of carpet, searching for a weapon. He glanced at Malek, who had his gun pressed into the policewoman's back. One false move could see her die. He must bide his time.

Lenski would soon realise they were no longer in the drawing room. He imagined the police officers closing in with guns drawn, wary that Malek had almost certainly set a trap for them. Once they realised the house was empty, the search would begin in earnest, breaking down the locked doors and finding, beyond them, the cellar.

Knowing Malek, this was not the end. By now he'd hustled

them behind an old wardrobe that hid another door and pushed them into a lit room. The geography of the cellar became clearer; Malek would try to escape through the small door hidden deep in the shrubbery at the side of the house. A desperate gamble, but with most of the police searching the house it could work.

'Over there, in the corner,' Malek said.

The constable was shaking; she looked young and vulnerable. Nothing in her career could have prepared her for this.

It was bad enough trying to second guess Malek, but as the police net tightened, he'd become more dangerous.

Knowing he had to maintain some pretence of cooperation, Dusty forced a question. 'What do we do now?'

'Put the bags over there. Get two pieces of rope.' Malek gestured first to a chair and then to a rafter above. 'Make a hangman's noose and thread it through that steel ring, then put the chair under it facing the wall.'

Malek's gun still pointed at Dusty. Under his curt direction, Dusty picked up the rope, hesitantly fashioned a noose, then climbed on the chair to thread the end through the steel ring in the rafter.

'Now tie it off.' Malek turned to the frightened policewoman. 'Now, girlie you're going to help us. Stand on the chair facing the wall. These cellars are riddled with passages and with your help, we'll be far away while your colleagues are still dithering.'

Malek slipped the noose over the woman's head and pulled it taut.

'Now, Rhodes, take one end of the other piece of rope and tie it to the door knob. Then pull it tight and tie the other end to the leg of the chair.'

The woman's shoulders tensed. 'What are you going to do?' she whispered.

'You may not have noticed, but the door that your colleagues will come through opens outwards,' Malek said. 'We have tied one end of the rope to the doorknob and the other to the leg of the chair. If you don't want to die, you'd better make sure they don't open it.' He chuckled to himself.

Finally, Malek walked to the door, his footsteps echoing loudly in the confined space.

'Now remember, if they open the door, it'll pull the chair from under you, and you'll swing. So, when you hear them coming, start shouting.'

He winked at Dusty. 'Come on, Rhodes, we're leaving. Goodbye, Miss ... eh ... oh dear, you never got around to introducing yourself.'

Lifting the bags again, Dusty wondered what would happen next. No way could Malek manage alone. He was needed; Malek would keep him alive.

With the briefcase in one hand, torch under his arm and the gun in the other, Malek took Dusty through another door, another room and then into a further room. It was empty, except for a pile of filthy rags in one corner. At the far end of the room was a square iron grate about eighty centimetres wide.

'Put the bags down and lift it,' Malek said.

'Why?'

'It's our way out. Down there is a drain that in the old days took waste from the house.'

Dusty lifted it and peered into the blackness. An idea formed in his mind.

'I can't. I'm terrified of confined places. What about that side door that opens onto the garden? They won't be expecting that ... you can easily get away.'

'Cut the crap. Get down there. There are toeholds. When you

reach the bottom, take a few steps into the drain. You can only go one way. I'll let the bags down and follow you after I set up one last obstacle for the police.'

Dusty hesitated. The gun poked his ribs.

'If I must, I will kill you. But I have good reason to keep you alive, so be thankful. Anyway, if you stay, the police will never believe you were a hostage. The policewoman would say that you helped me. Why do you think I want her alive? I could easily have killed her.'

Against the odds, Malek seemed to think of everything.

Dusty lowered himself into the opening. As he braced his back against the wall of the shaft, his feet searched for the first toehold. Toehold by toehold, he reached the bottom. A small rivulet of water flowed along the circular brick drain, but otherwise it seemed dry. The air was relatively fresh.

59

Dusty looked up to see Malek lowering the bags down the shaft. Soon he would climb down. It'd be a tight squeeze for someone of Malek's bulk, and he'd have to stow his gun for the descent. If Dusty timed it right, he could grab Malek's legs, jerk him down and smash his head into the brickwork. Was this his chance? The thought gave him a feeling of satisfaction.

As he moved the bags aside, Dusty heard a scraping sound. He could no longer see up the shaft. It must've been Malek dragging the grating back across the drain. Anyway, he couldn't hear him climbing down. Seconds passed – still nothing.

With a jolt, Dusty realised Malek must've used the outside door after all. Now free of him and the bags, it would take only minutes for him to escape.

He slumped against the wall. Tiredness flooded him. It'd been relatively easy coming down. It would be harder to get back up and harder still to shift the iron grate.

He heard a slight scuffling sound. A shiver ran through him. Rats. His mind ran through the options: try getting up the shaft or follow the drain and hope that there was a way to get out at the end. The drain travelled away from the house, but where did it lead? How far did it go? He had no idea. The best way would be to go back the way he'd come.

Malek would be well clear by now. If he could lift the grate, he'd soon be out, and with nothing to stop him, he could free the policewoman and alert the police.

Anxiously, his fingers explored the bricks above him, tracing the grooves, feeling his way back to the shaft. The darkness began to take on a new dimension and claustrophobia gripped him.

Suddenly, a beam of light hit him full in the face. He blinked rapidly, putting up a hand to shield his eyes from the glare. 'What the hell?'

From somewhere beyond the light, Malek's voice echoed harshly. 'On your feet, you idiot, and get moving.'

For a moment, the shock of Malek's dramatic appearance robbed him of speech.

Then Dusty said, 'How the hell did you get here?'

Malek ignored him and shone the light along the drain. 'That's where we are going, so take one bag. I'll manage the other. Just keep going until you see daylight.'

The torch beam dipped to light the bags. Dusty reached down, grasping the one closest to him.

In the peripheral light spill, he saw the gun in Malek's other hand and the shoes that hung by their laces around his neck. So that's how the bugger climbed down the shaft without a sound.

The torch shone ahead into the black void of the drain. Wherever the drain came out, at least Dusty would be in front. With Malek burdened by the other bag, he'd have a few brief seconds to get the upper hand.

Using his elbows against the brick walls as a guide, Dusty groped his way forward. Behind him, he could hear Malek grunting and panting, the beam of the torch jerking with every step.

After trudging through the drain for some time, Dusty felt a draught of fresh air on his face. It was a shaft to drain water from one of the property's many interior roads.

'We're halfway,' Malek said, flashing his torch on his watch. 'We have to push on or we'll lose what's left of the light.'

'It'd be a lot quicker without these bags.'

Dusty could hear Malek's breathing become more regular.

'They come with us. And don't forget this.' Malek shone his torch on the gun in his other hand.

Dusty stared at the gun, which despite Malek's exertion, was rock steady. The man had to be mad.

Malek's voice grated again. 'Get moving.'

Hunched over, Dusty resumed his passage along the drain. A sharp stabbing pain shot from his ankles to his thighs, his back ached, his head bumped against the roof, and the bag grew heavier with every step.

To take his mind off the pain, he tried to concentrate on what he would do when they hit daylight. The heavy bag might yet prove to be the weapon to disarm Malek.

They trudged on until Dusty sensed the floor of the drain beginning to slope a little more steeply. It became slippery; he almost lost his footing.

A little further along, he was soon knee-deep in water.

'Can you shine the torch ahead?' Dusty asked. 'The drain seems to be flooded.'

Malek directed the beam over his shoulder. A few metres ahead, water lapped the roof.

'What now?'

Malek ran the beam of light back and forth along the wall, stopping at a painted white line. He gave a grunt of satisfaction. 'The good news is we're only four metres from the end of the drain, which means the outlet is submerged. But we should be able to make it.'

Dusty's voice choked with disbelief. 'You've gotta be joking.'

'I never joke.'

'With the bags, there's not a hope in hell.'

Malek seemed to consider Dusty's words, then gave a deep sigh. 'I guess you're right. They stay behind. I'll come back for them later.'

'I don't believe it. We've dragged them all this way and you abandon them just like that.'

'Just like that. There's not a lot of choice.'

'Great. Pity we had to bring 'em this far.'

Malek sighed again. 'I didn't think the creek would still be up.'

'Who's going first?'

'You. I won't be far behind.'

'Hope you're right.'

'Trust me. It's my life on the line too.'

Distrust hit Dusty like a punch to the chest. His heart raced. What other tricks did Malek have up his sleeve? With the bags abandoned, Dusty's life would have lost its value in Malek's eyes.

He tried to suppress his darker thoughts. Wading deeper into the water, he crept forward until only his head was clear. The water chilled him to the bone. He closed his eyes as the water lapped around him. An image of Jenny and the boys – their faces anxious when he'd last seen them – made him grit his teeth. He had to make it.

He waited for his heartbeat to steady and to take several breaths, each time exhaling deeply. On the fourth breath, he plunged forward, running his free hand along the walls to give him direction.

The pressure from the water increased with every metre. The creek must be flowing strongly. Dusty emptied his mind of everything except putting one foot in front of the other. Counting his steps, he tried to gauge the distance and maintain his composure. His head started to pound. It was taking more effort than he thought. He hoped Malek was right about an exit.

Without warning, his feet slipped from under him, and he tumbled forward into a swiftly flowing current. In panic, he reached out for the drain walls, his fingers touching nothing. He raised his arms and kicked furiously towards a pale light above him. He burst to the surface.

Grass covered banks rose steeply from the water. A pale blue sky arched overhead. He filled his lungs with fresh air. With a few weary strokes, he reached the riverbank. He rested in the waist-deep water, leaning against the slope of the bank.

Looking around, he saw the surface water unbroken. Malek couldn't be far behind. Older and bulkier, he'd be doing it tough, but Dusty knew not to underestimate the man.

A couple of minutes passed before reality hit him. For the first time since he'd been jumped by Yanovic and Schokolov, he was free. The realisation gave him fresh energy.

Grasping a handful of the willow branches that drooped over the riverbank, Dusty hauled himself up. The relief of warm, dry earth under him drained his newfound energy. He fell to his knees and rolled over on his back. He cupped a handful of the sandy dirt and ran it through his fingers. He let out a broken, hysterical laugh that ended in a choking cough. He slowly got to his feet, his whole body shaking with the relief.

The river still flowed, swiftly and smoothly. There was no sign of Malek. He could've gone back, or he could've drowned. If the bastard was dead, he'd got what he deserved.

He looked to the west. The sun was not far off the horizon. Soon it would be dark. Dusty began to relax. He could scarcely believe it. Time to go home and leave it to the police. Time to pick up the shattered pieces of his life.

But a hook of indecision held him back. He wanted to walk away, to take the opportunity he'd been waiting for. He walked several paces, looking around to get his bearings.

But Malek's last words hammered in his brain. 'Trust me. It's my life on the line too.' He'd said it with grim conviction. Deep down, he knew Malek was alive.

It had been a good five minutes since he'd climbed out of the water. Even if Malek had allowed some time for him to get clear of the drain, he should have emerged by now.

He walked another two or three paces, stopped and turned round. Had Malek gone back for the bags? He walked back to the water's edge.

60

The sun cast pale shafts of light across the paddock, and the autumn chill from the deep shadows of the trees stabbed at Dusty's wet clothes, making him shiver. Stamping his feet and rubbing his hands to restore some circulation, he started to walk away from the river but, hearing a gurgling sound behind him, he stopped and looked back. At first, he saw only the unbroken surface, then bubbles. Seconds later, Malek's head bobbed to the surface, coughing and spluttering. He disappeared then came up a second time, his arms flailing desperately. Malek was drowning.

Let the bugger go. The world would be better for it. Yet he couldn't. Despite everything, he just couldn't stand by and watch a man die.

Malek came up and went under again.

In a few strides, Dusty was back at the riverbank. Taking a deep breath, eyes fixed on the spot where he'd last seen him, he jumped in.

The murky water revealed little, but his groping hands soon found him. Grabbing him, Dusty kicked up, pulling the limp form onto the riverbank. As they surfaced, Malek convulsed in a series of choking coughs and lurched from Dusty's grasp, then arched forward, vomiting into the muddy brown water before trying to stagger up the bank.

'You're too heavy to lift – grab these,' Dusty said. 'I'll try and help you out.' He took a handful of willow branches, pushed them towards Malek, and for a second time, hauled himself up onto the bank.

Malek nodded. With Dusty's help, he managed to crawl up the bank to finally collapse on the grass. Water streamed off him and his body shook with spasms of coughing. It was the end of the road.

Dusty waited for the coughing to subside. Although he felt no sympathy, he didn't want him to die before he could get the police. 'You okay?'

Malek looked up at Dusty, hugging himself to ease the pressure on his chest. 'Why are you still here?' he gasped.

Dusty shrugged. 'Drowning's too easy. I want you to pay for what you've done.'

Malek slumped forward. 'Do what you damn well like.'

Dusty turned on his heel. 'I will.'

It would take him a good twenty minutes to get to the house, but Malek was going nowhere.

'Not so fast.'

Despite the rasping wheeze, Malek's words still held a note of menace. Dusty looked back.

Malek was pointing his gun at Dusty's chest. In his other hand was the plastic bag, with his passport and money. No doubt it had kept the gun dry as well.

Slowly, Malek got to his feet. 'You're not going anywhere, yet.'

He bent down and loosened a rope he'd tied to his ankle. With the gun trained on him, he shook the rope towards Dusty.

'Pull that. I need what's on the other end.'

Dusty reeled in the slack, looping the spare length in his left hand until the rope became taut. He pulled hand over hand, stealing a quick glance at Malek, whose attention seemed fixed on the rope.

After a few minutes one of the bags appeared, soon followed by the other one. Under the pretext of taking a firmer grip for the final effort to get them up to the top of the bank, Dusty stepped sideways and with all his strength, flung the looped rope towards Malek's head.

Dusty's attempt to lasso him almost succeeded, instead the rope fell to the ground. Malek stepped over it and struck Dusty across the face with the muzzle of the gun.

Before he could regain his balance, Malek kicked him savagely in the shins. He waited for Dusty to get to his feet.

'Now, do as you're told. No more stunts.' Malek raised the gun. His eyes blazed.

Dusty shook his head in disbelief.

With a few heaves and a final pull on the rope, he retrieved the two bags.

Against all odds, Malek had taken his luck to the edge.

'Untie them. I have precious little time.'

Dusty gave himself the luxury of a malicious smile. 'And to think I could've let you drown.'

'You're not a killer, that's your problem, but I haven't got this far to let sentimentality get the better of me.'

Dusty thrust out his chin. 'I've had it up to here, you bastard. Carry them yourself.'

'If I must carry them, you're dead. They're worth a fortune.'

'Bronze replicas from some museum in Belgrade?'

Malek's eyes took on a steely glint. 'Your memory's impressive but they're not bronze. They're solid gold and the stones are diamonds, emeralds, rubies and sapphires. The statuettes are worth ten million each. There's a plane waiting for me in the long paddock. Soon it'll be too dark to take off.' He paused. 'It's our ticket out of here, Rhodes.'

'Your ticket maybe, but not mine. We part company here.'

Dusty barely registered Malek lifting his arm, but the gun fired. A bullet splintered the tree trunk beside him.

'You have three choices. Die here, carry the bags to the plane and stay behind, or come with me and make some money. What's it to be? I can't wait any longer. You have three seconds. One …'

Dusty stared into Malek's impassive face. My God, he was ready to risk everything. Surely there had to be a way to use it to his advantage.

'Two …'

If he went along with Malek, and Malek was hell-bent on protecting his treasure trove, there was a chance Dusty could bring the bastard to justice and settle the score for his family, Callaghan and the horses that had died.

But first, he had to buy time. The count of three hung in the air.

Malek raised the pistol, pointing it at him. He couldn't miss.

Dusty bent down and picked up the bags.

Malek vaguely indicated a way through the trees.

The long paddock was a fenced corridor about fifty metres wide and a kilometre long. A channel, probably full after the rain, ran along its southern boundary. They would need to cross a narrow wooden bridge near to where the channel emptied into the creek. The plane would be on the other side.

In the fading sunlight, Dusty and Malek negotiated the trees. Dusty's body trembled with fatigue. His wet clothes chafed his skin and water squelched in his sodden boots. He stole a glance at Malek. He was a sorry sight: damp hair, mud-stained clothes, yet eyes that held a febrile brightness. Malek's left hand still clutched the plastic bag, his right hand held the gun.

No matter what it took, Dusty knew the man would get himself on that plane.

He could try to delay him, but he might wind up dead. His only chance was a plan now taking shape in his mind. Malek still needed him; it was enough to keep him going.

After a bad stumble, Dusty had to put the bags down to catch his breath. They trudged through one paddock and across the next. Dusty hoped like hell his calculations were correct.

With relief, he found the gate that opened onto the long paddock – his first stroke of luck. Three horses grazing there lifted their heads in curiosity. Dusty pursed his lips in a soft whistle. The horses moved slowly towards them.

By the time he'd reached the gate, they were quite close. He opened the gate, easing his aching back. His spirits rose – the channel was almost full. The bridge was fifty metres to their left.

A bellow came from behind. He turned to see Malek waving his arms above his head.

'The plane.'

Dusty lifted the bags once more.

In the fading light he thought he saw a figure climb into the plane. A few seconds later, the plane's engines spluttered into life.

'Get a move on,' Malek snarled, waving the gun at Dusty. 'We're almost there.'

By the time Dusty got to the bridge, the plane was only a hundred metres away, its engine picking up a steady rhythm. He looked back again; the horses had followed them through the gate.

Dusty lurched forward, anxious to reach the bridge ahead of Malek. Once there, he stopped in the middle of the bridge and rested the bags on the edge.

'Don't stop,' Malek roared. 'Keep going.'

Dusty leaned down to pick up the bags, but instead, tipped them so they balanced precariously on the edge of the bridge.

'This is as far as we go. Don't come any closer,' Dusty said.

Malek raised the gun. 'I warned you.'

Dusty stared resolutely at Malek. 'Shoot and they'll fall. You'll never fish them out in time to get on that plane.'

61

Malek took two steps closer. Their eyes locked. Malek appeared to understand he was a hair's breadth away from losing them. The gun dropped to his side. Behind Dusty, the aircraft engines throbbed.

'You want a cut?' he snarled. 'Alright, take one and get lost.'

Dusty shook his head. 'I wasn't born yesterday. If I do, you'd shoot me like a dog.'

A look somewhere between anger and frustration flashed across Malek's face, then a sneer of contempt. 'What do you want? Both?'

'No. I just want my life. You can have the damned gold, but on my terms.'

Malek's eyes narrowed. 'And your terms are?' He edged a step closer.

'Keep back.' Dusty hoped his voice held more conviction than he felt. 'One more step and I drop one.'

Malek took a step back, his face breaking into a crooked grin. 'If I can't have the gold, why not shoot you now.'

It flashed through Dusty's mind that a quick jump into the water, bags and all, might be his only option. But that would allow Malek to get away. He hadn't come this far to let that happen. He'd gambled on Malek's greed, but now the chips were down.

It hardly mattered what Malek said, it's what he'd do that counted.

'I can retrieve them later.' Malek raised the gun and took careful aim at Dusty.

Dusty stared into his cold grey eyes, trying to read his thoughts. Malek didn't as much as a blink. Dusty had nothing to lose.

'Do your worst. The cops'll track you down wherever you hide and without the gold …' Dusty let the words hang in the air.

With every second of delay, a tiny ray of hope grew.

'There's a way out for both of us,' Dusty said. 'Toss the gun into the water and start walking towards the plane. When you're halfway there and I'm halfway across the paddock, you can come back for the bags. Or keep the gun and fly off without them. But I'm staying here until either that gun hits the water or you leave. Which is it?'

Malek hesitated; his brow furrowed.

Then Dusty saw something that sent his spirits soaring. The three horses he had whistled up when they were crossing the paddock had come to the gate, just as he'd hoped. He whistled again. The whipbird's call echoed through the trees. The horses' ears pricked as they trotted through the open gate, their hoofs softly rustling the leaves on the ground. They stopped as if to watch the drama playing out on the bridge.

Malek took no notice. The gun had drifted lower and was now aimed somewhere near Dusty's legs. 'It's a deal,' he said. 'One thing, though. Before I get rid of the gun, let me cross the bridge. You mightn't trust me, but I don't trust you.'

'Just keep well over there,' Dusty said, nodding towards the other side of the bridge.

He watched Malek edge past, the pistol still trained indifferently in Dusty's direction. Once on the other side, he saw Malek hold the gun high in the air. He gave it an elaborate flourish before arcing it towards the channel.

It dropped into the water with a reassuring splash.

Dusty eased the bags back onto the bridge. He was relieved to see Malek hurry away across the paddock towards the plane without looking back. In unison, the horses turned and started to move away. He whistled again. As one, they swung around and trotted back towards him.

He stripped off his belt and slowly walked back across the bridge. Stepping off the bridge he approached the horse closest to him. He reached out and stroked its forehead, then worked his hand down to the muzzle. He looped his belt gently over the horse's neck until his arms encircled its neck to do up the buckle. Muttering the soft flow of syllables he used to communicate trust and understanding to horses, he gradually coaxed it onto the bridge.

The hollow ring of its metal shoes striking the wooden planks made the big thoroughbred pull back. Dusty kept up his stream of reassuring words, stroking the soft velvety neck until, with gentle pressure from the belt, the horse took a tentative step forward, and then another step, until it crossed the remaining length of the bridge and walked onto the grass

With energy that belied his fatigue, Dusty sprang up onto the animal's back, one hand grasping the belt and the other grasping the horse's luxurious mane. He set off at a trot heading towards Stable Square.

He had gone perhaps two hundred metres along the paddock before he chanced a glance back. Sure enough, just as he thought, Malek had turned back from the plane.

Silhouetted against the backdrop of the darkening sky, he saw Malek retrieve the bags. He should have been on the plane by now, but he couldn't leave them behind.

Beyond the bridge, the cabin lights in the plane and its blinking navigation lights shone brightly.

Dusty slowed his mount to a walk. Malek had left the bridge and was making difficult progress back to the plane. At the pace he was going, it would take him several minutes to reach it. There was barely enough light for the plane to take off. Surely the pilot must abort his mission or stay stranded on the ground.

Once Dusty was certain Malek had no way to escape, it would take him only minutes to ride back to the house for help. But Malek was getting closer to the plane. The note of the engine seemed to be rising. If the pilot was prepared to take the risk, Malek would be gone – statuettes and all.

Swinging the horse in a half circle back towards the plane, Dusty dug in his heels and with a wild whoop, spurred it into a gallop, the wind stinging his face. The other two horses followed, having crossed the bridge to join the fun.

The gap between Dusty and Malek was lessening, but Malek was getting too close to the plane. Crouched low over the neck of his horse, Dusty raced towards Malek. He needed to run him down before he could scramble on board.

Within seconds, all three horses were running abreast, their manes and tails streaming in the wind. Dusty gave another whoop. The gap was closing fast.

Malek must have heard Dusty because he dropped the bags and began to stumble to the plane.

Becoming frightened by the noise of the planes' engines the other horses began to veer away, making it difficult for Dusty to hold his horse on course. He needed to get closer, but the frightened animal was fighting him every stride. He dropped close over the withers. Without warning, it propped and spun side to side, trying to shake him off. Dusty held on like he was part of the horse.

Malek had reached the steps of the plane. The engine's roar became deafening.

The horse reared in panic just short of the plane.

Clinging to mane and belt with all his strength, he heaved his feet and body outwards to throw the horse's weight away from the centre of gravity. It staggered, trying to keep its balance but tumbled sideways. Dusty jumped clear. The horse fell with a resounding thump – pawing the air as it struggled to regain its feet.

Dusty ran forward.

Malek heaved himself up the steps.

Dusty tried to push himself faster, but his legs were slow to respond.

Through a blur, he saw Malek at the top of the steps, turning back to pull the door shut.

He knew the steps folded up with the door.

If only he could reach them before they lifted off.

With a desperate lunge, Dusty threw himself against the steps, clutching at the edges for a handhold. Slowly, the steps sank to the ground. Somehow, he managed to gain a footing and scrambled up the steps.

The two adversaries came face to face.

62

MALEK STEPPED BACK, his face red with rage. Reaching out, Dusty managed to grab a handful of Malek's shirt but before he could get a firm grip, Malek drove his foot into Dusty's chest.

Dusty jerked back, losing his footing. He tumbled off the steps and landed on the ground with a sickening thud. Winded, he could only watch the door fuse into the side of the plane.

Despair overwhelmed him. So close, yet so far. In seconds, the plane would take off and fly Malek to freedom.

The cabin lights dimmed. In the gloom, Dusty's eyes became transfixed on the spill of light from the cockpit, which threw a kaleidoscopic pattern on the propeller. As if from a higher force, the image spun a frantic message: his last chance.

Rolling to his feet, Dusty frantically looked around for the bags Malek had abandoned.

With a herculean effort, he stumbled to the closest one not far from the plane's wing tip.

Heaving up the bag, he swung it with all his strength, hurling it into the spinning blades of the propeller.

The plane rolled forward. The engine spluttered, before revving furiously.

He watched with satisfaction as the aircraft came to a halt. The pilot cut the engines.

He dropped his head and offered up a silent prayer of thanks.

An eerie silence followed the engine's wind down. Nothing moved, like a movie on pause.

Dusty smiled wearily, savouring the irony. Malek, undone by the very object he'd valued so much.

Soon the door opened and Malek descended its steps. He began wandering aimlessly around the plane.

Under the mantle of darkness, Dusty worked his way back in a wide arc towards the other side of the plane.

Neither Malek nor the pilot could know what had happened; this gave him some slight advantage. But was the other man a Malek gang member or a commercial pilot?

The pilot climbed out and began to inspect the shattered propeller. Dusty saw he was wearing a uniform. He also noted that Malek ignored him, continuing his aimless circling until he stopped next to the second bag of statuettes. Malek heaved it up and carried it up onto the plane.

Dusty stayed on the blind side of the fuselage speculating his next move.

Looking under the plane, he saw Malek descend from it, presumably to look for the other bag. He joined the pilot. 'What happened?'

The pilot turned to Malek, the peripheral glow of a torch lighting his passenger's face. His words floated on the still air.

'Something's hit the propeller with great force. There's no other way it would shatter like that.'

Malek's voice came back quietly but firmly. 'It's Rhodes – this is his doing. The man's a killer and I'll bet he's still here.'

'What the hell do you mean?' asked the pilot, a note of panic in his voice.

'Why do you think I look like this? He tried to drown me, but I beat him off. Then he tried to trample me to death with one of our horses. He's homicidal. Got any sort of weapon?'

'A small fire extinguisher and hatchet. Not much against a homicidal maniac.'

'Better than nothing.'

Stunned by what he was hearing, Dusty crept forward.

The pilot ducked under the wing, the beam of his torch sweeping the ground.

Dusty looked down, horrified. The beam lit his legs and feet and stopped.

'What's the matter?' Malek hissed.

The pilot's voice was a whisper. 'He's on the other side of the plane.'

'Get the hatchet.'

Dusty back-pedalled, hoping to get as far away from the plane as possible. It was so simple for Malek to twist the truth and gain an ally.

He tried to run from the plane, hoping to gain some protection from the darkness, but had only gone a few metres before his legs gave way under him.

Malek was on top of him in an instant, kicking him and yelling to the pilot for help.

Dusty rolled clear of Malek's feet and tried to get up, but when he put weight on his right leg, he felt a stab of pain from his ankle.

The area around them was lit by the faint glow of the plane's cabin lights. Behind Malek, Dusty caught a glimpse of the pilot crouched in the cockpit, earphones on his head.

Malek towered over him.

'You're finished,' Malek said.

But Dusty twisted away. Biting his lip against the pain from his ankle, he struggled to his feet.

Malek came at him, bellowing and swinging wild punches.

Dusty ducked and drove a fist into Malek's solar plexus. He grunted, falling back a pace to drop into a crouch.

They circled each other like boxers. Dusty knew he couldn't run. His leg wouldn't let him. Somehow, he had to overcome Malek before the pilot returned. It would be no contest against two.

Malek swung a punch at Dusty's head, who ducked under it and counterpunched Malek's head who also swayed back, the punch landing only a glancing blow.

They circled again. Malek swung a wild punch over Dusty's head. Again, he dropped back, pain shooting up his leg, he stumbled. Malek's next punch caught Dusty full in the mouth. He tasted blood.

Things weren't going so well. Dusty dropped his hands to his sides and took a few faltering steps back.

'You win, you bastard.'

With a sadistic laugh, Malek wound up for the haymaker punch that would finish his defenceless opponent. But Dusty was ready.

Malek had dropped his guard.

The punch from Malek came towards Dusty.

He ducked, driving his jabbing fists hard into Malek's soft belly. At such close range, they had a telling effect – Malek doubled up.

Dusty clouted Malek on the jaw. Malek stumbled back, gasping for air and shaking his head.

In a frenzy, he delivered a flurry of blows to Malek's unprotected head, opening a cut on his right brow. Blood ran down to join the blood spilling from his split lip.

A red haze of fury clouded Dusty's mind. All he could see was the face of his hated adversary. Malek was wobbling on his feet, arms hanging limply by his side. But Dusty didn't let up, driving more punches into his body.

Malek's knees buckled and before he went down, Dusty landed

one last knockout blow to his battered face. Malek fell. He didn't move.

Barely able to see, overwhelmed with fatigue, he turned round to face his next foe. The pilot strode towards him.

Dusty dropped into a fighter's crouch, but he knew the tank was empty.

The pilot stopped and clapped. 'Well done, old boy.'

Dumbfounded, Dusty looked at him.

'I … I don't understand.'

'You're lucky, I'm a coward. When I got back to the plane I radioed for help. You being a "homicidal maniac" and all that. The police should be here any minute.'

Dusty shivered violently. His leg hurt with a vengeance, his whole body ached, and his knuckles were bleeding. He could barely stand.

'Take this,' the pilot said, handing Dusty the jacket he was wearing.

Dusty was grateful for its immediate warmth.

'I have a sweater in the plane,' the pilot said. 'I'll get that for myself. Should I get him a blanket?' He motioned to Malek on the ground.

'Let him suffer.'

The pilot looked behind Dusty. 'Here they come.'

Car headlights were rapidly approaching. The paddock lit up with red and blue streaks.

It was all over.

63

THE COFFEE WAS STONE COLD. For two hours Lenski and Bryant had taken Dusty through all that had happened since he'd left the racetrack. The police officer Malek had shot was alive, although in a critical condition. The policewoman was also alive but traumatised. Malek's tactic had wasted valuable time rescuing her. They were just leaving Mowbray Park when the pilot's call came through, hence their rapid response. Lenski and Bryant had accepted his explanations and praised him for his courage and resourcefulness. They had arrested Spetcevic, and were spreading their operations to tie up any loose ends. Jenny and the boys were safe and recovering from their ordeal.

'She's tough,' Lenski had said. 'She'd wheedled a lot of information out of Schokolov – enough to bust their drugs racket wide open.'

For the moment Dusty was alone. As he sat waiting for his statement to be typed, he tried to collect his thoughts and bring some perspective to his future.

When Bryant returned with the first sheets, he asked him how much longer they would need to keep him.

'I wouldn't think much longer. Another coffee?' Bryant said.

'How about a cold beer?'

Bryant shook his head. 'Sorry, not on the menu.'

A short while later Lenski returned. He looked at Dusty

sympathetically, shook his head and said, 'I'm sorry it's taken so long, you must feel completely buggered. Oh, and by the way, Leigh Woodward said to drop you over to his place when we've finished here. I'll run you over.'

Dusty slumped in his chair. All he wanted was to go home and be with Jenny and the boys.

Lenski left the room, returning twenty minutes later with fresh coffee and the remaining sheets of Dusty's statement. 'Check these, if they're okay, sign them, and then that's it.'

Dusty read through them, signing each page as he went. As he signed the last sheet, Bryant came in and muttered something to Lenski who grinned. 'Oh, I'm sorry, but you're not quite finished.'

Dusty groaned.

'Local reporter to interview you.'

Dusty flushed. Lenski appeared not to notice. 'She thinks very highly of you.'

Dusty gave a non-committal shrug. He didn't dare respond for fear of giving too much away, emotionally drained he was vulnerable. Kerry Suster was the last person he wanted to see.

When she walked in, Lenski left, shutting the door behind him.

Dusty recalled those desperate night visits they'd made to Murphy's office.

She sat demurely behind the desk opposite him and produced a small dictaphone. 'Mind if I use this?'

'I'd rather you didn't.'

'I'll be discreet, believe me, it'll help a lot.'

He didn't feel like pushing the matter.

'I am happy to turn it off at any time,' she said.

'I trust you.'

After the interview, Kerry pressed the stop button and looked up at Dusty.

'Not so bad, was it?'

Dusty shook his head. 'Painless. By the way, Woodward's having something at his place. Would you like to come?'

She rose and walked around the desk to give him a hug. 'No.' Her voice was thick; she fought back tears. 'It's time to say goodbye, Dusty.'

'Goodbye?' Dusty said. 'What do you mean?'

'I'm heading back to Sydney. I've been offered a job with one of the TV channels. It's the break I've always wanted.'

She looked at him through tears before she crossed to the door.

She turned to him one last time. 'I'll file this and leave tonight. Good luck. Perhaps you'll give me an interview when you bring home that Melbourne Cup winner.'

Dusty looked at her, almost unable to see for his own tears.

64

THE POLICE CAR PULLED UP outside the Woodward's house. Cars were parked in the yard and out in the street.

'Quite a party,' Lenski said as Dusty opened the door and got out.

Lenski drove off, leaving Dusty standing at the end of the driveway. With each step towards the front door, he struggled to compose himself and push back a flood of emotion. He knew what he had to do, but walking through Woodward's front door seemed an almost impossible task.

He heard laughter coming from inside. His spirits sank. The aftershock of all he'd been through was kicking in.

Woodward's generosity was well meant, but he needed time on his own – time with Jenny and the boys. He turned away and retraced his steps down the driveway.

A few clouds scudded across the night sky. The moon sailed in celestial splendour on a black sea. The stars seemed particularly luminous, as if reaching down to embrace him.

Immense gratitude welled within him – gratitude for the unseen hand that had guided him through a nightmare to the calm of this beautiful autumn night. He felt the touch of a higher being. Someone up there had looked after him and his little family.

Dusty turned and walked back to the open door of Woodward's house. He could smell the delicious aroma of food. Here was normality – kindness, generosity, friendship.

Among the babble of voices, he heard Jem calling out to one of his friends. He smiled and heaved a sigh. This was what he wanted. He'd quit racing, be a better husband, a better father. He would go back to his trade. Perhaps George Mitchell would give him his old job back.

No one noticed him at first and he was glad. He spotted Jenny just as some of the guests recognised him.

'Look who's here,' someone called out.

Those nearest the door crowded around Dusty to cheer for him, then parted to let Jenny through. She threw her arms around him and placed her head on his chest, so overcome she couldn't speak.

Dusty held her head in his hands and tilted it to kiss her.

In a soft voice, he said, 'I'm giving up racing, Jenny. That's a promise.'

She gazed up at him. 'I'm so proud of you.'

A voice he recognised as Vicky's struck up, 'For he's a jolly good fellow.'

Soon everyone was singing, laughing and cheering.

Jem and Rafe came barrelling through the sea of legs to hug their parents.

Dusty lifted one in each arm. The family was back together.

A little later, Tom Loftus arrived to join the celebration.

'Sorry I'm late,' he said, shaking Dusty's hand. 'I want to thank you for getting Fire King over the line.' He beamed. 'He ran a great race.'

'I don't know about that,' Dusty said. 'But I'll say this: I enjoyed working for you more than Malek.'

'Damned with faint praise,' Tom said with a wry smile. 'I'd jolly well hope so, but before anyone else nabs you, we have something to discuss. Let's nip outside for a few minutes.'

Once outside Tom began, 'The Race Club has so much to thank you for your help in exposing Malek's schemes, it was so significant.'

Dusty felt his face redden. 'Thanks,' he mumbled.

Tom stared ahead. 'What'll you do now?'

Dusty paused before answering, gazing out over the brightly lit swimming pool. 'Not work at Mowbray Park, that's for sure. Firstly, I'll take a few days off.' He sighed. 'Then I'll ask George for my old job back.'

Though Dusty didn't look at Tom, he was conscious the old man was looking at him.

'Take the job with Carisbrooke Ellis. I'll send Fire King down for the Melbourne Cup.'

Dusty found it difficult to breathe. The promise to Jenny pounded in his head. He gazed up at the sky, trying to find some strength. He closed his eyes, remembering the small boy walking beside his father. He remembered how he had asked his father how the horse would go in Thursday's race.

Dusty's lips quivered.

Tom's voice was soft. 'Fire King can do it, you know. If you train him.'

'He'll do it for anyone; he's got a big heart.'

'You don't want to train him? Or you won't.'

'Tom, there's nothing I want to do more, except –'

'Except what?'

'I've promised Jenny I'll give up the race game. If I've learnt anything from all this, it's that family comes first.'

'You've promised Jenny what?' said Jenny, who had come out to join them.

'That I'd quit racing.'

She put her arms around him. 'I know what you've been talking about. Take it.'

'I made a promise to you.'

'I know and I'm so proud you'd do it for us. But I love you, and I'd rather put up with a man who can sometimes be difficult, but is happy, than one who thinks he's doing the right thing and is miserable. And Dusty darling, you'd be miserable.'

He shook his head. 'That's not what you really think.'

'I know what I said.' She held his face and looked into his eyes. 'But it's what you need to do. It's your life, I won't take it from you.'

Dusty opened his mouth to protest.

Jenny put her fingers to his lips. 'Trust me. Tom, he'll take the job.'

Dusty looked steadily into his wife's face. 'You … you really mean it?'

'Of course. Our love has brought us this far; it'll carry us through whatever's ahead. Working for Carisbrooke Ellis will be totally different. I don't mind the racing, it's just that I hated you working for Malek. I knew he was crooked all along.'

'Let's put it to a vote?' Tom said.

'Yes,' said Jenny and Tom in unison.

The last remnant of Dusty's doubt fell away. He felt a huge surge of hope and joy.

'Yes.' He hugged and kissed her. 'On one condition.'

'What's that?'

'It's us … together. From now on, we're a team.'

'What I've always wanted,' she said, kissing him again.

They went back inside.

'Everyone,' Dusty called out. 'I've got an important announcement to make.